CW00499404

Nick began his literary career quite late in life, having his first novel published when he was forty-seven. Prior to that he enjoyed writing and illustrating from an early age. Despite attending art college, at the age of eighteen, he decided to pursue a career as a nurse, qualifying in 2003.

Although *The Freelance Chronicles: J'Ba Fofi* is his first novel, Nick has produced a popular social media illustrated story known as *The Unscratchables*. He lives in the north west of England.

For Olivia, who wanted to know what happened next. And for Georgia, who agreed.

Nick Hughes

The Freelance Chronicles: J'BA FOFI Book 1

Austin Macauley Publishers™
London * Cambridge * New York * Sharjah

A CIP catalogue record for this title is available from the British Library.

ISBN 9781398416499 (Paperback)
ISBN 9781398416505 (Hardback)
ISBN 9781398416710 (ePub e-book)

www.austinmacauley.com

First Published (2021)
Austin Macauley Publishers Ltd
25 Canada Square
Canary Wharf
London
E14 5LQ

I wish to thank my parents and family for their ongoing support whilst I was writing this book. To my many friends (Sonya, Marie, Lucy, Tash, Mandy, Michaela, Joe, Tanya, Wayne, Sara, Jo and Amy) who read the rough drafts with genuine interest and encouraged me to finish the story. To the publisher, who believed in my book after reading a few chapters. To Leanne, who gave me inside knowledge of Turkey without me visiting. To Susan and Kate, who both kindly wanted to be my PA/agent. To Claire, who was too scared to read the book, which made me realise it had potential. To Hannah, who was the very first person to read my opening chapter, but who also gave Lance his surname and suggested Ezzy as a character. To Corrina ,who told me Lewis would devour my book if I got around to putting it on paper. To my literary and artistic heroes John Wagner and the late great Carlos Ezquerra, whose names I honoured within a character. And finally to Narla and Macavity, who kept me company (and sane) whilst I completed most of the book during the 2020 COVID-19 pandemic. Thanks everyone. It was a team effort.

Tropical Rainforest,
The Democratic Republic of the Congo,
May 7

They waded through the endless vegetation. Two men, weary from three days of trekking through the forest. The light was fading, largely due to the thick undergrowth and heavy cloud cover. The rain was easing up, though it was warm and refreshing on their skin. Pausing for breath, they checked out their surroundings. It was a small clearing. Vast trees, letting in little light, circled the enclosed area.

'Think we should set down here?' the first man asked.

'Hmm. I guess. It'll be dark soon. I don't fancy pitching a tent by torchlight,' the second man replied. He had a strange feeling about this little exposed site. It was somehow different from what they had been walking through. He was unsure why.

'Agreed. Let me just take a look at this area close to those trees. Whilst we've got a bit of light.'

'Watch out for ch-bah foo fee!' the second man said laughing.

'I've got my camera just in case,' the first man said smiling.

'I'll get started,' the second man shouted, as his companion trudged away through the wet plants, disappearing behind a tree trunk. He looked around as he took his bag off, his gaze finding the misty tops of the trees, realising what was different. Birdsong. There was none. Throughout their journey, the forest had been alive with sounds of nature. Sounds of life. Birds mainly. He had gotten so used to the sound that he barely noticed it. Until it was no longer there. The silence of the forest unnerved him. He began unpacking their bags when a shout startled him.

'RUFUS!'

Rufus dropped the bag and instinctively grabbed the machete he was carrying to cut through the thick plants. He had sensed alarm in the other man's voice and felt the need to be armed with something. He waded his way around the tree to find the other man standing still, staring at something up ahead.

'What is it?' Rufus gasped.

'I don't know. What do you make of that?' The man pointed about fifteen metres ahead of them. A pale, white, almost transparent substance was covering a whole area of trees and bushes. It reminded Rufus of frost covering plants on a winter's morning. Rufus knew it was not frost as it was so humid here, even at night. Looking closer, he could make out that the substance appeared to be made up of thousands of very fine strands of a silky material, which were littered with various detritus from the plants. Leaves, branches, insects, dirt. The forest debris appeared stuck to this strange silk. Rufus's heart missed a beat. He swallowed hard and he felt a surge of fear rush through him, as he recognised what he was looking at. He stood frozen to the spot. Suddenly, feeling itchy as imaginary fingers of panic crawled up his back. A coldness gripped him. He tried to speak, but no words came out. His mouth and throat felt dry, like sandpaper. Finally, he managed a whisper.

'Duncan…'

Duncan turned his head slowly towards Rufus. It was obvious he was thinking exactly the same thing Rufus was. His face had a look of excited fear.

'It's a web…' Duncan croaked. 'A massive canopy of spider webs.'

Rufus stared at the enormous, pale structure, trying to make out any shapes he could recognise. Trying to remain calm, he turned to Duncan.

'Perhaps we shouldn't camp here tonight.' He laughed humourlessly.

'Probably not.'

'Head back towards the bridge?'

'For tonight, but I want a recording of whatever made these,' Duncan replied.

Rufus stared at him incredulously. 'You want a *video* of whatever made this? Are you mad? Let's at least go back over the bridge whilst we still have light.'

Duncan grinned. Any fear he may have been feeling appeared to have disappeared. 'This could be a world first! *The* most important zoological discovery of the century!'

Rufus wanted to share Duncan's excitement but had a very sickly feeling in his stomach. He could not help but be afraid. 'I'd rather watch it on YouTube. And I think you should keep your voice down.' Duncan's excitement was causing his voice to become gradually louder. Rufus was still whispering, his words coming out as a hiss.

'Don't panic, it's probably something quite unremarkable which has made these massive…' His voice ceased. They both looked towards a rustling sound in some dense bushes ten metres to their left. It sounded like footsteps. As if a group of four or five people were marching separately on the leafy, forest floor. The sound got closer and louder.

'Hand me your torch,' Duncan quickly whispered.

Rufus shook his head. 'Duncan. What on *earth* are you doing?' he whispered loudly. Duncan grabbed the torch from the other man's belt, as Rufus backed away slowly, gripping the machete tighter.

'Duncan, whatever you're thinking of doing. Don't!'

Duncan flicked the torch on. The bright blue, white beam fell upon the bushes. 'I just want to have a quick look.'

The noise had stopped. There was no movement.

'You see? Nothing. Can we get out of here now?' Panic was starting to grip Rufus. He backed further away.

'What's that? Looks like a tree root. And it's moving.' Duncan was holding the torch light at the bushes and recording on his camera, as the leaves suddenly trembled. There was something inside the bush. And it was big.

'Duncan, please! We'll come back tomorrow. When it's light!' Rufus could no longer hide his fear.

Duncan stood firm. 'It could be nocturnal, whatever it is. This could be a once in a lifetime…' His words trailed off. Duncan gasped, then spoke in a way Rufus had never heard before. A voice filled with pure terror. 'OH MY…'

His voice was drowned out by the vast dark shape, which sprang from the bushes and fell upon him.

The peace of the forest was shattered by Rufus's scream.

Sir Arthur Knightly's Residence,
Camlet Way,
London,
July 10,
11am

'Lance!' the woman's voice shouted up the grand staircase of the luxurious town house.

'*Yes*?' a well-spoken computerised voice replied.

'A call on the landline! Sounds pretty urgent.'

'*Message*?'

'Er… No. Firstly, I'm not your secretary. Secondly, do I have to repeat the *urgent* part of this call?'

There was a long pause.

'*And thirdly*?' the voice responded.

'Lance, it's Rufus Walcott's brother.'

A man descended the stairs quickly. Lancelot Knightly, known as Lance, was the youngest of five children. Their father was the billionaire philanthropist Sir Arthur Knightly. Financially secure, Lance had never needed to work, though he often found employment as a freelance journalist. Lance's passion in life was discovery. At twenty-seven, he could be considered as one of life's adventurers. As a child, he found communication on any level difficult, though he viewed life as a gift to be made the most of. He was also very intelligent, tall, handsome to many and athletic. Lance was an expert in outdoor survival, also enjoying extreme sports and was a lifelong animal lover. And he hated injustice in any form, against anyone or anything. A traumatic childhood event had caused Lance to unable to speak, though it was not a physical condition. This did not stop him in leading a full life however.

Lance took the phone from the woman. He was concerned about this phone call.

'You're welcome, little brother.'

Lance nodded stiffly. His sister walked away muttering, 'Not your answer phone…'

He took a device off his arm and placed it to the phone. It was a flexible wraparound screen. The words LANSPEAK were engraved on the side. He pressed it a few times and a voice spoke into the phone.

'*Myles, it is Lance. What is up*?'

There was a pause on the phone.

'Lance, I'm sorry to disturb you at the family home. I didn't have your mobile. I didn't know what else to do. I heard you were staying there for a couple of days.'

'That is fine. Do not worry. What is up? Have you heard from Rufus? I was starting to worry. He has not been in contact for weeks.'

'Lance, he's here, in London. The British Embassy in Kinshasa arranged for him to be flown back two days ago.'

'Arranged for him to be flown back? Is he all right?'

There was a pause at the end of the line.

'Myles, what has happened?' Lance asked.

When he spoke again, Myles's voice was strained. He was fighting back tears.

'I'm not sure. But Duncan isn't with him. He's missing. And Rufus…' His voice trailed off, turning into a sob.

'Missing? Myles, what is going on?'

Myles let out a cough, took a deep breath and continued.

'Lance, it looks like Rufus has cracked up. I mean totally lost his mind. A couple of weeks ago, he emerged alone from the forest he and Duncan were based in, barely conscious, dehydrated and talking gibberish. He kept saying Duncan has been taken. Duncan has been taken. Nobody could make any sense of it. The local police took him in for questioning, thinking he had something to do with Duncan's disappearance.'

Lance gripped the phone tight.

'Go on.'

Myles continued.

'Fortunately, the embassy got involved. They had him released and transferred to a hospital. That's what's taken so long. They didn't want to send him home until they were sure he didn't have some awful tropical disease. They even tested him for Ebola!'

Lance drew a large breath in.

'They do have to be cautious, Myles. Where is he now?'

'He's still in an isolation unit. The Royal Free Hospital in London.'

'And what has he said?'

A long pause.

'That's just it. He hasn't said anything.'

'What do you mean?'

'Most of the information we've got is from the embassy people. He appears to be in a catatonic state. He's barely even blinking. It's like he's in a state of shock. He looks absolutely terrified.'

'What are you saying, Myles?'

'I'm saying that I think he's seen something in that forest so shocking, that it's scared him, almost literally, to death.'

The Royal Free Hospital,
London,
July 10,
2pm

'Can I help you, sir?'

The nurse got up from his desk at the front of the closed doors of the isolation room as, Lance approached.

'Good afternoon. I am here to see Mister Walcott,' Lance replied via his LANSPEAK.

'Are you a family member, sir?' the nurse enquired, slightly taken aback by the computer reply.

'No, but I am a close family friend.'

'Sorry, sir, immediate family only I'm afraid.'

'I understand. Are you able to tell Mister Walcott's brother I am here? Inform him it is Lance Knightly, I think he is visiting right now.'

The nurse nodded and went to the phone on his desk. He spoke briefly then returned to Lance.

'There are some people coming out to talk to you now, Mister Knightly.'

Lance was puzzled. He said nothing but nodded a thank you and sat on a seat in the waiting area. Two well-dressed men in suits emerged from the isolation room. They did not acknowledge Lance, but walked over to a small sink and washed their hands in turn. They turned to Lance, as they were drying their hands. One of the men smiled. It was a professional smile with no warmth. Lance stood up, as they walked over.

'Mister Knightly?' the first man asked. He was older than Lance, perhaps in his fifties, with flecks of grey in his short jet-black hair. He was taller than the journalist and looked powerfully built under his suit. He smiled again and extended a hand in greeting to Lance, who shook it, though made no eye contact. Lance never made eye contact, finding it too difficult. The older man appeared not to notice.

'Lance Knightly,' he responded.

‘Ah, I’ve heard of you, sir. You covered some news stories in Cairo a few years ago, I believe? The Valley of the Kings cover-up if I recall?’ The man smiled, but again it was a cold, practiced grin. Lance felt uncomfortable as he did not recognise this man and disliked that he seemed to know about his past work. When Lance first started out as a journalist, he proudly used his own name. But it soon became apparent to him that when reporting on potential illegal activities he needed to become anonymous, even using one or more pseudonym.

‘That’s a handy little gadget I must say,’ the man commented, nodding at the LANSPEAK.

‘I am sorry, sir, have we met?’ Lance replied, ignoring the remark regarding his communicator.

‘Oh no, we’ve not *personally* been introduced. But I am familiar with your work. Brenton Stanmer. I work for the embassy in Kinshasa.’

He gestured to the man next to him. He was much shorter than Stanmer, but had the same professional appearance and looked roughly the same age as the Embassy man, though lacking the air of strength and power Stanmer seemed to possess so easily.

‘May I introduce Doctor Charak Khan? He’s a specialist in tropical diseases here in London.’

Doctor Khan shook Lance’s hand. The handshake was considerably weaker than Stanmer’s.

‘Tropical diseases? Is Rufus sick then? I thought he was cleared of any illness before he was flown back.’

Lance, being a journalist, had a sense of what people were like. It was his instinct. And he felt that Stanmer and Khan were acting cautious over something, but at the same time, curious as to what *he* was doing there. Lance had no intention of divulging anything until he was sure about what was happening with Rufus.

‘Well, we don’t think so, but we are very concerned about the poor fellow,’ replied Stanmer. Lance heard no trace of concern in the man’s voice. And his use of the phrase “poor fellow” felt like he was lightly mocking Lance’s well-spoken device. His journalist’s nose began to itch. There was much more to this than these men were letting on.

‘I am just wondering what your interest is in Mister Walcott. In fact, how did you find out about his location? It has not been made public.’ Stanmer’s practiced smile now appeared quite threatening. Lance was not intimidated. He had dealt with men like Stanmer many times in his work over the years.

‘Mister Walcott is a very dear friend of my family and me. Is he in danger, Mister Stanmer? I mean is there something I should know? And what exactly are Congolese embassy staff doing here?’

Stanmer now looked uncomfortable. When he spoke, his voice seemed to have lost some of its confidence, as if he was not expecting such direct questions.

‘Well, no. It’s just that with so many concerns recently over some of the world’s deadliest diseases, which are currently spreading throughout Africa, you understand we have to be cautious. And I’m here on official business. Requested personally.’

Lance outwardly showed no reaction. Inside, his mind was racing.

‘*I was told he was tested for Ebola. Does he have it? If not, what does he have, which requires such isolation and security?’* Lance looked towards Doctor Khan. The doctor turned to Stanmer as if asking what his reply should be, and it was Stanmer who answered. His smooth manner of authority had slipped. He leaned towards Lance intimidatingly.

‘Mister Walcott is undergoing more tests. And when he is well enough, will be questioned about the disappearance of his travelling companion. And I can’t tell you any more than that, owing to reasons of national security. Being a story writer, you will of course understand.’ Stanmer smirked and leaned closer. ‘Do you understand, young man?’ he asked very loudly, slowly and patronisingly as if he was talking to a child who was struggling to understand.

‘*I am neither deaf nor stupid, Mister Stanmer, please do not treat me as such.’*

The embassy official had no idea what to make of Lance and was disappointed his bullying manner was clearly wasted on him.

Knowing that further questions were pointless, Lance nodded and headed towards the exit, though turned as he reached the door.

‘*A pleasure to meet you, Mister Stanmer. I also, have been personally requested to find some answers. But I must be off. People to see, stories to write. And I feel I have just found an incredible story right here. I must begin to dig up as much information as I can, no matter how deeply it is buried.'* Lance had his usual inscrutable look.

Stanmer grinned in a sickly way. Lance nodded at the two men and left them staring at each other, looking worried.

Ezquerra Residence,
Floor 57,
The Shard,
London,
July 10,
9:30pm

'Not a bad view,' Lance said, as he took in the view of the London skyline at dusk.

'Yes, it's not too shabby, is it?' the woman's voice replied from a chair behind Lance. A mature, strong voice, with a mild Spanish accent. 'My name was down before it was built. I thought if I'm too old to travel far, then a nice view is a must.'

Lance turned around. An elegant lady was sitting in a comfortable armchair drinking green tea. At eighty years of age, she was much older than he was. Her hair was long, thick and dark with small, distinguished streaks of silvery white. She cut an impressive figure wearing a purple cocktail dress. She ran appraising eyes over Lance.

'So, what are you thinking? A potential story? It's often worth following the smallest instincts. It always worked for me.'

Lance nodded and looked at the photos on the table next to the woman. A few small black and white photos showed a strikingly beautiful lady in some famous locations around the world.

Wagner Ezquerra used to be a freelance journalist, back when being a young independent career woman was much less common than today. Wagner's father was Esteban Ezquerra, a famous Spanish architect, responsible for designing some of the finest buildings in Europe. Her mother was English. Charlotte Ezquerra had been a medical doctor. She was also a suffragist and Wagner's hero. Her strength and desire to stand up for people's rights became Wagner's lifelong plan. She had fought hard over the years to give a voice to people who often had no say. In her later years, she had become and still was an active member of numerous charities. Recently, Wagner had happily found herself becoming a life mentor to Lance. Wagner was the reason he became a journalist. She was also a mother figure to him, whose own mother had died when he was fourteen.

'To be honest with you, Ezzy, I do not know what to make of it.' Lance affectionately called Wagner Ezzy, as she said she always hated her first name.

'It's clearly niggling you. What's your gut telling you? My gut rarely let me down.'

Lance sipped a mug of tea he had and looked out at the fading light over the river.

'Something stinks. And it's not just Stanmer's aftershave.'

'Hmmm… Ezzy's rule number one. Put little trust in officials claiming to be on your side. He'll have told you only what he wanted you to know. Which sounds like very little. And probably mostly with lies.'

'That much I know. I am just puzzled as to why they are so interested in Rufus. He told me he was going on a Zoological Foundation trip to the Congo. How on earth could one man cause such a stir when coming back? Myles said he did not even have any kind of infection.'

'Lance. If there's one thing I've learnt about people in power over the years, they're excellent at convincing you and everyone else that everything they do is morally justified.'

Lance shook his head. Mankind's desire for power and wealth had never ceased to amaze and horrify Lance. Although Lance was one of five heirs to a vast personal fortune, he used his money for good whenever possible, supporting many charities in the UK and abroad. Even though his father was viewed an entrepreneur, he was also generous with his wealth. But it was Ezzy who had nurtured Lance's desire to spread his fortune fairly. The reason she had bought the apartment in the Shard was that she knew its price would remain high. All of Ezzy's assets would be auctioned for charity when she passed away. Everything she owned was going to many in need in her will.

Lance was always burdened with the thought that he could and should, always do more. Vast wealth sat uncomfortably with him, even though he was born into it. He took a deep breath.

'Well, the challenge has been laid down and I have accepted. Any idea where I should start?'

Ezzy put down her cup. She tilted her head in mock disappointment.

'My dear boy, if I've taught you *anything* over the years, you already know the answer to that.'

Lance stared over the city.

'The only person so far I feel has told me something remotely close to the truth.'

Walcott Residence
Tower Hamlets,
London,
July 11,
9am

'He's being moved.'

'Moved? When? Where?' Lance's questions were typed out as Myles Walcott's revelation momentarily stunned him.

'St Thomas',' Myles replied.

'The hospital?'

'Yes. And his ward is now under heavy security. I'm the only person allowed to see him.' Myles appeared to have aged decades since Lance saw him a few months ago. At twenty-five, he was younger than Lance. At the moment, he seemed to be carrying the weight of the world on his shoulders. His eyes were bloodshot, sunken with dark shadows beneath them. He had lost a lot of weight. His face was lined with stress and he acted like he was continuously exhausted. Myles was sitting in an armchair, gazing out of the window. He seemed to be in a daze. A cold mug of coffee sat on the table next to him. Lance took the chair opposite.

'Myles, something is going on. That man from the embassy was fishing for information, whilst almost certainly lying. What were Rufus and Duncan doing in that jungle? If you tell me what you know, I might be able to help. I assumed that is why you contacted me in the first place. Try and meet me halfway here.'

Myles sighed wearily. He gazed at last as if no longer caring who knew what.

'It probably doesn't matter anymore. But can I just state that Rufus *is* innocent of any wrongdoing in this? But he appears to have been made a scapegoat, for reasons I don't know.' The talk of his brother seemed to lift Myles out of his low mood. He focused on Lance.

'Yes, I did call you for help. And I'm hoping you can.'

Lance listened intently, as Myles revealed what he knew.

'Rufus and Duncan were working for the ZSL. The Zoological Society of London. They were on an expedition in some rain forest in the DRC. They were documenting destruction of habitats by big corporations. And the risk of extinction of some species due to this.'

'Were they looking for anything in particular?'

Myles shrugged. 'I don't know. But I think that any endangered wildlife they did find and document might have major consequences for these big companies. Which I'm thinking this is what the ZSL were hoping for.'

'And Rufus never gave any details?'

Myles paused. 'You might as well know. There's a couple of things.'

Lance leaned forward. *'Anything you know might help.'*

Myles took in a deep breath and spoke. 'Rufus mentioned they would be somewhere in the Salonga National Park. It's a UNESCO World Heritage Site. So technically, any corporations should have no business being there. Not that *that* is always the case.'

Lance now sighed. The corruption of large businesses in many poorer parts of the world was one of the many things he reported on as much as he could.

'Which company?'

Myles's concentration seemed to be fading again. He looked away. 'ACS was one. At least I think…' he said vaguely. Myles seemed to have withdrawn into himself again. Lance doubted he would get much more out of the man now.

'Myles, Rufus is a good man. And he is in good hands. I will do my best to find out what happened. I owe him that.' Lance shook the other man's hand, not surprised at the weakness of it. He stood and headed to the door. He paused as he heard Myles's tired, distant voice behind him.

'Oh, Lance. One more thing. Probably not important.'

Lance turned, not expecting much more, but listened.

'Rufus, as I've mentioned, has said very little. Well, anything that makes any sense anyway. But when he arrived back, he kept repeating something over and over. Usually during times when he appeared the most lucid. And the most terrified.'

'What did he say?' Lance asked with renewed interest.

'Nothing that I could understand. It sounded like he was saying ch-bah foo fee.'

The Fleet Street Press Coffee Shop,
Fleet Street,
London,
July 11,
10:05am

'Chabar what?' Lance's friend laughed, choking slightly on his coffee.

Lance smiled thinly. *'I know. It does not mean anything. There is not one match for Chabar Foofy on Google. Which is rare in itself.'*

'Are you sure you've spelled it correctly?' Blake asked, sensing Lance's disappointment. Blake Cudjoe was Editor-in-chief of "My Earth" magazine. An independent online publication where Lance had gotten his first news story published. A majority of his work was still published by them. Blake and Lance had become good friends in the eight years they had known each other. Lance valued his opinion and more importantly, trusted him. He had told Blake what he knew so far about Rufus's trip, which was, Lance pondered, very little.

'I am not even sure. It sounded like Myles said chabar foofy. I've typed in Chabba Foofy. Nothing. Jabba Foofy. Again, nothing. I have spelled Foofy; F-O-O-F-I. I have drawn a blank.' Lance sighed.

'It looks like Rufus was talking gibberish. Sadly,' he added.

Blake immediately regretted laughing. Rufus's apparent mental breakdown had affected Lance quite badly.

'In all seriousness, what *do* you think they found? You said it was something dreadful sounding. Perhaps it was what happened to this Duncan? From what you've told me, Rufus is an experienced traveller. Probably seen some sights in his life. Maybe a wild animal or a desperate local attacked them. This particular area of Africa *is* a dangerous place whichever way you look at it.'

Lance nodded. Blake then leaned closer and solemn look fell across his face. He lowered his voice. 'Lance. You don't want to hear this, but I'm going to ask anyway.'

Lance knew what was coming. He shook his head.

'Are you sure Rufus himself didn't have anything to do with Duncan disappearing?' he asked grimly.

'Yes.' Lance's definite answer was what Blake expected.

'I know he's your friend, but spending so long in a really inhospitable environment *can* have some shocking effects on people. Believe me, I've seen it happen.'

Lance appreciated Blake's honesty. He expected nothing less. And he hated to admit to himself that a nagging doubt regarding Rufus was slowly simmering away at the back of his mind. He pushed them away for now.

'I know,' he replied. *'But I am not convinced. Rufus saved my life once. And our Mister Stanmer is trying to protect something.'*

Blake nodded and smiled. 'You always have a nose for these things. You know, if I can help, I will.'

'Thanks.'

'Actually…' a sly look came across Blake's face. 'I think we can solve maybe one of your mysteries.'

Lance raised his eyebrows, though he was looking away.

'TOM!' Blake shouted over to the counter where a tall man was hunched over a laptop. He looked up.

'Everything okay?' he replied.

'Could you spare a minute, mate? Need your advice.'

Tombe Nantaba nodded and made his way to their table.

'You okay, my friends?' His voice was deep and slow. Both men seated shook Tom's hand.

'Tom, if I remember, you're from Uganda?'

The tall man smiled. 'I am. How can I help? But if you wanna know how 'Spurs are gonna do next season, I've no idea!' He laughed.

'Ah, nothing so serious. It's a question about the Democratic Republic of the Congo,' Blake replied.

Tom's face became serious. 'Hmmmm. Go on.'

'This is going to seem like a daft question, but have you ever heard of anything near the Congo called Chabba foofy? Or something similar?' Blake asked.

Tom raised his eyebrows. He looked at both men in turn. 'You mean Ch-bah foo fee.' It was a statement rather than a question.

'*That is it. That is how he said it. Ch-bah foo fee,*' Lance replied, taking his time typing a brand-new word.

Blake grinned. 'Ah ha. So what is it? And how do you even spell it?'

Tom dug out a small note pad and pen from his apron and quickly jotted something down.

'I'm sure it's spelled this way.' He handed the paper to Blake. He walked back to the counter laughing. 'And what is it? The stuff of nightmares brothers.' He was laughing, as he disappeared into a back room.

Lance looked at the words scribbled down. J'BA FOFI.

Blake took his tablet out of his bag and typed in what was written. They both glanced at the screen. What downloaded sent an icy wave of fear flood through Lance's body.

Temple Tube Station,
London,
July 11,
10:30am

'You're not *seriously* thinking those things might be real?' Blake asked incredulously.

'Of course not, but something in that jungle has sent Rufus half mad with terror. I owe it to him to clear his name,' Lance replied to Blake's question.

The train approached, both men stepped forward as the rush of noise and warm oily wind hit them. Blake had to shout as the tube slowed.

'You're not considering *going* out there?'

Lance shrugged, as they stepped onto the crowded carriage. Both men stood holding a bar as fellow passengers squeezed in around them. The train juddered out of the station.

Blake leaned closer, his voice more composed. 'Mate, seriously… The DRC? It's dangerous even by *your* standards. Civil war could break out any time.'

Lance sighed. *'I have known Rufus most of my life. I have not been able to even see him. If I cannot find out what happened from him, I will have to find out another way.'*

Blake knew that once Lance became focused on a story, he never let go. It was a good quality for a journalist to have. At the moment, however, Blake wished the man not to be so obsessed with getting to the truth.

'Lance, I get that. I do. But what you're thinking of doing sounds like an impossible task.'

Lance shook his head. *'I can be resourceful when I want to be.'*

'But this other thing? I get the feeling you think there may be some truth to what Rufus has been ranting about. My family are from Ghana and I've never heard of anything like this mentioned.'

Lance looked at his feet, agreeing that what Rufus was trying to communicate was impossible to believe, but also felt that many questions needed answering. He looked past Blake's ear, the closest he ever got to eye contact.

'You know me, boss. I always like to keep an open mind.'

Blake glared back at the younger man. Up until today, he had always trusted Lance's judgment. His instincts were rarely wrong. He now seemed determined to set off on a fool's errand.

'Lance, you're talking about flying to Africa in search of giant spiders!'

Blake's raised voice carried along the carriage. Passengers closest to the men heard. Most briefly glanced at them. One man smiled and a teenage girl snorted a small laugh. They both continued the journey to the next station in silence.

Westminster Tube Station,
London,
July 11,
10:45am

They both shuffled off the carriage alongside numerous other travellers and were swept along with the tide of people, remaining silent until they were on the escalator. Blake, considerably shorter than Lance, was on the moving step above. He turned to his friend. 'I'm sorry if I don't seem supportive. But I feel you're getting in above your head here.'

Lance smiled gratefully. *'I know. I am thinking the same thing.'*

Blake raised his eyebrows. 'But…'

Lance shrugged. *'But I have to find out what happened to Rufus.'*

Blake nodded resignedly. They exited the station. The Houses of Parliament loomed majestically above them. Blake turned to the younger man.

'Okay, my friend. I'll leave you to it. Will you call me later; let me know your plans?'

They shook hands. *'Of course. Do not worry. You know me.'* Lance smiled as best as he could.

'That's what worries me.' Blake laughed lightly. 'But seriously, if there's *anything...*' Blake trailed off.

'I will call.' Lance reassured him.

Blake nodded and walked away, instantly disappearing in the thick crowd.

Lance squinted in the morning sun and looked across Westminster Bridge. His gaze found the façade of St Thomas' Hospital. He swallowed hard, knowing Rufus was there. He shuddered as a chill flushed through him. The thought of his friend, lying in a hospital bed, possibly in some sort of shock troubled him deeply. But it was more than that. Something had nagged at him since he had exited the tube train. He had not let on to Blake. Feeling uneasy, Lance headed back into the station and through the barrier. He headed swiftly to the platform. He allowed himself a brief glance back before he got to the escalator. His instinct had been right. He was being followed.

South Kensington Tube Station,
London,
July 11,
11:00am

He looked slightly older than Lance. Mid-thirties perhaps. Short and stocky, long, red hair tied in a ponytail and a brown leather jacket. Nothing remarkable about the man, apart from the fact that he had followed Lance's route since he and Blake stepped on board the tube at Temple. He had noticed him since Blake had raised his voice regarding giant spiders. There was something different about his behaviour. He had no luggage or belongings. Sometimes he would appear to be talking on his phone. But even when Lance got off at Sloan Square station, pretended to look at the tube map, then rejoined the journey towards South Kensington, the man had never been more than thirty feet away. Lance was good at acting casual under pressure and he was sure that the man had not noticed that he had been spotted. Although Lance was quite intrigued as to why he was being followed, he was also unnerved. His family's fortune was well known worldwide and on more than one occasion, his father's security department had warned him about the dangers of being kidnapped and held for ransom, particularly when Lance visited countries alone with no protection. Which was a lot of the time. Lance knew he could handle himself, but he was starting to become more concerned about this man's determination. He boarded a Piccadilly line train and sat down. The pursuing man was at the other end of the carriage.

Lance had to think fast. He had a friend in Knightsbridge, but as he had no idea who this man following him was, he did not want anyone else put in potential danger. He thought back to his father's security firm. How they would be telling him "They told him so", as he tried to lose a potentially dangerous individual. But Lance could not shake the feeling that this man was tied up somehow with Rufus and his ill-fated trip. His mind now raced. Rufus, Stanmer, Mister's leather jacket, it felt like it all linked. He had to shake off this man quickly. He thought about getting off in Knightsbridge. It was a very built up place. He could lose him in Harrods he was sure. They had a lot of security. Security. That word repeated itself over in his head. He knew where he could get help.

Hyde Park Corner Tube Station,
London,
July 11,
11:15am

Lance walked as fast as he could out of the station. Running would have alerted the man and he needed to keep up the act as long as possible. The traffic was heavy as usual. He waited to cross the road within the dense crowds. He dared not look behind. Lance's new shadow would likely also be shuffling along with the tide of people. Quickening his pace once more as he weaved between tourists waving selfie sticks, Lance darted through Wellington Arch and was caught up in the next human wave crossing the other side of the roundabout. He headed up the tree lined-road of Constitution Hill, still not glancing back. He knew the man was following. The area was crowded. Tourists, city workers, souvenir sellers, school parties. Green Park appeared to his left, equally alive with people walking or relaxing on the benches, oblivious to Lance rushing as inconspicuously as he was able. The trees that adorned the road gave ample shade, but Lance was now sweating profusely. As his pace quickened, he guessed that his pursuer had realised his cover was blown, Lance still did not look behind.

The vast façade of Buckingham Palace appeared before him at the end of the road. A sudden thought struck the young journalist. He subtly reached into the bag he was carrying. He took out a cloth cap, which he used as a sun hat and a pair of sunglasses. He put them on and broke into a run. As he approached the Queen Victoria monument, he allowed himself a fleeting look behind. His pursuer was also running. This convinced Lance that drastic action was required. He sped towards the monument. Ignoring honks from cars and taxis, as he dodged his way through the traffic. He turned his head towards the guards based at the gate, raised his arms and leapt into the fountain. Not turning back, Lance trudged through the water, which surrounded the statue. His legs ached as he splashed his way to the other side. People stopped to stare. Many taking photos, unsure of what Lance was doing.

Guards in red uniforms had taken notice of Lance's apparent erratic behaviour. He could see them swiftly talking to themselves. More flashes from cameras continued. Two police officers casually approached him. This was not what he had planned. He splashed out of the water and ran towards the main gates of Buckingham Palace. The police jogged after him. Two guards approached, as Lance got closer. He slowed to a walk and held his hands up. As one the guards was about to speak, Lance pressed his LANSPEAK a single time. *'Merlin!'* shouted from the device.

Both guards looked at each other puzzled.

Lance looked around. The determined pursuer was nowhere to be seen. He was sure he was still being watched though. He smiled weakly at the confused guard, looking past him. *'Merlin,'* he repeated. *'Could you please inform Queen's guard Tristan Knightly that Merlin's assistance is required urgently by Lancelot?'*

Wellington Barracks,
Westminster,
London,
July 11,
2:00pm

‘What on Earth were you thinking?’ Tristan Knightly asked his younger brother exasperatedly.

Lance sheepishly stared at the lukewarm coffee in front of him. He shrugged. *‘It was all I could think of at the time.’* He looked up slowly. *‘I knew I was being followed. I knew you were stationed at the palace today. I got scared. I panicked.’*

Tristan sighed and shook his head. A faint smile slid across his face. ‘You? *You* panicked because you were scared? You sound like some of my men.’

Lance stared towards his brother, puzzled. Tristan continued to shake his head. A small laugh escaped him.

‘What?’ Lance enquired, bemused.

‘Lance Knightly. Extreme sports addict. Scared?’

Lance shifted uncomfortably in his chair. He began to speak; *‘Tris, I thought that a man—’*

Tristan interrupted the voice. ‘Lance Knightly. The same Lance Knightly who has reported from some of the most hostile and corrupt areas on Earth. The same guy who spends his spare time hanging out with my SAS pals, doing such crazy stuff that he can’t even tell his dad for fear it would give him a heart attack. The same guy that last year base jumped from the Burj Khalifa in Dubai.’

The younger man grinned. *‘You have made your point.’*

At forty years of age, SAS Staff Sergeant Tristan (Tris) Knightly was the oldest of the five Knightly siblings. He had always been closest to his youngest brother, despite their lives moving in very different directions. Lance had always admired his brother for not following in the family business, choosing to turn his back on the wealth and privilege his brothers and sisters enjoyed. The Lancelot/Merlin code words had been used by the two men since they were children. It was Lance’s way of contacting Tristan quickly without too much explanation. The older man sipped his tea and leaned towards his brother. He could see Lance was clearly shaken up and used his banter to relax him. The journalist briefly told his brother about what had happened since Myles contacted him.

‘So, someone was following you. But you don’t know who, or why?’

‘Yes. I have never seen him before. But it just felt connected to what has happened to Rufus.’

‘Hmm. I won’t ask you how you seem to know this, but you *are* usually right in these situations.’ Tristan stared at his brother. He did look more un-nerved than he had seen him in a long time. ‘Why did you pop around so quickly? Were you after my advice? Or protection?' He spoke sadly when he mentioned protection. He had never known his brother to ever need anything for years. Yet here he was, literally banging on his front door like a frightened child being chased by school bullies. In fact, he had not seen Lance in such a state since they were children.

Lance gazed ahead and sighed. *'I felt, for the first time, out of my comfort zone. Way out of my depth. This story seems to have found me. It is always normally the other way around. And I do not like it. I feel like I am digging myself into a hole.'*

'It's more than a story. From what you've explained, it sounds suspicious in many ways. It's personal for you because Rufus is your friend. And because you know very little about this man, Stanmer, you're convinced you've put yourself in some sort of danger?'

'Yes.' Lance sighed. *'And it has all happened in the past twenty-four hours.'*

Tristan cleared his throat. 'Okay, let me be clear about everything so far. Your friend Rufus has returned from Africa, after losing his friend *and* apparently, his mind after possibly seeing some mythical, cryptozoological giant spiders in the jungle, which nobody has *ever* proved actually exist. And due to the fact he's been smuggled back here, whilst under some sort of house arrest by some unscrupulous individuals who may or may not be working for the British embassy, who are now chasing *you* for reasons unknown. Possibly due to the fact that you've stated you're planning to travel to the Congo to try and find out what on earth happened out there, and to perhaps even find these spiders, which apparently have a five-foot long leg span. Is that about accurate?'

The two brothers looked in each other's direction for a moment. Then they both burst out laughing. It was the emotional release Lance needed. He rarely laughed. It was a laugh or cry moment. His brother had always been his best friend, so he felt a huge weight had been lifted from his mind. For the first time since this had all started, Lance felt he was back in control. Ideas and plans raced through his head. As his laughter waned, his excitement grew.

Tristan was still grinning to himself, as he gulped his last mouthful of tea. Lance leaned over the table smirking.

'Actually, I do need your help,' Lance asked.

His brother held up his hands, still smiling. 'If I can.'

'Are you still in contact with Iain Colquhoun? Now he is in Civvy Street?'

Tristan put his mug down. 'Er, I am. Why do you ask?'

'And he still runs that company?'

'Insanity Sports? He does… Why?'

'I have a really bad idea.' Lance grinned slightly.

Lancelot Knightley's Residence,
The Clock House,
Gipsy Hill,
London,
July 11,
9:45pm

'Hoon. Come in.' Lance was pleased to see his old friend, as he opened the large front door of his home.

'Thanks, mate,' replied the man, as he walked through the impressive doorway, shaking Lance's hand. Iain (Hoon) Colquhoun was a short very muscular man in his early fifties. With cropped greying hair, he looked every part the soldier. He was still extremely fit since leaving the military four years ago. Lance and his older brother used to enjoy many outdoor pursuits with Hoon and other members of the regiment. Since leaving, he had founded a very successful extreme sports supplies business. Lance regretted his loss of contact with him since he had left the SAS.

'Nice bit.' The older man smiled, as he looked around Lance's spacious home.

'*Thank you. My very own castle in London.*' Lance smiled inwardly.

'A bit small for my tastes, but I could live with it!' Hoon laughed.

'Wait until you see the view,' Lance said, as he gestured the older man up the spiral staircase of the converted clock tower, which was his permanent home. On the fourth floor, there was a roof terrace. The two men stepped out into the late evening dusk, taking in the view of endless streetlights of the sprawling capital.

'Tea?' Lance asked, as he poured two hot drinks from a flask on the outdoor table.

'Perfect,' Hoon replied, as he settled into one of the comfortable terrace chairs, still taking in the views of the rapidly cooling summer night. Lance brought two steaming mugs over to the small table next to the other man and sat in the opposite chair.

'Well, cheers.' Hoon raised his mug and took a sip. Lance nodded and smiled.

'How is business?'

'Booming! Just opened my second place last month. Fort William, near the canal. Branching out into water sports. The JJS should be in the prototype stage next year hopefully.' Hoon smiled contentedly.

'I shall have to check it out.' Lance typed, pleased for his friend.

'So. Even though it's good to see you, mate, and it has been too long, I know this isn't a purely social visit,' he stated in his broad Glaswegian accent.

Lance shook his head and smiled thinly at what his friend had just said.

'I am sorry, my friend. I should have contacted you earlier, not when I needed a favour.'

'Mate, what are friends for if you can't call on them for help? Besides, Tris said it was an urgent, no questions asked sort of situation.'

'It is.' Lance sighed.

Hoon put down his mug and leaned closer to his young friend and grinned. 'Well, that sounds like my kind of favour. What do you need from me?'

Lance stood up and walked over to the terrace wall. He sipped his tea and exhaled. *'I need some of your latest equipment. Probably even the prototype stuff.'* He turned towards the older man. *'That is if it is as insane as Tristan has told me. It needs to be.'*

Hoon stood up. 'Well, now I'm intrigued. What do you need and why?'

Lance turned around, a sly look of excitement on his face. *'I need your latest abseiling gear, low level flight suits and some stealth tools.'*

His friend laughed lightly. 'Well, this sounds good! And seeing as this is all hush hush, dare I enquire what you're planning?'

Lance put his mug down and put his hands out in a mock blasé gesture.

'Ah, nothing much. I was just planning to break into that large building that is directly opposite the Houses of Parliament.'

Westminster Bridge,
London,
July 12,
7:00am

The vast modern building of Saint Thomas' hospital began to come to life in the early summer morning. Staff, patients and visitors were already surging through the main entrance to the busy London hospital. Lance examined its frontage through the zoom lenses of his camera whilst blending in with the tourists and commuters who were even now, filling up the bridge. The majority of cameras were aimed at the impressive gothic structure that was Parliament and Big Ben. Lance knew he would not stand out at this tourist hot spot though.

The hospital building was larger than he had always thought. Then he had never looked at it in the way he was currently. The view was filling him with questions. A few he now hoped to answer, as he called a number on his phone. It rang for over a minute before a weary, weak voice answered.

'Uh, morning. Myles speaking.'

'Myles, it is Lance. Are you free to talk?'

A pause and what sounded like a stifled yawn.

'Ah, er, Lance?' Myles Walcott replied, as if he had no idea who he was speaking to. Lance heard a deep sigh, then, 'Er, hi. Sorry, it's just early.' Another pause. 'Um yeh, what's up?'

'Are you at home?'

'Well, yeah. You just woke me up actually. What's… Is something wrong?'

Myles was clearly not fully awake. Lance expected this, as he found during the last time they spoke, the man was not much more alert then.

'Myles, I need to know if you are visiting your brother this Sunday.'

Myles replied much more clearly. 'Er yeah, of course, I go every day.' A shorter pause followed. 'Why?'

Lance had carefully considered his answer. *'I have an idea about helping Rufus. But it is probably not what you had in mind.'*

Myles's lethargic mood immediately lifted. 'Oh, mate, really? You think you can help? That would be so great! Thank you! Thank you!'

'Do not thank me just yet. My idea is crazy. But after what I discovered yesterday, drastic measures are required.'

Lance heard Myles take a few deep breaths. 'What have you found out? Should I be worried?'

Not wanting to lie to the man, but not wanting to worry him, Lance moved the conversation in a different direction.

'Well, I have just been digging around for information and come up with a few concerns. And I will be needing your help.'

The journalist heard the man sigh. 'Anything. Anything you need.'

'That is good to hear. Now what I am asking may sound insane. But I need you to get hold of some certain items of clothing. Some very specific things.'

'Clothing? What on Earth f—'

'Myles.' Lance cut the other man short. *'Just trust me. I will explain more when I see you. You are also going to need a particular design of window sticker.'*

After hearing a brief outline of his friend's plan, Myles hung up feeling quite bemused. Lance felt he was taking a risk even telling Myles about his idea. But he knew it could not be done without the other man's help. Even though he did not know Myles that well, he knew Rufus as well as anyone could know a person. Rufus only ever had positive things to say about his brother. For Lance, that was good enough. As he briefly glanced back at the hospital on his way to Westminster tube station, Lance went over his plan in his head. *I must be insane,* he thought to himself, as he entered the subterranean world of the London Underground.

Gipsy Hill Tavern,
Gipsy Hill,
London,
July 12,
2:00pm

'You *are* insane! I thought I'd talked you out of this crazy idea the other day. In fact, I sort of hoped you weren't serious in the first place. Now it looks like you've added another layer of shear lunacy on top of this. You *honestly* think you can actually pull this off?' Tristan could scarcely believe what his younger brother was telling him. The two men stared at each other for a moment, as they sat opposite one another in a quiet area of the tavern.

'*It is mad, I know. And, no, I am not sure if I can get away with this. But things have changed since I last saw you. I discovered some scary things last night.'* Lance understood his brother's concern. His own mind, however, was already made up.

'What have you discovered? That those giant spiders actually *do* exist according to Wikipedia?' Tristan asked sarcastically, shaking his head in despair.

There was more than a trace of concern in the man's voice also, which was not lost on Lance.

'No. Forget that for now. I have uncovered some facts about some real monsters. Our very own Brenton Stanmer being one of them.'

Tristan sipped his coffee and leaned closer. 'Okay. Convince me.' Sounding genuinely unconvinced.

His brother took a gulp from his tea and nodded. *'Brenton Stanmer does not work for the British Embassy in the DRC. Or any British embassy for that matter.'*

The older man raised his eyebrows. 'Go on.'

Lance sighed, shaking his head, as if repeating what he had found out was emotionally draining. Which it was to him. *'Stanmer is CEO of a multi-national company called Company Expansion Services. Better known as CES.'*

'Never heard of 'em.' Tristan stated, leaning back in his chair.

'Not surprising. They have only been trading under that name for about eight months. I am not sure when they were established, but they have changed company names more times than I can count. They were previously called ACS. Stanmer has always been CEO though.'

'Sounds like you're average unscrupulous multinational company. I'm guessing there's more to it.'

'They are a legitimate company. Legal in the eyes of international law. What they do however is usually anything but legal.'

Tristan nodded, not sounding particularly surprised. 'So what's their M.O.?'

Lance sighed. *'Where do I begin? Theft and plundering the natural world would cover it. They basically find natural resources, foreign business locations and cheap labour for large international companies. They specialise in third world countries. They find areas high in natural resources but have poor economies and corrupt governments.'*

Tristan shook his head. He knew where this was leading. 'Let me guess. They move in and take what they want.'

'Literally, yes. Oh all in the 'guise of legal business dealings. They basically do the dirty work for the well-known companies, who are so wealthy that they can pay off whole governments and protect CES with any legal wrangles. If CES,

or whatever they are called, gets too close to being discovered globally, a legal army declares them bankrupt and they disappear from the business world, only to pop up at a later date with a new identity, but the same CEO. And the same Modus Operandi as you say.'

Tristan took another drink and stared at his younger brother over his glass. It was his turn to be worried. What Lance was telling him was frightening. He needed to know more. 'Any examples of what they've done?'

'Nothing I could begin to prove. But it looks like nothing is beyond them. Lying, cheating, bribing, intimidating. There are no depths to which they will stoop. I am certain that last year in Bolivia, they displaced an entire small town, claiming that the area was unfit for human habitation due to dangerous gasses leaking from a nearby abandoned mine. They bribed local government officials to arrange the evacuation. It was a ghost town inside a fortnight. Straight away, CES moved in and began mining the rich deposits of lithium which many of the homes were built upon.'

Tristan stared in disbelief. He had no words.

'It is all almost impossible to prove of course. Some of the companies CES works for are the media. They control what is made public news. They have their own security, who do not mess around when it comes to nosey people like me.'

Tristan looked puzzled. 'Have you never come across them in your work? You've always been a world class snooper.'

'I have. It was a few years ago. They were trading under a different name then. They were called PIT. Property, Infrastructure, Trade. I was in Bangladesh trying to report on a large multinational company who were dealing in petroleum products, but the landowners were getting nothing. Same sort of story. But I could not even get close. Their legal team is a monster. I had no chance. No proof meant no story.' Lance looked away listlessly. *'One story that got away.'*

Tristan lay back in his chair. He had always admired his younger brother for the work he does regarding exposing injustices in the world. He finished his drink and sighed heavily, shaking his head.

'Thoughts?' Lance enquired.

Grave concern spread across the older man's face. 'You *are* out of your depth like you said earlier. You've entered a whole new level of dangerous. This is nothing like anything you've done before.' He looked down. 'I don't think you're ready for this. I'm not sure anyone could be.'

Lance appreciated his brother's concern. And he agreed with him. He was way out of his depth. His mind, however, was already made up. *'I understand how you feel. I do. But I am doing this. With or without your help.'* The two men stared at each other. Tristan never made eye contact either, making it easier for Lance.

'But I really would like your help if you can,' Lance said.

Tristan shook his head and half smiled. 'My baby brother. As stubborn as *I* am. Latches onto a story like a dog with a bone. Okay. How can I help?' he asked, almost wearily.

Lance sat forward, an excitement in his eyes. *'I need to draw on your practical knowledge of my trip to the DRC. To ensure I can get there as soon as possible.'*

'Sure.'

'Okay. What immunisations will I need?'

Tristan raised his eyebrows. 'That I do know. Hepatitis A, Hepatitis B, Typhoid, Yellow Fever, Polio, Rabies. And the MMR vaccine. Tetanus, I think. We needed all of them before we were posted to Central Africa. But Lance, these jabs are needed up to eight weeks before you fly.'

Lance nodded. *'No problem there. I had those shots two months ago prior to my Costa Rica trip I was planning next month.'*

'Lucky. How about arranging a visa?'

'*It is sorted. Pop some money in the right pockets; you will be amazed how fast an entry visa can be obtained.'* Lance grinned inwardly.

Tristan stood up. He was shocked at his brother's apparent blasé attitude to this obviously dangerous trip. 'Lance. This isn't one of our adventures. And you're not Indiana Jones. You're planning to head into one of the most dangerous places on the planet. I know because I've been there. And I was armed and had an elite SAS team with me. You're heading out there with what? A camera, some money and your irresistible wit and charm? You don't even know where you're heading. Are you taking this seriously at all?' Tristan could not contain his anger. Although it was not anger. It was fear. He was terrified for his younger brother.

Lance looked toward his brother guiltily. *'I am sorry. I know why you are worried. Believe me, I am too. I would not normally choose to take a trip like this. But I feel I have to. I owe it to Rufus at the very least. And if I can get any evidence of dodgy dealings from Stanmer or CES, it will be worth it. But please do not talk to me about places that are Hell on Earth. I know those places. I have reported from them. Lived in them.'*

Tristan regretted his outburst. He knew the lengths his younger brother went to, trying to expose the horrors that went on in the world. He admired him for it. That was the main reason they were so close. In many ways, Lance had also turned his back on the family privileges to pursue more out of life. He sat down and sighed heavily.

'I know you have. I'm always in awe of the things you do. I'm very proud of you. Even if I forget to say it sometimes.'

'It is nice you care. And in all fairness, if it were you planning this trip, I would be trying to talk you out of it. And if we are handing out compliments, I think you are one of the bravest men I have ever known. Or likely to know.'

Without a word, the two men stood up and hugged each other fiercely. They both knew the dangers of what lay ahead for Lance. A thousand silent words were exchanged in the brother's embrace. As they headed out of the building, Lance turned to Tristan. *'There is one more thing I have to do which is going to bug you.'*

Tristan shook his head. 'I think I'm way past the shockable stage. What else have you planned?'

'I have to make a brief visit to Morgan,' Lance stated, looking sheepish.

His brother's face darkened. 'Why?' he asked dejectedly.

'I think she will be able to do me a favour. And she owes me one.'

Tristan held his hands up. 'You do what you have to do, little brother. Just make sure she doesn't expect anything in return. Though she probably will.'

'Do not worry. I think it will appeal to her ambitious nature.'

'That's one way to describe her,' Tristan said wearily, as the men headed out into the bright London streets.

Caelia Godalming-Knightly's Residence,
Cambridge House,
One Tower Bridge,
London,
July 12,
10pm

'Dearest brother. To what do I owe this unexpected pleasure?' asked Lance's oldest sister, as she opened the door to her private apartment.

'*Well, I am here with a big ask,*' Lance replied, as he entered one of the most lavish homes he had ever been in. The immaculate room was luxurious in every way. He made his way over to the huge windows and gazed at the stunning view of Tower Bridge, shining elegantly over the dark River Thames. Although Lance lived in a very large classic building in London, his sister's home was another level of opulence. He turned and smiled courteously.

Caelia Godalming-Knightly was an exceptionally beautiful woman. Wearing a tailored three-piece suit and her long, dark hair tied neatly in a bun, she looked every part the business owner, which she was. Caelia had taken over the running of the majority of the Knightly business empire since their father had taken semi-retirement to concentrate on charity work. Her relationship with her other siblings had grown more distant over the years. She saw Lance, their brother Andred and sister Lynette very infrequently. Tristan, however, had not spoken to his eldest sister since their mother died. A fact that had always saddened Lance. He had never quite understood what had happened between them, as they both refused to talk about it. Tristan's loathing for his eldest sister had only grown over the years. It had come to the point that he refused to even mention her name. He and Lance came to calling her Morgan-Le-Fay, though only ever between the two of them. Lance went along with it for Tristan's sake, although he felt it rather childish and always reminded Lance how stubborn his brother could be.

'So, you're here to call in a favour? For a moment there, you had me trying to remember who's birthday it was today.' She smiled thinly.

Lance raised his hands. '*Sorry if it seems like I am only here on business. But I do really need your help. Is Seb not here?*' Lance added the last comment to make the request sound less formal.

Caelia raised her eyebrows. 'He's in Hong Kong. Business trip. Back next week.' Her voice, as always, was clear and to the point. Her accent polished. Despite being very well spoken, Lance always felt that there was a coldness to his sister's voice. It had a controlling tone, lacking any warmth.

'So, what does our little globe-trotting reporter need from his big sister?'

The mocking tone was not lost on Lance. He was in a hurry so had to humour her.

'Has you-know-who been in contact with you? I read he was in London promoting the new film.'

The person Lance was enquiring about was an A-list Hollywood actor. Caelia and her husband were close friends of his. The older woman walked over to the settee. She poured herself a drink and sat down. Taking a large sip, Caelia looked up in false thoughtfulness. Lance knew this flippant attitude was her little game. A mini punishment for daring to ask for something which offered no reward. Lance had to patiently let it play out.

'Hmmm. You-know-who?' She sat up in mock surprise. 'You're not talking about the baddie in Harry Potter, are you?' She smirked.

Lance grinned weakly. He joined her on the other end of the settee. *'Is he free? I need to know if he will—'*

'Would you like a drink?' she interrupted.

Lance shook his head. *'No thank you. Caelia, I need him for a charity appearance. An hour at the most. In a couple of days.'*

She took another large gulp of her drink and lay back, staring at her brother over the rim of her glass. 'Where?'

Lance was relieved the game was over. It could have dragged out. He preferred his sister business-like. *'Saint Thomas' Hospital. I know he has visited there before.'*

She nodded. 'Yes. He's been in a few times. Charity events. Usually when he's over to watch Wimbledon. We often have dinner when he's here. He and Seb always have their own little match arguing over who'll pay.' She smiled smugly, knowing her little boast would not impress him, but saying it anyway.

Pretending to be impressed, Lance continued. *'Amazing... So he will do it?'*

Caelia got up and walked to the window. Gazing out at the multi-million-pound view. 'I'll ask him. No promises.'

Lance knew the event was secured. He trusted his sister's aggressive nature and ability to make things happen. He stood up. *'Thank you so much. It means a lot. And it will to the hospital too.'*

He did not want to ask any more from his sister, but he had one more question he thought she might be able to help with. It could do no harm, he concluded.

'Caelia. I have something else you may be able to help me with before I go.'

A short laugh escaped her. 'You *are* taking liberties, baby brother.' She turned and faced him. She drained her glass and glared coolly. 'Go on.'

'You probably cannot help. But have you ever had any business dealings with a company called CES? Or heard of a man called Brenton Stanmer?'

Lowering her glass slowly, Lance's sister stared inscrutably for a few moments then turned back to the window. 'No.'

Slightly puzzled, Lance asked. *'Are you sure?'*

'I *know* who we do business with,' she said after a short pause without turning around.

Not wanting to stay any longer than he had to, Lance headed to the door. *'Well, thank you so much again. I really appreciate the help. I will text the details when I have them.'*

His sister said nothing, nor turned around.

The younger man shook his head, as he opened the door. *'Well. See you again.'*

Caelia still did not acknowledge him as he left.

Hearing the door close and her brother descending the stairs, she put her glass down and reached her phone from her bag. Caelia punched in a well-used number.

Wellington Barracks,
Westminster,
London,
July 13,
8:00pm

'I asked these three to assist with any logistical jobs which may arise,' Tristan said, waving a hand towards the only three people in the room other than Lance and himself. 'Is this cool?' he asked.

'If you trust them, I trust them,' Lance replied gratefully. The younger man glanced over to the seated men, smiled and nodded swiftly. The men all nodded back simultaneously.

'Anything to help out a brother of Sir Shouts-a-lot.' One of the men laughed, causing all three of them to chuckle to themselves. It was clear these men were serving soldiers. Their appearance and manner was obvious to Lance, as his brother was the same.

Tristan laughed too. 'I wouldn't shout so much if you lot followed orders more!'

Cries of "Oooo!" came from the men.

Lance approached his brother. *'The fast boat and skipper you said you could arrange?'* he asked, knowing what he was asking was bizarre and also illegal. Though he trusted Tristan to vouch for these men.

Tristan grinned. 'It's all sorted. Young Taffy over there. He's standing by.' The older man said, winking at the youngest of the men, who returned the gesture with a broad grin and raised thumb.

Lance looked at his brother. Despite Tristan disagreeing with everything Lance had planned, he was helping as much as possible. He could not have gotten anywhere without him. *'Thank you for the whole "no questions asked" help you are giving me,'* he said smiling sincerely. *'And you do know all three of these men are here only if I have to switch to plan B.'*

'Of course.'

'And plan B is the worst possible case scenario. You know that too, right?'

'The four musketeers will be standing by just in case it all goes pear shaped.' Tristan grinned.

Lance shrugged. *'I still cannot believe what I am about to do. I am trying not to think about it too much. If I did, I would talk myself out of it.'*

'You can back out anytime. Nobody would think less of you,' Tristan said, putting a hand on his younger brother's shoulder.

'I know, but I feel I—' Lance was cut short by the buzzing from his mobile. He looked at the number then glanced at his brother. Tristan knew the caller by the look on Lance's face.

'Morgan-Le-Fay I presume?' he asked dryly.

Lance nodded humbly.

'Let's hope she's true to her word,' he said. 'For once,' he added, walking over to his friends.

'Hello,' Lance answered.

There was a short pause at the other end. Then Caelia's unmistakably sharp voice replied. 'It's all arranged. He'll be there tomorrow. Between midday and one.

Westminster Bridge,
London,
July 14,
11:30am

A lump formed in his throat. The fear he now felt was uncomfortably close to panic. All the advice from his brother and friends over the past few days now seemed like obvious sense. Knowing they were right made him feel queasy. Lance closed his eyes and tried to clear his mind. He took slow deep breaths as he slowly opened his eyes and gazed at huge building that was Saint Thomas' Hospital. The feeling of hopelessness, which had crept into his mind since he had woken up this morning, now grew with every step he made along the bridge towards his destination. His heart began to race and throb in his throat, hands sweating and he felt both legs weaken.

'Come on, keep it together,' he encouraged himself. He reminded himself of all the situations he has been in over the years. Extreme sports, reporting from war zones, crossing boarders in secret. None had ever felt like this. There was something disturbing about what he was about to do, largely due to with the people he was about to cross.

Lance joined the steady flowing crowd, as he made his way towards the hospital's main entrance. He suddenly felt paranoid, as he imagined security cameras were now watching him and had a sinking feeling that the authorities already knew what he was up to. Pushing negative thoughts aside, he paused and checked himself. Wearing a boiler suit, complete with a bogus logo stitched on, sunglasses and a cap, Lance looked like a random deliveryman. His equipment was packed into two large black cases, which he wheeled along in front of him. Having managed to gain online access to the internal layout of the building, he glanced at his phone and examined his route once he had entered the hospital. It looked straightforward on the map. Personal experience had made Lance cautious of anything that seemed easy. Most likely, they were quite the opposite.

He glanced right, the Palace of Westminster rose grandly over the river, shining a reddish gold in the late morning light. Lance felt a pang of envy when seeing the swarms of people shuffling over Westminster Bridge. *Why am I not living a simple life?* he questioned himself. There was nothing stopping him abandoning this absurd plan and returning to normality right now. The thought of feeling safe and living a stress-free existence almost persuaded him to turn around. Then thoughts of one of his most loyal lifelong friends laying in a hospital bed a few floors up shook him from his doubts. He had never laid down and ignored difficult decisions. "Welcome to St Thomas' Hospital" was written over a modern glass entrance. With a last look around at everyday life, and feeling completely unwelcome, Lance took a deep breath and entered the building.

St Thomas' Hospital,
London,
July 14,
11:35am

The foyer was cool after the humid walk from the tube. Glancing up through the glass ceiling of the entrance, Lance got a real feeling of how high the building was. It did little to calm his nerves. He knew his friend was on a ward on the twelfth floor. The reception desk was straight ahead. A man and woman were sat talking to each other. Lance had a panicked thought that they were about to stop him and foil his whole ridiculous plan. As he approached the desk, Lance felt cold sweat prickle from his forehead and neck. A nurse went up to the receptionists to ask something. *A perfect distraction,* he reasoned and swiftly turned right towards the lifts. A small group of people were waiting for the next lift. Lance looked at the control panel. Level 12 was now so close. But he needed to get as high up as possible. If he was acting suspicious, nobody had noticed. And Lance was excellent at reading body language. He glanced at his watch. *Right about now,* he thought.

The lift opened and people poured out. Standing aside, he picked up on a surge of excitement from the crowd. Some people were on phones. Talking or hurriedly texting. A few people saw people they knew and grabbed their arms and steered them back towards the entrance. Lance caught brief parts of conversations.

'No way!'

'Is it really him?'

'What's he doing here?'

'Is he filming?'

Very quickly, he found he was standing in front of an empty lift. Only two other people were now entering it alongside him, looking rather confused. Lance wheeled his equipment to the back as the doors closed. A thin, tired looking man wearing surgical scrubs glanced at him, as he brushed his fingers of the control panel. 'Floor?' he asked.

Lance held up a piece of card with the words; 'I am without speech. Floor 12 please.'

Lance knew his speaking device could be his biggest giveaway, so he would not use it, hiding it under his sleeve.

The man nodded, then pressed a few buttons. For a couple of seconds, nothing happened. Lance's heart leapt into his mouth. *I've been found out,* he irrationally thought. A cold sweat surged through him just as the lift slowly pulled upwards. The other man began quietly talking to the other passenger, a woman, also in scrubs. Lance was aware he still had his sunglasses on. The two people seemed not to notice. The lift journey seemed to take an eternity. On the 10th floor, the lift slid smoothly to a stop. The two people swiftly exited without looking back, and Lance was relieved that nobody else had entered the lift. Quickly jabbing the button for floor 12, Lance took a breath and tried to clear his head. Rufus was on floor 12. His heart quickened. He felt he was passing a point of no return. *Keep it together,* he thought to himself. As the lift eased into a stop, Lance felt his body had been left on the floor below. His legs felt weak. As the doors rattled open, Lance looked up. And was now staring into the face of Brenton Stanmer.

The Westminster Unit,
12th Floor,
St Thomas' Hospital,
London,
July 14,
11:38am

A thousand thoughts stampeded through Lance's head. At first, he thought Stanmer had recognised him immediately. Then it instantly became obvious to him that the older man was not making eye contact, partly due to the fact that Lance was still wearing sunglasses. For a moment, time seemed to stand still, then Stanmer spoke. 'Yeah. Yeah, I understand.' It took a second for him to realise the other man was on his phone. It then occurred to him that he was actually blocking his way to the lift. He put his head down and wheeled his bags into the corridor. The man he was beginning to loathe so much brushed passed him. An alarming thought struck Lance. Stanmer could be revealing valuable information. He considered following him back into the lift, but quickly dismissed that idea. Stanmer could recognise him and he had come too far to ruin everything. He pretended to check his phone whilst listening intently. 'It's not a problem; I know the boss is kicking off. We'll get 'im moved tomorrow. I know just how to handle…' His voice faded away as the lift doors hissed shut.

Any thoughts of backing out had now vanished. Seeing the smug Mister Stanmer, obviously discussing his friend, had more than strengthened his resolve.

Lance gathered his thoughts and looked around. The ward entrance lay before him, though he had no intention of using it as three security men were sitting at the door. Two were reading newspapers, the other sat at a desk observing a monitor. Possibly viewing CCTV, Lance guessed, then quickly moved away from the entrance before they had a chance to look up and now checked his onward route. He had gained inside plans to access to the hospital roof. However, there was one more hurdle to jump, he mused. Feeling an uncomfortable rush of irresponsibility mixed with irrationality, Lance smashed his fist into the fire alarm mounted on the wall. *No going back now,* he thought.

The Westminster Unit,
12th Floor,
St Thomas' Hospital,
London,
July 14,
11:40am

The alarm shrieked to life. Louder than Lance had thought it would be, but the noise was strangely comforting to him. It was the distraction he wanted. He also knew the noise would draw people from the surrounding areas. People would be investigating the source quickly. He had to move fast. Quickly finding an access door and pushing through, Lance saw what he was looking for. A sign displaying 'TO ROOF' next to a short built in ladder. He parked his cases and ascended the steps. A simple hatch was at the top. He released the bolt and pushed the small door, coughing as a cloud of dust and grit rushed into his face. Then a fresh breeze blew in and he blinked at the daylight. He smiled inwardly, as he realised his planning had been accurate so far.

Flipping the hatch fully open, Lance briefly surveyed the hospital's vast roof, before descending quickly and unpacked both cases. He took all the equipment out and brought them to the roof. He pushed the cases to the side, wearing gloves the whole time as to not link him with them when found. Once out in the open, he closed the hatch and placed a few bricks, which he had brought with him on top to weigh it down slightly. The view over the Thames to Westminster was spectacular, but he had no time to appreciate it, as he busied himself checking his equipment. Rope, harness, belay devices, various tools, thick gloves, helmet and goggles. And one last bit of kit, which he really hoped he would not need, which he put on first. He was now ready to abseil down the side of the hospital.

Working quickly, as he could still hear the fire alarm beneath him, Lance found the most solid structures on the roof and swiftly attached the ropes required. Now, too busy to feel regret, he took all he needed to the roof edge and counted the windows from his right to left. Finding the right number, he looked around and down. There were a sparse number of people below, but they appeared too busy adhering to the fire alarm to notice him. He sighed. *Here we go*, he whispered in his head and jumped.

He reached the window in seconds. Knowing it was the right window, as a large smiley-faced sticker, with the logo "HELLO PRIME MINISTER" stared back at him. Lance tapped the grimy glass. Myles Walcott's bemused face appeared behind the sticker. Lance gestured for him to step back, as he fished out a hand-held device and began digging at the window seal. It was a cutting tool, which used heat and vibrations to quickly undo the join. The device was lent to him by Mac. The window seal weakened, cracked in places. It took a surprisingly short time for the entire pane to lean into the room. Lance took its weight but was grateful when Myles used a bed sheet to break its fall into the ward and not shattering.

'Lance, this is crazy, what're we…' Myles stuttered, as the younger man swung inside.

'No time. Have you wedged the door shut?' he replied. Myles nodded quickly. Lance winced, as he saw Rufus in a chair rocking back and forth, muttering to himself. The ward was empty. He knelt next to his friend and removed his goggles. *'Rufus.'* No obvious recognition. *'Rufus, it is Lance. Remember? Lance. You know me.'* Rufus locked eyes with Lance. Eye contact was painful but he managed to hold his gaze for his friend's sake, difficult as it was. There appeared to be a brief awareness, then a glazed look covered Rufus's face.

'He's been like this since he came back,' Myles said sadly. Lance gazed at the open window. *'You both need to leave. Right now.'*

'Both of us? Lance, what's going on?'

'Just trust me. Our Mister Stanmer is a dangerous man to know. Questions are for later,' Lance said, as he began undoing his harness and unravelling another one. *'Put this on and help me strap the other one to Rufus,'* Lance quickly communicated, his mind working overtime.

Myles was more alert and focused than Lance had seen him since his brother's return and was grateful for it. Both Myles and Rufus were wearing simple boiler suits as Lance requested. They made good time strapping the harness to Rufus, as he offered no resistance, just moving limply. Myles was strapped up quickly and secured himself and his brother to the abseil ropes. Lance helped Myles walk Rufus towards the window. It was slow as Rufus could only manage a weak shuffle, his body sagging, leading to the other men taking most of his weight. He got slower as the natural light touched his face. Then Rufus stopped completely. His whole body became rooted in fear. A look of horror began to spread across his face, as he appeared to recall a faraway terror. His eyes rolled back and he screamed. A loud, guttural sound, which sent ice cold waves through Lance. He wanted to calm his friend, but he was supporting him and was unable to reach his LANSPEAK. 'Rufus. It's okay. It's okay you're safe,' Myles pleadingly spoke to his brother. The screaming continued. Louder and more constant. 'Rufus. Please! Please don't shout. We're nearly home.' Myles desperately tried to comfort his brother. Then the loud knocks at the ward door could be heard over the terrified wails.

'Open the door! It's the police!' Lance's heart dropped out of his stomach. A feeling of hopelessness surged through him. He could feel Myles staring at him, imagining him feeling the same. The banging on the door increased. Louder. They were trying to break through, which Lance knew would not take long. Without thinking, he eased Rufus closer to his brother and touched his LANSPEAK. Two pre-recorded words loudly came out. *'J'ba Fofi!'*

Without warning, Rufus pushed his brother toward the window. Lance had no time to react as he heard Rufus shout "Noooo!", as he and Myles fell out of the open window.

The sound of Myles now screaming in horror instinctively made Lance grab the ropes used for ascending. Pulling them in and anchoring both around a bed leg. He winced when it took the weight whilst jerking his arms, pulling at his joints. He secured the weight and glanced outside and looked down. Myles and Rufus were dangling above the ground. They looked stunned but uninjured Myles even managed a small wave.

He sighed with relief when he saw one of Tristan's men on the ground looking up. He had a wheelchair next to him and was frantically waving for the men to be lowered. Lance wasted no time in releasing the rope gradually, feeling the weight of the two men lower until he felt it slacken. Looking out and down, he saw Rufus lifted into a wheelchair and the three men headed towards the road. His relief was short lived when he heard the ward door crack open and footsteps hurrying his way. Hurriedly attaching a protective head and facemask, he typed into his LANSPEAK *Plan B.* The message automatically synced with Tristan's phone. Lance simultaneously heard a voice behind him shout, 'Hold it right there!' Followed by Tristan's voice message, 'Oh terrific,' as he ran at the window and leapt out headfirst.

The River Thames,
London,
July 14,
11:44am

A rush of wind and adrenaline hit Lance, as he dived from the hospital window. He immediately pressed a release button on his belt and a wing-suit opened. It was a prototype designed by Mac. It was suitable for low-level gliding. It worked perfectly. Or it would have worked perfectly if he had jumped from the roof, Lance quickly thought. The line of trees rushed closer, as he guided himself towards Westminster Bridge. If he hit the trees, he would never make it. Lance tilted in mid-air and he shot over the river losing height at a steady rate.

The bridge loomed closer and he immediately knew he would not clear it. He did his best to steer towards one of the decorative lamps, which were placed regularly across the structure. Heading towards a lamp opposite the south bank lion, Lance attempted a landing. As he levelled out, an open topped double decker bus crossed his path. He collided with it as it slowed for the traffic. His wing-suit shrunk back, as he grabbed the top rail of the bus and climbed into the moving vehicle.

It was almost full with tourists enjoying the view in the warm weather. Lance was glad his face was not on show. A woman gasped in surprise when he launched himself onto the deck between the seats. A few people laughed nervously, then Lance felt a number of cameras and phones taking his picture and filming him. He had to get off right away. The bus then sped up and he almost lost his balance as it headed towards Westminster. The wrong direction, he realised. Squinting in the brightness of the day, he saw an identical bus heading towards them on the opposite side of the bridge. As the buses drew alongside each other, Lance did not hesitate, and to the sound of more gasps and a couple of screams, he jumped from the top deck to the other buses deck, to be met with identical gasps and a scream.

He was now heading away from Westminster. Police and fire engines were clustered around the hospital entrance, slowing the traffic down. As they approached the end of the bridge, Lance held his breath as he jumped from the bus towards the river. He briefly opened the wing-suit to act as a windbreak, hoping everything was timed to perfection.

The river rushed up to meet him, but at the last minute, a small speedboat sped underneath in time for Lance to land on its small canopy. 'Need a lift, mate?' Taffy asked, briefly looking up as he turned the vessel around and sped away from the bridge. Lance could only raise his thumb in appreciation. The boat swiftly turned around and cut through the river, past Westminster, towards the rendezvous point. He looked back at the bridge, hoping Rufus and Myles made it out safely. His LANSPEAK beeped a message. 'You're insane.'

Lance smiled at his brother's voice. He closed his eyes and worked on controlling the rush of adrenaline coursing through him. The boat powered towards its destination.

Under Vauxhall Bridge,
London,
July 14,
Midday

The boat sped up to a small wharf and docked long enough for Lance to jump off, then sped away. 'Double O seven, we've been expecting you,' a familiar voice called out about the sound of the lapping water. Lance looked up to see Tristan smiling, looking relieved.

'*I am happy to be expected.*' Lance typed wearily. '*And double O Seven does not usually cock things up and head for plan B.*'

'Lance, it worked. Rufus is on his way to Manchester. He'll get the care he needs. It's all taken care of.'

Lance walked swiftly up the steps and faced his brother. He looked past his head.

'*The ball has started rolling. I need to act fast.*'

'I know,' Tristan replied, sighing. 'I can't change your mind, I suppose?'

'*After seeing Rufus like that. No way.*'

Tristan nodded and led his brother into the hidden doorway under the bridge. They ascended some old stone steps, which led to a road where a car was waiting. They got in and drove north over the bridge.

'So where to now?' Tristan enquired.

'*You need to drop me off.*'

Tristan turned to Lance, who was staring straight ahead, a determined focused look on his face.

'Uh, sure. Where are you going?' Tristan asked.

Lance paused before replying.

'*I cannot involve you any further.*'

Tristan laughed humourlessly. 'What're you saying? My help is no longer required?'

They drove in silence until LANSPEAK broke the tension. '*I do not want to involve you further. I have put you and your soldiers in danger.*'

Tristan laughed. 'Danger? We're SAS! We eat danger for breakfast!'

'*This is different. This is not war danger. It is big business danger. Which is much worse.*'

'Oh you'd know, would you? Been in many war zones, have you?' Tristan retorted angrily.

'*I have wars inside my head on a daily basis. I do know real fear.*'

Tristan stared ahead, feeling embarrassed. He knew more than most people how hard life had been for his younger brother. The years of therapy Lance underwent just to learn to communicate, to even interact on a basic level. He had fought harder and longer than any soldier he knew. And he was still battling.

'I know. I'm sorry.' They drove for the longest thirty seconds Tristan had ever known before he asked, 'So, where do I drop you?'

'*London Zoo.*'

They drove the rest of the journey in silence.

ZSL London Zoo,
Regent's Park,
London,
July 14,
1:10pm

The car pulled up to the quietest area they could find. The traffic was heavy and the day was getting warmer.

'Well. This is where we part company I guess,' Tristan stated, knowing offering his brother any further assistance was pointless.

'*Thank you for everything,*' was all Lance could reply. He was extremely grateful to Tristan and his men, but he always had difficulty showing sincere gratitude.

'You can thank me by coming back in one piece, little brother,' Tristan said, trying to keep his concerns to himself, not wanting to stress his brother.

Lance looked as closely as he could to his brother's eyes. '*I will.*'

Tristan sighed as his younger brother climbed out of the car and headed into the crowds lining up to enter the zoo.

'Lance!' Tristan could not help shouting to his brother's back. Lance stopped and tilted his head, but did not turn around.

'Try not to become a fly huh!' Tristan shouted, smiling humourlessly.

Lance half-smiled to himself, nodded and continued walking, feeling a pang of sadness, as he heard his brother's car drive away.

He patiently queued at the entrance, once again feeling envious of the people around him, enjoying a pleasant day out, unburdened of the stresses that he was constantly feeling now. But right now, personal feelings had to be pushed aside to enable him to focus. Paying the entrance fee and entering the zoo, Lance now began to concentrate his mind. Since adolescence, Lance knew he had an almost photographic memory. And it had proved very useful over the years, travelling the world. Today was no exception, as he searched his subconscious memory for the day Rufus told him about his trip. Fresh information flooded into his head and he knew where he was headed.

The Office of Doctor Fimi Kazadi,
London Zoo,
London,
July 14,
1:20pm

The door to the small office was open wide, though Lance courteously knocked.

'Come in,' a cheerful female voice called out. He entered the office, which felt only slightly cooler as it was in the shade. The room was small and had little light. Every inch of the walls was decorated in posters of African wildlife or African art. Books and box files filled any remaining desk and table space. A short woman was sat in one of only two chairs in the room, hunched over a laptop. She was dressed in a bright, colourful dress with a matching head covering worn over very long braided hair. The woman did not initially look up as Lance entered but raised a hand in a wave, causing her large number of metal bracelets to clink loudly.

'One second, honey. Just let me save this, if it'll let me.' She pressed the last key firmly. 'Done.'

The woman finally looked up, her large earrings waving with the motion of her head. She smiled warmly. Lance immediately looked to her shoulder, hating his difficulty to make eye contact. He tapped his LANSPEAK.

'I am sorry to disturb you, Doctor Kazadi. My name is Lance Knightly. And I would be grateful if I could speak with you.'

The woman stood and stepped closer. 'Lance. I've heard about you from Rufus.'

She walked closer but stopped when she was at a distance she knew Lance would feel comfortable with. She sighed.

'And I have sort of been expecting you to drop by, honey. That's if everything Rufus has told me about you is true. Which I'm sure it is, as Rufus is a decent man.'

She breathed deeply again. 'And a good friend.'

Lance was relieved that he did not have to explain the situation with Rufus again. But he was now curious as to how much this woman knew. Before he could type again, the woman spoke,

'And please, call me Fim.' Although he could not look at her face, Lance could feel Fim's warm smile again.

'Honey. You want to know what Rufus and Duncan were doing out there in the DRC? A dangerous place by all accounts.'

Lance nodded.

'Well. What I *can* tell you is what they were looking for out there. Which was almost as a special favour to me and my team here. But what I can't understand, are the bizarre circumstances regarding their disappearance and Rufus coming back alone.'

Lance was pleased that Fim knew quite a bit already, but he did not want to alarm her by telling her what he already knew.

'But before we do anything, let's have a cup of tea,' Fim stated, gesturing to Lance to sit in the only other chair. She poured water from the freshly boiled kettle into a large teapot and sat back down.

'Now, honey, whilst that's brewing, let's try to unravel some of these mysteries you've been caught up in.'

The Office of Doctor Jonathan Drachmann,
London Zoo,
London,
July 14,
2:40pm

'The door's open,' came the reply from within the office after Lance had knocked. He entered a similar sized room to the one he had just left, though not as colourful as Fim's. It was more like a museum, with specimen jars with various insects and similar creatures unevenly placed along bookshelves and small tables. Books and files were scattered wherever they could stand or lay. It had a musty smell, reminding Lance of old books and furnishings. He could not immediately locate the source of the voice, so stepped further in. Some of the specimens in the jars appeared to be large spiders. A particularly big, black hairy tarantula like creature caught his eye and he leaned forward. A faded label hung from the jar. "Theraphosa Blondi" was hand written on it.

'Marvellous creatures, aren't they?' The voice from behind startled Lance slightly. His general senses could usually identify a person so close to him. He turned around. The man was stood only a few feet away. Much older than himself, with long white hair and an equally white, but neatly trimmed beard and a weather-aged face. Small half-moon glasses were resting on his large, rather hooked nose. He wore a tweed suit and light brown boots. The man was writing on a small jar, so Lance was able to see the man fully before he looked up. He placed the jar in his pocket and finally raised his head. Lance looked past him, feeling rude, but unable to help it.

'*Doctor Drachmann?*' Lance typed.

The man smiled broadly and strode forward, extending a hand, which Lance obligingly shook, though stepped back once they had officially greeted.

'Nope,' the man replied, still smiling. Before he could type, the man spoke again.

'I'm Drach. I'm only *doctor* Drachmann when I'm forced to attend tedious lectures or presenting research. Which is all rather dull,' he said, motioning Lance towards two armchairs.

'Have a seat, as long as you don't sit in my favourite chair,' he said chuckling. Unsure of how to take him, Lance sat in the nearest armchair.

'Good choice!' Drach bellowed and slumped into the next chair, exhaling loudly. Without looking at Lance, he spoke. 'I'd offer you some refreshment, but I know you've just come from Fim's. So I know you'll be full to bursting from that lovely fruit tea she brews so well.'

'*Yes, I am fine thank you,*' Lance replied.

Drach leaned towards him and pointed to the back door, 'Talking of bursting, the loo is just through there.'

'*Thank you, I am okay right now.*' Lance was still puzzled by this man. His eccentricity was so obvious he wondered if he was going to get honest, plain answers from him. He felt like he was about to interview Doctor Who. But before he could ask anything, it was Drach who spoke. The older man removed his glasses and leaned forward in his chair, not looking at Lance as he spoke, which he was grateful for.

'Fim phoned me and told me you were coming to see me. She told me about Rufus. I admit I didn't know him well, but I am sorry to hear what's happened to your good friend.' Lance nodded gratefully.

Drach continued, 'Though, as Fim said, we don't actually know what's happened. And when people look for answers, they grasp at anything they feel may help them. No matter how unlikely.' Lance knew where this was going but he needed to hear it.

'Let me tell you something, young man. I'm an arachnologist, amongst other things. I'm a member of the British Arachnological Society and know members of the African Arachnological society.' He smiled slightly. 'I've always loved and been fascinated by arachnids, particularly spiders. The fear of spiders is taught to us, you see. It's not natural to fear something that can do us no real harm for the most part.' Drach then sighed and leaned back in his chair, tilting his head in Lance's direction and continued, as Lance listened, glad that this man was as knowledgeable as Fim said he was.

'Let me tell you this. There are approximately forty-five thousand species of spiders in the world. Forty-five thousand. That we *know* of. There are possibly many thousands more yet to be discovered. They are vital to the eco-system of this planet. If there were no spiders on earth, we'd be knee deep in flies. And considering how many flies carry diseases harmful and even deadly to us, we have a lot to be grateful to our eight-legged friends for.'

Lance reached toward his LANSPEAK but stopped when Drach said something unexpected.

'You want to know about the existence of the J'ba Fofi?'

The younger man was surprised at the directness of the question. But it was why he was here.

'Let me share a few facts with you. The largest spider on earth is the goliath bird-eating spider. Terribly and inaccurately named, but there you go. You've probably seen many documentaries about them. A tarantula with a leg span the size of a dinner plate is the stuff of nightmares to many people. They've been found in South America. There *is* a larger spider, though not in terms of weight. The giant huntsman. Yes, an even *more* inaccurate name. This spider's leg span has been measured at a foot. But it is mostly leg. It was found in Laos. Following me so far?'

Lance nodded.

'There are some creatures on this earth that can make people believe in giant arachnids. The Japanese spider crab can measure twelve feet claw to claw. A coconut crab is also a very large arthropod. Do you see how rumours, folklore, myths and stories can become perceived as fact? The Internet has a lot to answer for.'

Lance again nodded. He felt reassured by these facts and this practical thinking.

'So J'ba Fofi. The Congolese giant spider. Is it real?'

Lance now felt embarrassed that he had come to this man with an opinion on this.

'This giant spider is as real as the Loch Ness Monster. Or Big Foot. I don't claim to know cryptozoology. But this animal *can't* exist. It's scientifically impossible. The claim that a tarantula like spider can exist which has a five-foot leg span is nonsense. It would be impossible for its legs to support its weight. It would collapse. It also wouldn't be able to breathe. Its body would simply suffocate. Evolution of such an animal would've ground to a halt millions of years ago.'

All of this made sense to Lance, but it still did not answer what actually did happen to Rufus. Before he could reply, Drach seemed to pick up on what Lance was thinking.

'What has happened to your friend is a puzzle. But in my opinion, he's suffering some sort of long-term delirium or mental breakdown.'

'*Caused by what?*' Lance finally asked.

'The Congo is a hotbed of diseases. There are some nasty tropical infections any outsider can get, even with the right vaccinations. Dehydration can also exacerbate this. And it's pretty hot in those jungles.'

Lance took all of this in. It did make sense. But he still had doubts about certain aspects.

'Diseases and severe heat exposure can cause terrifying hallucinations. Your friend may have been told of the J'ba Fofi story before he set off. And when he became ill, he imagined this animal to be real. As real as I am sitting before you. And that is an upsetting thought for you to hear.'

Lance looked down. This all could be true. Probably was true. But Lance was still going to find out what happened. There was more to this than Rufus falling ill. Brenton Stanmer confirmed that. He stood up and shook Drach's hand gratefully.

'I hope I've been of some help,' the older man stated.

'*Very helpful,*' Lance replied and meant it. As he walked toward the door, he came in, the doctor called after him.

'One more thing!' Lance turned but said nothing.

'If you'd like another piece of proof of this creature's unlikeliness to exist, you must know this too.'

Lance nodded.

'Well, it's a well-known theory amongst my fellow peers at the BAS, that if spiders were as large as cats, just domestic cats, they would be the dominant species on this planet.'

Lance raised an eyebrow sceptically. This seemed far-fetched. Drach picked up on this. 'It sounds absurd, I know. But they really are the most efficient predators. Humans wouldn't have stood a chance. Spiders would have ruled the earth!' The last line was delivered in the flamboyant way Drach had been when Lance first met him.

The younger man nodded gratefully once more and stepped out into the warm afternoon sun. He was pleased to get an impartial opinion on this aspect of what Rufus appeared to be saying. It was hard not to agree with everything Drach had said. Lance himself had always had a lateral thinking mind. He believed in facts, but facts he could understand, theorise and, if able, prove. This cryptid idea did not sit well with his way of thinking at all, but Lance felt he needed to find out the truth of Rufus's story. And why his friend was now living in an almost permanent state of pure terror. He closed his eyes and immediately Rufus's tortured face was staring at him. Lance could see his pain. His fear. His loss. He opened his eyes and a determined feeling rushed through him. It was time to go home and pack. It was time to leave.

Lancelot Knightly's Residence,
The Clock Tower,
Gipsy Hill,
London,
July 14,
7:45pm

He had travelled around the city for the rest of the afternoon. Not going anywhere, but trying to clear his head. The past few days had been a physical and mental roller coaster. He knew now he could not leave this, but must see it through to its conclusion. Lance felt like he had opened Pandora's Box and it could now not ever be closed. His life had suddenly changed permanently, so he was doing his best to rationalise how his life would be over the next few weeks, even months. Looking too far ahead was too much strain. But thoughts of Rufus pushed aside any feelings of regret, making way for resolve, helping him focus.

As Lance walked out of Gipsy Hill train station and along Gipsy Hill towards his home, he made a mental list of what he needed to do, such as book the flight. He reasoned a last-minute booking would leave less of a trail to follow and had decided to fly to Turkey to get a flight to the DRC. His mind raced with plans, decisions, scenarios, until he caught sight of his imposing home. The Clock Tower was purchased by Lance five years ago. A huge part of him felt guilty for buying such a large imposing building to live in, but he had reasons for this. Lance easily feels claustrophobic in certain spaces. It is not true claustrophobia, as he has found himself in confined spaces throughout his work as a journalist. But if it is a prolonged feeling of lack of space, he feels shut in and anxious. He previously lived in a small apartment, but felt that a large, airy building would lessen this anxiety when he was home for long periods. The roof terrace is his most relaxing place in his home for him and he often slept out on it regardless of the seasons or weather.

The building itself, a former church clock tower, stood on a corner of two roads. As he approached his front door, a large arched structure, facing the road that turned off the main road, Lance noticed a man standing on the pavement immediately outside. As his mind was making multiple decisions, it took a few seconds for him to focus and see the man. A short stocky man, with a long, red ponytail and a brown leather jacket. He saw Lance and smiled.

Lancelot Knightly's Residence,
The Clock Tower,
Gipsy Hill,
London,
July 14,
7:48pm

The man waved as Lance stopped at the kerb, looking over and gesturing him to cross the road, but the younger man did not move, his mind began to evaluate and discuss the situation quickly. When he last saw this man, which seemed like a lifetime ago now, it was in a panicked state. Feelings of being out of his depth and in real danger now seemed much less powerful. Lance did not feel fear; it was now more cautious curiosity. Perhaps the fact that he had planned and executed an outrageously bold and dangerous rescue and escape from a place opposite one of the most secure buildings in the country this morning filled him with slightly more confidence.

Lance decided he wanted to talk with this man. He looked around quickly. The place was public and busy, with people enjoying the warm, summer evening. It was the most neutral ground as he could hope for. Though Lance wondered how this stranger knew his address, it was not as important at this time, he mused. Raising a hand and inviting him to cross the road, Lance prepared to gain some insight into this man's interest in him.

The older man quickly glanced both ways and then swiftly jogged across the road.

'Mister Knightly!' he shouted excitedly, smiling broadly and extending a hand, as he approached. Lance did not like people coming close to him too quickly and backed away two steps. The man stopped, mistaking this gesture for fear.

'I'm sorry, mate. I think I scared you the other day. I never meant to.' He had a West Country accent, rolling his words. Lance looked past his face, trying to read him.

'I'm Quentin Roth. And I'm sorry again I startled you before. I only just wanted a chat.' It was hard to establish any motives at present. Lance stepped forward and slowly extended a hand, which the man shook vigorously.

'*Lance Knightly.*' He typed, once his hand was free.

‘Call me Quent,’ the other man replied, appearing fascinated by the LANSPEAK.

‘Does that need Wi-Fi?’ he asked randomly. Lance thought quickly.

‘*Yes, though I have a good signal here. But I am sure you not here to discuss my communication device,*’ Lance replied, rather impatiently.

‘Er, yeah. Yeah, right,’ Quent replied, looking quite bemused. He composed himself and spoke.

‘You don’t remember me, do you?’ he asked, though it was more a statement. Although Lance could not make eye contact, he had Quent’s face pictured in his head. It was a face he did not recognise.

‘*I have an almost photographic memory. I do not recognise you because I do not know you. We have never met.*’

Quent seemed quite taken aback and mildly offended by the reply.

‘Let me jog your memory. Seven years ago, or thereabouts, I attended the same lecture you and Rufus Walcott did at UCL in London. Hosted by the ZSL. Sound familiar?’ It was a mildly aggressive statement and Lance felt like his photographic memory was being scrutinised. But he was much more interested in Quent’s mention of Rufus.

‘*I have an excellent memory. I am not psychic or omnipotent. There were four-hundred and seventy-two people at that lecture if I recall. You were only one of them. If we did not meet, how would I remember you?*’ Lance typed calmly. Quent appeared flustered, exhaling loudly before he replied.

‘Well, I asked a question. The panel answered honestly. It was about western involvement in the DRC.’

‘Twenty-nine people asked questions that night. Mostly about the same thing. Be more specific.’

Quent paused as small group of teenagers passed between them, laughing and talking loudly. They turned around the corner and he continued.

‘Well, it was a broad question. What I really wanted to ask would’ve been laughed out of the hall.’ He looked down, looking dejected. Lance found a trace of pity for him and was becoming interested in where he was going.

‘*What was the question, Quent?*’ he asked, wishing that the LANSPEAK could verbalise with more empathy right now. The older man looked up. He looked like an embarrassed child.

‘I was going to ask if there was any evidence of the J’ba Fofi in the area they were discussing,’ he said in a guilty tone, as if confessing a shameful secret.

Lance's mind sped up. He knew there was a connection between Rufus and this particular area of the DRC, but something had also caught the attention of some powerful and dangerous people. Lance was now intrigued at what else Quent could tell him. But not here.

'*Let us go somewhere and talk.*'

'We're talking here,' Quent replied puzzled.

'*These streets have ears.*' Lance typed, as he began to cross the road, gesturing the other man to follow, which he did. It was strange, Lance thought, how circumstances change. How different this was to their first meeting. Quentin Roth was now following *him,* who was now unsure what to make of this unassuming journalist.

Dulwich Upper Wood,
Farquhar Road,
London,
July 14,
8:15pm

They walked in silence, Quent guessing that they should not talk until they got to where they were going. He felt hot in his leather jacket and removed it, though he still felt warm. Lance appeared to not be affected by the heat, as he strode along at a brisk pace. It was clear to Quent that this man was extremely fit, very intelligent and virtually impossible to see any obvious emotions in him. Unbeknown to Lance, Quent had followed him, through his work, for many years. This was due to the fact that the journalist was not afraid to visit places few people dared to in the desire to uncover truths and establish facts. He secretly hoped that Lance would one day uncover some of the secrets he had always believed in. Though he knew Lance would get the credit, it would redeem himself to many of his peers, who largely viewed Quent as a laughing stock. *The truth is waiting to be discovered,* he thought to himself.

They entered the wooded area and the trees offered a cool relief from the evening heat. Lance paused in a grassed area. Looking around cautiously, he sat down on a bench and looked toward Quent. The older man slumped next to him, grateful to be sitting and out of the heat. He turned to Lance.

'You got a signal on that thing?' he asked, nodding towards the LANSPEAK.

'*It looks like it.*' Lance typed, looking straight ahead.

‘Clever. Where’d you get it?’ he asked genuinely interested.

‘I constructed it.’

‘Wow. Are you some sort of genius?’ The child-like personality of Quent was becoming more apparent. Lance did not have time for small talk.

‘I have an above average IQ. But you did not come to me to discuss my technical skills. You came to talk about what Rufus and Duncan were looking for in that particular area of the DRC. And your question about the J’ba Fofi leads me to believe you are a cryptozoologist. Am I correct?’ Lance remained staring forward, though could feel Quent shifting uncomfortably on the seat.

‘My *learned* friends call me a pseudoscientist. Which I think is meant as an insult. But I’ve adopted that title. I’m a proud pseudoscientist. Or cryptozoologist if that makes you feel more comfortable,’ he stated proudly and confidently.

‘What qualifications do you have in this area?’ Lance asked, knowing cryptozoology was not recognised in a specific academic field, but hoped Quent had some genuine knowledge or experience in a scientific area.

‘The university of life,’ was his only answer. Lance’s heart sank. This man, who Lance hoped would be able to answer some of the questions surrounding Rufus, appeared to be no more than a fantasist.

‘Oh, I know what you’re thinking. I’m a crazy nut who wastes his time trying to prove the existence of Bigfoot, Nessie and other improbable creatures.’

‘I did not think nut.’

‘Oh laugh and scoff, mister high IQ, but even a learned man like you can’t argue with the bumblebee paradox,’ Quent said, almost arrogantly.

‘That is a statement I am not familiar with.’ Lance found himself humouring the man.

‘Well, for years, people couldn’t figure out how a bumblebee could fly. It’s a short chubby insect and people believed it was defying the laws of physics by actually getting off the ground. But we’ve all seen one, hovering around a flower, showing off with its impossible antics,’ Quent replied smugly.

‘If I recall, the bumblebee’s flight has been explained scientifically.’

‘Exactly my point!’ Quent excitedly shouted. ‘So many things are deemed impossible, until someone comes along, thinking outside the box and proves us all wrong. People like me.’ He spoke as if he had just discovered how to make fire.

‘How do you think I can help you?’ Lance asked, wishing to conclude this conversation as soon as possible.

'You don't beat about the bush, do you?' the older man asked. 'Okay, I won't either. I want to come with you,' he stated slyly.

'*Come with me where?*' Lance asked, feeling genuinely puzzled.

'To the DRC of course. To find out what really happened to Rufus and Duncan,' he stated matter-of-factly. Lance was taken aback by this man's boldness and apparent knowledge of his immediate plans. This was a concerning development. Either Quent genuinely knew he was going to the DRC, or he was guessing. He hoped it was the latter. He thought quickly about his answer.

'*What makes you think I am going to Africa anytime soon?*'

'Mate, it's obvious. You're a thorough journalist. You want answers about what happened to your friend. Nobody's sharing information, so you're clearly going to take matters into your own hands, fly out to The Congo and find out yourself. Tell me I'm wrong?' Quent asked confidently, almost excitedly. Lance was intrigued and worried at the same time. Each time this man spoke, it added another layer of interest to him. He decided to find out exactly what Quentin Roth was all about.

'How much do you know about what happened to Rufus? It has not been made public knowledge as far as I know.'

'I have connections to the ZSL. I'd not actually met Rufus, though a mutual colleague informed me of his bizarre return to the UK. Which is all rather cloak-and-dagger I must say. I'm sure it was his brother that told a few people at the zoo. Well, what little he knew. I did know about some of the work Rufus was involved in. And as I've followed *your* work over the years, I put two and two together.'

Lance was trying to decide if this man was either a convincing liar, or genuine. It troubled Lance that he was not able to read Quent as easily as he could with others.

'*Why would you not just go to the DRC, regardless of whether I went? Is it a question of funding?*' Lance enquired, trying to gain an insight into this man's thinking. Quent laughed humourlessly.

'Funding? Well, I know your family are loaded but I can pay my own way thanks. Despite being a joke to most of my contemporaries, I have managed to get some private sponsorship to continue my unique research,' Quent arrogantly stated.

'*So why would going with me benefit you? You clearly do not need anything I can offer.'* Lance typed, but was eager to find out the real reason Quent wanted to accompany him.

'I just thought we could work well together. We're both looking for the truth in many ways. Time is no hurdle. Money isn't a problem. You're well-funded and I've now got corporate sponsorship.' He stopped speaking quickly after the last revelation. It was not lost on Lance.

'*Corporate sponsorship? Who is exactly funding your expedition?'*

'I'm not at liberty to divulge. Suffice to say, it'll be worth my while,' Quent replied, grinning and winking.

Lance had heard more than enough. The very first time he encountered Quent, Lance felt there was a connection between him and Brenton Stanmer. It was purely a gut feeling, but it was strong. Whether Stanmer was behind Quent, pulling his strings, Lance had no idea. But anyone heading to the DRC with a large company and their interests funding them, was not good. He stood up but did not face the older man.

'*I can be of no help to you, Mister Roth. I always work alone anyway. How you know so much about me, including where I live, concerns me. I feel you are not being honest with me, but have another agenda. One you know would go against my way of seeing things. I wish you good luck in your future endeavours. Though I am politely asking you not to follow or contact me again. Good evening.'* Lance had begun to walk away, as he finished sentence. He heard Quent mutter something but was out of hearing range very quickly, as he was briskly heading out of the park and then home. He did not look back as he quickened his pace and found himself jogging quickly. It was not to get away from Quent. It was to get home, pack and secure his house. He had to leave straight away.

Lancelot Knightly's Residence,
The Clock Tower,
Gipsy Hill,
London,
July 14,
10:00pm

He began to pack and book his flights as soon as he got home, suddenly feeling that he was racing against a deadline. Which was not something he was unused to, but this was more serious than submitting a story for publication. The truth he was seeking could be hugely significant for an entire country and countless people's lives. Having no idea how long he would be out of the country, he packed accordingly, but also mindful he had to travel light. He packed essentials, but also equipment he had borrowed from Mac at the same time as he had loaned him the wing-suit. Other items included headphones for music. Lance often had music playing whilst out in busy places. It shut out unwelcome noise, distracted his thoughts and he enjoyed it. The music was almost always classical, nineteen-eighties pop or nineteen-nineties dance. For some reason, these three groups suited his needs when travelling.

Another item he never left without was his camera, though this was a unique model. His own GoPro. Lance had designed and constructed it using recycled materials from similar well-known models. This had been his evidence-collecting device ever since he built it. Tough and waterproof, it was exactly what he needed on most of his trips, this current one included.

Lance removed his LANSPEAK and examined it. Apart from some light dirt, it was in good condition. This particular device was known only to him as the LANSPEAK prototype, as there were nine others almost identical to it in various secret locations known only to him. He could only guess their monetary value, as Caelia was very fond of reminding him, more than once telling him he should mass produce them and sell for profit. And Lance had considered this on some level, though not the profit part, knowing the LANSPEAK could change the lives of countless people throughout the world, who were also without speech. He knew of course, that this could not be done. The communicator was far too complex for most people to use. It was designed specifically for Lance too, who had such a high intellect in this field of technology and he used it as easy as talking. The device also had a built-in computer, which allowed him Internet communications, though used only with a select few people. Before he stopped physically speaking, Lance was fluent in seventeen languages, though most people were unaware of this and it was not public knowledge. Fortunately, his device could be programmed to an almost limitless amount of languages. Lance felt it much easier to communicate with the world this way.

Having a near photographic memory was also advantageous when it came to documentation. Lance required no files, backup computer systems, passwords or information storage of any kind (except for evidence for legal purposes). It was all contained in his mind. Anything confidential or private merely needed to be remembered. This also made following him extremely difficult. He left no paper trails and very little, if any, evidence behind of his activities, which ultimately made him an extremely efficient journalist. At this moment, he was grateful for all the advantages he had, as they would all be needed for what lay ahead. He had a last look around his spacious home. Although he set the alarms, security cameras, light timers and locked everything, he had a suspicion his home was at high risk from being broken into. By who exactly, he was not sure. He even considered asking Tristan to stay there while he was away, who would have gladly done so. But he did not want to involve him, or anyone else from this point on.

He packed everything. Took his passport and travel documents. He went online that evening and booked six flights, all one way. Three from Gatwick, to Athens, Oslo and Berlin. One from Stansted to Amsterdam and two from Heathrow, to Brussels and Istanbul. He did this as he felt that he was now being closely watched, by whom, he did not yet know. But too many people were involved in his decision to investigate Rufus's story that he had to assume that his every move was being considered. He knew to take public transport to the airport, so Lance had one last look at his home, then exited into the warm London night.

Looking around cautiously, he had never before felt so acutely aware of his environment. How he could be watched, followed or tracked. But he felt he had made adequate precautions to make it as difficult as possible to be traced. He walked up the street at a brisk pace.

Brixton Tube Station,
London,
July 14,
11pm

He took the train from Gipsy Hill. He remembered back to when Quent was following him on the underground and how it was easy to notice his pursuer. Lance felt that he was now under the watchful eye of more powerful individuals, and feared they would be much harder to notice, if he could at all. He looked around the station, observing all the people, suspicious behaviour, ways in or out and decided he could only do so much to shake off a tail.

The night was cooler, but still very mild, so there were still plenty of people around. Lance saw this as good and bad. It was harder to follow someone in a large crowd and equally easier to disappear into one. But it was also more difficult to spot a possible tail when there were more people to blend in with. Knowing he could be being watched right now, Lance decided not to hang around and as the train pulled in, he shuffled on with the rest of the passengers. It set off and he took a seat in the quietest carriage. Although he felt overwhelmed at the decisions he had made and was still making, Lance felt in control. He was focused, determined and confident in his plans to find the answers to what had happened to his friend.

Thoughts of Rufus overtook him and he closed his eyes. He kept thinking of the haunted, terrified look in his eyes. It was more painful as Lance never normally made eye contact. It was disturbing to see. But it strengthened his resolution in finding out what happened on that fateful trip.

He opened his eyes and looked around. Nobody appeared to be interested in him, or even looking in his direction. He pondered where to get off, knowing the changes to get him to Heathrow, but felt he should not be making his route too obvious. The train slowed, as it neared the first stop, Stockwell. Lance debated getting off, even changing routes. In the end, he decided to get off, pretend he had changed his mind and get back on again. Nobody did the same or even appeared to notice him. The train trundled out of the station. Lance decided to get where he was going directly. If he were being followed or watched, it would be harder to do outside of the UK.

Heathrow Airport Tube Station,
Terminal 5,
London,
July 15,
11:40pm

It felt as late as it was. Lance carried his luggage into the airport and checked in. Security personnel and cameras were everywhere. He was being continuously monitored, as was everyone else in the airport, but Lance wondered if more unwelcome eyes were on him. Though, it felt virtually impossible to tell at this time. He checked in and proceeded to the departure lounge. A television was playing nearby; though it had no sound, Lance's heart skipped a beat as he saw a news report of a security incident at St Thomas's Hospital that day. Though he knew he had covered his tracks well, it still unnerved him. And uncomfortably reminded him of how deeply involved he was in a situation he still did not fully understand.

Finding a seat in the quieter area, Lance gathered his thoughts. He had to mentally plan his onward journey, as everything up until this moment had been rushed and made up as he went along. Which he hated. Closing his eyes, the trip was laid out before him. A photographic memory was extremely helpful, as he could picture Istanbul as clearly as if he was walking through it. Though Lance used technology as little as he could, he was extremely competent in all areas of technologies of the world. He had numerous online pseudonyms when he is investigating anything. Anonymity in the cyber world was one of his best protections he felt. Lance even had an alias when publishing in "My Earth". Calling himself "BLACK EYED BOY", the name stemming from Lance's incredibly dark eyes. Only Blake knew his identity at "My Earth". And he had numerous contacts in the cyber world who he could turn to when needed, one whom he would be contacting in Turkey. Planning and organising gave him a little well needed peace and he felt in control once more. This new calm made him feel sleepy and Lance realised he had not slept well for a while. He let a tranquil restfulness sweep over him.

Though he did not fall asleep, the announcement of his flight stirred him suddenly. Heading towards his gate, Lance was reminded that he never enjoyed flying, though he did it often, as he had to for his work. But he felt uncomfortable being in an enclosed space for such a long time. Plus, he was in the hands of someone he had never met. Though always having every faith in the pilot's capabilities, it still felt like he was putting his whole life in their hands. People who knew Lance found this bizarre, as he had no problems base jumping, skydiving and involving himself in all manner of extreme sports which would terrify most people. But this was because Lance was always in control. And he had confidence in himself, as he approached all these activities from practical, scientific and mathematical points of view, so always felt safe.

As he headed to the aeroplane's door, he was reminded how turbulence was the part of flying he hated the most. He knew scientifically it was nothing to worry about, but that did not stop him feeling anxious with each bump the flight made. Once, on a previous trip, a fellow passenger noticed his nervousness during a particularly rough period of turbulence. Lance distinctively remembered the well-meaning man saying that flying was less dangerous than crossing a road. And he also remembers nodding to thank the man, but actually thinking that he does not normally cross a road at fifty thousand feet in the air, inside a giant metal tube filled with flammable liquid, in the hands of someone he has never met.

Taking a deep breath, Lance took his seat and concentrated on the onward journey, as the plane taxied across the runway and lifted smoothly into the air, flying him towards his destination.

Atatürk Airport,
Istanbul,
Turkey,
July 16,
7:30am (Turkish time)

The sun was already up and looking warm, as the plane gradually descended toward the Turkish city. Lance could see a busy looking sea, and as they lowered, he could make out numerous buildings he recognised, as he had been here numerous times. Familiar landmarks such as the Bosphorus Bridge and the Blue Mosque swam into view as the plane touched down, much to Lance's relief.

Disembarking with the rest of the passengers, he made good time funnelling through security and customs, which Lance was grateful for as large crowds made him uncomfortable and headed into the city. The heat hit his whole body, as he left the comfort of the air-conditioned building. A taxi rank was close by and Lance entered the nearest car, once again grateful to be cooler. He handed the driver a hand written note in Turkish with his destination's address on and a footnote saying he is without speech. Any use of the LANSPEAK was an obvious give way to him. As soon as he had left customs, he had covered his speech device in a pale plain cover, so that it resembled a plaster cast. This disguise had been useful many times on his travels. Hiding the LANSPEAK helped with anonymity.

The driver nodded and soon they were crawling through the heavy city traffic. Time was not too important to Lance today in fact he had time to kill, which was fortunate, as they shuffled through the gridlock.

Sitting in the back seat, he began to unpack certain things. His camera he mounted onto a special clip on his shoulder. Lance felt that this needed to be online and ready whenever possible. Throughout his work, he had discovered that an active digital camera was an invaluable tool in providing evidence and gaining proof against people or organisations, whom he had found were often extremely unscrupulous.

His backpack was secure and various papers were pulled out from his luggage. His hotel booking confirmation, passport and cash were all at the ready. Lance always felt being prepared on any level gave him a slight advantage over those who were not. As the car drew closer to the destination, he felt that, if he needed to, he could exit the taxi quickly and proceed to any number of destinations on foot. That was how poised he felt as the taxi pulled up to the hotel.

Sultan Suites,
Istanbul,
Turkey,
July 16
8:30am (Turkish time)

Lance was hyper vigilant, as he approached the building. Of course, if he was being watched from a distance or with the assistance of technology, there was not a great deal he could do about it. He had one last look around the busy streets, at the mass of people going about their everyday business, realising it would be almost impossible to spot a potential tail, then entered the cool foyer.

This was one of four accommodations he had booked and paid for to try and throw any pursuers off the trail. Lance chose this one as he had never been before and it was not a top budget hotel, which would often the obvious choice for a man of his means.

He had considered using a false identity on this trip, which is something he had not done before. But the reason he did not was that he *partly* wanted to be followed. On some level, Lance was intrigued to know who was behind all these clandestine decisions. He wanted to know but did not want to risk exposing his plan, or finding out the truth about Rufus.

After eating a large breakfast, Lance checked in. It was much earlier than the standard check in time, but he had paid extra for the room to be ready early in the morning. Any activities which were slightly unusual in everyday life could help to conceal Lance's plans.

The room was comfortable and felt cool as he entered. Once freshened up, Lance took out his camera, which was also a sophisticated computer. Lance only ever used this for Internet access unless he had access to a public device whilst travelling. Though not believing himself to be paranoid, it was obvious to him that for anonymity and protection, his online self should be as hidden as possible. He never wanted to leave any trail to protect himself and any vulnerable people or groups, which he often encountered.

Despite being very adept at working online covertly, Lance had, on occasion, used other online individuals to help him. Often they were people similar to him, wanting to make a difference in the world often just via social media or blogs. Though he was also acutely aware that he should exercise extreme caution, as the anonymity of cyberspace was very good at hiding people with nefarious intentions. Though Lance had assisted in exposing some of these individuals, the smarter ones were often ten steps ahead.

The most important online support Lance used was the one he was about to contact. He (who once stated he was male) was obviously a technological genius. The journalist had worked alongside him numerous times with a lot of success in exposing criminal activity. Though he did not know him and knew they would probably never meet, his actions spoke volumes about his character. Lance felt he could trust him as much as he could. He logged on. It was time to contact TEX.

****

He was walking through the thick undergrowth, growing more tired with each step. The jungle was humid, though he felt a clammy chill on his skin. It was still light, though the thick trees hid most of the sun. His backpack felt heavy and he was aware of the silence around him. Only the noise of his footsteps, his own heavy breathing and a few insect sounds were all that could be heard. The trees felt over bearing and claustrophobic. Though he suffered from claustrophobia, he had never felt it whilst outside.

Lance felt as unfit as he ever had and each leg got heavier with each step. His skin flushed cold. The light suddenly became less as a cold dank feeling swept over the area. Lance found himself walking through a clearing with the darkest twisted trees at the edge of it. Then he heard it. Something that made his blood run cold. A scream. A man's voice, shrieking in terror. Lance's heart pounded, as he recognised the horrible cry. It was Rufus. Rufus was screaming a guttural cry of fear. It was coming from the shadowy trees. Lance tried to run towards them but he found it too difficult. His legs were sinking into a swamp, sucking him in up to his knees, as he tried to move. 'Lance!' Rufus cried with renewed anguish. 'Help me!' the pitiful voice screamed. Lance felt helpless as he tried to move. 'Lance, it's coming!' the voice shrieked with renewed horror. 'Lance, it's coming for me!' These cries for help stung Lance in the heart. He tried to move but the marshy ground pulled him deeper. 'Noooo!' The last word ended with a scream. Lance then found he could move again, though something else moved out of the trees that stopped him dead.

The spider swiftly scuttled out of the branches and stealthily crept around the swampy edge. It began making its way towards Lance. Though this was no ordinary spider. It was unnaturally huge. Its gigantic body was over two feet long, with huge thick legs over five feet across. It looked roughly the size of a dining table, hairy like a tarantula and with large, black fangs over six inches long. And it was heading straight for him.

Lance managed to turn around and sluggishly wade out of the sinking mud. He found solid ground and ran, though his legs felt weak, feeling like he could collapse at any moment. He briefly looked back. The colossal spider was pursuing him at a frightening speed. Just as he thought he was gaining ground, he slammed into something. It was strong and sticky. As he tried to free himself, he turned to face where he had come from, but in the process getting further tangled. Both arms were trapped. He could not reach his LANSPEAK. He wanted to cry for help. He opened his mouth to scream but no sound came. Lance looked up. The spider was twenty feet away and crawling stealthily towards him.

Fifteen feet, he tried to scream. Nothing. His hands felt like they were glued to his sides. He tried to wriggle free. It only made him more constrained. Ten feet. A silent scream again. He could hear its fangs clicking together. The creature made a large hissing sound. Five feet. He felt faint but squirmed as he felt the arachnid's front legs brush his neck; the thick wiry hair sent icy shivers through him. The fangs were close to his face, as he finally let out a scream.

Sultan Suites,
Istanbul,
Turkey,
July 16,
8:45pm (Turkish time)

Lance awoke suddenly and sat up quickly. He had screamed in the nightmare, but not when awake. His clothes were soaked in sweat. Taking a few seconds to orientate himself, Lance glanced around the room, which was darkening with the setting of the sun. Breathing rapidly, he had to stop himself from shivering. Pouring himself a glass of water, Lance sat and stared at the reddening sky and tried to focus his mind. His head felt foggy but he was starting to orientate and rationalise his thoughts.

Nightmares were something Lance had suffered from in the past but not recently. The vividness of the dream was fresh in his mind. He gradually pushed the horror of that unwelcome mind invasion away but then found that the guilt remained. In fact, it was stronger than it had been. He was not sure why he felt such guilt towards Rufus's situation. This trip he was on was, Lance was hoping, would go some way to alleviate some of the guilt.

Pushing the unpleasant thoughts of giant spiders to the back of his mind, Lance knew he was ready to proceed with his journey. Before he had fallen asleep, Lance had contacted TEX. It had only been a few weeks since their last conversation. TEX was informed about all the main aspects of what had led Lance to this point. What Lance required from TEX was even further anonymity. A direct and secret route directly to the area of the DRC where Rufus had last visited. An incredibly complicated and detailed task ordinarily, but add to that, it allowed only a few hours' notice would be virtually impossible for most people. But for TEX, barely a challenge Lance knew.

It was the arrangements at the very last minute that made it much harder for anyone to trace or infiltrate the journey. TEX arranged the final part of the planned expedition in fifteen minutes. This was no surprise to Lance. He was used to TEX's ability to tap into any technological resource to fulfil his aims. What did always intrigue the journalist were the varying methods of communication TEX used when conversing online to Lance.

Over the two years since TEX and BLACK-EYED BOY had worked mutually and anonymously from time to time, they had communicated via online games, social media cryptic clues, online blogs and even via a crossword, which Lance sometimes wrote in "My Earth". It was obvious that TEX was as highly intelligent as Lance but superior when it came to the technological and cyber world. It never ceased to surprise Lance how much TEX could achieve just from a keyboard anywhere in the world. It was also very alarming to him. Lance knew that if TEX could use this cyber world for genuine positive and good reasons, in someone else's hands this secret power was extremely dangerous.

Lance suppressed a shudder of fear at what was happening in this world at this very moment. But he had to stay grounded and focused. He packed what he needed and headed out of his room to the taxi he had just called. The journey had quickened its pace once more.

Istanbul,
Turkey,
July 16,
9:10pm (Turkish time)

TEX had given Lance instructions to take a taxi down a certain road at a certain time, which was where he was headed right now. The driver knew the roads well and was happy to follow the first direction given, which Lance had written down on paper from TEX's instructions. To limit the use of the LANSPEAK was important to maintain any secrecy at this time.

The car headed towards the street as night swept over the city and the streetlights gradually lit up. The traffic was lighter than the morning but the roads were still busy. Lance was in the front seat looking out for a sign from TEX. The driver just assumed the younger man was admiring the night's scenery. Just then, up ahead at the next junction, a streetlight began to flash regularly. To anyone else, this was just a fault or an electrical surge. But Lance knew what it was. TEX had outdone himself this time, as he had promised. Controlling a section of the electrical grid of a major city to make certain selected lamps flash. It was on the left of the road, so Lance tapped the driver's arm and pointed left.

The car turned in the direction of the flashing light, oblivious to its rhythmic signalling. This was a quieter road but still a main highway. Another flashing lamp indicated the route forward. The taxi driver was happy to follow Lance's direction. The older man guessed that Lance knew where he was going from memory but had forgotten street names. As long as the meter was running, the driver drove through every street Lance pointed to.

This bizarre signalling happened numerous times until the final destination came into view. It was an office building, illuminated by a garish-green light. The taxi pulled up, Lance paid the driver and headed into the building. Lance looked for what he was expecting to find. He quickly located the safety deposit box. It had a key code to unlock it. Lance punched in the correct numbers and retrieved the documents he knew would be inside.

He walked back out into the warm night. The taxi had gone. Lance pocked the papers and headed back to the hotel. He was feeling quite exhilarated at how easy that had been so far. He needed to leave first thing in the morning. Lance proceeded to run at a steady pace back to his accommodation.

Sultan Suites,
Istanbul,
Turkey,
July 17,
7:30pm (Turkish time)

The sun was already warm in the sky, as Lance checked out after an early breakfast. Climbing into a taxi, he felt like he was now one-step ahead of whomever he thought might be following him. His over cautiousness and forward planning must surely have thrown even the most determined pursuer off the scent. As the car headed to the airport, Lance pondered on the outlandish ways TEX and he communicated, but also how effective it was.

With minimum information relayed over the Internet, TEX was able to book, print and almost hand tickets to Lance personally for a private charter plane from Kinshasa Airport to the area he wanted to get to in the DRC. Lance had a renewed admiration and respect for TEX. His skill at obtaining these documents in such a short time was quite incredible in Lance's mind. But it did get him wondering at just how TEX was able to operate in such an efficient manner. It was clear that he had access to extremely confidential material, though he appeared to use his knowledge for good, it always felt uncomfortable for Lance at how much knowledge, information and power one individual could have.

The fact that they used this power for the greater good did not excuse the fact that one person could have such potential influence on the world with a few presses of a keyboard. Though at this very moment, Lance had to put aside his misgivings and was just grateful he had TEX on his side during this complicated period of his career, if not his life.

As the taxi approached Atatürk Airport, Lance pondered on the ease of obtaining a secret pass to the area of the DRC he needed to get to. TEX had communicated the details of the collection to Lance (as BLACK-EYED BOY) in the form of a game. Cryptic messages were sent to Lance, which both men knew how to decipher easily. TEX simply informed Lance to secretly follow the flashing lights to the green building. Though any codes or ciphers could be cracked over time by an outside party, it would take too long for them to catch up with Lance once they had figured it out. At least, that is what he hoped.

The airport rose into view as the taxi slowed as it entered the drop off point. Lance paid the driver and headed into the building with his luggage. Another small trip which is less dangerous than crossing the road apparently. Lance sighed and headed towards the check in. *Time to find some answers,* he told himself.

N'djili International Airport,
Kinshasa,
The Democratic Republic of the Congo,
July 17,
3:50pm (Congolese and UK time)

The flight was uneventful, though Lance was very relieved to be back on the ground. He collected his luggage and headed towards his pre-planned destination. Back in Turkey, Lance had exchanged some currency. He was only allowed to take a certain amount of cash on the flight, so he obtained American dollars, South African rand and Congolese francs. Lance hoped that the second part of the plan TEX and he had put together was going to run equally as smooth.

The destination was in sight. A private runway, used only for official flights. Though Lance knew for the right price, a charter could be arranged. And had been. The fake plaster cast was still on to disguise the LANSPEAK, so he was hoping no verbal negotiations were required. A number of armed guards were stood in the doorway to the private entrance. Lance acted as relaxed as he possibly could when he took his documents out and handed them to an official looking man who eyed the younger man and his paperwork meticulously.

The ticket was for a small aeroplane, which was ordinarily used to fly a small group of people from Kinshasa to Kisangani. Officially, there was only one flight per week between these cities, however, an undisclosed number of private and official flights regularly made the journey between them. That route took them directly over the Salonga National Park, which was Lance's final destination.

The official began shaking his head as if to suggest that the documents were not enough to board this flight. Lance had been expecting this and held out a hand, turned upwards, so the older man could see a number of American dollar bills. The man sighed and pretended to shake the younger man's hand whilst grasping the bribe subtly. He expertly counted the cash, which were mixed with Lance's papers, pretending to examine them further.

Lance was beginning to feel uncomfortable. Everything had been relatively simple up until now, perhaps too easy. The manmade inscrutable facial expressions whilst counting his unofficial fee and Lance had to subdue a feeling of dread. If he were not let on this flight, all his efforts up to this point could be for nothing. Time, as he knew it for this current task, had a limited time frame. The man was now making exaggerated faces, much to Lance's annoyance. The official was acting like he was unimpressed with the offered amount and appeared to be debating whether it was an appropriate sum offered.

Lance was about to get some more money out, which he did not want to do, as he guessed this would not be the first person who would require "financial persuasion", a term TEX used often. The man finally grunted, though acting disappointed, he handed Lance his papers and motioned him to head to the runway. The younger man nodded gratefully and made his way to the waiting transport.

The Monsoon,
N'djili Private Runway,
Kinshasa,
The Democratic Republic of the Congo,
July 17,
4:10pm (Congolese and UK time)

The humidity hit Lance like a wet towel in the face. This place had a whole new level of heat. It was much hotter than Turkey, or so it felt. He checked his watch. It was helpful that Congolese time was also UK time. Somehow, it felt easier to orientate to a country with the same time zone. It was also worth remembering, he thought, that the sunset time was in approximately two hours here, three hours earlier than the UK at this time of year. Lance surveyed his surroundings. A single strip runway spread out before him. Then he saw his transport.

It was a Gulfstream III business jet. “The Monsoon” was printed along the side of the aircraft. It looked like an older model, but one that had been well maintained on its outward appearance. There were only three men that Lance could see. One man standing under the nose of the aeroplane with a clipboard making notes, the other at the open door performing what looked like final safety checks. Both men were in boiler suits. The third man was dressed like a security guard. No other passengers or officials seemed to be waiting for the flight.

An uneasy feeling crept into Lance’s head. He was not sure why but he just felt not everything was sitting right in what he could see. Though everything about this trip, he reasoned, did not sit right. He had never done so much with so little planning before. So far, he felt he had been remarkably lucky. Though how long that luck would last was what Lance was turning over in his head.

He knew there may or may not be other passengers on this flight, though he had no way of knowing who they were if they were accompanying him. Just then, a fourth person, a young woman, exited the aircraft from the door close to the cockpit and waved at Lance to come forward. He felt like there was no turning back now, though that had never really been an option for him.

The young woman, unlike the men was dressed in a smart flight attendant’s uniform. Smiling warmly as Lance approached she held out her hand for his ticket. He handed her the documents, half expecting her to then ask for an extra payment. To his surprise, she swiftly handed his papers back and with an official but warm smile, gestured Lance to climb on board. ‘Thank you, *monsieur*, enjoy your flight,’ she said with a strong French accent. Just before he boarded, the security guard patted him up and down his body, poking his fingers into pockets, though it was a brief search and the man nodded and gestured him to continue.

Lance had a long last look at his surroundings, beginning to feel more and more unsettled at the ease of the journey since he had left England. There appeared to be nothing out of the ordinary to concern him, so he shrugged internally and boarded The Monsoon.

The Monsoon,
N'djili Private Runway,
Kinshasa,
The Democratic Republic of the Congo,
July 17,
4:13pm (Congolese and UK time)

The interior of the transport was cooler, mainly because it was dark and out of the humid sun, though it was still uncomfortably warm. Lance hoped that some air conditioning would commence once the engines started up. He surveyed his new surroundings. The cabin was small but looked comfortable enough. Large luxurious looking chairs were randomly placed around the compact area. Some were single, others double and most had tables next to them.

A reclining sofa was against the wall next to the door he had entered through. The cockpit door was closed and had a sign "Entrée Interdite" in red letters written on it. On further entering the cabin, Lance noticed another door at the opposite end of the aeroplane. It looked to be part of a partitioned wall, as if the end section of the cabin had been sealed off from the rest of it. Taking a few steps closer, he could read another sign on this door. "Strictement Privé."

This was looking more and more like an official government transport than one for private leisure. Though this was always going to be a possibility, he knew that. Lance just hoped that the money TEX had put into this flight would secure the no questions asked deal he required.

Sitting in a single chair, Lance surveyed the cabin with his keen eye. The only thing which struck him as strange were the three bright orange coloured bags secured over the doorway. He had seen enough of these in his life to know they were parachutes. Though they looked like very old and outdated packs. Seeing them hanging over the door only confirmed that this was more of an official transport, a parachute being a last means of escape in an emergency. Why there were only three seemed strange to him. Surely all members of staff should be able to escape if the aeroplane was crashing. *Curious*, he thought.

What was even more puzzling was that Lance knew that a door like this could not be opened whilst the aircraft is in flight, the cabin pressure would not allow it. So, the presence of parachutes hanging above the door was a mystery.

Before he could ponder further, the cabin lights flicked on and a voice over the loud speaker made Lance jump. In English, with a French accent, the male voice spoke, 'Ladies and gentlemen, please take your seat and fasten your seatbelt, as we are preparing for take-off.'

Lance suddenly felt alarmed. He was alone, yet this trip should have been booked as a charter flight. It was meant to make an unofficial stopover in the Salonga National Park, his destination. He stood up and headed towards the door, which was then promptly shut and in front of him.

He had to stifle a feeling of panic as the engines started. Everything now seemed very wrong. He was expecting other passengers and probably some staff on this flight. This felt like he had suddenly become a prisoner. A hundred thoughts raced through his head. What had TEX done? Who had planned this? Where was he now headed? Could he just open the door right now and get out? Trying to clear his mind and focus on the present, Lance felt the aeroplane move. It was taxiing along the small runway. The French voice boomed out again, 'Seatbelts, please.'

The cabin shook uncontrollably. He had no choice. It was too late to try and open the door now, so he returned to his seat and strapped himself in. Looking out of the window, the airport rushed by. His stomach sank as the aircraft lifted off the ground, gaining height very quickly. The buildings shrunk below him. A stretch of water shone in the early evening light. The Congo River.

Lance suddenly felt out of control once more, which he hated. Having been so careful since he had left England, he felt frustrated and quite angry that he appeared to have been stalled. His mind swam, as he looked out of the window. The river was now a silvery line, snaking through a vast green landscape.

Closing his eyes and calming himself, Lance focused his thoughts. Though he knew something was wrong, he could not be quite sure what situation he was in. Though on the positive side, he was very close to where he needed to get to. Rationalising his thoughts, it did occur to him that this trip could be exactly what TEX had organised all along. One last misdirection to make following him even harder.

Feeling calmer, he checked his compass. They were heading in the direction planned. It was roughly two hours to Kisangani, though he was planning on getting off sooner than that. Lance began to feel like he had panicked when the aeroplane had set off, though he was still not totally convinced he was not in a potentially serious situation.

The aircraft went through a patch of turbulence, making Lance feel slightly nauseous. Safer than crossing the road someone once told him. Lance really doubted that at this exact time.

Aboard the Monsoon,
The Democratic Republic of the Congo,
July 17,
5:28pm (Congolese and UK time)

The past hour and fifteen minutes had passed quickly and uneventfully. The flight was feeling surreal. No further messages from the (he assumed) pilot. Lance was tracking his journey. They were flying towards Kisangani, passing over the Salonga National Park. His thoughts had continued to return to those parachutes and the door below which they were hanging. It had seemed strange that when the door closed, it had neither swung in nor out, but from the side, having been hidden in the body of the aircraft.

Knowing this was a government transport, Lance had some ideas why this was the design. His work over the years had led him to study many aspects of official security measures in different countries. One constant trend was that the people at the top always had escape routes planned in advance before travelling. Some methods extremely advanced, others quite simple. It was starting to become obvious that this door could be opened whilst in flight to enable the escape of the most important passengers. How it could be opened, he had no idea. And he had absolutely no inclination to try it.

The small plane was cruising at thirty thousand feet and flying in a north-easterly direction, according to a small screen near his chair, though the feeling of unease grew rapidly in Lance. They should be descending right about now.

He knew where his starting point should be following his conversation with Fim, which now seemed like an age ago. Did TEX get it wrong? Were others currently taking control of this journey now? Lance took the fake cast off and checked his LANSPEAK. His heart skipped a beat as a small flashing light alerted him to an incoming message.

He knew it was from TEX, as his messages were colour coded (TEX's was red) and he also knew TEX had no need to message him again for a while. How long had it had been flashing? There had been no signal since he had taken off. He cursed himself for letting his panic cloud his concentration. With a shaky hand, Lance opened the message. It was in the form of a game one which they had designed between them. The "game" was simply called FRUITS. They had created it about a year ago. It was very simple in its concept. The message always opened as a screen. It had twenty-six fruit items on the screen ready to be placed into a basket, which then revealed the message. Each fruit represented a letter of the alphabet. They were never laid out in alphabetical order, and the letter for each fruit changed after each time they used FRUITS to communicate.

This was secure aspect of the game. To inform one another of what each fruit/letter was each time, the two men used many methods of revealing the new codes to each other. The simplest one was to write a paragraph of text, which had to include all letters in the alphabet. The text could appear online or on social media, or as a letter in "My Earth". In another part of the Internet, often in games magazines, they would publish the exact same paragraph of text in fruit form, which would reveal what letter each fruit represented. The messages were always very short, often no more than five or six words. If letters were used more than once, the fruit would have both or more numbers on in the order they were to be used. Lance only had to read the text once and look at the fruit image once to memorise both. It was an elaborate way to communicate, but they had used it with good effect on numerous occasions.

FRUITS appeared on the LANSPEAK. The fruits, which were to go into the basket were numbered and flashed. Though Lance would often place the fruits into the basket to look like he was actually playing a game, which meant he could openly communicate secretly whilst in a very public place. As he was alone, he looked at each numbered fruit and instantly knew the letter.

1.T - 2.H - 3.E - 4.Y, once it had spelled out THEY, his head spun. He already guessed the rest but hazily went through the motions of the message.

5.K - 6.N - 7.O - 8.W.

THEY KNOW

Lance felt faint as he tried to process it all. Just then, the door at the back of the cabin opened. Lance, to his disbelief, found himself staring up at Brenton Stanmer.

Aboard the Monsoon,
The Democratic Republic of the Congo,
July 17,
5:30pm (Congolese and UK time)

The tall man Lance had begun to loathe simply stared down at him with a cruel smile spread across his face. 'Mister Knightly,' he simply said and no hand was offered in greeting. The younger man stayed seated, feeling too overwhelmed to physically move. Stanmer ran appraising eyes over the journalist. It was difficult for Lance to read his manner, though it was obvious it this was the man's true persona. Without another word, he sat in the chair nearest to Lance and began to hum tunelessly, trying but failing to make eye contact with the younger man. This felt oddly unnerving to Lance. The older man was clearly more in control of this situation than could be imagined.

Finally Stanmer spoke. 'Well, you're a difficult quarry to hunt young man,' he arrogantly stated. The patronising manner was still there, but now it had a sinister undertone. Referring to Lance as a quarry to be hunted filled him with a sickening dread. 'And smart too. Very smart,' he coldly continued. The younger man felt like he was being interrogated without any questions being asked. Stanmer lay back in his chair, clasped his hands together and looked up. 'And there was me thinking you were dumb.' He sniggered humourlessly then leaned forward. 'Oh of course, we aren't supposed to say dumb these days, are we?' he said with mock surprise.

'My apologies, young man, I should've said I thought you were just a thick mute,' he cruelly continued. 'But you've proved me wrong. In fact, you're like a Stephen Hawking. As in you're super smart.' He pretended to ponder. 'Well super smart but handicapped,' he added. Lance was not surprised that Stanmer was talking to him like this. He knew the man was vile from the moment they first met. He had been spoken to like this many times over the years and it was no longer hurtful, it just reaffirmed what he knew about Brenton Stanmer. He was a man with little, if any conscience.

The older man then stood and paced up and down the cabin. This seemed like a little performance from him, a grim warm up prior to revealing to Lance what the situation actually was. Stanmer's hand then rested on Lance's shoulder, feigning affection and making him shudder. 'I've always wondered that about evolution,' he spoke as if reciting philosophy. 'Why lock brilliant minds away in people like you? Such a waste if you ask me. It's like nature has a sick sense of humour.' These foul comments were going over Lance's head. He was waiting for him to finally talk about what he was planning.

Sitting down again, a ruthless look crept over his face and body language. It looked like he was finally getting down to business after his nasty small talk.

'Yes. I do work for CES, not the British consulate. And yes, we have control of numerous companies internationally.' Stanmer spoke in a boastful way, clearly proud of the man he was and in his position. 'But what I'm interested in right now is you. And why you're poking your nose into things that don't concern you. And as that funny little thing on your wrist needs Wi-Fi, you're not able to answer my questions. We have no Wi-Fi on board I'm afraid as there's infrequent signal in this jungle for many miles. So we'll head to Kisangani and you can tell me exactly what you're up to.'

Lance wondered how the man thought the LANSPEAK needed Wi-Fi. His internal question was answered when the door from which Stanmer had entered from opened again. Lance found he was not totally surprised to be staring up at a rather guilty looking Quentin Roth.

Aboard the Monsoon,
The Democratic Republic of the Congo,
July 17,
5:32pm (Congolese and UK time)

Quent could not even look Lance in the eye, acting like someone who was forced to be there. He stood behind the older man's chair like a child waiting to receive a punishment.

'What can I say? I guess everyone has a price,' Stanmer said with a sickly smirk. Quent stared down at the CEO, a look of bewilderment on his face.

'You said y-you believed in my work,' he stuttered. 'You asked me to help—
'

'And you have. You are,' Stanmer snapped an interruption.

Quent looked crestfallen. Lance almost felt pity for him. It appeared that he had been used. Which was always going to happen if you choose CES as your corporate sponsorship.

'Oh, don't feel too disappointed in your stalker here,' Stanmer said waving a hand at the dejected Quent, who now slumped into the chair next to him. 'It wasn't he who has the tech to be two steps ahead of you all this time. A company like ours has limitless access to anything we need.' The CEO seemed happy to continue talking about his reasons for being here, so Lance now focused his mind and began to listen intently. 'Young Roth here informed us that you were heading off immediately. All we had to do was follow you,' Stanmer said to Lance, clearly happy to reveal more and more. 'And I must admit; your efforts of trying to cover your tracks were quite ingenious. You led us quite a merry dance at times!' he chuckled darkly.

Please expose more of your methods, Lance said to himself.

'In fact, I'd ask you to come and work for us. But I know you won't, being a spoiled little rich boy.' The last sentence was spoken with clear resentment from Stanmer.

'Of course most of it wasn't down to you,' he continued 'This cyber genius you use are really something, aren't they?' Stanmer's tone had changed with that last statement. He seemed angry. It made Lance feel that although they were able to trace every step of his journey, the identity of TEX had actually escaped them, which gave him a trace of comfort and some hope. Though how TEX knew they had been exposed was still a mystery.

'I wish he or she were working for us. That would be something,' Stanmer said, almost to himself. 'Anyway. Enough about you, let's talk about why we're all here,' Stanmer said, as if he was addressing a room full of people. Leaning forward in his chair, his face adopted a serious, professional look. His corporate face, Lance reasoned. 'Did you know that the DRC is one of the richest places on earth?' he proclaimed confidently. This should have puzzled Lance, but he actually understood. The DRC was a country defined as poor in most descriptions. Many of its people suffered poverty, conflict and displacement. It was the type of country Lance reported from. Like many countries, it had so much potential to improve life for its people, but many factors stopped this from happening. Lance nodded at Stanmer's words.

'I thought you might understand. The DRC, like many African countries, is rich in many natural resources.' Even Quent seemed interested in this fact. 'Oh yes, lads. It's rich.' Stanmer spoke to both men like a father talking frankly to his sons. This repulsed Lance, but he listened inquisitively. 'Oh, it's got it all,' Stanmer said with increasing excitement. 'Diamonds, gold, copper, timber, oil. All there for the taking.' What he had just stated sickened Lance to his stomach. Many people like Stanmer viewed the planet as an infinite amount of resources to be plundered by anyone who is able, often by illegal means and at the cost of the native people, habitat, wildlife, in fact the whole ecosystem at times. Planet destroyers he knew them as.

The look on Lance's face was not lost on Stanmer. 'Oh, what a disapproving face. But you don't seem to see the good we're planning on doing. With the backing of the government, I'll let you know,' Stanmer smugly informed them. Lance had found that the most dangerous people in power were the ones who believed their own lies.

'There's a small area in the Salonga National Park which is rich in cassiterite, which is a tin oxide mineral and one of the many raw materials that this planet is hungry for. One of our companies plan to mine this area.' Stanmer spoke as if everything he suggested had no consequences. Lance was not surprised that the CEO of CES would be behind such a project. The thought of mining in a tropical rainforest made Lance want to weep. The damage to such a fragile area would be catastrophic. He placed his head in his hands and wondered where he went from here. They sat in silence for what seemed like hours, but it was less than a minute.

'Oh don't worry, young man. With the latest technologies, the environmental damage will be kept to an absolute minimum. And we're providing much needed work for potentially thousands of locals.' Stanmer's voice shook him from his slump and with a renewed interest watched as the arrogant CEO stood up and walked towards a map Lance had noticed hanging on the cabin wall. The map was of the Salonga National Park and a few areas were highlighted with red ink.

Standing proudly in front of the map, Stanmer used his pen to point to certain areas as if addressing his board of directors regarding a business plan. Lance listened intently despite his loathing for this arrogant man.

'Here we have it,' he boastfully highlighted an area at the edge of the National Park.

'The area rich in the product we need. And the square footage we'll be mining it from.' Stanmer's statement repulsed Lance, but it was also a revelation. He had seen an almost identical map in Fim's office only a couple of days ago. Everything she had told him was true. The reasons Rufus and Duncan were out there, what they were looking for, the proof they needed to protect that whole area. And now, why CES were so interested in finding out everything Rufus knew for themselves and nobody else, including the whereabouts of Duncan. It all fitted into place.

The area of planned mining looked small, but Lance knew the scale of the map and it was a devastatingly large area of rainforest CES were planning to decimate. But he also knew now they were getting desperate to start and more and more obstacles were being put in their way. Himself being one of them, he gladly thought.

'Impressive, isn't it, young man?' Stanmer was smugly looking down at him. 'I bet you wish you had Wi-Fi for that thing now,' he maliciously asked. 'So you could reply with a smart, morally confident argument. But the ball is well and truly in our court now, you annoying little snoop.' His dislike for Lance was equal to Lance's for him.

'And, to prove just how well planned we are, take a look at that,' the CEO sneered, as he took his smartphone out and pointed to the screen near Lance's chair, which had been displaying the aircraft's flight statistics. He looked as the data disappeared in a haze of static, to be replaced by the image of a small aeroplane in flight. The footage was grainy but it began to zoom in. His heart sank as the image became clearer and he saw writing along the side of the craft. "The Monsoon." Lance was looking at a live camera from outside of the aircraft he was actually travelling in. Stanmer read the younger man's face, as he looked up.

'Impressive or what?' He had the smug look of a spoilt child showing off his latest expensive toy. 'A jet-drone! A prototype capable of keeping up with this flight, at this speed and height.' He was clearly relishing telling Lance about CES's latest weapon. And it was a weapon in the younger man's eyes. 'This is going to speed things up. Literally,' he boasted. 'It can do low-level information gathering. It'll film all the areas we want to work on and all data we find will be presented to the authorities.' He was talking hurriedly, almost excitedly. 'And the footage we show will of course be edited by us. Leaving out anything your pals may have found in that area. As far as the evidence is concerned, it'll reveal nothing of interest ecologically, giving us free rein to take as much as we wish. And when I say it'll speed things up, I mean just that. It's equipped with explosives, which will, how can I put it? Get the ball rolling with the new mines.' An evil grin spread across Stanmer's face, shocking even Quent.

Lance knew CES would do anything to get their way, but to hear it presented like the evil scheme it clearly was utterly shocked him. The drone he had witnessed was another twisted tool CES were using to break laws and rules to get their hands on anything they desired.

He slumped back in the chair, feeling defeated. CES really was the monster corporation he knew it to be. The power they wielded in the world chilled him to the bone. Something on his LANSPEAK distracted him. It was a flashing light red light. Despite there being no signal here, TEX was messaging him.

Aboard the Monsoon,
The Democratic Republic of the Congo,
July 17,
5:40pm (Congolese and UK time)

Trying his best to be subtle, Lance opened the message, which was encrypted with FRUITS. It was clearly the longest FRUITS message TEX had ever sent. As he deciphered the letters, he noticed Stanmer standing above him. In Lance's haste, he did not see the older man walk his way. He had the same triumphant grin. 'Oh it plays games too, does it?' Lance did not acknowledge him. 'Well, you're used to that I guess. You've certainly toyed with us, haven't you?' The younger man still did not look up. 'Enjoy playing as we'll probably confiscate that thing when we land. I'm sure you understand why.'

Stanmer's statement about the LANSPEAK had a deeper significance to it. If they took the device, they would literally be stealing his voice. Which is something CES have done to thousands of people throughout the world. This callous immoral company, he decided there and then, was his enemy. And he was going to do anything in his power to get in their way. Lance was still puzzled as to how TEX was getting a signal through in such a remote area. As Stamner sat back down, Lance quickly revealed the message.

THE DRONE
IT CAN BE CONTROLLED REMOTELY
I WILL LET YOU HACK IN
STAND BY

Lance's heart was in his throat as he read the message in his head. He felt a rush of excitement but also concern. TEX clearly knew far too much than any individual should. TEX was clearly a computer genius but this level of knowledge was frightening. It was as if he was there with them.

Lance suddenly felt faint as a horrendous thought hit him. It *was* as if TEX was right there with them. He looked up at Stanmer who was engrossed in a newspaper. Quent was reading a magazine looking sullen. What if TEX worked for CES? That was it. The easiest way to get him into the clutches of CES was to have one of their own lead him straight onto Stanmer's aeroplane. How could he have been so stupid? TEX had been following him for years. All along, he had been pretending to be on his side but it all could be a front.

But what about all the people TEX had helped with Lance? He knew TEX had done genuinely good things. Was this all one big lie? A façade to lure BLACK EYED BOY into the open? It made sense. It made horrible, sickening sense.

CES was clearly an international monster company. This was an obvious method to control people like him. Control was their main weapon. And they wielded it brutally and powerfully.

Anger rose in him. Lance rarely felt this emotion as he had learned how to control it many years ago. But right now a dark fury filled him. He decided to play things out. He had nothing to lose. He messaged TEX, whoever or whatever TEX was.

HOW LONG HAVE YOU WORKED FOR CES?

He kept the message encrypted with FRUITS, though unsure why. The pause in TEX's reply seemed to take forever to Lance, though in fact it was a few seconds and also encrypted.

FOUR YEARS

Lance gazed at the message. Confused at TEX's apparent honesty, initially assuming the other person would vehemently deny being involved with CES. But here was an apparent full confession. Though with a heavy heart, Lance reasoned that TEX had no more need to hide now, CES had proved their power and, at the same time, Lance's vulnerability. Then another messaged flashed, still encrypted.

THEN I FOUND OUT WHAT THEY WERE DOING
I LEFT SEVEN YEARS AGO

New confusion now overcame Lance. This could all be part of the sick charade. He so much wanted to believe this, but it seemed too easy to claim such a thing. Another message flashed.

DO NOT TAKE MY WORD FOR IT
I WILL GIVE YOU PROOF

Before Lance could reply, another encrypted message was being sent through. This was not a simple message. It was computer data and Lance understood what it was. It was a language computer hackers used. It was written to gain control of the drone he guessed. This would be proof if it did work.

He turned his chair towards the two other men when the LANSPEAK became a blank screen, which he swiftly typed in the complicated lines of code. Typing fast was easy for Lance, though he felt he could not go quickly enough.

Once the data had been uploaded, nothing seemed to happen. For a brief second, Lance wondered if TEX had actually sent him a computer virus to attack his speaking device, which should actually be impossible, since he had designed the device himself.

All of a sudden, a camera view flashed onto the LANSPEAK. It was the drone's view of the aircraft. The drone footage was live streaming to the device on his arm. At the base of the image were direction icons. When Lance touched them, the drone shifted its course in the same path. There was also a small red round icon on the screen, which had written below it "HOME" in small letters He had control of this highly sophisticated CES hardware. He let out an involuntary chuckle. Something he rarely did. Quent briefly looked up at the noise, but quickly returned to his reading.

CONVINCED?

Lance almost let out another laugh as the encrypted messaged flashed at the side of the screen.

YES

This was all he could reply, as he was overwhelmed with excitement. Looking over at Stanmer, a thought entered his head. *The ball is back in my court now,* he thought.

Before he could focus on what he had to do next, the red light flashed and TEX messaged again.

IT IS TIME FOR YOU TO LEAVE

Puzzled, he replied,

LEAVE HOW

There was a pause before TEX answered.

THE DOOR

Lance thought he had deciphered the message incorrectly. He rechecked it twice. The answer was the same.

PLEASE EXPLAIN

There was a pause. Lance hoped TEX was misspelling the code. But the next message reaffirmed he was not.

YOU NEED TO JUMP OUT OF THE PLANE IN FIVE MINS

Before Lance could question this, he heard Stanmer and Quent speaking loudly to each other. They clearly had gotten into an argument.

'Give me a break Roth, we needed your help to locate mute boy quicker. Your reward is a year's funding and transport to this dump of a country,' Stanmer bellowed to the younger man.

'You said you believed in my work!' Quent replied with a renewed vim.

'Oh come off it! Even you surely don't believe this cryptid garbage? Giant spiders? What planet you living on son? I think you've read too many fantasy books.'

'Evidence suggests—'

'Evidence? Listen to me, you sad little loser. The only evidence we'll be finding on this trip is the edited version, which that drone outside will be recording. And my company will no longer be associated with a nutter like you gobbing off about monsters. It's bad publicity, sunshine.'

Quent looked tearful but he continued to angrily retort, 'I have done research into this area for years. I have researched…'

The argument trailed off to Lance. He mentally shut out the pointless argument between the men as he broke down the next message.

THEY WILL NOT LAND UNTIL KISANGANI
THEY WILL HAVE PEOPLE WAITING FOR YOU
YOUR DESTINATION IS NEAR HERE
YOU NEED TO LEAVE THE PLANE IN THREE MINS
YOU HIT TURBULANCE IN TWO MINS

THE ONLY WAY IS DOWN BLACK-EYED BOY

The message felt sinister but truthful. The two men were still arguing. Almost subconsciously, Lance gathered his belongings up, which he had not unpacked. His LANSPEAK was still projecting the drone outside. His camera was secure in his pack. In the pack, he had some goggles and an altimeter. He always carried them due to the many times he was working at great heights. He secured them to his head and wrist. His backpack was fastened around his waist, leaving his back free.

He was suddenly uneasy about trusting TEX again. The whole drone control could be an elaborate plan to gain his trust quickly. Though he also knew that Stanmer would have people waiting at the next airport to put a definite stopper on any plans he had.

The craft began to shudder. A message, not encrypted flashed.

TURBULANCE NOW

And as if TEX was controlling the weather, the aeroplane began to shudder and sway up and down. The French voice crackled out of the tannoy. 'Seatbelts, please.'

The two other men promptly sat down and fastened themselves to their chairs. Stanmer looked, to Lance's pleasure, rather queasy.

The aircraft shuddered quite violently and another messaged came through,

POOR SIGNAL
YOU NEED DOOR CODE

Lance looked at the door. A small keypad was next to it, which he was surprised he did not notice before.

DOOR CODE FOUR NUMBERS
I TRY AND SEND DOOR CODE OTET WAY

The last message proved the signal was poor or that TEX was in some difficulty himself. The aircraft was jerking quite considerably. Quent and Stanmer looked sickly and worried. Lance, unsure of what he should be doing next, quickly took out a pair of goggles he used during his extreme sports and which he always travelled with.

After securing them to his forehead, he strapped his backpack to his belt so it hung behind his legs. He checked the path of the drone on the LANSPEAK. The image of The Monsoon was much further away from the drone now. The turbulence was clearly affecting its flight. Then a wild thought hit him. The drone. That was it. TEX was possibly able to send messages by piggybacking his signal off the drone's own in-built navigation computer. Or something similar, he reasoned. Only someone like TEX could do this, though now nature was putting a huge obstacle in the way of their communications.

The aircraft was getting further away on the screen. He tried to control it, to bring it, and the signal, closer but the shaking of the aeroplane was making it very difficult to type. Then a different message flashed up.

DOOR CODE
STAR WARS DAY
THIS MEAN ANYTJI

Lance was momentarily puzzled. Then it dawned on him. International Star Wars Day, an important time of the year for fans worldwide of those films. And a day he knew well as he was also a fan. It appeared that TEX was not also a fan. May the fourth every year. The code was 0405.

YES. MAY 4

TEX had handed him the code, which was obviously hacked to open the door and leave Stanmer's apparent custody. A renewed confidence filled him. He could do this. Lance had base-jumped, parachuted and wing-suited all over the world. This was a relatively simple task compared to many of his previous jumps.

The other two men were still looking nauseous. Stanmer actually had his head in his hands. This was it, he thought, as he shakily made his way towards the door, though the turbulence was easing up now. Quent looked up and stared at him, a bewildered look upon his face, as he watched Lance take one of the parachutes from the hook above the door.

Quite suddenly, the aircraft flight became smooth again. Stanmer looked up with a similar bemused expression to Quent, though mixed with anger.

'What are you up to, boy?' He wearily shook his head.

A surge of defiance rose up as he saw the CEO still strapped to his chair looking pale.

The LANSPEAK spoke for the first time in days.

'*You are wrong. This thing does not require WIFI.*'

Stanmer stared aghast. Quent had a look of mild amusement.

'*Also, I am not mute, the expression is without speech.*'

He knew he had to go right away, but letting Stanmer know he still was not in control was slightly too satisfying. The aircraft had cleared the turbulence and Lance saw Stanmer fumbling with his seatbelt. He knew he could not open the door if both men were not secured to their seats. Realising he did not have time to fully strap the unusually heavy feeling parachute to his back before the CEO freed himself, he held it tight under one arm.

'*Fasten your seatbelt.*' Was his last word, causing the older man to pause briefly in his task. Lance steadied himself at the door, put his goggles over his eyes, raised his free hand and tapped 0405 into the door.

Aboard the Monsoon, The Democratic Republic of the Congo, July 17, 5:45pm (Congolese and UK time)

Nothing happened. Lance's heart almost stopped. Thoughts flooded his head. He could see Stanmer was still fastened in and was not attempting to stand anymore. A smug half smile spread across his face. Quent appeared to be disappointed.

'Door locked?' The older man shook his head patronisingly. 'Tut tut.'

Had TEX purposely done this? Why? There was no reason. The drone was still a distance away from the aircraft on his LANSPEAK screen. Stanmer began to speak, 'Did you really think you could…' The voice trailed away as Lance concentrated. There had to be something he had not thought of, TEX *was* trying to help him. TEX, why did the name mean something suddenly? TEX. It hit him like a thunderbolt. TEX is American. He knew that. Americans write the date differently to the British. Perhaps the code was in the American order of writing the date.

Without a second thought, he pressed 0504 into the keypad.

'You'll be questioned by the—' Stanmer's words were suddenly cut off as the aeroplane door slid open to the side alarmingly fast. The noise was explosively loud. The very atmosphere seemed to get sucked out through the small doorway. An alarm rang around the cabin as it lurched to its side, causing anything loose to clatter and smash to the wall. The two men were still strapped in, though Quent might have been screaming. It was impossible to hear over the roaring of the freezing air circulating around the cabin.

Lance was holding the bar by the doorway, being violently pulled out of the aircraft, which felt terrifying as he had not strapped his parachute on, which was slowly being pulled from his grasp. This was not good, he thought. Not good at all. The craft suddenly lurched to the opposite side and he was now hanging outside of the craft, being pulled into the vacuum, the heavy parachute now in his other hand.

Stanmer's voice bellowed over the rushing freezing air. He was speaking into a tannoy by his chair.

'Frederic! Frederic! Close the door! Now! Close it!' he screamed.

To Lance's horror, the door began to close slowly. He had no time to think if Stanmer intended him to be either inside or outside of the cabin when it closed. The door slowly pressed on his side, but the vacuum was still wrenching him away from the exit.

The parachute was sucked from his grasp, and the last thing from that flight Lance remembered was Quent screaming something inaudible, as he was pulled out into the freezing air and began falling from thirty thousand feet up with no parachute.

Above the Democratic Republic of the Congo,
July 17,
5:46pm (Congolese and UK time)

Oblivion overcame Lance. No thoughts or feelings were there. He had no sensation of falling through the icy air at one hundred and twenty miles an hour. He had briefly passed out in the freezing sky. Plunging towards the forest at fifty-two metres a second, a slow awareness overcame him. He thought momentarily that he was submerged in icy water, as he was unable to breathe and his skin felt numb.

Almost instantly, the horror of what was happening hit him. He was freefalling without a parachute. The Salonga National Park was spread out beneath him, looking very similar to the map that Stanmer had been pointing at earlier.

Lance tried to breathe but when he did draw breath, it was like freezing smoke filled his throat and chest. This was not good. Holding in what breath he could, knowing he had to focus quickly if he was to survive. Freefalling is something Lance had done countless times. So he imagined this was just another standard jump. How he would land was something he had to figure out. In about two and a half minutes.

He looked at the altimeter on his wrist.

Twenty thousand feet.

In fact, he had two minutes until he hit the trees. He pushed panic to one side. Panic would be the end of him. The thought of the parachute was his next thought. That heavy, bright orange bag had just been in his grasp before falling he remembered. *It must be nearby,* he reasoned, *though seeing it would be impossible*, he thought grimly.

At last, the air felt less intense. He was able to breathe slightly better but his body still felt under huge pressure. The rushing air was cold but not as icy as before. Though he could still be numb, he thought.

Nineteen thousand feet.

Look, Lance, look. The stern voice in his head forced him to scan the entire area around him. Turning three hundred and sixty-degrees for any signs of that little orange bag. It was still light but it was like looking for an orange grain of sand on a green and blue beach. He searched and searched.

Eighteen thousand feet.

Do not let panic overtake and distract your focus, he ordered himself. Orange bag. Keep scanning the sky. It is here and should not be too far away. Lance had excellent eyesight but he felt he needed more to find this parachute.

Seventeen thousand feet.

The green forest looked closer. Which it was. The Salonga National Park was rushing up to meet him. He needed to get there but not this fast, he told himself.

Sixteen thousand feet.

It was difficult to fathom just how fast he was falling, but the altimeter did not lie. *Do not panic*, he kept telling himself. But with each second, Lance was fifty metres closer to crashing into the forest at a deadly speed.

Fifteen thousand feet.

Other thoughts flooded his head. Could he land without a parachute? It had been done in the past and Lance knew of each time this had occurred. He also knew how rare it was. Thinking about scenarios where this was possible, his mind wandered. Trees breaking his fall. Landing at a cliff side and sliding down into water. Landing in snow.

Focus, Lance. Focus. The last impossible scenario shook him from deeper thoughts. *Be realistic,* he mused. The parachute is the best option. That tiny scrap of hope was the only thing keeping panic and irrational behaviour at bay.

Fourteen thousand feet.

Keep looking. It has to be—

And there it was. He thought at least. An orange speck, slightly lower than him but over one hundred feet away. As it was lighter, it seemed to be catching him up. If he falls below it, all is lost, he thought. Lance streamlined his body and dipped his head and slowly glided towards the orange object.

Thirteen thousand feet.

Lance was making progress. Arms flat by his side and head dipped, his body was approaching the luminous bag. Hope filled him, but he had to remain focused. The air felt warmer, though still cold. The forest looked more detailed now. Not a featureless map but a real forest, which made it look all the more foreboding.

Twelve thousand feet.

He was gaining on the bag, but unfortunately, the bag was also gaining on him. It could not get above him. It was slowly getting level with his height. He was about fifty feet from him now. *Come on,* he urged himself. At that moment, he wished that flapping his arms would help, but he knew he was getting closer as fast as he could.

Eleven thousand feet.

It was clearly in sight, he could see tags and fabric flapping in the turbulent wind. It was twenty feet away but almost getting too high. Lance stiffened his body. Come on he urged his body. It was close, fifteen feet. So very close. His lifeline was within reach. He had to try and not panic and lose control.

Ten thousand feet.

The bag was almost above him. Five feet away. Grabbing fistfuls of air trying to climb up to it, Lance's body was thrashing around. *Do not panic,* he warned himself. Stretching his whole body, he reached up and felt an overwhelming surge of relief as his had grabbed the strap of the bag. He pulled it to his body like a new mother cradling her new-born child. With difficulty in the pounding wind, Lance eased the pack onto his back. The tension from the wind made fastening the belt difficult.

Using all his strength to pull the straps together against such pressure, the parachute was finally secured to his back. He was under ten thousand feet. It was time to slow down, he thought with relief. Lance gratefully pulled the tag to deploy the chute. Nothing happened.

Nine thousand feet.

Above the Democratic Republic of the Congo,
July 17,
5:47pm (Congolese and UK time)

Lance almost passed out a second time. Time itself stood still, as he continued to plummet towards the forest. Before another thought could enter his head, the pack on his back made a clunking sound and he felt something loosen. Then the parachute shot out of the pack to the sound of metal clanking against itself.

Any relief he felt was short lived. The parachute did not open. Looking up, it was flapping vertically in the wind like a sock on a washing line. Lance saw it was torn, frayed and tangled. It would never open.

Eight thousand feet.

Sheer panic flashed through his head. Looking down at the approaching mass of green, he briefly glanced at his LANSPEAK. The drone was still flying, though not in sight of The Monsoon. The drone. It was flying with the sun on the right side of it. A wave of clarity flushed through him. The sun was also on his right. Almost without thinking, Lance pressed the red HOME icon. And he watched in awe as the drone immediately and swiftly changed direction.

Seven thousand feet.

The speed of the machine was incredible. It was cutting through the air at an inverted angle. With renewed hope, Lance saw that the sun was now on the drone's left. It was heading straight for him. At least he hoped it was.

Six thousand feet.

Ignoring how close the ground was and how quickly he was falling towards it, Lance's eyes were fixed on the drone's progress. The speed of the thing was encouraging. But could it reach him before he hit the ground? Looking up briefly, he scanned the skies for his rescue craft. No sign of it, but the sun's glare did not help.

Five thousand feet.

He now had about thirty seconds left. The drone was rocketing towards him. He knew it could keep up with an aeroplane, so it had speed, but he had no idea how far away it was coming from. He would find out one way or another in a few seconds, he grimly thought.

Four thousand feet.

He saw the speed of the drone on his LANSPEAK. A new fear hit him. If this thing hit him at the speed it was clearly going, it would probably cut him in half. It was like a giant bullet. He almost thought he would more likely survive if he took his chances with the trees. No, the drone was his best hope for survival.

How ironic that a multimillion-pound piece of technology designed to assist CES could actually save his life. The expensive thing itself was hurtling towards him he saw on the screen. It was still not in his visual range, though that did not mean it was close by. He hoped it was.

Three thousand feet.

His time was almost up. Then he saw on the screen, a thin white vertical shape dropping at speed. His failed parachute. The drone was within sight. He looked up but still could not see it. He looked at the controls. He was sure there would be a way to slow it in some way, but he was out of time. He could change the direction at the last minute. That was his best option.

Two thousand feet.

He could now see birds flying far below. The forest looked huge now. An overgrown wilderness, which looked too dangerous to even attempt a controlled landing. Those ancient trees and rocks would rip him to shreds if he fell straight into them. Lance scanned for the drone. There it was. A small red light blinked on and off. *Thank goodness for that light,* he thought desperately.

One thousand feet.

He could now hear the sounds of wildlife rise up from below. A moist humid heat began to filter up and the numerous smells of nature began to fill his nostrils. This feeling of being so close to the ground instilled an unwelcome feeling of panic. He anxiously looked at the drone. It was shooting towards him. Lance flattened himself and prepared to alter the course at the last second.

Five hundred feet.

He felt like he was right on top of the trees now, though he still was not. The drone seemed to be taking ages covering the last short distance. Then it occurred to him. It was actually slowing down. It was clearly designed to do this, to stop it crashing into the place it was being recalled to. Which was technologically impressive and important. But did not help Lance right now and he still could not actually control the speed.

Four hundred feet.

Hurry up, he thought. Lance now realised the drone reaching him before he hit the ground would be a split-second moment. Though he knew he had above average reflexes, this was going to be a challenge. *Focus, Lance,* he thought. *Focus*.

Three hundred feet.

Focus. Focus. The drone looked to be about one hundred feet away, but travelling at half the speed Lance was falling at. This was purely him guessing. It was going to be very close.

Two hundred feet.

Focus. Focus. The drone was gaining. But so was the ground. Focus. It was about fifty feet away. It seemed to slow even further. No. Get here. Follow the signal. Come home.

One hundred feet.

The trees were coming up to meet him. He could hear loud shrieks from various animals. It felt like they were warning him of the danger. He dared to look down. The tops of the tallest trees were directly under him, as some were at least one hundred feet high.

Too late, he solemnly thought. Lance tucked his knees into his chest and braced for a violent impact into those high gnarled trees.

The Salonga National Park,
The Democratic Republic of the Congo,
July 17,
5:48pm (Congolese and UK time)

His body jerked violently sideways as the speeding drone crashed into his useless parachute. He was catapulted sideways, his feet brushing the tops of the wild trees. Lance looked up. The drone was still incredibly fast despite slowing down. The parachute was helplessly tangled into the machine, which was by far one of the largest drones in existence.

He was being dragged through the air, just above the forest. The drone was travelling horizontally, as if it was confused as to where to stop.

The cords were caught onto the front of the speeding device. But Lance saw with renewed concern, that the flapping torn silk was dangerously close to one of the spinning propellers. Although it was jet powered, two propellers were on top, clearly to guide it at lower levels. And Lance's faulty chute was about to get sucked into the front one.

Lance braced himself as the rotating blades began churning up the ragged silk he was hanging from. His body began to spin as the drone started to shudder and veer downwards. He was spiralling towards the ground at about forty-five degrees.

The trees had given way to rocky bushes, which lead down to the river. The blades were consuming the cords now and to Lance's horror, were pulling him into the sharp propellers. Although they were clogging up the mechanism, slowing them down, it would still mean he would be killed if he were to be pulled in.

Whilst frantically searching for the release on his belt, the drone started to shudder alarmingly as black smoke began to thickly pump from the clogged propeller. *Time to leave,* he told himself. Before Lance had time to release himself, the cords burst into flames. The momentum of the drone's speed, Lance's body weight, his own pack and the unusually heavy chute bag caused the burning cords to snap in one swift motion.

He was once again falling to earth, just seeing the drone shoot away like a smoky rocket, ready to explode. The river looked dangerously far away, but the large trees protruding from the rocky edge of the water were rapidly coming up to meet him.

He was not sure how far he had fallen when he crashed into a massive tree, which was over hanging the river. Leaves, branches and thousands of insects suddenly hit him. Lance collided with the heavy boughs of the tree as he tumbled through the foliage, his body scratched and bruised as his fall was broken by numerous branches, each one stunning him slightly.

Without realising it, Lance found himself hanging by one hand on a branch over the steep edge of the river. He was exhausted but knew he had to stay in control. The water was not flowing fast but it still looked deep.

Before having time to think, the branch snapped unexpectedly and Lance was suddenly plummeting towards the river. It was not far but a small but solid tree rose up to meet him. Although it broke his fall, he knew he would have been better off falling straight into the river, as he instinctively grabbed the thick branch, which protruded at a ninety-degree angle from the high bank.

A sudden intense pain shot through his body like an electric shock. It started at the top of his right arm, which had grabbed the tree. Lance was very good at controlling pain in the past. He saw it as something to rationalise and thus control. But in his exhausted state, it was difficult to control this, as his shoulder was actually dislocated. Lance knew this, as it had happened in the past.

The pain and weakness were too much to bear and he let go. A short drop before landing in the river. The water felt cool and not unpleasant, though when he felt the current drag him along, Lance knew he needed to get to the bank, as he was too tired to swim.

Pushing to the surface, he felt like he was going nowhere. The pack on his back felt even heavier. It was pulling him down and he was almost out of air, the pain in his shoulder now burning. Black dots swam before him. He knew he was close to passing out again. Lance tried to fight it. If he fainted in the river, he would drown.

He had never felt so weak as he did right now, kicking and thrashing his arms to try and break the surface. Each movement caused searing pain to shoot up his arm, but he ignored it as he struggled to the surface. Lance's lungs were on fire as with one last thrust of his body, his head broke the surface and he gulped and gasped at the sweet air. Then the weight of his packs pulled him back under.

With lungs full of precious air, he tried to release the pack's belt and free him from the excess weight. It was too difficult as the undercurrent was rolling his body in different directions. Then, through his blurred, watery vision, Lance noticed the bank was close by. Using the current to assist him, he half swam, half glided towards the edge, the pain in his shoulder keeping him conscious he imagined. It seemed to take an eternity and his lungs felt empty once more.

With his last ounce of strength, he grasped at the slick mud of the river edge. Grabbing at roots, grass, anything he could find, Lance pulled himself free of the flowing water. His breathing was rapid, but he needed to do one more thing.

Barely able to stand, but mustering enough strength to do so, Lance walked towards a dead tree stump. Without giving himself time to think about what he was doing, he rammed his right shoulder, as hard as he could into the gnarled wood.

Lance let out a silent scream, as his shoulder popped back into its socket. The pain washed over him like a heated blanket. Collapsing on the ground, a darkness filled his vision.

Sweet relief, he thought to himself, as he passed out on the banks of the river.

The Salonga National Park,
The Democratic Republic of the Congo,
July 17,
9:10pm (Congolese and UK time)

The rest was so welcome. Though Lance had no idea where he was as it was dark when he opened his eyes. Every inch of his body ached. His right shoulder was extremely tender when he moved it to sit up. He winced when he touched it. Where was he? He was totally confused, the utterly black darkness not helping him re-orientate.

He took a few deep breaths and tried to focus his mind. Patches of information began to filter in. The trip to Istanbul. The flight to the DRC. And the disaster of falling out of a moving aircraft without a parachute. Lance lay down and sighed. He had not felt so foolish for a long time. His brother had been right to warn him against this insane plan. His behaviour had been insane these past few days, he thought to himself.

He had very nearly died more than once. And now, he was sat, soaking wet, on the banks of a river, in a dangerous forest, in the middle of the night, with not another soul on earth knowing where he was, two people in fact thinking he was dead. *Great job, Lance*, he thought to himself.

Feelings of guilt then overcame him. His actions on the aeroplane could have caused it to crash. It still might have, he thought solemnly. Lance had never wanted to put people in any danger, even vile people like Stanmer. And Quent had clearly been duped into helping CES.

He felt utterly ashamed. For a man who liked to stay rational and focused, this entire trip had been mainly controlled by his emotions. Which was never a good idea he had learned in the past. He was sat here purely because of his love for his friend Rufus. Yet how was this helping him? He had no idea where to go from here. A renewed exhaustion hit him. He did not even know what time it was. It was not important. Lance lay on his back and stared up at the stars. He had never seen them this clear before. It was a comforting sight, he thought.

He knew he could not wallow in self-pity as he had come too far. And more questions still needed asking. But more importantly, CES needed to be exposed for their monstrous plans for the country he was now in. He needed to re-evaluate his plans. He had to find out where he was and how far to his destination. Lance wondered if he was fit enough for the rest of the journey. His body ached like it was broken.

He guessed he would found out in the harsh light of day. Looking up at the brilliant light of the stars, a restful feeling overcame him. Lance was in a deep sleep very soon, unaware that curious eyes were watching him.

The Salonga National Park,
The Democratic Republic of the Congo,
July 18,
6:15am (Congolese and UK time)

The infinite sounds of the forest stirred him slightly. But it was the light and warmth of the newly rising sun that roused Lance to finally blink himself awake, the brilliant light of the new dawn making it impossible for him to open his eyes straight away. He tried to stand and coughed from a dry throat and even drier mouth. Then the pain hit. And the pain was everywhere. The previously dislocated shoulder was by far the worst. The achingly stiff neck was not far behind.

Trying to stretch, Lance found himself on his belly, shielding his eyes from the blinding sun. He knew he had slept for around nine hours. Which was foolish. He had no cover, no way to observe for signs of danger. Anything could have happened, as he slept the night away. In fact, he was lucky to have awoken at all, he pondered grimly. Lance could actually hear Tristan's voice in his ear shouting at how utterly stupid he has been on this entire trip.

Knowing he had to move, but not wanting to at all, Lance moved his battered body into a sitting position. It felt like every bone in his body was bruised. Opening his bleary eyes, he finally looked around. The river flowed swiftly behind him and the trees filtered the early light down onto him. The forest was so thick and rich with vegetation. The sounds of various animals were constantly vibrating through the plants. Insects swam around his head. It was a true wilderness. A beautiful but dangerous place.

The warm beams of light became hotter on his skin. It felt like it was energising his shattered body. Lance basked in the fresh new light, feeling his mind re orientate itself. Focus and clarity found his thought again. He assessed the situation. The original destination of his journey was quite a few miles away, though he had to work out how far he still had to go.

Thoughts of working this out led him to think about his equipment and supplies. How much had survived the fall. Then the realisation hit him. The faulty parachute and his own pack were not strapped to him. It had taken time to realise this. A sinking feeling overcame him as he glanced back to the fast-flowing water. He was so dazed last night. He feared all his supplies were lost to the river. No food or drink. No protective clothing. No navigation equipment. No money. No evidence gathering technology. He might as well have fallen naked out of the sky. This trip was really beginning to feel hopeless now.

Although Lance had excellent basic survival skills, taught by his brother, he had not planned on having to use much of them on this expedition. Before he could form another thought, a sound ahead of him made him look up. It was the sound of numerous close footsteps moving through the undergrowth. The sun was in his vision and he squinted to find the source of the sounds.

Painfully lifting onto one knee, Lance concentrated his vision on the single area of bushes ahead of him. What finally emerged from the thick plants made his blood run cold.

The Salonga National Park,
The Democratic Republic of the Congo,
July 18,
6:19am (Congolese and UK time)

Lance was staring up at the barrel of a gun, a very large gun. He hated guns, always seeing them as an evil invention created for a single purpose. He had never held or even touched one, but his knowledge of these weapons was considerable. Largely through his brother, who, much to Lance's dislike, used guns in his duties as a soldier. Though Tristan often explained to Lance that not using a gun was always the favoured option in any situation.

As his eyes focused, the sight of who was holding this deadly weapon made him want to weep. The high-powered machine-gun was held firmly in the shaking hands of a child. A small boy who looked, to Lance, to be about twelve years of age. The expression on the child's face was one of fear. Almost terror as he aimed the deadly weapon at Lance's face. The journalist could not look the boy directly in the eyes. But the child was not looking directly at him either, as his whole body was trembling. He was looking all around Lance, to see if he was alone he guessed.

The fearful eyes finally settled on Lance. The boy then spoke in French. It was a weak nervous voice. That of a frightened child, Lance thought tragically.

'Who are you?' he blurted out, trying to sound older and stronger than he was. Lance could not reply, but merely held his hands up and adopted a weary half smile.

'Who are you?' he repeated. 'Where you come from?' The young voice sounded more desperate, almost panicked. Lance stood slowly, his muscles burning with every movement. The gun was raised as Lance finally reached his full height. The boy looked even smaller and vulnerable with the heavy weapon held in his shivering hands.

‘Where you from?’ Lance raised his hands again and shook his head as much as the pain would allow. But before he could think of how to resolve this potentially volatile situation, he was suddenly drawn to two more figures nervously entering the area from the thick forest the boy had emerged from. Lance’s heart almost broke, as he saw the two other boys were even younger than the first child. They looked no older than eight or nine. They also had the same expression of fear as the older boy, but thankfully, Lance thought, they were not carrying weapons as far as he could see.

What they were holding, to his slight relief, were his belongings. One boy held his pack, the other was holding, rather clumsily in his small hands, the remains of the heavy parachute bag.

‘Did you come from the rocket?’ the older child asked. Lance was puzzled at this question, but saw the boy point to an area in the distance. A dark plume of thick smoke was rising up from the tree line. *The crashed drone,* he guiltily thought. Lance dreaded to imagine the damage the crash had caused to the area. The fire had obviously attracted the children.

He could only nod slowly in the boy’s direction.

‘What you want here?’ the child asked desperately. The situation was becoming more serious by the second. Lance flicked open the fake cast and without thinking, he touched a pre-arranged word, one he had not used since London, a lifetime ago, it felt.

‘J’ba Fofi.’

The Salonga National Park,

The Democratic Republic of the Congo,

July 18,

6:20am (Congolese and UK time)

These words had an immediate effect on the boy. He appeared relieved and lowered his gun slightly, unsure what to think of the LANSPEAK, but more interested in what was said, as the speaking device was now set to French.

‘You know J’ba Fofi?’ the boy asked eagerly.

‘*Yes,*’ Lance replied, knowing he had nothing to lose. A look of strained hope spread across the boy’s face.

‘You are looking for J’ba Fofi?’

‘*I am.*’

'You will let me take you to J'ba Fofi?'

'*I want you to,*' Lance replied, feeling like he was making renewed progress on this disastrous trip. The boy seemed almost excited now. He waved to his younger companions to follow him.

'That way.' The boy pointed with his gun to a well-worn track, which ran along the river edge. Lance raised his hands, ignoring the pain in his muscles and headed through the grassy path.

'Move.' He heard the boy behind him speak with a renewed confidence, trying to speak aggressively and sound older than he was. Lance felt such sorrow for the lost innocence of all three of these children. He could not begin to imagine the horrors they had seen in their short lives, and, he sadly imagined, were still seeing.

The sun was feeling hot now and as he walked, Lance realised how exhausted and dehydrated he felt. But he tried to ignore his physical problems and began to focus on what situation he was currently in. The fact that this boy recognised the name J'ba Fofi, made him feel like he was closer to getting answers to what happened to Rufus and Duncan. Though he was struggling to imagine where the boy was taking him.

It felt like a long walk, though in fact, it had only been about forty minutes, but his aching thirsty body being exposed to the now fierce heat of the sun was beginning to feel worn out. He slowed down at times, but felt the gun poke him in his lower back, forcing him to keep going.

They walked further along the riverside, insects biting Lance continuously, his body feeling pain with every weary step. It was becoming difficult to focus his mind and try to evaluate the current situation. His own questions were answered when the boy shouted at Lance to stop, which he gratefully did, almost falling to his knees.

'We wait.' He heard the child shout from behind him. The noise of the flowing river and forest sounds were interrupted by the sound of an engine. Lance looked in every direction trying to locate the sound. It was coming from the river. Then it appeared. A sight that filled Lance with genuine fear. A boat was heading towards the bank they were waiting on.

As it approached, Lance got a clear view. It was a large metal motorboat. And it was filled with about ten heavily armed adult men, most whom now had their guns aimed at him. *Out of the frying pan,* Lance wearily told himself, as the transport thudded into the muddy banks of the river.

The Salonga National Park,
The Democratic Republic of the Congo,
July 18,
7:11am (Congolese and UK time)

The boat looked old and in need of serious repairs. Three men jumped out and headed straight towards Lance. They were dressed for war, he thought. Huge machine guns, bullet belts wrapped around their chests, combat clothing. They were intimidating in their appearance. Two of the men stopped walking, but the third man walked straight up to Lance and stood close to his face. He removed the sunglasses and ran his eyes up and down him with a look of disgust. Lance found it impossible to look into this man's eyes, though he felt his penetrating glare all over him.

The man then turned to the older boy and spoke in French.

'What is this?' he demanded, gesturing to Lance. The man's use of the word "what" instead of "who" made Lance feel queasy.

'He was by the river. We found him. Near the rocket,' the boy stated, all bravado and confidence now gone from his voice. He now sounded like the frightened child he was, trying to talk his way out of trouble. The man sneered, which looked almost like a snarl, as he marched towards the quivering boy.

'The rocket. You found it?' the man demanded.

'Yes,' the boy pitifully answered. The man glared at the scared child.

'What did you find?' he barked at him.

'Nothing. It was just fire. Just fire.'

'Fire? It was on fire? You found nothing?' the man aggressively asked.

'Just fire,' was the meek reply. The man gave the boy the same look of contempt he gave Lance.

'You are useless,' he said whilst looking away. The boy was about to say something, but the man then slapped the boy hard across his cheek, causing him to fall back. Lance felt a surge of anger, but could do nothing. The boy looked up, pain etched across his frightened face.

'Sir.' A high-pitched voice broke through the air. The man looked at the small boy who was carrying the parachute bag.

'The man was carrying this.' He nervously raised the bag towards the man, who snatched it from his grasp violently, causing the child to stumble back in fear. The man looked into the bag. A greedy grin spread across his cruel face. He looked at Lance.

'This yours?' he asked calmly. Lance nodded slowly, not making eye contact. The man then strode over and was once more so close Lance felt his breath on his face.

'Where you get this?' he whispered menacingly. Lance could only shrug. The look of revulsion returned to the man's face.

'I ask you a question. You answer, man. Where you get this?' The question felt like a serious threat. Lance felt his heart in his throat as the man's hands gripped his gun, moving it towards Lance's body.

'You answer me now, man!' he demanded loudly.

'He cannot speak. He does not speak!' the boy shouted from behind. The man looked around, genuine interest on his face. Looking at the boy and then back at Lance.

'You don't speak, man?' he asked, almost looking amused. Lance quickly nodded.

The man let out a cruel raspy laugh.

'Ha. It don't speak. This is stupid!' He laughed more, pointing at Lance as he looked at the two other men, who also laughed.

'It's real stupid,' the man finally said, poking his finger into Lance's chest.

'We move!' the man shouted into the air. On that single instruction, the three boys headed towards the boat. One of the three men snatched Lance's pack from the boy holding it, as he scurried passed nervously. The two men then followed the boys to the boat.

The man stood in front of Lance, leaned closer to him and whispered chillingly into his ear.

'We find out where you get this stuff,' his quiet voice more menacing than when he was shouting. He gripped the parachute bag to his chest, the bag, which Lance still had no idea of the contents. Though he did know the contents of the bag had almost killed him more than once.

'Yeah, man, we make you show us where you get this stuff.'

Lance knew he was in serious danger being in the company of these men and had no idea how he would escape them right now. He could not focus any more thoughts, as the men began aggressively marching him towards the rickety over crowded boat.

The Salonga National Park,
The Democratic Republic of the Congo,
July 18,
7:32am (Congolese and UK time)

The boat was faster than Lance thought it would be. It cut through the flowing river at a steady pace. He sat on the floor of the deck, thankfully in the shade. His hands were tied behind his back with rope. The knot clumsily looped over the fake cast he could feel. All eyes were on him. Varying looks of disgust, curiosity and humour. Most of the men looked to be about the same age as Lance, some slightly younger. A couple of men looked like teenagers, Lance thought sadly. The man who had questioned Lance was sat on the other side of the deck, the threatening smile still on his face. The man looked older than him, closer to Tristan's age. Lance did not want to think about the type of life this man, in fact everyone on this boat, had led up to this point.

The three boys were nowhere to be seen and Lance began to wonder why the older boy had defended Lance against the older man, possibly saving his life. And why he did not tell the older man about the LANSPEAK. As Lance knew that would have been removed from his arm as soon as the man had laid his greedy eyes upon it. He had a lot to thank the boy for, despite him leading Lance to this group in the first place.

Despite feeling utterly drained, Lance tried to use this time to focus and plan his next move. He could tell they were heading east due to the position of the sun. He guessed the boat was moving at around seventeen knots. The boat was travelling in the general direction he had planned to since he arrived in the country. *Though being kidnapped was never part of this plan*, he humourlessly thought. He was struggling to figure out a way to escape. These men were heavily armed and looked like they would not hesitate to shoot him if he tried to get away. He closed his burning eyes and tried to conserve energy.

Time seemed to stand still on the boat, possibly due to his lethargy and dehydration he thought. He tried to fight his fatigue, knowing he was in an extremely dangerous situation. Feeling pure exhaustion, Lance fell into a restless sleep, with the sound of laughing men in his ears.

J'ba Fofi's Territory,
The Salonga National Park,
The Democratic Republic of the Congo,
July 18,
10:15am (Congolese and UK time)

The same laughter he had passed out to was now jarring him awake. But not just laughter, something else. Something cool on his head. It took him a while to realise water was being poured onto him from above. Lance turned his head up and almost choked as the stream splashed his face, much to the amusement of whoever was soaking him.

Coughing and choking he shook his head, blinking the stinging fluid from his eyes. The flow had stopped and he looked around. A young man was walking away chuckling to his companions, pouring the last drops of water out of a metal canister. The burning aches in his muscles re ignited the moment he tried to move. He could barely stay conscious and tried to swallow a few beads of water, which had trickled into his mouth, but it felt like sipping on sand.

A shadow blocked out the hot sun and he was able to focus on the person who crouched in front of him. It was the older boy. A look of concern was etched over his young face. Lance tried a weary smile, but it felt like his face would crack. A small hand found his aching shoulder, giving him support he did not realise he needed until then. A cold metal object touched his lips.

'Drink,' was all Lance heard. And as the cool fresh liquid poured down his parched throat, he found himself gripping the bottle and gratefully drinking the offered water. He ravenously swallowed every drop, feeling the fluid filling his very muscles, waking him from chronic daze.

Dropping the empty bottle, he saw the boy smile lightly.

'Pod! Pod! Bring it!' The older man's bellowing voice behind the boy caused him to stand up suddenly. Lance saw the gun pointed at him. A look of miserable guilt on Pod's innocent face was tragic to see, as he waved the gun at Lance, indicating him to leave the boat.

With every ounce of strength, Lance stood his agonised body up and headed towards the muddy bank, the sun feeling fierce now he was directly under it. The brief drink felt like it had lubricated his aching joints as he made his way up the bank, Pod close behind him. The older man was just ahead, coughing and spitting but not looking behind. A pile of thick long logs were stacked neatly away from the river's edge.

A gap in the small trees at the river's edge led into a very large grassy field. The whole area had the mark of men on it, Lance sadly saw. Tree stumps, ripped up earth, crude muddy roads and a number of tents positioned around a few poorly constructed buildings. The buildings were no more than large huts. They appeared to have been built using any materials that could be found anywhere. Wood, metal bars, corrugated iron roofs, sheet glass, rope and grass. None looked like they were able to withstand monsoon rains. Many did not even look waterproof.

There were many men in this makeshift camp. Almost all were young and armed. It was a frightening place. He was thankful he could not see any more child soldiers. The older man turned but did not look at Lance, but at Pod behind him. 'Put it in the box,' he snarled, indicating a crumbling half-metal half-stone shack about fifty yards away. Pod poked the gun into Lance's back and led him towards the "box".

'And make sure he is fed today! I want him fat and strong when he meets J'ba Fofi!' the older man shouted and laughed, as Lance was led into the building. The use of the words J'ba Fofi was significant. The phrase clearly has meaning in this part of the world. Though when the man required Lance to be fat and strong when they met, a crazy thought entered his head. He envisioned himself, fat and bloated, dangling from a rope over the web of a hungry giant spider like some twisted fairy tale.

And though he half smiled at that ridiculous image, he reasoned that this ludicrous fantasy was more of a desirable situation to be in than the one he was currently facing he darkly thought.

The "box" was aptly named he thought, as he entered a single stone room. Over ten feet high, smooth dry walls led up to a roof of sheet metal, which did not cover the ceiling the whole way. A gap of about a foot revealed the hot sky. Very little light could enter, but it still felt like an outside dwelling. There was very little in the room apart from a metal bucket on the sandy floor and a few bits of metal and plastic rubbish scattered around the edges. The bucket was his toilet, he queasily thought. Although it was hot outside, the room only felt warm, largely due to the thick walls and lack of direct sunlight.

He turned to look towards Pod, who still had the sad guilty face he had from the boat. Lance tried to smile but could not make eye contact. The child nodded and closed the high metal gate, locking it with a rusty key, which he put in his pocket.

The gate had thick bars supporting it. Pod looked through and stared at Lance.

'I am Podestin,' he proclaimed proudly. Lance quickly opened the cast.

'*I am Lancelot.*' He was unsure why he used his full name, possibly to make Podestin trust him more. The boy's eyes widened with excitement at hearing Lance's full name. A full warm smile spread across his young face. Then he was gone.

Lance looked through the gate bars. He could see parts of the camp from here. As he was looking for possible ways to escape as quickly as possible, an armed man came into view. He gave Lance a look of curiosity, then turned his back and stood against the building. *An armed guard is going to make escaping slightly more difficult*, he thought.

He had to get out of here. Ideally, before he was brought before whatever J'ba Fofi was. If the hysterical state of Rufus was in on returning from this area was anything to go by, it did not sound like a pleasant meeting. He sat on the cool floor and tried to focus his mind. He entered a peaceful state, the first for many hours. He mentally planned ways of escaping, going over numerous scenarios.

Just then, he heard the gate lock open and was surprised to see Podestin walk in with a large tray of food and some bottles of water. Lance was relieved to see that his gun was gone. The absence of the deadly weapon, coupled with the smile on the boy's face made him look more like the young child he knew he was. In a different world, he could have been proudly bringing food to his mother in bed as a birthday treat. This evil world, Lance sighed. Podestin put the tray at his feet. Lance was about to stand when the guard poked his head into the cell. 'Eat!' he ordered. The boy's smile faded slightly, but when he turned to leave, he called out, 'Eat! Eat and get strong, Lancelot!' For some reason, this boy's words gave him renewed hope about the situation.

The food was a selection of raw vegetables, many of which were unfamiliar to him. He ate and drank gratefully, feeling energy returning to him gradually. Though one recent memory kept finding its way into Lance's thoughts. It was what Tom said in the coffee shop, ages ago it seemed. When asked what J'ba Fofi was, "The stuff of nightmares brothers" was his only description, he remembered with a shudder.

**J'ba Fofi's Territory,
The Salonga National Park,
The Democratic Republic of the Congo,
July 18,
1:10pm (Congolese and UK time)**

The gate clanked openly suddenly, the noise rousing him from his thoughts. The guard entered the room and motioned him to follow. Lance stood his aching body and exited the box. The sun was harsh, its heat intense. Following the man, he looked around. All eyes were on him. There were so many men that they formed almost a guard of honour for the celebrity prisoner, which was precisely how he felt.

The walk in the relentless sun seemed to take forever, but it was only to the other side of the field, where the largest of the makeshift buildings stood at the tree line. Constructed largely from stone, it was reinforced at all sides by sheet metal plates. There were no windows to be seen and it looked to house more than one floor. The roof was corrugated iron patched with grass.

Two guards with machine guns flanked the only obvious entrance to the place. A wide doorway with no door, only a shabby curtain tied to the side of the entrance. His guard left him to walk towards this dark doorway. The guards both stared, as he approached, one indicating to go in with a look of curiosity.

The room felt pitch black for a moment once he was out of the blinding sun. A few seconds to focus and he looked at the back wall of the room. Two metal stands with a tray of burning wood about six feet high were posted either side of a large throne-like chair. The rest of the room was sparsely furnished, though there was a set of rickety steps leading up to a dark landing. His eyes settled on the figure sat in the huge chair, his body now illuminated slightly in the poor flickering light.

He was an older man, possibly in his mid-fifties. Stockily built and wearing similar combat clothes to the other men, though he also wore a pale-yellow animal skin over his shoulder. It gave him the impression that was a man of authority. His short hair and neatly trimmed beard both were flecked with white. Although it was dark in the room, he was wearing sunglasses. One leg was across the other and he was half slouching in his seat. Two more guards stood behind the chair, their guns deliberately on show.

He had an intimidating grin on his face. Lance was able to focus on what he had resting on his leg, both hands securing the brightly coloured parachute bag. He clicked his fingers and motioned Lance to approach. He gingerly stepped forward a few paces until one of the guards held a hand up but said nothing. He stopped a few feet from the man. It was now obvious what this man was. A warlord. And he was clearly in charge of this small army. His grin widened and it looked like he had numerous gold teeth, though it was hard to see in the limited flame light.

Then for no reason, the man let out a loud rasping laugh, as if Lance had said or done something amusing. The laugh lasted for over thirty seconds. The men behind joining in to the mystery joke, leaving Lance bewildered. Once he was done laughing at whatever he found so amusing, he looked at Lance again. He was still smiling but it had an even more sinister edge to it now.

He quickly snapped his fingers together and one of the guards shouted something inaudible towards the dark landing. A second later, Pod slowly walked down the creaking staircase. The look of hope and excitement from earlier now gone. He meekly went towards the man and stood by his leg. The man chuckled and finally spoke. 'So, you came to my place from somewhere far away?' His voice was incredibly deep. He spoke slowly and controlled. His French was excellent but it had a strong accent to it, one Lance could not pinpoint. French was clearly a second language to him, unlike Pod and the other men. 'The boy tells me you don't speak.' He nodded towards Pod. Lance simply nodded, not making eye contact.

'You must be stupid.' This comment caused the guards to laugh slightly. 'You must be *real* stupid to come to my place man.' This was more of a general statement not directed at Lance. The grin vanished, to be replaced by a defiant snarl. 'I am J'ba Fofi. And I own this place. I own this forest. I will own this country soon enough.' The deep slow words clearly believed what they were saying. *This is a desperate power-hungry man,* Lance wearily thought. Was this the man that had reduced Rufus to his current state? The evil grin returned and he continued. 'But to do anything, I need men,' he stated like he was justified by what he was doing. *Need men? Boys more like,* Lance angrily thought. 'And to get men, I need money. Lots of money.' He laughed deeply once more. Then he looked straight at Lance. 'This is where you can help, man.' The puzzled look on Lance's face caused more laughter to erupt from J'ba Fofi. He suddenly stood up, causing Pod to jump back startled. With a golden toothy smile, he emptied the contents of the parachute bag onto the dusty floor.

The older man laughed at the look on Lance's face once more. The bag contained two large gold bars and some bags of solid gold looking coins. He could scarcely believe what he was seeing. Realising he had jumped from a moving aeroplane with a bag of gold stuffed into a parachute bag. He really was lucky to have survived. The hearty laugh echoed around the room. Lance quickly thought what this was. He could only imagine that a member of the crew or a passenger from a previous trip was trying to smuggle this treasure between destinations. Or maybe it was an official bag, to be used for emergency currency at any point.

None of this actually mattered right now. What did matter was that J'ba Fofi thought that this gold was Lance's. The greedy bright smile spread across his face only confirmed this. 'This is good, but not enough. This won't even cover my new teeth.' He laughed once more. 'What I need to know, is how you're going to get me more.' This was what Lance was dreading. He had suddenly become this man's latest source of income. At least that was what he was thinking. 'So. You clearly do not come from this place. I guess you come from far away. America maybe. That is not important. What is important is how you can get me more of this. Lots more.' His smile was covetous. 'You may not want to help me. But you will, man. You will.' His face twisted into a menacing sneer. 'I *will* make you do as I want man. People always do what I want.' The Last statement was a clear threat.

Pod glanced at Lance, a frightened look on his face, Lance replied with a slight nod. The older man noticed the interaction and walked up to Lance, his face inches from him. 'I can tell you do not like me using these boys for my work. They are too young, you think?' It was not worded as a question. Lance could only look away. 'I take them young and turn them into men. Fighting men. I have to be tough. It is a tough world.' Lance was sickened. This man was describing turning children into killers as some sort of tough love. As if he did not take them, they would be worse off. Evil people believing that they are always justified in their actions. 'I have to treat them badly otherwise they are useless to me. Useless things are extra weight I cannot afford to keep around. Lance shuddered at this man's flippant attitude to the lives of other human beings. He was utterly cold. Lance knew he had made another enemy, just like Stanmer.

J'ba Fofi could read the look of revulsion on the younger man's face. He went and sat back down again. 'I shall tell you something you need to understand. About why I do this,' he nodded curtly at Pod. Lance was almost intrigued to hear this self-justification. 'My father was the lord of these lands before me. Like me, he had enemies everywhere. So he had to fight these enemies.' His deep voice was calm as if explaining an interesting historical period. 'And one day, after a good day of destroying many enemies, he asked me what the greatest weapon against your enemies was. I held up my gun and knife. And my father laughed.' The older man actually laughed at this recollection. 'Of course not, they are useless without your best weapon, he told me.' His penetrating glare now cut through Lance. 'Fear boy, he said. Fear is your best weapon. If they fear you, they can never defeat you,' he boastfully repeated his father's words.

Lance actually agreed with this in many ways, but could never condone the behaviour of a man like this. 'So, I took the name J'ba Fofi, a legend in this jungle. And it works.' *So J'ba Fofi has another meaning in this area,* he fleetingly thought. 'But of course, a name does not win a war. Real fear does. So when my father died, I did what he did. Recruit my soldiers young and either make them or break them.' Lance could not comprehend his use of the words "recruit" and "soldiers" when describing this ghastly practice. The older man laughed lightly. 'My father told me something I now know to be very true. It works when training the soldiers harshly.' He knew he had got Lance's attention now. He stood up and walked up to face the younger man. Although Lance could not look him in the eye, his piercing gaze bored into him. 'If you spend long enough in Hell, even the Devil will fear you.'

J'ba Fofi's Territory,
The Salonga National Park,
The Democratic Republic of the Congo,
July 18,
1:30pm (Congolese and UK time)

That phrase made Lance's blood run cold. Whilst being marched back to the box the blazing sun could barely warm the chill, which was coursing down his spine. This man was clearly a product of his environment, but was more than that. He was pure evil in Lance's eyes. His own sweat made him shiver as he was pushed back into the stone cell he was being held in.

It was humid and full of humming insects. Trying to find the coolest part of the tiny building, Lance sat on the dusty floor and gathered his thoughts once more. He evaluated his current situation. J'ba Fofi was holding him so he could somehow get more gold or money from him. Lance shuddered to think how the man was planning on doing this. Torture? To reveal where more wealth was? Asking for a ransom? If J'ba Fofi ever found out how rich Lance *actually* was, he would be seen as a source of limitless cash to be used to fund his war. The thought of the man having access to endless funds to finance his violent quest was a disturbing thought indeed.

And the thought of Caelia handing over her beloved money to ensure Lance's freedom was about as farfetched an idea as giant spiders living here, he thought, smiling grimly to himself.

Thoughts of Caelia quickly turned to thoughts of other people in his life. He could hear Tristan's voice, 'I told you it was dangerous there.'

Blake, 'No story is worth your life.' Then his mind focused on Ezzy. Her gentle wise Spanish accent swam into his head.

'You can do this. Too many people need you to find out the truth. The Stanmers of this world only thrive when good people do nothing. You are a good person. You have come so far. You have to finish this.' It was as if she was actually sat next to him. Lance had always valued her opinion. Now he had to follow her advice, which was actually *his* advice, but it made sense in his head. Knowing he had to get away from here as quickly as he could.

Night would be the easiest time to escape, he reasoned. He knew where the boats were. It was figuring out a way to get out of the building without being seen. Cautiously walking towards the metal gate, Lance peered through the bars. His heart sank when he realised how serious J'ba Fofi was at protecting his "investment". The guard had been increased from one man to eight heavily armed men.

'You need to think outside the box,' this voice was from his brother Andred, who was known for his puns. It was also no help whatsoever. *Think, Lance, think.*

Ezzy spoke into his ear again. 'You think a few men and a high wall can stop a fit athletic resourceful man like you?' *Though that would actually be more like something Tristan would say,* he thought. His mind was swimming now. He had to get out tonight. He looked up at the smooth high wall. *I will get out. But I will not be leaving alone*, he determinedly thought.

J'ba Fofi's Territory,
The Salonga National Park,
The Democratic Republic of the Congo,
July 18,
6:30pm (Congolese and UK time)

The sun had gone down, though it was still hot. Lance had patiently waited for the darkness. He had eaten the food, which had been offered. J'ba Fofi clearly wanted fat profits, judging by the large amounts. He wondered if any of the warlord's young men and boys had gone without eating to ensure his plate was full. Probably quite a few was his grim assumption.

The men outside had gradually gotten louder with their voices and laughter as the evening wore on. At one point, a child's voice could be heard conversing with the men earlier. It could have been Pod, but it was difficult to hear over the men's noise. As the voices and laughs became louder, Lance heard the chinking of glass on glass. Often the sound of smashing glass cut through the raised conversations.

These men were getting drunk, Lance quickly realised. This was good news for him. Drunk men make poor guards he reckoned. At least he hoped they did. Not daring to look through the gate, he looked at the sheer wall and felt the surface. It was soft like dry packed mud. It had been built from stone but packed with a layer of mud at some point, possibly to keep it cool. Quickly looking around the small dark floor, his eyes settled on a twisted old metal spoon.

The men's loud conversations were now an adequate cover for what he was about to do. He began to gouge and scrape at the solid mud with the metal tool. He was directly underneath the ceiling gap. Nothing happened at first. Then with more pressure, he was able to dig out a small section, making a narrow hole. Lance began to hack at the wall in different places. He was an experienced rock climber, so was able to scale a surface with minimal grips. It was forming holes higher up that was proving more challenging to him.

As he was figuring out a solution, a sudden burst of noise made him pause in his task. Extremely loud music was blaring out from something outside the wall, accompanied by cheers and laughter from the guards. It was pop music, which clearly sounded like the men's favourite choice.

A boy's voice was heard over the excited chatter, though it was not clear if it was Pod. The gate suddenly clinked open and Pod ran in, a beaming smile on his face. He was carrying three black plastic bags. He placed them on the floor and silently closed the gate, turning the key, then pocketing it. 'More rubbish for the rubbish,' he shouted so the men could hear. Pod held a finger to his mouth, indicating Lance to be silent, which was quite easy for him to do, he wryly thought. Pod quickly emptied two bags of food waste and various tied bags onto the floor, laughing exaggeratedly. Louder laughter could be heard from outside.

Lance was puzzled until the last bag was emptied and his pack fell out, just visible in the fading light. He was stunned to see it but mainly relieved. Pod then looked pleadingly at him. 'Help us escape, Sir Lancelot,' he whispered, his eyes moistening.

Without another thought, Lance pocked the pack up and checked its contents. It had clearly been emptied and re packed hurriedly. 'I got it from the father's house. But he is keeping hold of your gold,' the boy said breathlessly. Hearing this child refer to that vile warlord as "father" repulsed him but he had to think fast.

He picked up the bucket and laid it face down under the wall, which had the new holes in it. Lance stood on it and realised it was too high to jump and he had not hand holes that high. Pod tugged on his belt and held up a thin length of rope, obviously from one of the bags he had emptied. Without thinking, Lance lifted Pod up and placed him on his shoulders, feeling a pang of sadness at how underweight he felt.

Ignoring the agony in his previously dislocated shoulder and the various other cuts, bruises and injuries his body had sustained, Lance hoisted the boy higher. He was now standing with his feet on each open hand and using his considerable strength and wincing through the burning of his muscles, pushed Pod above his head. The boy was able to reach and grab the edge of the roof and began shuffling through the gap.

He turned around when he was through and Lance threw the rope up. '*Tie it to something solid.*' He quickly typed, as the boy took it with a huge smile. Pod looked around and began to wrap the rope around something out of sight. The thin rope fell into Lance's grasp and he let it take his weight. It held. Pushing up hard, the bucket clattered loudly in the room. To his horror, he heard the music suddenly switch off. He looked up at Pod's terrified face. The men outside suddenly started shouting angrily. The party had ended suddenly, Lance fearfully thought.

He pulled himself up the rope as the gate was being banged on loudly. The chilling sound of metal on metal. Guns at the door, he guessed. 'Quickly!' Pod shouted. Lance was quick, despite his body crying out in pain, and he reached Pod in seconds as he heard the door being forced open. The boy reached for Lance's hand. They touched fingers but before they could grip, the rope jerked suddenly. Whilst he had a firm hold, the rope slid limply down the wall and Lance fell to the floor, pain wracking his whole body. The rope had snapped. Pod looked tearful and lost.

The door could be heard being forcibly opened. They would be inside in seconds. Lance wearily stood and lifted his stiff neck toward the frightened boy. He then did something he almost never did. He looked Pod straight in the eye. It was much easier looking children in the eyes. He was never sure why, but he guessed it was because there was always honesty in a child's eyes. They had an open innocence, which he found he could relate to, much easier than an adult who can hide emotions too easily.

Pod locked eyes with him and instantly became calm. Lance held the child's gaze, gaining his attention. He needed Pod to trust him. '*Pod. You have done very well. But right now, you need to run. Grab the other boys and run. Go to the river. Get onto the boat we came in on. And the long logs stacked nearby, try and get them on the boat. Now go. I will meet you.*' Lance threw his pack up to Pod, which he caught skilfully, though he looked even more scared, knowing Lance was now staying to be captured again. He pleaded. 'No. Jump up, Lancelot! You don't know father! He's a bad man. He's the devil! You don't know him! He will hurt you! Please try!' The pitiful pleas from this frightened child made keeping his gaze more difficult but he held it. '*He is a bad man, but he has never met Lancelot before.*' Lance managed a half smile and a wink, which he also never did. He stared at Pod intensely. '*Run.*' With a morose nod, Pod disappeared from view.

The door burst open and four of the drunken but armed men stood before him. 'You come now!' None of them appeared to be wondering where Pod had gone. Lance no longer felt fear. He felt anger. Anger towards the warlord and his men. Rage surged in his ears. These men were about to discover exactly what the LANSPEAK is capable of doing, he furiously thought.

J'ba Fofi's Territory,
The Salonga National Park,
The Democratic Republic of the Congo,
July 18,
6:40pm (Congolese and UK time)

Lance knew he was too valuable to the warlord to be killed, but that did not mean he would not be harmed. This escape attempt would obviously anger him. But he knew that if Pod or any of the other boys were caught helping him, their fate would be much worse, he thought despairingly. Knowing Pod had others with him by the use of the words "help us escape", Lance hoped they were not being pursued. But looking at the condition of his drunken guards, he doubted they were going after them.

The walk across the dark field was slow. None of the men appeared to have torches, which confirmed to him how disorganised this group was. The light was poor but he knew where the river was. He glanced in the direction of it, hidden by dark trees. He let them lead him for a few minutes longer, hopefully giving Pod and the others time to get to the boat and possibly find the logs he suggested.

As the men stumbled in the dark uneven ground, Lance subtly slowed down and edged away from the group. In their drunken haze, they were not paying attention as well as they should have been. It was a good a time as any, he boldly thought. He jumped to one side and fell to the ground, ignoring the pain this caused. A couple of men raised their guns, unsure of where Lance was. He flipped open the fake cast and punched in a few commands.

The LANSPEAK could not only recreate his own actual voice as closely as possibly, it could speak in many voices. Lance had built this program into the device for moments such as this. '*Stand where you are! We have the area surrounded!*' The voice which boomed out of the darkness was a very deep older man's voice, speaking in English. Sounding a lot like Tristan's when shouting at his soldiers. '*Drop your weapons and lay on the ground!*' The volume was turned up higher than normal. The men looked at each other confused. Two dropped their guns and held their arms up clumsily. Others raised their weapons and shakily pointed them in all directions. '*Drop your guns or we open fire!*' Lance hated violence in any form. Even threatening violence was difficult. But these men only responded to this way of life. Thanks to people like J'ba Fofi.

The remaining men looked ready to start shooting. The drunken state the men were in had clouded their judgement. Tristan had once told him about the term "Dutch courage". A man with Dutch courage and a machine gun was a lethally dangerous combination. *Time to up the threat level,* he firmly thought. The LANSPEAK could produce more than voices. It could produce sounds. Animals, machines and various random noises. He typed in a code and pushed the volume higher.

The thunderous sound of a firing machine gun filled the night. Its relentless noise cut through the warm air. To Lance's relief, the remaining men threw their guns down and dived into the mud and grass. They cowered with their hands on their heads. It was half-satisfying to see these thugs hiding in fear but also sad that he had to do this. *The twisted humans that we are*, he sadly thought.

Pitiful cries of "don't shoot" and "we surrender" cut through the night once the machine gun noise stopped. Despite himself, Lance found himself feeling slightly sorry for these violent men. They possibly were young and torn away from their home and families like Pod was. *Raised in Hell to scare the Devil,* he thought darkly. Torchlights from the direction of the main camp were heading towards them now. Lance wasted no time in running as fast as he could towards the river. As he ran, he continued with the machine gun sound, increasing the volume as he ran, so it would hopefully still sound close by.

The dark patch of the trees grew closer. Lance realised the machine gun fire could scare the boys, so he turned it off as he entered the cooler canopy of branches, hoping prolonged fear and confusion would keep the men at bay for longer. The light was poorer here but he could still make out the dark shape of the three boats, silhouetted against the pale flowing river. Small figures could be seen lifting, what he guessed to be logs onto the nearest boat deck.

'*Pod,*' Lance called out, the volume much lower now.

'Lancelot!' Pod's voice was a loud whisper, the excitement evident in his tone.

The boy raced up to him and collided clumsily in the dark, almost knocking Lance over. 'You came as you said! Here is your pack!'

'*I said I would, but we must move now.*' Lance was acutely aware that the men could be following them within a minute. He tied his pack to his back. '*How many of you are there*?'

'Me and three of my brothers.'

Lance had no idea how many children the warlord kept here but going back to find out was sadly not an option.

'*Did you load some logs?*'

'We loaded four! We are strong men!' Though Pod was clearly proud of his efforts, it was sad to hear him talk about himself and the other children as men. *J'ba Fofi must feel so proud,* Lance thought despairingly.

'*Let's get on board.*' Pod made a whistling sound and suddenly small muddy footsteps could be heard scurrying to the boat. They headed to the waiting craft. As Pod climbed onboard, Lance took his pack off his pack and rummaged through it. He always packed everything in a particular way, so it was obvious the bag's contents had been removed and then randomly repacked. Lance got the feeling Pod had been in charge of the bag and its contents. And J'ba Fofi was obviously more interested in finding gold than anything else. Thinking that a lot of items had been kept, Lance was relieved to find what he was looking for.

He pulled the small ice pick from the pack and headed to the next boat. He crouched as low as he could above the water line and began to hack at the hull with the metal tool. It was difficult to do this without creating revealing noise. Managing to rip a few holes in this boat, he quickly moved to the next one. As he began to open up the underside of this one, he heard a frightened shout from Pod.

'Lancelot! They are coming!'

To his horror, Lance saw about twenty torches, their beams waving sporadically into the darkening sky, heading in their direction. They were no more than fifty feet away and were clearly running quite fast.

They would reach the river in seconds.

J'ba Fofi's Territory,
The Salonga National Park,
The Democratic Republic of the Congo,
July 18,
6:42pm (Congolese and UK time)

Lance sprinted to the first boat and pushed it into the flowing river. Once he could feel the boat float and catch the current, he leapt onto the deck. '*Is everyone on board*?' he urgently asked.

'Yes!' was Pod's frightened reply.

He grabbed one of the logs and ignoring the burning pain in his muscles, thrust it over the side. Mustering all his strength, he pushed the log down to the riverbed and heaved the boat further into the fast-flowing water. The craft bobbed for a moment, then it caught the current and began to drift slowly in the direction of the river. Not fast enough, he feared, as the first torchlight cut through the tree line at the far edge of the bank.

Three or four beams of light searched aimlessly around the muddy bank. Thankfully, no lights landed on the boat and Lance was relieved that the children were being quiet. The sound of the water was quite loud, which also helped to aid their escape. More torches broke through to the bank, their lights searching.

Lance knew that they were not certain he or the boys had come in this direction, though it was the obvious choice. He hoped they would quickly give up and look for alternate escape routes. The boat was drifting far too slowly to give Lance any reassurance that they were in the clear.

Shouts and arguments could be heard from the bank. They appeared to be confused and frustrated, giving Lance a tiny feeling of hope that they would soon give up. Then it occurred to him. It was obvious one of the boats was missing. Though there were many men in this camp, Lance feared at least one of them would know they were a transport down. The boat continued to ebb along with flow of the river, slowly but at least putting distance between them and the warlord's men.

His heart suddenly thudded in his throat as a bright beam found the boat, accompanied by excited cries. He heard numerous voices. 'They are there! Get them back!'

A cold feeling of terror rushed through him, as he heard the night pierced by machine gun fire. '*Get down!'* The LANSPEAK roared and all the tiny shapes fell flat on the deck, terrified whimpers ringing in his ears. The gunfire stopped almost immediately, followed by angry shouts. 'He is to be kept alive!' The gun was clearly aimed into the air but Lance motioned for the boys to stay down, as he was himself.

The lights, as there were more than one now, continued to illuminate the vessel as it drifted downriver. The sound of the moored boats' engines being started up filled him with a renewed dread. It quickly occurred to him that they had lost their secrecy, so he stealthily crept to the small cabin and turned the ignition key, which he was relieved was left in the lock. After a few attempts, the vehicle spluttered to life.

Sitting up on his knees, Lance steered the craft straight ahead. Daring to glance back at the men pushing out their boats, he hoped that the leaks would not be noticed and would disable their transports sooner rather than later.

The boat reached its top speed quite quickly, which unfortunately was not as particularly fast as he thought. Lance felt confident enough to stand and steer the boat adequately through the water. A quick glance back confirmed that the men were pursuing at a similar pace, though the light on the river was now very poor. The torches in both boats made it easier for Lance to locate them.

It was unclear how many men were aboard each vessel, but Lance hoped that their extra weight would serve as an advantage to the escape. No further gunfire was heard, but the boys were still crouched low on the small deck. The craft bounced through the water, the torch lit boats remaining about thirty feet behind.

More thoughts on the situation crept into Lance's head. Which boats had the least fuel? How far would this transport take them? What would happen to him and the boys if they were captured again? He pushed these thoughts to his subconscious. He had to focus on what was happening right now. His life and the lives of four others depended on him right now.

Loud shouts from behind caused him to look back once more. The boat in front was slowing down rapidly. The boat behind quickly pulled up alongside. The torch beams were mainly being pointed downwards. *They have discovered the leaks,* Lance thought hopefully. The distance between the escape boat and both the pursuers was growing rapidly, much to his relief.

They turned around a bend in the river and the torchlights disappeared from view, leading the boys to cautiously stand up. Lance was now suddenly aware of how dark it now was. The silvery shimmer of the river still contrasted against the inky black banks. He could not keep going if it got much darker. Not being able to see the bank would certainly risk crashing into it, possibly destroying their best means of escape.

As if sensing what he was thinking, Pod reached into a bag stored at the side of the deck and pulled out something, which he held up towards Lance. Slowing the boat and taking the item, he was surprised to be holding a pair of night vision goggles. They looked like a pair of binoculars with a head strap attached.

Tristan had once loaned him a similar pair a few years ago. These were obviously military grade and expensive. J'ba Fofi was clearly able to get hold of quality equipment to aid him in his twisted campaign. He put them on and the world turned an unnatural shade of green. The river, the banks, the forest were all clear for him to see. *A bit of good luck on this trip at last,* he thought gratefully.

He looked down and saw Pod grinning up at him, knowing he had done well. Lance ruffled his hair and smiled as best he could. '*Good work, Podestin.*'

The boy beamed broadly then went back to sit with the other boys who were huddled together on the deck. He sped the boat back up to its maximum speed. The world now looked like a bizarre computer screen. Time to break free from the spider's web, he told himself. The boat sliced through the water, heading for a destination unknown.

A River,
The Salonga National Park,
The Democratic Republic of the Congo,
July 18,
9:05pm (Congolese and UK time)

They had been travelling for over two hours. The fuel gage on the dashboard had not moved at all, which led Lance to think it was not working, so he had no idea when they would run out. The journey had been stressful, particularly for the boys, as they were in constant fear of the pursuing boats.

The three other boys were called Dosufe (Doz), Carhel (Car) and Amadou (Am). Doz and Car were the two youngsters who were accompanying Pod when they first met. They still seemed terrified, but Pod had insisted that they could trust Lance. It saddened Lance greatly that none of the boys knew exactly how old they were, as none of them knew when their birthdays were.

The river never seemed to end. Though of course the Congo River itself was huge and they were travelling on one of its tributary rivers. It was difficult to get data from his LANSPEAK so he did not know which river this was. They really were travelling through a wilderness, but if they roughly kept heading east, they should find safety soon enough. The sounds of the forest were less vibrant than during the day, but it was still alive with nature's songs. The LANSPEAK was mostly solar powered so he knew he had to ensure he did not consume too much power during the night, as it had proven very useful in many ways on this trip.

The three boys had lay down to sleep, though Pod was still awake and excitedly standing next to Lance. 'Where are we going, Lancelot?'

Lance wished he could say more, but at the moment, he was heading northeast as much as he could tell. '*I do not know, Pod,*' was all he could reply. '*You should get some sleep,*' Lance suggested gently.

'I want to help,' he replied eagerly.

'*You have. You helped save me and your three brothers, but we all need rest after working so hard.*' Pod nodded dutifully at this and went to join the others. Despite his excitement, Pod looked exhausted. Lance hoped he would have the most peaceful sleep he had gotten in a long time.

He looked at his LANSPEAK. A map was glowing up at him. It had their estimated position. And their destination. Lance had memorised the locations from the map he had seen in Fim's office only three days ago. Three days? It felt like a lifetime. The destination was a small village on the edge of the forest. The starting point for Rufus and Duncan back in May. Would the answers he was seeking be found there? Or had they already been answered back at that Hellish warlord's camp?

He glanced over at the sleeping boys. Pod had already joined his brothers in a deep slumber. His green vision focused on Car. Though all of the boys had said very little since their escape, he had heard each of them speak. Pod, Doz and Am all spoke fluent French. But Car had a distinct accent when he spoke. Like J'ba Fofi, he had a very good grasp of French, but with an accent. As though French was a second language to him. Lance wondered how old he was when the warlord kidnapped him for his personal army. He guessed that Car must have some local knowledge, which could be useful in the days to come. But for now, he looked at the sleeping children, hoping their dreams were as innocent as they should be for their tender years.

A River,
The Salonga National Park,
The Democratic Republic of the Congo,
July 19,
2:25am (Congolese and UK time)

The endless river took the small boat through the thick forest. They had no choice but follow its flow, he thought. But anywhere away from the warlord's territory was always good. The boys were sleeping. The forest was still alive with sound, which felt strangely comforting to Lance. There had been no sign of any boats since they left, though he could not relax, knowing desperate men could still be close by.

The night vision goggles were beginning to feel uncomfortable, so he took them off. The pitch black was almost oppressive. There was no moonlight and no manmade lights for hundreds of miles, he guessed. It felt like he was floating in a pool of black ink. He had to suppress a feeling of panic. He slowed the boat right down. He dared not turn the engine off but he let the boat lazily drift with the river's energy.

The initial disorientation dispersed and Lance found himself embracing the natural darkness. The place suddenly felt less threatening and more welcoming. He realised that this was a beautiful natural environment. No disruptive interference from human technology. Lance felt his senses were reduced and enhanced at the same time. Sensory deprivation was used in some of the therapy he had in the past. Lance felt he was getting a free relaxation session by being here.

He let his eyes adjust to the darkness. He could barely make out the river, but he felt comfortable letting the boat drift with the water's energy. If they did not have distance to make, he would have happily turned the engine off and let nature guide them along the river's route.

Lance wondered how far behind them the men were. Had they given up the chase, or were they just delayed? He was feeling exhausted now and knew he too needed rest. Was it safe to moor the boat for a few hours whilst he slept? It was impossible to know how away the men were. But also, he had to rest at some point. He reasoned that the dark of night was the safest time to take a break.

Steering the boat towards the bank, Lance glanced back to see if he could make out any sign of torchlight in the empty blackness of the forest. Satisfied he could see none, Lance nudged the boat against the west bank. He loosely tied the craft up to some thick branches. The children never stirred as the boat bobbed against the muddy river's edge.

Setting an alarm on his LANSPEAK, Lance lay himself down and felt sleep overcome him. As he drifted off, he hoped that his nightmares would not be too long or disturbing.

A River,
The Salonga National Park,
The Democratic Republic of the Congo,
July 19,
05:45am (Congolese and UK time)

The alarm chimes suddenly roused Lance from a deep and (thankfully) nightmare free sleep. He winced as he moved, jarring his aching muscles. His whole body was stiff and sore, though he felt that the sleep had been worthwhile, even if it was a short rest. The boys all woke with the sound of the alarm. Each one of them looked like they wanted to sleep longer, but Lance knew sunrise was in about fifteen minutes as he looked at the lightening horizon through the trees.

Pod was the first to stand and he quickly busied himself opening a bag on the deck, which he had obviously packed with provisions earlier. He took out canisters of water, some fruit and packs of dry biscuits. Lance had not asked him to prepare such a bag but was grateful for the boy's resourcefulness.

All four of them ate in silence as the sun began to burn through the treetops, reminding Lance of how hot the days were in this part of the world. Once he had eaten, he stood. Pain flashed through his body with each movement. Limping weakly to the front of the boat, Lance reached for a dry, faded map which was hanging on the wall of the cabin. He had noticed it yesterday, but was relying on the LANSPEAK for navigation through the night.

The crusty paper almost came apart in his hands when he pulled it down. What intrigued him were the various scribbles of blue and red ink dotted all over the map. Some areas were circled, others shaded. But more importantly, words, in a language he did not recognise, labelled many points on the page. Lance thought Car could possibly help, as he hoped he might speak this unfamiliar language.

Car was, like the other boys, still eating and looking, Lance gratefully thought, more relaxed than he had ever seen him. Not wanting to cause the boy any new stress, Lance sat down next to Pod, who looked up happily, as he unfolded the map. '*Do you think Car can understand these words, Pod?*' Pod put down the biscuit he was eating and looked over at Car, who had also stopped eating and looked nervously at Lance.

Pod then did something that surprised him. He spoke to Car in another language. It was clearly a local dialect. Lance wondered if Pod had learned this second language from J'ba Fofi, who also had an accent like Car, or from Car himself. It did not matter, as it was fortunate that Pod had this skill.

Car replied readily to Pod's questions, though still had a cautious, even fearful look about him.

'Yes, Lancelot, this is Car's language, he is a Bayaka. Though he does not read so well, he can tell you what these words say.'

Lance nodded gratefully at Car who looked slightly less anxious, as he took the map off Pod and looked at it. It was hard for Lance to read Car's expression, as he had always appeared frightened. The boy's eyes widened as he looked at the faded text, drawing his small fingers over the dry paper, as he muttered to himself.

Patiently, Lance waited, hoping for any new information, which would lead him closer to the truth of what happened to Rufus and Duncan. Car's mutterings became louder and faster, now talking to himself in his own language and shaking his head.

He began to get more agitated and almost frightened the more he read, which Lance did not want. Pod also noticed the growing anguish in the other boy's voice and spoke softly to Car in his own language. Car seemed not to notice and began gasping and repeating the same few words over and over, gradually getting louder.

Before Lance could ask Pod to speak to Car, the younger boy stopped talking suddenly and pointed to a section of the map, a look of pure terror on his face. Rarely had Lance seen such a look of fear etched across such a young face. He went to take the map from him, but as he reached for the crumbling parchment, Car let out an ear-piercing scream, horrible to hear and threw the map in the air.

He quickly withdrew into himself and huddled on the deck, trembling and repeating the same words, though now more like a whimper. Lance felt disgusted with himself. He looked over at the shivering child, who was now being comforted by Doz and Am. These boys had been through more pain and trauma than any person, of any age, should go through. He felt like he had opened a barely healed wound.

Pod picked up the map, a puzzled look on his face. Car was quietly sobbing, but looked up at Lance with a face of despair mixed with guilt. He smiled as best he could and spoke to the boy. '*Thank you, Car. You have been very helpful. And very brave.*' He noticed the boy's mouth twitch slightly in what could have turned into a smile. Pod moved closer to Lance and pointed to the map. The document was suddenly familiar to Lance. His heart pounded as he recognised the location, for he had seen a larger, more up-to-date one hanging on the wall of Fim's office when he was there.

Barely able to contain his excitement, the map, which he knew they were now located in, thanks to the LANSPEAK navigation, was showing the area where Rufus and Duncan had last visited. They were perhaps half a day from their destination.

Pod looked worried, as he pointed at the points on the map. It showed a vast area of forest with the river they were currently on, snaking and winding around the edge of it.

The map showed the location, on the banks of the river, where Rufus and Duncan had set off from back in May. It was a large village, possibly even a small town. It had small crude sketches in blue ink of houses, clearly an attempt to update this ancient document. From this settlement, according to the map, the forest spread out in a southwestern direction. The river acted as a natural boundary to the south. Lance noticed that the wider forest area was separated by two wavy lines, splitting the forest into three distinct sections.

Lance knew, from Fim, that these were natural borders. They looked from a distance like rivers, but they were in fact huge canyons. Natural rocky gaps in the forest that Fim and her team referred to as creating "land islands". It was these three land islands that Pod was now showing Lance, a troubled look on his face. There was blue and red ink symbols on these land islands. Pod pointed at the first "island", which contained the settlement. It had a simple drawing of a figure, which resembled a crouching man. 'Car says this is known as the sacred forest,' Pod informed Lance, his voice growing with trepidation. Pod then pointed to the third island, which had red scribbles, which were obviously guns. 'This is controlled by J'ba Fofi,' Pod said, a look of loathing on his face. And Lance found it pleasing that Pod referred to the warlord as "J'ba Fofi" and not "father". He then looked at the middle island. It too had red ink scribbles dotted throughout it. Pod's face became grim as he looked over at Car, who was looking over at them, repeating the same words over and over, renewed fear upon his face.

'*What is he saying, Pod?*' Lance asked, part of him not wanting to hear the answer. Pod pointed at the middle land island. At the red shapes, which now became clear to Lance what they were meant to be. Dotted throughout the dense jungle of the middle island were red circles, all of which had four lines on each side. A crude, childlike drawing of a spider. And they were spread evenly throughout the middle island.

Lance grimaced and forced himself to look into Pod's eyes, which now were filled with genuine fear. The young boy swallowed as Lance glanced over to Car. He was repeating the same phrase over and over. Almost reluctant to discover what he was saying, Lance looked at the map and pressed his fingers into the spider island.

'*What does it mean?*' Pod sighed wearily.

'The silent place.'

Lance looked over to Car, who appeared even more frightened. Pod touched Lance on the arm. 'The silent place. The bad place. The place where nobody returns from Lancelot,' Pod informed him, the fear in his voice causing it to tremble.

A River,
The Salonga National park,
The Democratic Republic of the Congo,
July 19,
6:30am (Congolese and UK time)

The newly risen sun was already hot, though Lance felt a strange chill in his bones. And he knew it was not the environment causing this feeling, but the words spoken by a terrified young boy. What on earth was in this forest that had instilled such fear in Car? He understood his fear of the warlord and his men. But these gigantic spiders of myth cannot exist in the real world, at least according to an expert like Drach.

He had an idea what was hidden in the first land island forest, following his conversation with Fim, but something in this place had shattered Rufus's mind. The crazed fear his friend was constantly in was very real indeed. And the truth was always what he tried to seek out over the years. This was just another story he told himself firmly. Though of course it was not, he also reminded himself. This was the most personal and baffling story he had ever attempted to uncover. And already the most dangerous.

He looked over at the four boys, who were now packing away the remains of their food into a single bag, Car was helping, though he appeared very weak, Lance sadly observed.

They had to get moving, he thought and headed to the front of the boat. He saw the boys were now waiting on the deck, clearly anxious to get moving. He started the ignition. The boat engine spluttered for a second, then shut down. The boys all looked fearfully at Lance. A cold feeling of dread coursed through his body. He was already apprehensive about heading towards their destination but it was still more appealing than staying here.

He turned the ignition over a few more times. It turned over but never started. The boys were beginning to look more frightened as Lance composed himself, though he had to stifle a feeling of panic. Pod quickly approached him and put his hand on his arm. 'Do not keep doing that, Lancelot. These engines can flood easily. They are not good machines. They often take time to start in the early mornings. They say it is the moisture.'

Lance nodded gratefully. He truly hoped this was the reason. Pod's inside knowledge was invaluable. He sat on the deck, wondering if the day warming up may increase the chances of this old boat starting soon.

The other boys all still looked frightened. Lance managed a half smile whilst looking in their general direction.

The smile vanished from his face as soon as he heard the noise. A low humming, barely audible amongst the noises of the forest. The humming became louder, the boys hearing it, Doz and Car moaned in despair, Am looked towards the source, which was the bend of the river. Pod raced up to Lance, who was frantically fumbling with the ignition. 'He is coming! Try the boat now!' His voice pleading, almost breaking with emotion.

Lance could hear the humming getting even louder, as he continued to turn the ignition, the engine ticking over but not engaging.

He dared to glance at the turn in the river. All fours boys cried out in fear as the boat swiftly cruised into view. It was one of J'ba Fofi's; it was instantly recognisable. The children ran to the cabin and crouched down; two of the boys were in tears.

He continued to try the engine. Nothing.

Pod looked imploringly at Lance. Suddenly, a spark of memory flashed across his small face, momentarily distracting him from his fear. 'Lancelot! We must rock the boat! That is what the men do sometimes! They say it loosens the fuel! We must try!'

Before Lance could reply, Pod frantically spoke to the three other boys and without hesitation, two raced to each edge of the boat and began to try and rock the boat.

'Do not try it until we rock it, Lancelot!' Pod shouted over to Lance. The boys, though only small, began to work in unison, and the boat began to sway from side to side. It bobbed from left to right. The boys had clearly done this for J'ba Fofi in the past.

Lance glanced at the approaching men. They were about two hundred feet away and heading towards them. Everyone on the boat appeared to be armed. He looked away, the sight of these desperate thugs horrifying him. The rocking of the craft became more pronounced. 'Keep going, brothers!' Pod called to the others, but fear now echoed in his voice.

One hundred and ninety feet, Lance saw with a cautious glance. He saw a man at the front of the boat, shouting and pointing towards them. The little vessel rocked deeply from side to side. Lance went to try the ignition. 'Not yet, Lancelot!' Pod called over desperately.

One hundred and eighty feet. The humming was now a steady rattling engine noise.

They were now listing heavily from side to side as the boys almost jumping up and down to increase the momentum.

One hundred and seventy feet. '*Pod!*' the LANSPEAK screamed, though Lance was grateful his electronic voice could not sound panicked, which he was now rapidly becoming.

'Try it now, Lancelot!' Pod screamed. Lance tried the ignition. It turned over, spluttered again, then cut out.

One hundred and sixty feet. Lance could now just make out the forbidding face of J'ba Fofi himself, standing at the head of the boat, shouting orders and angrily waving his fists towards them. The look of pure hatred and anger filled Lance with a fear he had known few times in his life.

'Lancelot! Keep trying!' Pod's voice mingled with tears. The boys now stopped moving the boat, Lance guessed that they had given up. Escape now seemed hopeless. A vacant, lost expression was on the three boy's faces. Pod was shouting at Lance, though he could not make out what he was saying, his mind now focused on what was happening. J'ba Fofi's snarling voice carried over the noise of the engine.

‘I have you now, rich man!’ he bellowed triumphantly. Lance did not even gaze up at the man.

One hundred and fifty feet. Some of the men had jumped off the boat into the shallow water and were slowly wading towards the shore, ready to run along the bank to their boat. Lance closed his eyes and tried the engine again.

A River,
The Salonga National park,
The Democratic Republic of the Congo,
July 19,
6:34am (Congolese and UK time)

The engine spluttered to life. The boys looked up amazed. Lance thrust the vessel into full throttle and sped the boat into the flowing river. The pursuing boat, which had not slowed down, crashed into the muddy bank. The warlord let out an enraged scream as the small craft grounded itself, sending some of his men falling into the river.

Lance glanced back as he saw a number of men in the water hurriedly pushing at the bow, trying to get it floating again. Some weapons were aimed in their direction, but he guessed they had orders not to shoot, not to harm “the money”, which Lance knew that was all he was to the warlord.

He hoped that the boat had sustained damage when it hit the edge. He was not, however, going to hang around to find out, as he steered their boat around the next turn in the river. The angry shouts gradually disappearing with the noise of the flowing water.

They were still in serious danger. He knew that, though it seemed that their boat was faster than the warlord’s, even though they appeared to be the same model. He guessed it could be due to the fact that his boat was overloaded with men and heavy weapons.

Pod and the other boys had joined him in the cabin. They were clearly frightened but now had looks of hope on their young faces, a welcome change to the despairing look they had only moments ago. None of the boys looked back, that also gave Lance a feeling of renewed optimism.

He pushed the boat forward, desperate to increase the distance between them and the warlord. He knew it would be harder to hear the approaching boat over the noise of their own engine, so he asked Pod to sit at the back of the craft and watch for the pursuing vessel. Pod was happy to do this, eager to help in their escape.

Lance humbly realised that Pod and the other boys had saved them all. Pod's quick thinking and the boys working so well together to help start the boat had more than likely saved their lives. The children often looked at Lance as some kind of hero, a saviour who had rescued them from their Hellish existence. But if it were not for Pod and his brothers, they would now be in the clutches of J'ba Fofi. The boys were as much their own saviours as he was perceived to be. They overcame their own terrors to help him help them. Lance felt a surge of pride for these children. He now felt that he owed it to them to ensure they stayed safe. Whatever it took.

They were making good progress, as J'ba Fofi's boat was still nowhere to be seen, as they sliced through the river, heading towards their destination. Lance felt renewed strength, as he steered their transport closer to the starting point on the map.

The pursuing boat was still nowhere to be seen. Which did not mean they were not following closely. He could do no more than head towards the next stage of his journey. And the port of call, which he hoped would be a safe place for Pod and the others. A final destination where they could finally find permanent safety, something cruelly denied them so far in their young lives.

A River,
The Salonga National Park,
The Democratic Republic of the Congo,
July 19,
7:10am (Congolese and UK time)

Over half an hour had passed and still no sign of the warlord. This could be either good or bad in Lance's mind. The sun was even hotter now, though he still felt a chill throughout his body. His mind searched for their next move. He had no idea how much fuel they had left and the thought of running out at any time filled him with a sickening dread.

Pushing negative scenarios to the back of his mind, Lance looked at the crispy, flaking map, which had always been on this boat many years, he assumed. He checked the LANSPEAK and compared the two. They were perhaps five or six hours from their destination. How safe their final stop would be, he could not know, though it surely had to be safer than anywhere within J'ba Fofi's reach.

Pushing the boat at full speed into the centre of the river, hoping the stronger current here would help them make optimum time, Lance could not shake off the feeling that even worse danger could be facing them. He did not believe the stories that Quent clearly did, but there were clearly many dangers in this place and not just from the crazed warlord pursuing them.

The boys all looked exhausted, which was no surprise, though Pod was keeping a keen eye on the river behind. Lance was expecting the boat following them to appear anytime. Now all they could do was hope luck would bring them to where they were planning to.

Lance's thoughts drifted towards Quent and Stanmer. He wondered where they had ended up. The aircraft was not damaged, he was quite certain of that but how far had they travelled, or where they were now remained a mystery. Though a mystery which felt much less important to him at this moment in time.

On closer inspection of the map, Lance realised that the edge of J'ba Fofi's territory was very close. He hoped that the final area under the warlord's control was not regularly patrolled by his men, thus offering them an easy escape from his domain.

After less than an hour, Lance felt he could breathe a cautious sigh of relief. There were no further signs of their pursuers and they were now approaching the invisible border between the land controlled by the warlord and the unknown forest beyond it, that was if the map was to be believed.

The heat of the day was now intense, but he pushed the boat forward, eager to be away from J'ba Fofi and his men.

As they steered through another bend in the river, Lance's worst fears about this final part of the journey suddenly and horribly became a reality. This last section of J'ba Fofi's territory actually looked more like a stronghold. This area of forest had been almost destroyed. But more disturbing were the amount of armed men camped in the middle of it. Many of whom had spotted the small boat and were now running angrily towards the river.

A River,
The Salonga National Park,
The Democratic Republic of the Congo,
July 19,
8:05am (Congolese and UK time)

As the men slowed to a jog, Lance still knew they would reach the bank before their boat could make it past the next river bend. Pod and the boys were all stood next to him, apparently resigned to their grim fate. He had to stifle a feeling of real panic when it occurred to him that these men probably have no idea who he was, or of his importance to the warlord. They could simply view their arrival as hostile and just open fire.

To try and distract himself from those terrifying thoughts, Lance focused on the spoiled land, which was the men's camp.

Almost all plant life next to the middle land island had been stripped. A few dead tree stumps jutted out over a vast ravaged landscape. Very little vegetation grew in what was now a wasteland. The forest was completely gone in this small area. Mud and scorched earth revealing that fire had been used with devastating effect on the place.

A few small fires could be seen dotted around the makeshift camp. Small tents, similar to where he had met J'ba Fofi, now littered the decimated area. The edge of this camp had a tree line, stretching into the distance and disappearing over the crest of the sloping land. But as Lance looked closer, he was fascinated to see a crudely built fence run along the entire edge of the forest.

Wire mesh and various other materials were secured between the gnarly trees, in no particular order. It was a hastily built, fragile looking structure. Natural and manmade litter covered the makeshift barrier.

Whilst he briefly puzzled at the reason for this bizarre structure, Pod tugged desperately at his sleeve as the boy pointed at the growing number of men congregating on the banks of the river only thirty feet away. Many were now laughing and waving at the boat to come closer, whilst simultaneously waving their guns at them.

A few of the men actually looked frightened themselves. And Lance was struck at how young many of these so-called soldiers were. Some did not look much older than Pod and Lance thought uncomfortably that this would be the young boys' fate if J'ba Fofi gets his hands on them again. Which right now, unfortunately, was looking more and more likely.

He continued to scan the camp, looking at any possible escape routes, anything that could help them. Preferably, before the warlord arrived. Though it looked quite hopeless from where they were, he grimly thought.

The boys all had tears in their eyes, though they were all clearly trying to put on their bravest faces. Pod's expression was more fear mingled with anger. Which, for some reason, saddened him even more.

The boat was bobbing up and down with the current, though the engine was still running. Part of him wanted to just keep going, calling the bluff of the men waiting for them. But then, one of the older men suddenly shouted angrily and shot his gun into the air. The rattle of the automatic weapon pierced the natural calm of the area. The boys all jumped and any bravado suddenly disappeared. They were clearly terrified, as was Lance now but trying desperately to stay in focused control.

The man now pointed the gun directly at them and aggressively waved them to steer the boat to him. He now had a viscously angry look. *A man as dangerous as J'ba Fofi himself,* Lance confidently guessed. As he reluctantly turned the small craft towards the bank, he thought the engine began making a strange noise. The boat breaking down now would be the icing on top of this hideous cake he humourlessly thought. The strange noise grew louder until he realised it was not coming from the boat but from somewhere else. Something Pod was now excitedly pointing at. The men on the bank had also seen it and were looking at one another in confused panic. Lance's vision finally located the source of the noise. A helicopter was swiftly approaching from the east.

A River,
The Salonga National Park,
The Democratic Republic of the Congo,
July 19,
8:07am (Congolese and UK time)

Before Lance could comprehend what he was seeing, the aircraft was now hovering over their boat, the powerful rotors churning the river water up. Cool spray splashed across his face, blurring his vision temporarily. Quickly blinking his stinging eyes, Lance focused on the craft, which was roughly thirty feet above them. His knowledge of military vehicles was limited, but spending time with Tristan over the years had given him some knowledge.

This helicopter looked like one of the super pumas, though it was not painted in military colours. An avalanche of thoughts rushed through his head. Who was this? Were they now in even more danger? Was this J'ba Fofi's men? The boys all looked scared, clearly not seeing this new arrival as anything good.

The boat rocked in the choppy river as he looked over at the camp. Most of the men were fleeing. A few remained on the bank, guns aimed at the aircraft, though all confidence and aggression was gone from them. Fear and confusion was all these desperate men were now feeling. As Lance looked closer at the puma, he quickly understood the men's fear. Mounted on the side of the craft was one of the largest machine guns Lance had ever seen and was aimed directly at the camp. A monstrous weapon constructed for one sole purpose. To spray instant death to anyone who was unfortunate enough to be anywhere near it.

Though he hated guns and he knew the damage this one could do, right now Lance felt a guilty relief that the mere sight of this killing machine was probably saving their lives right now. A twisted irony. The last few men were now sprinting back to camp, knowing this fearsome weapon was no match for theirs. Though Lance was very grateful that whoever was in the helicopter had not fired a single shot.

The craft then suddenly began to drop lower. It was suddenly thirty feet away, facing them directly. The wind and water blasted his face, obscuring the view into the vehicle. Through watery eyes, Lance could see a couple of figures inside. One was sat at the gun, which was thankfully aimed down. Another, his or her head hidden behind a helmet and goggles was holding up what appeared to be a white board.

Blinking the cool spray from his eyes, he briefly focused on the figure. It looked like they were holding a poster, as it had writing on it. Lance could scarcely believe what he was seeing. It had a message written in English.

LANCE
FOLLOW US

A River,
The Salonga National Park,
The Democratic Republic of the Congo,
July 19,
8:10am (Congolese and UK time)

The initial shock of this message was suddenly replaced by a thousand questions. Though right now, he had no way of them being answered. The helicopter ascended and hovered, as if awaiting a reply. Lance looked at the boys. They all looked less frightened, but still cautious about this sudden change in circumstances. It was impossible to follow the helicopter in this boat, he knew that, but they clearly wanted to assist them in guiding them in the direction they were already going.

The puma slowly flew away, following the line of the river. Lance looked at the boys. He owed it to them to get as far away from this place as possible. They had nothing to lose. And if the people in the helicopter had meant them harm, that gun would have effectively accomplished that. He pushed the boat up to its full speed and steered it through the flowing water.

There was still no sign of the warlord behind them. Lance took one last glance at the camp before it was lost from view. It appeared almost deserted. A few anxious faces could be seen between the tents. They were clearly still afraid of the puma and its gun, even though the aircraft could no longer be heard. The ravaged patch of land, with its bewildered men living a brutal existence was one of the saddest things Lance had seen in a long time. He looked at the boys, who were clearly relieved to be moving again.

The cruelty inflicted on so many people around the world had never ceased to surprise and horrify Lance. Seeing first-hand the mental and (he knew) physical damage people like J'ba Fofi inflict on so many throughout the world only strengthened his resolve in doing all he could to put a stop to people and regimes which cause nothing but misery. Though he sadly knew it was an impossible task. Human history repeatedly reminded him that people will always seem to be greedy, power hungry and, in many cases, pure evil.

Lance pushed these thoughts aside and focused. The boat was slicing through the river. Pod was dutifully looking out for anyone pursuing them. Despite the soaking with cool water they just had, Lance suddenly realised how hot the day was. The sunlight beat down mercilessly, though thankfully the boys were clearly used to it.

The helicopter was on the horizon now, though there was only one route to take, east along the river. Whilst he wondered how much fuel was left, Lance casually looked to the thick tree line to his left. Something caught his eye. A thick wooden post, clearly manmade, protruded up on the muddy bank. A square wooden sign with red writing on it was crudely nailed to the post. Above the sign was a shape, which looked from a distance to be a bundle of rags.

Curiosity took the better of Lance and he steered the craft closer to the edge. He immediately regretted getting too close. The red writing looked like French, but it was so worn and faded it was illegible. But perched on top of this sign, which was now clearly a warning to anyone who saw it, there appeared to be a skull. A human skull and a few bones tied together. The bones were moist with vegetation growing through them. Insects were buzzing around this grisly sight. He tried to quickly decipher any words to read the warning. Though, seeing that it had a rotting human corpse perched on top of it, it was unlikely to be a friendly welcome or directions.

Lance shook his head in bewilderment. It seemed to be one horror after another since he arrived. And though he was sure that they were leaving J'ba Fofi's domain, Lance had to wonder if the danger would ever be over. Had he brought himself and the boys from one menace to another? Possibly to an even more hazardous place.

His fears were immediately confirmed when a scream pierced the air. Lance turned to see Car, a look of pure terror on his young face, shrieking at the sign and its gruesome adornment. Pod, Doz and Am were all holding the boy as his fear was turning to hysteria. Lance quickly steered the boat away from the sign as quickly possible, hoping putting some distance between Car and the grim warning may help calm him.

His terrified screams continued. He slowed the craft and gently approached Car. His eyes were wide and full of an unseen dread. A horror known only to him.

'*You are safe now, Car. I will not let anything hurt you,*' Lance wished this to be true. But he knew there could be real danger around the next corner. Though he would try and protect Car and the others at all costs. The boys screaming slowed to laboured gasps, though the fear in his eyes remained. Lance approached him. It was too difficult for him to look into this child's fearful eyes so he placed a hand on his shoulder, feeling the wracking sobs, which now followed.

Car had been through a lifetime of trauma, as had all the boys here. But this was something different. Lance guessed it was not the sight of the skull, which had set off the boys panic, but what was written beneath it. He felt that the boy already knew what was written. Wanting to know, but not wanting to cause fresh anguish, Lance looked towards Pod. The boy nodded, as if guessing what he was thinking.

Lance, Doz and Am stood and gave Car space as Pod quietly spoke to him. A few sobs and gasps came from Car, as he replied in his own language. Lance took control of the boat again and pushed it forward, hoping even more distance between the sign could calm Car further. He was focused on the river ahead when Pod appeared by his side. His young face full of concern. 'Lancelot. That thing we saw. It was a warning.' Lance nodded, listening for what was coming next. 'It is for the local people. It says if you enter here, the devil will find you.' Lance looked down towards Pod, sensing he was more afraid than he was letting on. His voice was a strained whisper, as if saying it out loud would make it seem more real. 'Lancelot, this is the entrance to Hell.'

A River,
The Salonga National Park,
The Democratic Republic of the Congo,
July 19,
8:30am (Congolese and UK time)

Pod's frightened description of what Car had said was disturbing to Lance. It was clearly a warning to keep people out. But a warning from who? And a warning *to* who for that matter. This trip was becoming more bizarre by the hour. It felt surreal what he had been through in the past seventy-two hours. And the trip was far from over.

Car appeared to have calmed down. Pod continued to look behind for followers. There was nothing else for him to do except guide the boat along the water, though he kept as far to the right edge of the river as much as he felt he could without grounding them. Lance had a feeling that they may not have seen the last of that "warning" and it would be best if Car and the others did not see them.

His suspicions were confirmed when from the corner of his eye he spotted what was unmistakably another gruesome warning. It was quite camouflaged sitting amongst the thick shaded trees. He glanced at the boys. Car was dosing, Pod listlessly looking at the boat's wake. The two other boys were muttering to each other. He steered the boat as far away from the grisly sign, relieved when it was out of sight before the boys had time to look up.

Throughout the day, a further four of these sick warnings were placed roughly twenty miles apart along the bank, he worked out from the speed they were probably travelling. Thankfully, the boys never saw any of them.

The journey had been hot but uneventful. They all ate and drank water and Lance wrapped some cloth over his head to try to avoid sunburn. He checked his LANSPEAK. It was five thirty-five pm. Sunset was about six pm here and the sun was now low in the sky. A red ball hanging over the trees behind them, turning the river a deep crimson, beautiful to look at. Lance watched the boys gazing at the darkening sky. They all looked in a sort of peaceful daze. He was thankful for this because it would be fully dark in an hour and he had no idea where they could stop for the night. Also he could not imagine any of the boys would want to stay this close to "Hell".

He looked at the map in the poor light. According the LANSPEAK, their destination was very close. Though he saw no sign of anything up ahead. As if he guessed what he was thinking, Pod walked over and tugged his belt. 'Lancelot! Listen!' he excitedly said. All Lance could hear was the gentle sound of the river lapping against the boat. Then he heard it. In the distance, the sound of a helicopter. He assumed it must be the puma, but on this trip, nothing was guaranteed. When the boat rounded the bend, the puma was there, hovering above the bright red river. Lights were shining from it and one in particular appeared to be searching the river. *Looking for this boat,* he imagined.

As they drew nearer, he noticed more lights. Not from the aircraft but on the left bank of the river. Emerging from the clearing in the forest was some kind of settlement. Not a makeshift camp like the ones he had met J'ba Fofi and his men, but brick buildings. It appeared to be a large village, possibly even a small town. The sight filled him with more relief than he could have imagined. This was it. The place Rufus and Duncan began their trip, according to Fim. He suddenly felt so much closer to finding out what happened to the two men back in May.

A small, wooden jetty came into view. Five men were standing on it, waving them forward. It was reassuring to see that none of them appeared to be armed.

The boys had all come to join him and Pod at the wheel. They were all smiling. Something he had never seen them all do together. The helicopter slowly glided to a landing strip behind one of the buildings and gracefully descended. The boat approached the jetty and two of the men grabbed the vessel, securing it with rope. They were all young men apart from one, but wearing the same uniform. Not a military uniform but possibly security. At closer inspection, Lance could see they were all in fact armed. Pistols holstered at their sides merely confirmed they were some sort of security.

A couple of the men were smiling genuinely as they offered hands to assist the boys out of the boat. All four of the children eagerly climbed out and waited for Lance to pull himself ashore. He was greeted by the oldest man, his white hair and neatly trimmed beard still visible in the low light. He smiled warmly and offered his hand to Lance, which he shook happily, though not giving eye contact. 'Mr Knightly, we've been expecting you, sir.' His voice was deep and clear and he spoke in French, though with an accent he did recognise. French was a second language, but unlike the one J'ba Fofi had. Lance half smiled and nodded, somehow reluctant to expose his LANSPEAK until he was more aware of what exactly was going on, as right now he was more confused than he ever had been.

As if to answer many questions, Lance was surprised but not shocked to see Quent jogging towards them from the direction of the helicopter. He was smiling broadly, waving both hands as if he was about to be reunited with a long-lost dear friend. The men on the jetty walked towards the village, leaving the boys with Lance. Quent ran up and attempted to embrace him like a beloved family member, though changed his mind when Lance backed off, though he was laughing excitedly, puzzling Lance completely. 'Aw man, how are you still alive? Falling out of an aircraft from *that* height? You should be dead, mate! You should resemble raspberry jam right now!' Lance was utterly bewildered at this greeting. The last time they had seen each other, Quent was ashamed to admit he had been working with Stanmer all along, as if pretending to be interested in the local cryptid legend near here. Yet here he was acting like none of that had happened, speaking to Lance like he had amnesia.

He flipped open the LANSPEAK and typed quickly. '*I did fall out of that plane, and you seem to think I landed on my head, erasing all memory of our last meeting.*'

Quent's smile faltered but he still seemed optimistic thinking they should continue to talk like old friends. 'Yeah, but you saw that Stanmer had used me. I was as shocked as you were, mate. All I wanted was funding for this trip. To prove what I know to exist.'

His excitement had subdued, this was now the Quent Lance knew. 'Mate, I have to find out the truth. And I'm nearly there. I've waited for this moment most of my life.' Lance barely looked up. He actually felt a pang of pity for the man. For he almost knew that J'ba Fofi were not some mythical giant spiders, but a ruthless warlord who used the name to instil fear into anyone who may want to challenge him. A reputation based on fear, keeping people away from the area so as to not interfere in his evil business. Lance almost admired the simplicity of the set up. He guessed those vile warnings were his doing. Pretending to be something terrifying to hide actions that were genuinely monstrous. It was a plan, which would have fitted perfectly into every episode of "Scooby Doo". And this was what Quent had devoted most of his adult life into looking for. *Poor deluded man,* Lance wearily thought. To establish what Quent was up to, Lance spoke again, '*Where is Stanmer now?'*

'Kisangani. His bosses called him there as soon as they discovered that the drone had crashed and burned! And it had cost the company sixty million quid to build! Ah gutted!' Quent spoke with a twisted relish. He clearly had no loyalty left for Stanmer and his company. Lance smiled inwardly, though he regretted the damage the drone had done to the forest.

'So, who are these guys?' Quent asked, nodding towards the boys who were staring at this new man with looks of intrigue on their face.

'*Casualties of war. And they need to be kept safe from this point on.'* Quent looked puzzled, he was not aware of any war raging in this part of the world. Lance guessed what he was pondering and was staggered at his naivety. He did not want to talk about the boys, as he was more interested in what Quent was doing here. '*How did you find me?'* Lance enquired, genuinely interested. Quent's eyes lit up, as if about to reveal a sophisticated plan.

'We bugged you, mate. How else?' The statement baffled Lance.

'*What are you talking about?'*

'Remember just before you boarded the plane? A security guard frisked you? He managed to pop a high-tech tracker into one of your pockets,' Quent informed him with an air of smugness. Lance was aghast. How long had they been following him? He instinctively felt his pockets. In a small, obscure leg pocket sealed with Velcro, he felt a lump. He reached in and pulled out a grey plastic disc, not much larger than a two-pound coin. *High tech indeed*, he mused. How it had stayed on him after the fall, the river and J'ba Fofi's men was quite a mystery in itself.

Pod looked at the tracker and smiled slyly. 'When we searched you, we found this. But we gave it back. It was yours, Lancelot. We told the men we found nothing else on you,' Pod beamed, feeling he had helped in some way. And he had and despite everything, Quent tracking him had saved their lives, though he felt he was once again in Pod's debt not Quent's. Lance squeezed Pod's shoulder and turned to the older man. '*So, what happens now?*'

'Well, I think you should all rest tonight and if you like, tomorrow you can come with me on my journey. I assume you're still eager to discover the truth about what happened to Rufus and Duncan?'

This was true, but Lance had never envisaged Quent accompanying him on the trip. He always worked alone. Having the older man by his side, trying desperately to prove his outlandish theories would not work. How he could set off from here without him would take some planning. Though more questions pushed their way into Lance's head. '*So what are you really doing here, Quent? Really?*' It was a broad question, but one that needed answering. It was almost impossible to believe that Stanmer had left Quent (whom Stanmer had confessed to seeing as little more than a joke) in charge of this place, which CES were planning to mine as soon as they felt they could without interruption.

Quent shook his head sadly, as if revealing the truth was more difficult to explain than any elaborate lie, though Quent never struck Lance as a liar. In fact, Lance knew the man believed his own theories, despite being laughed at by anyone he revealed them to.

'I told Stanmer that I would survey the place. Give them concrete proof that this area is appropriate to be salvaged of its natural resources. That it has no significant ecological significance.'

Those words "ecological significance" stung Lance. Companies like CES used phrases like this to justify destroying natural habitats throughout the world. There was no place on earth, in his opinion, that did not have *some* ecological significance. But this area of Africa certainly did have such significance. Fim asked Rufus and Duncan to document such significance. Though what they did discover was why he was now here. And Quent, who had little experience in this field, was now asked to prove that this whole area was ripe to be plundered of its natural resources was too much for Lance to take in. It was almost laughable that Quent could be held responsible for proving that this entire place was simply no more than an a few trees, ready to be cut down and mined for the minerals beneath their roots.

Quent seemed to be reading Lance's thoughts, as when he spoke again his real reason for being here was made clear.

'I couldn't care less about Stanmer or his company. They all used me to get to you easier. Once we landed in Kisangani, CES's people hauled him in to explain what had happened. They gave me these instructions to survey the place. Which I have no intention of doing. I'm now using them. Oh, I said I'd come here to carry out some sort of evaluation of the place. Which meant that I had use of their helicopter to get me here. Of course, we took a slight detour when I saw that your tracker was moving. I knew you couldn't have survived but… I don't know. Maybe I had a shred of hope. I thought if you're injured, I could redeem myself by rescuing you. And I feel I have. I think this makes us even, mate. And tomorrow I go on my journey of discovery. To show the world what's out there.' Quent pointed to the forest, a smug look spread across his face.

Lance decided at that moment that he would accompany Quent on his "survey" the following day. He felt an overwhelming responsibility to Fim, Rufus and Duncan to prove the importance of preserving this place and protecting it from companies like CES. And anything Quent found, or more likely did not find, would make any difference to what he himself discovered. Lance felt he was destined to be here. He owed it to Rufus. He would reveal the truth of this place.

Rivertown,
The Democratic Republic of the Congo,
July 19,
8:40pm (Congolese and UK time)

Rivertown. That was the name of this place; Fim had informed him. It had grown from being a small fishing village but it was now starting to resemble a small hurriedly built town. Some of the buildings looked crudely built from concrete with metal roofs, though there were a number of what appeared to be mud-built dwellings, which, though looking older, Lance guessed were far superior constructions. These traditional houses looked safer and more permanent.

One such building was a beautiful looking church. The modern block buildings only added ugliness to what would have been quite an idyllic, unspoiled place, existing in harmony with nature, not destroying it. Lance wondered who had funded and built these modern additions, believing CES could easily have their grubby hands all over this.

His day spent in Rivertown had been interesting, answering a few questions that were swirling around his head. Though it was Quent who had answered some of them. Quent was many things but a good liar was not one of them. He claimed that CES had indeed hired the security guards who had met him and the boys from the boat. The concrete buildings had been quickly built by the local government, which had largely happened in the past two years.

The reasons had been vague, suggesting CES had been behind this "development", thinking long term. Lance knew how good CES were at manipulating and controlling governments. They really did ruin everything they touched he thought sadly. Though some hope for the place did still exist. He knew this from Fim.

The boys, who were all exhausted, were resting in a simple building next to the church. It was a communal meeting place, though it had some beds and they would also be fed. Food, shelter and safety. The boys needed all three. Though love, family, hope, which was what all children deserved, may sadly be more difficult to find for them. He had found himself extremely tired and sore once he took the time to rest late in the morning. Having slept from late morning until the sun was setting, Lance woke up rested but his whole body was stiff and sore. Having eaten and drunk he checked on the boys, who were still asleep.

Pushing thoughts of what will happen to the boys temporarily to the back of his mind, he set out to find someone. A person Fim had informed him could hopefully clarify a few details of this place and what was going on. It was dark but still very warm as Lance headed to a small cluster of single-story buildings close to the edge of the settlement. A few pockets of light from various dwellings offered the only sources of illumination.

Fim had given him rough directions to the place, but now, in such poor light, Lance found himself disorientated. He approached the lights that were nestled near some trees. Making out some mud brick buildings he heard talking and laughter from the general direction. Before he could decide where to start, a bright torch flicked on and shone a white beam of light his way. Shielding his eyes, Lance heard a voice from the darkness. A deep voice, speaking English with a strong accent.

'Mister Knightly, I presume.'

The Office of Doctor Dante Santu,
Rivertown,
The Democratic Republic of the Congo,
July 19,
8:50pm (Congolese and UK time)

The man holding the torch held it up to his face, illuminating a man in his mid-fifties Lance guessed. Long silvery white hair hug over his shoulders and an even longer beard grew down his chest, looking even whiter next to his dark skin. He was roughly the same height as Lance, though his body was much more thick set and powerful looking. He was wearing a pink polo shirt and long, white shorts. His feet were bare.

'*Doctor Santu?*' Lance enquired adjusting his eyes once more.

'The one and only young man, but please call me Dan.' His deep voice was warm and welcoming. He stepped forward.

'May I shake your hand?' Lance was appreciative of the doctor's respect for his personal space. They shook hands and he was also grateful that Dan did not make eye contact.

'*Lance Knightly,*' he said formerly, as Dan clearly knew who he was.

'Come in, come in. It's slightly less hot inside.' He gestured to the closest building.

The mud brick office was about the size of two garages, though oval in shape. The ceiling was tidily constructed using wood and metal sheets. It was a single room, lit by numerous oil lamps and candles. The dry walls were covered in maps, anatomical pictures of various animals and graphs of various sizes. Three large full bookcases were evenly placed around the building. At one end of the room, there was a small sofa and an armchair. A tall narrow wooden table with some bottles of water and glasses on it was between the seats. At the opposite side was a large wooden desk, which had a computer, an electric lamp, a traditional looking telephone and various textbooks on. A single swivel chair was pushed up to the desk. And Dan was correct in saying it was only slightly cooler inside.

The electrical cords from the computer and lamp, along with the telephone cable ran out of the building through a hole at the base of the wall. None of the equipment seemed to be turned on. Dan noticed Lance staring at the desk. 'They're powered by a generator a few buildings away, though it's turned off for about fifteen hours a day.' He smiled and shrugged. 'Technology is slow at reaching some parts of the world still.'

Lance nodded but he actually did not want technology reaching many parts of the world. Dan gestured Lance to sit on the sofa while he sat next to him on the armchair. The younger man was grateful for the cool, comfortable seat, easing some of the burning aches in his body. Dan poured Lance some water and handed it to him.

'It's boiled. I am probably immune to any bugs in the local water, which comes from a well. But I didn't think I could risk it with you.'

'*Thank you.*'

Dan looked at the LANSPEAK. 'Now that *is* impressive technology. Fim told me about it. I wish a few people I know wore one of those,' he said seriously.

'*Do you know people without speech?*' Lance asked with a pang of pity.

'Oh no. It's just some people I know could do with a switch off button!' Dan said, breaking into a hearty laugh, causing Lance to smile and then chuckle to himself. It was a refreshing change to hear genuine laughter from true humour. So different from the cruel laughter J'ba Fofi and his men engaged in. Once he had settled down, Dan's face became suddenly quite serious. Leaning forward and placing his hands up to his bearded mouth, he gazed in Lance's direction.

'I was told you've had a tough journey getting this far. I hope your journey has not been a wasted one.'

Lance leaned forward, unsure at what Dan meant.

'I know Fim told you what Rufus and Duncan were looking for here.' The man nodded his head in the direction of the forest. It was right next to them. So close it hardly seemed real.

'I know why that other Englishman is here and who he's working for.'

Lance nodded solemnly. '*Quent. Though now he claims he is not working for them anymore.*'

The older man nodded grimly, clearly not convinced of Quent's true intentions.

‘Companies like CES have almost destroyed countries like this. I don’t want them to get a foothold here. Their plans to mine this area will be the end of this place.’

Lance nodded, knowing this to be tragically true.

‘If we prove what Fim, myself and many others know to be true about what is living in that wilderness, the international community will be forced to act. Many will wish to. There are a lot of people on our side.’

This was a comforting thought for Lance, though he knew how ruthless companies like CES were. Dan leaned back in his chair and sighed wearily. Looking away, he spoke as if he was close to tears, his voice choking with emotion.

‘I was one of the first people to see Rufus when he finally crawled out of that jungle.’

Lance leaned even closer. Could this man have some answers he had been seeking since he had found out about his friend?

‘That day last May will haunt me until the end of my days.’ His voice strained.

‘Rufus and Duncan were also friends of mine. Good men, both. And Fim trusted them, which was good enough for me. They came here wanting to help Fim and her team. And probably looking for a bit of adventure too.’ Dan smiled humourlessly.

‘Though they had good intentions, I warned them not to go. In fact, I begged them not to go.’ This surprised Lance, but he continued to listen.

‘Two men from another country cannot comprehend the dangers of a place like this. Yes, it’s unspoiled and beautiful. But its dangers are endless.’ He sighed again, as if reliving a painful memory.

‘So they left, with good intentions in their hearts. They set off not far from here.’ He wiped a single tear from his eye.

‘And only one came back.’ Dan’s voiced trembling with grief. Lance stared at the floor, trying to imagine what had happened on that fateful trip. Composing himself as best he could, the older man continued.

‘Seven days after they set off, Rufus returned alone. He was starving, dehydrated, injured. And he…’ Dan trailed off. Lance listened. Dan shook his head despairingly.

‘He was… He was…’ He looked up and gazed directly into Lance’s eyes. A coldness had replaced the previous warmth in his eyes. He almost shouted the last statement. ‘He was mad! Totally and utterly mad!’

The Office of Doctor Dante Santu,
Rivertown,
The Democratic Republic of the Congo,
July 19,
9:00pm (Congolese and UK time)

Though Lance knew this, the doctor’s words made him shiver, despite the heat.

Dan was shaking his head, tears rolling down his face. The two men sat in silence for a few minutes. Dan finally looked up and cleared his throat.

‘And it was fear, Lance. In fact, pure terror in my opinion that had destroyed this man’s mind. Pure terror can do that. I have seen it.’ Lance did not like the phrase “destroyed”. It gave the impression that Rufus was beyond all help. He did not want to accept that. He could *not* accept that. His mind was damaged, yes, but not destroyed. He felt Rufus could be brought back with the right help. As if Dan could sense what the younger man was thinking, he continued.

‘There is a phrase in this part of the country which is well known.’ Lance listened, but was shocked by what Dan said.

‘If you spend long enough in Hell, even the Devil will fear you.’ The phrase, which he had heard boasted threateningly by the warlord J’ba Fofi only recently, was surreal when spoken by Dan. The doctor noticed the surprise on his face.

‘I take it you have heard this said before.’ Lance could only nod, feeling stunned.

‘I know you met J’ba Fofi. It’s what he likes to tell anyone he thinks may cross him. It is sadly well known in this area, as is he. How you managed to escape him is a miracle to be honest.’ Lance shrugged, though he did realise his escape with the boys was largely down luck to say the least.

‘Rivertown is too far from his territory for him to feel comfortable enough to attack us. Hopefully, that will not change soon.’ Lance nodded, hoping for the same.

‘But other terrors are closer to us than any warlord. I know you know what I am talking about.’ Dan stared closely at the younger man. Lance was at a loss at what to say.

‘*Do you mean the legend near here? Of some gigantic spiders?’* He felt foolish even mentioning it.

Dan however nodded briskly and stood up suddenly, facing Lance, but looking over his head.

‘Yes. That’s exactly what I am referring to,’ he said with all seriousness.

‘*But they do not exist. They cannot exist according to expert opinion.’*

Dan smiled but it was devoid of any warmth.

‘Experts. Yes, I know what they say. I am considered an expert myself. But I also have an open mind and know there are things in this world that cannot be explained rationally. Things that defy science, even logic.’ Lance was surprised that this man, who was clearly academic, seemed to believe in myths. Puzzled, he asked him a direct question.

‘*Do you believe these giant spiders exist?’* Again, he felt ridiculous even asking such a question. To his surprise, Dan laughed deeply.

‘My dear boy, yes I do,’ he stated proudly. Lance was aghast. He now felt differently towards this man. How could an intelligent, scientific man believe in something so outlandish? Lance was actually eager to hear his rationale on this subject. Dan continued to gaze over Lance’s head, which he was grateful for.

‘I admit, it is a difficult concept to even comprehend, but there is far too much evidence to dismiss the facts.’ Lance felt compelled to ask further questions, despite his misgivings.

‘*And what are the facts, doctor? Have you seen one of these animals?’* He felt using his title as a doctor could at least remind him that he was a professional. Dan merely smiled slightly and replied.

‘No. I have not seen one personally. Though I have spoken to many people who have. Ones who have survived a sighting that is, which sadly is very rare.’ Dan was talking about something, which was, in Lance’s opinion, absurd in professional reasoning.

‘*People saying they have seen them is not evidence, doctor. And if you will forgive me, you know this.’* Lance hated speaking like this to the man, but he came here for information. Facts. Not to discuss local superstitions.

‘Oh, I agree. But you see, the people I have spoken to have many things in common. Firstly, they are all members of a church. Some even attend that one you may have seen earlier. These people are mostly devout Christians. God-fearing and honest, so they have no reason to lie. Secondly, why would they lie? They have never been offered any financial incentive to speak about what they have seen. In fact, they have never been offered anything to persuade them to talk about it. Thirdly, most of them do not actually like talking about what they have seen. Most have been terrified by the experience, as you have seen with Rufus.' Lance was struggling to take Dan's statements seriously on any level, but he let him continue.

'Finally, all of the witnesses have described the spiders in exactly the same way. Bearing in mind these are people from many different areas, who have not met or spoken to each other. Yet they all describe the same creatures in detail.' Dan was talking exactly like Quent. Yet it was strange to hear it from someone who actually was a genuine doctor. Lance had to state his opinion.

'With respect, doctor, I believe Rufus and Duncan were not attacked by giant spiders. Which I do not think are real. My opinion is that they met the warlord called J'ba Fofi. Duncan was either killed or captured and Rufus escaped, though has been severely traumatised by this. And tomorrow I plan to find out what did happen to them, but at the same time get the evidence Fim and her team need.' The older man raised his eyebrows, mildly surprised at Lance's stubbornness.

'I was afraid you would think like this. But you are wrong on this. The warlord you refer to does not have any power in this area. Rufus and Duncan could not have crossed paths with him and his men. It's impossible.' Lance found himself becoming frustrated, even agitated with Dan.

'*I am not so sure. I have seen warnings. Sick warnings, not far from Rivertown. Dead bodies tied to posts, saying that this patch of jungle is controlled by this warlord or a similar one. Warning anyone to stay away from whatever they are getting up to in there. Saying that the place is literally Hell.'*

'What have I just been saying about the people here? Deeply religious. God-fearing. If they think that place is Hell, with the Devil himself living there, then they will keep away. And they should keep away. Everyone should. You will only ever find death there!' Dan's voice became louder and louder. Though Lance was horrified at what the man had just said, he did not want to believe it. But he had almost confessed. Lance wasted no time in asking.

'*It was you, doctor. You put those warning signs up. You do actually believe this myth.'*

'Believe it? I know it! And I have to make sure people do not go anywhere near that part of the forest. Ever.' The older man was almost frenzied in his speaking. Lance had to ask the next question.

'*Where did those skeletons come from? It seems an extreme level to go to warn people of something.*' To his surprise, Dan laughed.

'Oh goodness, they're not real! The skulls are made of hard resin. I asked Fim to send me a few over from London. It took months! They were part of a display no longer in use at the zoo. Though as a favour, she had extras made for me. I told her they were part of my teaching in the village here. The rest of the skeletons are animal bones and a few rags. The weather and wildlife does the rest. They clearly fooled you!' Dan said laughing even more. Lance was relieved to hear this, even managing a smile though his mind had not been changed by Dan's revelation.

'*I still plan to head into the forest tomorrow. I have to learn the truth for myself.*'

The older man exhaled deeply and sat down again. His face was sad as he slowly shook his head. He finally spoke.

'Lance. I know you to be a decent, generous and extremely brave young man. I am in awe of you in many ways. But I am pleading with you. Begging you if I have to. Please, please do not enter that forest tomorrow. I know Fim wants you to go, but she has no idea what awaits you in that unforgiving place. If she knew, she'd agree with me. I cannot go through that again. What I went through with Rufus.' Lance was genuinely touched by Dan's concern, but his mind was made up the moment he saw Rufus back in London.

'*I am sorry.*' Dan signed and slouched back in his chair and closed his eyes solemnly.

'I am sorry too. For this will be your last night on this earth, Lancelot Knightly. For tomorrow, you will enter Hell.'

Rivertown,
The Democratic Republic of the Congo,
July 19,
9:15pm (Congolese and UK time)

Lance walked slowly back to the community building near the church. Dan had lent him his torch to find is way back as well as a large machete. The darkness was almost total. Living in a large city, he rarely saw such natural dark nights, unless he was away from large human settlements. The lack of any moonlight gave the darkness an almost liquid feel. Lance felt he could have been in a pool of black ink such was the total lack of light when before he had switched the torch on.

Normally, he would have embraced such a peaceful and natural sensation, gently refining his senses. But the unexpected conversation he had just had with Dan caused Lance to feel uneasy. He still did not believe in what the doctor told him. An intelligent man swearing that these cryptids were as real as any other animal on earth was preposterous but the feelings of fear and dread the older man was clearly harbouring for this place were very real. He was sure of that.

It took very little time to return to the building where the boys were. They were still sleeping, which he was grateful for. Lance picked up his backpack and checked all the equipment he would be taking with him in the morning. Pod had managed to salvage almost all of his belongings when he escaped the warlord.

He had three large water bottle, complete with water purification tablets and a good supply of food rations. There was sunscreen lotion, insect repellent and a change of clothes, which unfortunately were still damp. Small binoculars, a compass, along with the map taken from the boat. A notepad and pencil, which were kept in a waterproof bag. Sunglasses and the night vision goggles they had taken from the boat. His GoPro camera was still working. This device would record the evidence when he hopefully discovered what was actually living in this largely undisturbed forest. He had Dan's powerful torch and the machete he had given him. Lance thought about the doctor's expression when he had handed him the large blade. It was obviously an invaluable tool to have when you had to hack your way through such thick vegetation. But the almost look on the older man's face was one that indicated that Lance may be forced to use this tool as a weapon. Which disturbed Lance in many ways. Using such a thing as a weapon was repulsive to him and was certain it could never be the case. He hated even cutting through plants, but at least they grow back, he thought reassuringly.

The night was still hot. Lance sat against the outer wall and turned off the torch. The darkest night he had known in a long time instantly enveloped him. This time, he embraced it gratefully. The lightless night made him feel instantly cooler. He knew this was only psychological but it was welcome nonetheless.

The sounds of the forest seemed louder, clearer. To his vision, it was like his eyes were firmly closed. He knew they were not when he blinked slowly.

This calm place was as refreshing as a cold shower. His mind relaxed and he let it focus. Lance visualised his journey in the morning. It began where Rufus and Duncan had set off from in May. It was a small clearing leading into the forest, not far from the riverbank. They would start at first light, which was just after six in the morning.

He tried not to dwell on Quent. He was unsure how prepared he was for a trip such as this. He had guessed not very. He was only slightly older than Lance but did not seem very fit, nor did he seem like he spent a lot of time in the outdoors. As much as he wanted to find out what CES was up to through Quent, Lance could not help that the man could easily become a burden, hindering him throughout the trip.

Weighing it up, he knew Quent had to come along, if for no other reason than to prove to him that J'ba Fofi are *not* some mythical giant spiders, but just a name adopted by an evil man to protect his foul activities.

The impenetrable night was becoming more soothing. The sounds of various nocturnal animals became like music. His weary aching body felt itself relax for the first time since he arrived in the country. Closing his eyes, Lance embraced an overwhelming sensation of peace. He felt that he was nearing the end of his journey. This whole stressful nightmarish trip was nearing its conclusion. The next few days would wrap up the loose ends. Confirm what Fim, Rufus, Duncan and even Dan knew to be true. Hopefully prove what had happened to Rufus and Duncan back in May. And at the same time, disprove the existence of impossibly sized spiders.

He knew it was still dangerous, as he suspected J'ba Fofi's men to be behind a lot of what happened in May. Though right now, Lance felt more confident when he thought about meeting men like them. Or not actually meeting them, which would be hopefully more likely. Not having the children to protect would make things much easier. Though when Lance thought of Quent by his side, he cynically guessed that Pod and the other boys could take care of themselves better than Quent ever could.

Pushing problem scenarios to the back of his mind, Lance lay flat on the dusty ground and welcomed the natural, peaceful sleep which overcame him.

Rivertown,
The Democratic Republic of the Congo,
July 20,
6:10am (Congolese and UK time)

Lance felt the hand on his shoulder as he gradually woke up. He blinked whilst looking up at Pod's concerned face. He sat up feeling new aches in his body.

'Lancelot, you are not going in there, are you?' The boy asked pointing at the forest. The light was poor, but the rising sun could be seen through the thick trees and it was already warm. Trying to blink his bleary eyes clear, Lance looked at the other boys surrounding him. Car, Doz and Am all looked equally concerned. Behind the children were about five other people, locals he guessed, though Dan was amongst them.

'Please tell us you are not going in there, my good friend.' Pod's repeated question was more pleading. Lance pushed his stiff body to a stand and looked around at his morning audience. They were all adults, men and women. Dan stood looking solemn but saying nothing. A few of the people were clutching crucifixes; some seemed to be praying silently. Pod grabbed his arm.

'Please, my good friend. You cannot go there. Car, he knows. It is Hell. The Devil is there. It is known.' Pod now had tears in his eyes. Lance felt overwhelmed with guilt. He had brought the boys to safety but now they feared he was returning to the danger they had all escaped from. It was difficult for anyone to understand. Lance took Pod's hand and leaned close to him. He so wanted to make eye contact but he had just woken and found it too difficult. Pod seemed to understand and looked past Lance's face.

'*My good friend. I have to tell you, a few months ago another good friend of mine and his friend went into that forest. A few days later, my friend came back alone. Something happened to him and his friend. I am going to find out what happened to them.*'

Pod looked crestfallen. What Lance had told him merely confirmed that the forest close to Rivertown was indeed evil. 'You see. It is Hell like Car says! You must stay here and be safe, my friend!' Pod was becoming almost hysterical. Lance had no idea how to reassure the boy. The mood of the group was broken by a man walking up to the small gathering.

Quent clearly felt prepared for the trip. He was dressed in what was clearly expensive outdoor clothing. Similar to what Lance was wearing but immaculately clean, obviously unused. A belt with various pouches and holders was firmly strapped to his waist. A large machete was hanging by his side. Thick brown boots without a trace of dirt on them almost shone in the early light. A backpack, twice the size of Lance's was secured to his back.

Quent waved, as he approached the group. He had a look of excited arrogance on his face.

'This is who you are travelling with?' Pod asked puzzled, momentarily distracted.

Lance smiled inwardly and nodded to the boy. Pod shrugged almost despairingly.

'You are doomed, my friend,' he said resignedly. Lance almost found this comment amusing. Then on studying Quent's outfit closely, the man looked like he was modelling for an outdoor clothing catalogue and he realised Pod could be right once more.

'Good morning!' Quent spoke to everyone in the group, acting as if they had all been waiting for his arrival. Many strange glances welcomed his arrival. Lance saw a man completely unprepared for what lay ahead. He looked like he was about to embark on an orienteering exercise on the Yorkshire moors. His clothes indicated he had no concept of the challenging environment that awaited them.

'Are you ready?' the older man asked, as if Lance was the one who was dressed for a camping trip. The younger man nodded, feeling that this trip was going to be more complicated than he first thought.

'Is that all you're bringing?' Quent asked, looking at Lance's compact backpack. Again, he nodded, not wanting to even engage with him right now. Quent shrugged his shoulders and waved a hand towards the forest clearing, the journey's starting point. With a sly smile, he turned and headed towards the forest.

Lance looked around. People were praying and Dan was shaking his head vigorously, mouthing the word "no" over and over. Pod looked up at him. He knew nothing he could say would stop him from leaving, so he simply hugged Lance tightly.

'My brother. My brother, come back safe. We love you.' Those last words stung him. Lance had always struggled to express affection. Giving or receiving loving feelings was difficult for him. Though Pod opening up with his feelings touched him deeply. He embraced the boy firmly before heading to join Quent.

Looking back, all the boys had tears in their eyes, though were clearly trying to look brave. From a distance, it was easy to look in their direction. He lifted the LANSPEAK into the air and used it. '*Do not worry. This is a powerful thing. It can fight off evil. It protects me from many bad things. I will be kept safe under the protection of this.*' The boys seemed to take some comfort from this small speech.

Though as he approached the forest he had been seeking for so long, Lance actually wished his LANSPEAK really were as powerful as he had pretended.

Tropical Rainforest,
The Democratic Republic of the Congo,
July 20,
6:20am (Congolese and UK time)

The sun was rapidly rising, heating up an already very warm morning. The two men entered the tangle of trees and bushes around the edge of the forest. The thick vegetation offered little respite from the burning sun. The sound of birds, insects and various other animals was constant, giving the feeling that the forest was waking up and coming to life.

Despite the heat, Lance briskly walked as well as he could, though there was no path to follow. The LANSPEAK was being used as a compass and map. He roughly knew the route Rufus and Duncan had taken over two months ago, thanks to Fim's information. They were retracing their tracks.

It began to feel eerie to Lance. Following in the footsteps of a horribly failed expedition. He was already on his guard, conscious of this new environment. Every sight, sound and smell was being analysed by him. Lance felt like he could not ignore any detail of this place. Looking up at the vast overhanging trees, he felt this truly was a jungle. An unspoiled wilderness full of wonder and danger in equal measure.

Glancing over at Quent, he was not surprised to see the man already looked uncomfortable. Sweat was pouring down his face and he kept slapping flies and other insects away from his face, neck and arms. It was clear he was already struggling to keep up with Lance's quick pace, though he knew the older man would be too proud or too stubborn to ask him to slow down.

To be fair to Quent, Lance thought, it was difficult terrain to walk through. The route consisted of thick roots growing up from rocky uneven ground. Branches, vines, leaves and thick grass surrounded them at all times. They made good use of the machetes to carve crude paths through the constant undergrowth. It made their progress slow and tiring. Lance thought how fit Rufus and Duncan must have been prior to setting off on the same journey.

It was an unsettling thought that two extremely fit young men could have had their trip so suddenly and possibly violently cut short. Lance glanced over at the panting sweating figure of Quent and wondered if he had made a big mistake accompanying him. If whatever the two men in May found had defeated them so easily, then Quent had no chance. Neither did he, for that matter.

Though one thing was in his favour, he thought, trying to remain optimistic. He was more prepared. Rufus and Duncan were on a zoological expedition. Lance himself was searching for them and the danger they had found. He was on his guard and prepared for the unexpected. Quent was searching for a fairy tale, but at least he too was hopeful.

Tropical Rainforest,
The Democratic Republic of the Congo,
July 20,
1:10pm (Congolese and UK time)

They had been travelling consistently for over six hours, taking rest breaks regularly. The breaks were important largely due to the constant heat. The sun barely penetrated the forest canopy, but the humidity was exhausting. They kept themselves rehydrated but flies and other insects swarming around them made the journey extremely uncomfortable.

Lance shared with Quent his insect repellent and sunscreen. It was no surprise to him that his companion had not packed either essential item, despite his very fair skin. Lance got the impression that the man had viewed this trip as an exciting adventure, just like in a film. And now, the reality of being in such a hostile environment was quickly dawning on him. And he knew there was a lot more ground to cover but began to wonder if the older man was even up to the challenge.

As if he could sense what Lance was thinking, Quent suddenly took the lead, cutting his way through the endless plants through the route they were taking.

Trekking at Quent's pace gave Lance more time to take notice of the environment. Glancing around at limitless flora and fauna, he spotted something, which made him stop suddenly. Quent obliviously hacked his way forward.

He noticed some thicker branches and vines had been neatly cut. Not by himself or Quent just now, but sometime in the past few months or weeks.

Looking further ahead, he noticed more areas. Even though the plant's regrowth had almost hidden this evidence of previous travel, it was clear to him where they were. They had found the exact path Rufus and Duncan had taken. He was standing directly in the path cut through by the men back in May. Assuming it *was* made by them. Though judging by the state of mass fear regarding this place felt by the people living closest to here, making it a no-go area, it was the obvious choice.

Quent paused and glanced back looking slightly confused. 'Problem?' he asked, almost impatiently. Lance glanced at his LANSPEAK and almost cursed himself for his own disorganisation. The device he relied so much on required solar power in fact direct sunlight, to keep it charged. It could be charged from a power source from an electrical device specially designed for it. But there was no way of doing that anywhere near here. Having been hidden in the fake plaster cast for most of the trip, it was down to the last four percent of power. He removed the cast and packed it away for future use.

Quent was wondering what the holdup was. Lance strode over to him and pointed at the LANSPEAK. The older man saw the four percent on the display but merely shrugged. 'Ah well, you're not the most talkative guy anyway. We know where we're going, don't we?' Aghast at the man's ignorance, Lance shoved the device up to Quent's face and pointed out the built-in map and compass he had been using to guide them this far. The other man's face dropped, a look of panic spread across his reddening face. 'You mean once that thing conks out we're lost? Stuck in the middle of nowhere with nobody knowing where we are or how to get back?' His voice was rising with ill hidden fear as he looked around at the surrounding forest, it suddenly feeling more foreboding than it ever had. Quent reached into his pocket and pulled his smartphone out. 'This is dead too. There's nowhere to charge stuff in this backwards place.'

Lance glared at the man a new loathing. The adventure was not so fun now, was it? Though Lance unfortunately did share similar feelings of concern but he was staying focused and began to think practically. Taking off his backpack, he rummaged inside and pulled out the map and compass. It was not ideal but it was good enough, he thought, as he used the compass to get their bearings.

Quent looked at him as if he was about to try and start a fire underwater. 'Are you kidding? We're using those to navigate through this wilderness?' His fear had been taken over by disbelief. Frustrated with the man's sudden defeatist attitude on a trip, which was as much his idea as it was Lance's, he took out the notepad, pencil, wrote furiously and handed the paper to a bemused Quent.

'The LANSPEAK is almost useless when it is less than 10% power. It will take up to 8 hours of sunlight to take it up to 100%. Shall we wait?'

Quent read but it only seemed to add to his worry. 'Maybe we should go back? Get some locals to help us?' His voice was quivering. He was genuinely scared. Lance sighed at wrote more.

'Nobody in Rivertown will help us. They are all scared of this place. You wanted to come on this trip. If you want to go back, off you go. I am going on to find out what happened.' Quent looked fearfully at the note and swallowed hard.

'You're right, I did want to come.' He took a deep breath in. 'Okay, lead the way,' he said, regaining some composure in his voice. To try and reassure the man, Lance pointed at the sliced plants. He seemed to take comfort in the fact that they were following an already used path. 'Rufus and Duncan came this way! We can do this. Our prize awaits us. We'll be rewarded for our discovery,' Quent confidently but arrogantly stated whilst following closely behind.

Lance knew exactly why Quent was here. The man clearly had no interest in what CES was planning. He was of course looking to prove his cryptid theories to the world and vindicate himself from years of ridicule. But there was more. He was after glory. It was clear he was seeking fame, fortune and anything else that went with it. *Very shallow and quite immoral reasons for being here, particularly from someone who continues to claim he is only interested in wildlife and furthering knowledge of such matters,* he thought.

Lance turned back to see Quent sweating and panting but eagerly trying to keep pace with him. Fame and fortune were clearly powerful incentives. They trekked deeper into the forest, the route of the previous men appearing at regular intervals, enough for them to follow, though the compass and map were his true guides.

Fim had given him grid references, which he had memorised. The area he was seeking could probably be reached by evening, though more realistically tomorrow if Quent was setting the pace. They continued in silence, Lance held the LANSPEAK above his head when they walked through areas of direct sunlight to try and charge the device but he knew it was a slow process.

They continued through the forest at a steady pace. The device was about seven percent charged. He pushed the self-blame regarding his disorganisation to the back of his head. He told himself that the past few days had been very distracting to say the least. They headed deeper into the unknown, watching as the reddening sun slowly sunk behind the endless tangle of trees and vegetation. Watching the thick, impenetrable darkness swallow everything around them, Lance had a strong gut feeling that tomorrow could answer the questions he has been asking himself for the past ten days.

Tropical Rainforest,
The Democratic Republic of the Congo,
July 20,
6:45pm (Congolese and UK time)

Once the sunlight was gone, the darkness felt like they were surrounded by thick black smoke. Lance welcomed the peace and sensory stimulation. Quent, clearly feeling exposed, wasted no time in switching on Dan's torch. Lance had let him carry it, as it was clear that the man needed anything to reassure him. The white light made them feel like they were encased inside a small, dimly lit bubble floating in a sea of ink.

The forest was settling down for the night. The endless sounds lessened with each minute that passed. The new quietness seemed to spook Quent further. He kept aiming the torch at various patches of darkness. What he was looking for, Lance had no idea. Though once again he wondered what Quent thought this journey would be like. It was clearly not the exciting adventure he had planned out in his head.

Once the older man was convinced there was nothing ready to pounce at them from the darkness, he produced a huge sleeping bag from his backpack. It was clear that this had taken up a majority of room in his bag. Lance genuinely wondered with mild amusement that Quent thought they may find a youth hostel or similar in this dense forest. His poor insight and lack of preparations for such an arduous trip were quite shocking. What disturbed Lance even more was the fact that if Quent had embarked on this journey alone so ill-prepared, it could have actually put his life in danger.

In fact, Lance guessed that if he decided to abandon Quent right now, his chances of surviving an onward or return journey would be dangerously slim.

The feeling that Quent was currently so dependent on him more than the older man could ever have imagined was another responsibility he had unexpectedly been handed. He watched, almost pityingly as Quent shook his sleeping bag several times before he clumsily climbed into it and began eating the rations, which Lance had shared with him. The food Quent had brought along consisted mainly of just snacks. Bars of chocolate and crisps mostly, though a few energy bars, which were mostly just sugar, were among his meagre supplies. What Lance was surprised and relieved to see was that in Quent's pack were a significant number of canisters of fresh water. Quent had informed him that Dan had insisted he take the supplies with him. Lance had enough water for himself but was counting on finding numerous sources of fresh water on their journey, which were, he was disappointed to discover, much more scarce than he imagined.

Lance wondered if Stanmer and CES knew they had sent Quent into a dangerous place completely unprepared. He began to feel sorry quite sorry for the man, this feeling added to by the fact that in the next couple of days, he would find out that these mythical giant spiders do not, nor ever have existed. Lance was actually dreading the moment when Quent finally realised that he has been wasting many years trying to prove the existence of an absurd rumour and that all the scorn and disrespect over the years had been, though cruel at times, been justified.

Lance continued to watch as the man tried to make himself comfortable on the forest floor. He was clearly going to be too hot in the thick bag, but he was obviously not prepared to expose an inch of skin to the elements. Lance himself was laid against a dead tree stump. He had packed no such sleeping bag, as it was far too hot even at night. He watched as Quent nodded off, the torch slipping from his grasp.

The light fell to the ground with a clump, stirring him suddenly. Quent turned off the torch and the pure dark enveloped them. Lance heard him mutter, 'Night, mate.' The darkness which Lance was now embracing did not make him feel sleepy, quite the opposite in fact. His body, though aching as usual, felt energised. His mind was calm and focused. The thought that long days of unanswered questions would soon be answered gave him a feeling of contentment.

He sat there in the darkness, letting a natural restfulness wash over him. Closing his eyes, he felt the energy of the forest embrace him, nature at its purest balancing his own energies. This was the safest he had felt since he had met Stanmer, which was when this can of worms had been opened. He felt so far away from the pain and stresses of the world, if only for the briefest of moments.

Drifting off into a welcome sleep, he began to feel a strong sensation. It had begun as soon as the light went out. It was not a frightening feeling but it was a curious one. He had no idea why he felt this, or that it was not disturbing or concerning him but as sleep overcame him, Lance felt, with a clear certainty what he knew. That at this moment in time, Lance knew, without a doubt, that Quent and himself were being watched.

Tropical Rainforest,
The Democratic Republic of the Congo,
July 21,
6:10am (Congolese and UK time)

Unsure if it was the morning light or heat which stirred him from his sleep, but Lance felt very well rested and his body ached less than it had since he had injured himself. Quent was also waking up slowly, though he looked like someone who had not slept well. His face was flushed and weary, his eyes sunken and bloodshot.

The sensation of being watched was still with him, though he kept it to himself. The other man did not need anything else for him to panic over. And for some reason he could not explain, Lance felt that the watchers were not immediately dangerous. The warlord's men or similar would have attacked straight away. The feeling of curious eyes, not threatening, felt strangely reassuring. As if the forest was looking out for them somehow.

Lance shared rations and clean water with him, the feelings of pity he had felt for the man last night were still there. Right now, he felt he was now obliged to keep Quent alive for the rest of this journey, as if the responsibility had been suddenly thrust upon him. He would of course do his utmost to ensure the man's safety, though it was, in Lance's mind, just more work for him. Though he could see no way out, so he resigned himself to the extra task.

Once they had eaten and freshened up, the two men continued their onward trip. Lance setting a pace Quent could keep up with. He checked the LANSPEAK. The complete darkness of last night had not helped to keep the power up. It was only at seven percent. The compass and map though were good enough to guide them through the next stage of their travels.

Keeping the LANSPEAK above his head to try and catch any sunlight, Lance pushed through the subtle trail Rufus and Duncan had made in May, though he guessed roughly two-thirds of the evidence had simply grown over. Though he knew he was not a tracker, Tristan had taught him a few tips of navigating through wild places during their many adventures together.

His thoughts drifted to Tristan and what he would have to say about this trip so far. Anger and disbelief would be Lance's first guess. He shook thoughts of home out of his head, as he could easily get distracted by dwelling on future scenarios. Right now, this journey required him to focus totally on it. His and Quent's life actually depended on him.

The lack of power in the LANSPEAK was almost beneficial, he thought. Quent knew he could not speak, so they trekked onwards in silence. There was no time wasting talking, debating or discussing the journey. Quent trusted the younger man to lead them forward, so the only breaks in the travel were for rest and refreshments.

Lance was impressed at Quent's determination to push forward, though he did look exhausted but he guessed that the man felt he had something to prove. That perhaps he was up to the challenge after all. *Time will tell,* he thought seriously.

The day got hotter and they were both grateful for the shade the thick trees offered, though it did not help charge the LANSPEAK, which was only eight percent at midday. He pushed thoughts of how he should have designed the device better to the back of his mind. It was pointless imagining "what ifs". Though a small mental note was made to update the devices when he returned.

They continued to trudge through the endless plants. Insects were trying their best to bite every inch of their exposed skin, clearly ignoring the repellent. Despite regular rests and hydrating, Quent was beginning to show his fatigue. His face was flushed, sweaty and his breathing was rapid. He stopped walking to try and control his laboured breathing. Lance looked towards him with renewed concern. It was easy not to make eye contact as the exhausted man was staring vacantly around. He strode towards him swiftly, as he saw Quent's knees buckle as the man collapsed onto the soft ground.

Tropical Rainforest,
The Democratic Republic of the Congo,
July 21,
1:10pm (Congolese and UK time)

He ran up to Quent, who was breathing rapidly and quickly checked for any obvious injuries, particularly on his head. Finding none, he sat him up, trying to ensure he was able to take in decent breaths. The man was semi-conscious and moaning slightly, his skin clammy to the touch. Lance felt the pulse. It was fast but regular, though it felt weak. Quent had appeared to have simply fainted.

He had seen this before and he guessed it was a combination of heat and exhaustion. Lance was patiently waiting until the man became more alert until he finally sat up looking like he was about to vomit, his face pale and sweaty, the flushed appearance temporarily gone. He thankfully did not throw up, which he knew would dehydrate him more.

Finally gaining some slight colour in his face, Quent gratefully drank the water offered. Lance then fed him one of his energy bars. He needed the sugar for an energy burst.

'What happened?' the older man asked, his voice trembling slightly.

Lance did not want to waste any LANSPEAK power, so he merely put the back of his hand to his forehead and overacted a swoon. Quent smiled dryly and shrugged.

'Fainting. Not clever. And not needed on this trip.' He sighed and looked up at Lance who looked away. 'I bet you wish I'd not come along now, eh mate?'

The younger man shrugged and held his hands out in an acceptance. But Quent was exactly right. He did wish he had come alone. This excitable but unfit man was rapidly becoming a liability on this trip, though there was nothing either of the men could do about it now. As Quent lay back, trying to feel more energised, Lance stood and contemplated the current situation. The sensible thing to do would be to turn back, the older man was in no fit state to continue.

Though he knew he himself had come too far to give up now. Duncan could be only twenty-four hours away.

Then leave Quent here? The man would struggle to cope alone. He could come back and find he had wandered off somewhere, never to be seen again. As if providing a definite answer, Quent stood and took some deep breaths in.

'If we take it a bit slower and rest more, I should be okay,' he proclaimed with a quiet confidence. Lance was dubious in thinking Quent was ever going to be "okay" on this journey. But as the man had made up his mind, they set off once more into the unknown.

Tropical Rainforest,
The Democratic Republic of the Congo,
July 21,
4:50pm (Congolese and UK time)

Despite Quent's weakened state, they made steady progress over the next few hours. They stopped more regularly and Lance ensured the other man was hydrated well. Looking at the map, he could see they were almost at the edge of the first land island. With renewed excitement, he studied the map closer. They were in what Car had described as the sacred forest.

This "island" was alongside the area Car had been terrified of. The bad place, which on the map was dotted with crude sketches of what appeared to be spiders, which were not enough to convince him of the existence of mythical creatures. Of course, they would find out themselves soon enough, he mused.

The third "island" was actually familiar to him. This was where they had seen the enormous fence separating the forest from the makeshift camp. J'ba Fofi's territory. The map showed a line, possibly another gorge right next to where the barrier was. He knew that if they went as far as that fence, they were at a very high risk of being captured by the warlord and his men. Whatever answers he was seeking must be found in the middle of the land islands, or as everyone around here seems to believe it to be, Hell.

The area they were currently in was slightly more open, offering the LANSPEAK some sun to charge it, as it was only on eleven percent. Lance surveyed their latest surroundings. It was a relatively spacious area. Small bushes, grass and various roots gave the impression they were in a natural clearing. Quent took the opportunity to rest, slumping against a fallen tree.

On closer inspection, Lance noticed that a lot of the forest here had been disturbed recently, more recently than Rufus and Duncan by the look of it. The grass and smaller plants appeared to have been trampled in places. Much of the surrounding vegetation had been stripped in places. Many leaves and small branches clearly had been ripped and pulled off completely.

A disturbing thought entered his head. People could have done this, a large number of people. He looked around suddenly, scrutinising every detail of the place. There were no obvious tracks on their way into here, except the fading evidence Rufus and Duncan had left behind. They could of course have come from the direction they were heading.

He pushed thoughts of running into a patrol of J'ba Fofi's men in such an exposed place to the back of his mind. Lance saw no evidence of human interference when looking closely. No litter, no traces of a camp. No fires had been lit here recently, if at all. No dead animals or food scraps. He was beginning to feel reassured that this was no more than a natural clearing when that feeling of being watched suddenly overwhelmed him. There were eyes on him and Quent; he actually felt them.

Lance scanned the trees. Nothing. The other man was still slumped against the tree trying to cool himself by using a flat piece of bark as a fan. His heart skipped a beat when he saw it. Movement a few feet away from Quent. The grass was long at the tree line, which was now being rapidly disturbed by a large shape cutting through it rapidly.

The older man was oblivious to the shape approaching him, which was now only about twenty feet from him. Lance did not want to use the LANSPEAK to alert Quent, unnatural noise could expose them both quicker. He picked up a small branch and threw it at the other man, striking him on the shoulder.

He looked up, a look of confusion on his sweating face, which immediately changed to fear as he saw the look of worry on Lance's face. A look of panic spread across his face when his gaze followed the direction Lance was pointing at, finally seeing the grass rustling towards him, now only ten feet away.

He went to stand but slipped and fell back clumsily, letting out a loud grunt. The approaching shape stopped suddenly at this new sound. Quent looked pleadingly at Lance as if asking what he should do. Lance simply put one finger to his mouth to indicate he should be quiet. When the shape still did not move, he motioned for the older man to stand up quietly and slowly walk towards him.

It was difficult to give such instructions with hand gestures, but Quent seemed to understand, as he gingerly stood and crept towards Lance. As soon as the older man was standing behind him, Lance surveyed the area further, focusing on the grass, which was clearly concealing something quite sizeable.

Nothing moved for what felt like ages. The two men barely breathing were both staring at the grass, looking for any signs of movement. Eventually, the shape continued its course to the clearing, though much slowly this time. Lance could hear the other man's breathing become more rapid, as they watched the thick grass part and a large hairy animal stealthily emerge from it. Quent gasped.

Tropical Rainforest,
The Democratic Republic of the Congo,
July 21,
4:52pm (Congolese and UK time)

It was a gorilla. A female gorilla judging by her size. She was covered in black fur with a large head but with a bald face with very flat nostrils. Her chest, hands and feet were also hairless, both arms were long and powerful looking. Lance guessed she would be roughly five feet high if standing upright.

She was a magnificent sight in Lance's eyes and one he had wished to see, as Fim and Dan were primatologists and had informed him of what he may find in this forest. It was the reason Rufus and Duncan had come here. Working for Fim, they were hoping to find evidence of these rare animals living here and report their findings back to her.

The large ape remained on all fours, staring curiously at the men. Lance had no problem making eye contact with animals and this was no exception. Though looking into the gorilla's intelligent eyes, he saw an almost human level of curiosity. She looked gentle, peaceful and confident. As she should, he thought. This was her territory.

That thought made him pause and look around. He was suddenly aware they were in the middle of their habitat, and there was no way to know how many were living here. The female ape simply stared, not appearing frightened just unsure of the new arrivals.

Lance did not feel unsafe but he did feel he should be cautious now. He took his GoPro out of his bag, strapped it to his shoulder and began filming. This footage could offer conclusive proof of a newly discovered group of these apes.

And armed with this evidence, Fim could hopefully have more influence in the fight against CES and other companies who would seek to destroy this place and everything in it.

He was now more pleased than ever that he had destroyed that drone Stanmer was so proud of. Quent was watching the gorilla intently, clearly fascinated by what they had discovered, though Lance wondered if the man was disappointed that these animals are the ones they had found instead of his fantasy spiders.

Lance then remembered the advice Fim had given him back in London. That he should not make eye contact if possible as that can feel threatening to them. Quent clearly had other ideas as he was staring intently at the female ape. Just then, the grass around her shook and two baby gorillas cautiously crept out of the hiding place, joining their mother, one climbing onto her back. They did not acknowledge the men but Quent was clearly taken with these new arrivals, letting out a loud excited "Ha!" then laughing, which startled all three of the animals.

The older man slowly began to walk towards the apes, trying to focus the camera he had produced from his bag. Before Lance could warn him to stop, he had begun taking photographs. In the shaded area, they were in an automatic flash engaged, the sudden bright lights distressing the mother. She let out a large grunt and waved her arms a number of times.

Quent looked back at Lance, a lopsided grin on his face as if asking what this behaviour meant. The younger man felt the anger rising in him as he waved his thumb at the man to come back. Ignoring him, the older man continued to take more photographs, much to the distress of the apes and the anger of Lance, who now was slowly walking towards Quent, feeling ready to snatch the camera out of his hands. He continued to film, knowing that it was important to film these animals in their natural environment. The other man, however, was acting like he was at the circus and that these animals were performing for his enjoyment. Quent however did stop using his camera and Lance also stopped in his tracks when a powerful fierce roar echoed through the jungle.

Tropical Rainforest,
The Democratic Republic of the Congo,
July 21,
4:55 pm (Congolese and UK time)

The roar even frightened the mother and her babies, who quickly retreated back into the long grass. Quent looked at Lance in horror. His eyes wide, as it really was a loud menacing roar. A large animal had obviously made it and it was clearly not very happy.

'What was that? A big cat?' Quent asked, his voice shaking. Lance shook his head. He knew what had made that sound and he knew they had to get out of there. He motioned for Quent to move quickly towards him and the man wasted no time in following. Lance secured the GoPro and began to jog away from where the roar had come from, which was in the direction they had first arrived.

Hearing Quent puffing behind him, they headed towards the same route they had been taking. Glancing behind, he watched the grass move in various places as a number of gorillas now entered the clearing. Females mainly, though a few young-looking males had joined them.

The men quickened their pace, eager to be away from any immediate danger. Another roar, louder this time echoed through them. Daring to look back once more, the owner of the fearsome sound was now at the edge of the grass, standing over six feet tall and looking directly at them was a male gorilla and clearly the head of this family of apes.

Quent made a sobbing sound as he broke out into a run, keeping up with Lance as much as he could. Another roar caused Lance to look back, dreading what he was going to see. The huge ape half ran, half beat his huge bald chest whilst heading in their direction. Lance knew that one way to deal with a gorilla's aggression is to make yourself small and not make eye contact, which was far too late now. Another method was to put distance between yourself and the ape, which they were trying to do right now.

The older man was running beside Lance but they were making slow progress as the ground was so uneven and they kept stumbling. The pursuing gorilla was clearly used to running on such terrain so was catching them up fast. He knew a gorilla could run up to twenty-five miles per hour and humans could run faster. But Quent and himself, running through roots, plants and rocks had no chance of outrunning the ape. He only hoped he would chase them until he was sure they were away from his territory and family.

A quick look back and the great primate was only twenty feet behind and gaining rapidly, angry grunts and snarls added to the feeling that this was an angry and hostile animal, which made it extremely dangerous. Lance thought quickly. *How do we get out of this situation?* Quent was crying out in pure panic now. 'It's coming! It's coming!' he blurted out between gasps.

Fifteen feet and Lance knew outrunning the animal was not an option, though neither was trying to stand up to him. *Think, Lance*, he thought with increasing desperation. The snarls became louder. He glanced at the LANSPEAK. Twelve percent. He had nothing to lose. He stopped running and turned to face the charging ape. His sheer size close up was frightening. He must have weighed over two hundred kilograms and looked simply unstoppable. Quent kept running, not looking back. The gorilla looked angrily at him but slowed his pace significantly when he saw Lance facing up to him. Fiddling with the LANSPEAK, he quickly found the sound effect he was searching for. The device roared loudly, bellowing out the sound of a large jungle cat, one of the few animals that were known to hunt gorillas.

The huge animal stopped as suddenly as Lance had and quickly looked around. He had momentarily lost his angry look and was searching the trees with curiosity but not fear, he thought. It took the ape mere seconds to try and find the source of the roar then looked back at Lance, appearing unconvinced. The aggressive face returned, clearly not fooled by this tactic.

Clearly, an intelligent animal, he thought briefly, just before the colossal creature strode forward with its arms raised. Lance just had time to turn and try and duck when a most powerful arm struck the side of his chest, knocking the wind out of him and sending the man tumbling down a sloping area of land, rocks and sharp roots crashing into him, as he rolled though the vegetation.

Though dazed and sore, he was not knocked out or seriously injured. Sitting up, he gasped for breath, taking in short gasps. The GoPro was still attached and looked, thankfully, undamaged. Lance then saw the gigantic gorilla roar and head towards Quent, who was now stood, transfixed, unable to move with pure terror. The younger man got up and raced towards them both, ignoring his aching body and holding his breath as another idea flashed through his mind. The animal was about to swipe at Quent's head, which could easily be a killing blow.

The LANSPEAK made another sound. This time, an unnatural high-pitched wail, the volume turned up high. The piercing screech cut through the forest, causing birds to fly out of their trees. The gorilla suddenly stopped and crouched low, looking around with a look of confused anger on his face. The consistent sound was hurting his own ears now though Quent merely looked bewildered.

Wasting no time and letting the LANSPEAK continue to scream its polluting noise, Lance ran up to the older man and grabbed his arm, urging him to run. They set off once more, Lance unable to run at his usual speed due to him being winded. Each breath hurt when he took one and every muscle ached with each stride. The gorilla had brutally reminded him that he was still recovering from his fall from the drone.

Glancing back, the ape was still crouched, but staring at them as they put distance between them.

As they entered the tree line, they allowed themselves a brief pause to catch their breath. The huge animal was no longer in sight and Lance hoped that he had given the animal second thoughts, satisfied that they were out of his territory. Without warning, the LANSPEAK became suddenly silent. The power was nine percent, not enough to continue making a high-volume sound. The sounds of the forest were alive once more. The birds and other small animals, clearly disturbed by the sound, were filling the trees with a thousand different calls.

Then they heard it. The roar. Louder, closer and angrier. The gorilla was still in pursuit. Quent looked like he was ready to give up as they heard the snarls getting closer. Despite feeling like they were in a hopeless situation, they began to run through the thick trees, knowing that if the gigantic ape caught up with them, not even the LANSPEAK could protect them.

Tropical Rainforest,
The Democratic Republic of the Congo,
July 21,
5:01pm (Congolese and UK time)

Lance hoped that the thick plants could help slow the pursuing animal, enough to give them the advantage. That thought stayed with him, as he guided Quent and himself through the smallest gaps between trees and bushes, knowing the huge ape would struggle to follow them directly.

They could hear the gorilla, his snarls reverberating through the forest, though they could not see him. It appeared to be working as when Lance finally glanced back, he saw the animal trying to get to them, but hindered by thick vegetation and letting out a frustrated roar as the men gradually put a larger distance between them and the ape.

They continued a steady run, though both exhausted, Lance concerned at times for Quent, but the older man was probably running on pure adrenaline now, though he hoped that the gorilla would be far enough away when the man finally crashed.

They had been running and jogging for over twenty minutes, though the protective animal was still doggedly following, not giving up the chase so easily. Lance wondered where they would end up, as it would be dark soon, he thought worriedly. Thoughts of Rufus and Duncan came to mind. Was this what had happened back in May? An aggressive alpha male gorilla putting a sudden stop to their expedition? It seemed unlikely somehow as both men were trained to know how to behave in such situations. After all, this was what they were looking for.

His train of thought was suddenly broken by a roar from behind. The ape had made up ground between them. He was gaining rapidly, despite the two men giving him the hardest path to follow. But this was *his* territory clearly knowing how to transverse it as efficiently as the men ever could.

Up ahead, the tree line thinned out revealing the last ray of sun for the day. And giving them less cover, Lance thought grimly. They pushed on desperately until they burst out of the forest onto the edge of a deep rocky gorge. Lance recognised it from the simple map. They had reached the end of the first land island, the edge of the sacred forest. Quent stopped at the top of the deep crevice, looking ready to collapse.

On the other side was an almost identical thick tree line to the one they had emerged from. Then he saw it, twenty feet to their left. A simple ancient looking rope bridge spanning the length of the gorge.

Quent wasted no time in running towards it, spurred on by another roar from very close by. Lance followed, realising they had very little choice of where to go now. They reached the bridge and he could see how deep the rocky gap was. Thirty feet approximately, mainly rock but with huge chunks of vegetation sparsely growing randomly throughout it. It reminded Lance of a dried up river.

From the forest behind them, the huge ape burst forth but suddenly stopped, a look of caution in his eyes, though he continued to snarl. This was all Quent needed to make his mind up, as he sprinted across the rickety bridge. The gorilla's behaviour had changed suddenly. He was acting defensive but still aggressive. But there was something else. Lance realised what it was. This gigantic animal was afraid. He bared his teeth and looked over at the opposite tree line, waving those huge powerful arms wildly, seemingly to have forgotten about the man stood only ten feet away. Lance cautiously glanced at the other side, seeing nothing but Quent trotting over the dry wooden bridge. When he looked back, the gorilla was gone, having disappeared back into the forest. This bizarre behaviour felt almost as worrying as being chased by the animal.

This huge powerful beast had literally run away in what appeared to be fear. But fear of what? Quent was on the other side now, waving at Lance to join him. It was then he noticed the sign. A small wooden sign, no more than a wooden board nailed and tied to the post holding the rope of the bridge. It was weathered but the writing was still legible. The words in French were carved into the wood, faded black paint just visible in the indentations. His heart raced as he read it.

SI VOUS PASSEZ ASSEZ
DE TEMPS EN ENFER,
MÊME LE DIABLE
VOUS CRAINDRA

(IF YOU SPEND LONG
ENOUGH IN HELL,
EVEN THE DEVIL
WILL FEAR YOU)

What was going on? Was he about to enter the warlord's territory? This felt very wrong as an uneasy feeling crept through him. This could potentially be a dangerous place. He was reluctant to cross the bridge. He needed time to think and assess the situation. As he looked up, he could see Quent entering the jungle opposite. He waved at him to come back. He had no idea what lay beyond here but he noticed at the bottom of the sign, something he thought was a paint blob. It was actually a crude drawing, similar the ones dotted around this area of the map. It was an image of a spider.

Tropical Rainforest,
The Democratic Republic of the Congo,
July 21,
5:05pm (Congolese and UK time)

Lance had no idea what to think. Was this sign just more superstition or a genuine warning? Before his mind began processing numerous possibilities, his gaze fell upon the forest on the other side of the bridge. Equally as dense as the one they had trekked through, though this place felt somehow infinitely more dangerous, though he had no idea why.

Quent was nowhere to be seen. The man clearly eager to put as much space between himself and the gorilla, though probably unaware that the pursuing animal appeared to have given up the chase, at least for now. With one last glance back to where they had come from, Lance followed Quent's route across the bridge.

The structure, roughly twenty-feet in length, felt ancient and unsafe. It swung erratically with each step and each step was slippery with moist green moss. Quent had clearly been in a panicked state, judging by the speed he traversed the bridge. Risking an unsafe bridge was obviously more preferable to facing a rampaging gorilla. He quickened his pace and was soon stepping off the shaking wooden structure and followed the route Quent had taken into the tree line.

The other man was slumped against a tree, a rapid gasping wheeze bursting from his gaping mouth. Lance approached and the older man glanced up suddenly, a look of vacant fear on his red sweating face. On seeing the younger man, he slid further down the tree and began half coughing, half laughing. Though the laughs were short and humourless, almost delirious.

'Ah, mate, I wasn't expecting that! Running into King Kong and his family!' he said between dry gasps. 'Man, I had no idea we'd find them angry beasts.' He glanced up at Lance, some focus now in his eyes. 'Did you?' he asked suspiciously. Lance was not making eye contact, but simply shrugged. Quent looked intently at him for a few seconds more, clearly guessing the younger man knew more than he had previously revealed.

Of course, Lance *did* know more. He was actually hoping to find these apes in the exact area Fim had believed them to be. What Lance had not counted on was being accompanied by a man who really had no business being in such a place. A rare, delicate environment did not need Quent trampling through it like a loud clumsy tourist who obviously had no respect for a potentially fragile ecosystem.

Then he immediately felt the familiar guilt regarding the older man. Quent had been in many ways, encouraged to come here, completely unprepared by a number of utterly ruthless people. But Lance felt right now that he was holding onto a powerful weapon against such people. CES, Stanmer and their ilk would now be facing international opposition to their monstrous plans to destroy this area with a mining operation.

That was, of course, if Lance could return to forward this evidence of some of the rarest gorillas on the planet living close to the area CES were planning to destroy.

The proof he had recorded was priceless, but he knew he still had to find out what had happened to Rufus and Duncan. Which unfortunately meant heading further into this foreboding forest. Quent was clearly keen to continue their journey, as he was now standing, awaiting Lance to join him. 'What'll we find *now,* mate?' he asked like an excited child. It was hard to believe that this man could still believe they were going to find some mythical giant spiders, which a learned expert had clearly stated could not and would not ever have existed. Lance felt more pity for this deluded man. Though as they entered this next stage of the journey, he was extremely apprehensive about what they could be heading into.

The map, which he had been his only reference of local knowledge, was old and outdated. The areas controlled by the warlord could have grown. It was more than likely that this land island was under his brutal control. Lance increasingly believed that they were heading into his hostile territory. On the plus side, he was not going to meet his army at gunpoint, half drowned and battered from falling out of an aeroplane. On the negative side, he had Quent with him. And he knew that Quent would be harder to look after than the children who had been with him the last time he had faced the warlord's men.

Tropical Rainforest,
The Democratic Republic of the Congo,
July 21,
5:45pm (Congolese and UK time)

Despite their exhaustion, both men kept a brisk pace through the dense jungle, Quent spurred on by the thought of discovering his outlandish spiders. Lance himself was encouraged by seeing plants that had clearly been cut and chopped quite recently. They must still be following Rufus and Duncan's route, he thought optimistically. Having survived the gorillas' domain, the previous two men had obviously crossed the bridge to seek out perhaps more rare apes and possibly other animals.

The older man was now racing ahead, clearly in no doubt that the gigantic spiders he believed in were close by. Lance was trying to charge the LANSPEAK at every opportunity, though it was painfully slow at recharging, as it was only at ten percent.

An uncomfortable thought had continued to nag at his head since they had crossed the bridge. The thought that they should turn around and head straight back. It was a confusing feeling. From the day he first heard Rufus and Duncan had run into trouble, Lance had doggedly pursued the truth of what had happened. And he guessed he was close to discovering what had happened to the two men here in May.

And although he was still determined to know what had gone on here, Lance could not control a dreadful feeling that Quent and himself were walking into mortal danger. His intuition told him that this place was somewhere people rarely returned from. Lance could not pinpoint in his mind exactly why it was such a hostile area. But deep down, he felt he knew the grim truth. That the warlord had taken over this particular part of the forest. And he did not want to admit to himself that he guessed that the two men had confronted J'ba Fofi and his men. And worse, what they had done to them to drive Rufus out of his mind.

Lance swallowed hard and slowed his pace. He knew it would be dark soon. Quent was still striding ahead into the darkening trees but paused when he looked back and saw the younger man now stop and shake his head. Breathless and sweating profusely, the older man trudged back to him.

'Why have you stopped? It'll be dark soon; we need to make up more ground.' His voice was more determined than Lance had ever heard it. He shook his head and wrote quickly on the paper pad he had with him.

'We need to go back. I'm sure the warlord controls this part of the forest. And he's evil. I think we are walking into danger.'

Quent's face distorted to one of confusion mixed with disgust.

'Are you serious? You're actually afraid? You? The guy that survived falling out of a plane *and* squared up to a mountain gorilla, all in the same week? This is a joke, right?' His voice was rising with anger. Lance shook his head firmly. Quent let out a large snort and laughed coldly.

'You know, I don't pretend that I've ever been able to work you out, but one thing's for sure, I never figured you for a coward!' The last word was spat with pure loathing. Lance was not surprised to hear the other man speak in such a way. In Quent's mind, he was about to complete his life's work.

'Well, you can stay here or crawl back with your tail between your legs like a loser but I'm carrying on.' With that, he headed back the way he had previously been walking.

Lance was afraid of this. Quent was the main reason why he wanted to turn around. The older man was in so fit shape to outrun the warlord's desperate men. In fact, Quent heading off alone would probably be then end of him even if he did not meet any of J'ba Fofi's soldiers.

As he watched him stubbornly head towards the ominous trees with no compass, map or any other form of navigation, Lance realised that this man was now obsessed with finding his fantasy goal. Thoughts of how to persuade him to abandon his insane quest were quickly pushed aside. Quent would clearly not listen to reason now. The man had physically and mentally given everything he had to get to this point.

Thoughts of how to physically stop Quent now overtook his mind. Lance was an expert in many forms of martial arts, so he knew he could restrain him. Bringing him back could be more of a problem, as he was heavier than himself. As he pondered numerous scenarios of getting Quent to give up and return with him, he noticed that he was no longer in sight.

Lance trotted towards the shadowed trees and entered the gloom of the heavy plants. Quent had stopped and was stood transfixed in front of a huge tree. He was staring at the thick overgrown trunk and did not seem to notice when Lance joined him at his side. A look of wonder was etched across the man's face, staring at one particular area. Lance followed his gaze, not seeing what the other man was until movement on the gnarled vegetation made him gasp inwardly.

The poor light and darkness of the bark was the perfect camouflage for the animal clinging to the side of the tree about ten feet from the forest floor. He continued to stare in bewilderment at the largest spider he had ever seen in his life.

Tropical Rainforest,
The Democratic Republic of the Congo,
July 21,
5:48pm (Congolese and UK time)

He could not take his eyes of the huge arachnid. The massive spider had a leg span of at least ten inches and was covered in thick brown hair, which was yellowish in places. The abdomen was darker but solid looking. It was facing upwards and now unmoving, as it had probably sensed their presence Lance thought.

Quent sheathed his machete and shone his torch on the animal, which moved slightly in the glare. The light revealed its sheer size. It had to be as big as the goliath bird-eating spider Lance guessed in fascination. The hair looked brighter now it was illuminated and the plump abdomen looked almost purple in colour. It was an impressive but intimidating animal and one he did not want to get too close to.

Quent though had no such misgivings and noisily marched towards the tree, the torchlight shaking with each step. As the man got nearer, the gigantic arachnid quickly scuttled into the vegetation behind the trunk and out of sight. Quent approached and attempted to locate the creature by walking around the entire circumference of the tree, though it was nowhere to be seen.

The older man glanced back, a look of manic excitement on his face. 'Did you see the size of that thing? I've never seen anything like it!' His voice almost cracking with emotion. Lance merely shrugged. The spider was very big but no larger than other similar species already known. If Quent thought that what they had just seen was some sort of proof of the mythical J'ba Fofi, he was fooling himself.

With even more renewed energy, Quent set of at a jog towards the denser plants. Right now, all Lance could do was follow reluctantly. Though as he caught up with the exhilarated man, an ominous feeling came over him. Two thoughts suddenly struck him at the same time. The first was about the sounds of the forest. Or lack of them, he thought. Since they had crossed the bridge, he had been distracted by different concerns.

His thoughts now were acutely focused on the eerily quiet forest. Since they had entered this wilderness, it had been alive with infinite sounds. Insects, birds, small and large animals moving noisily through their habitat. These were now almost completely absent. All he could hear were their own movements through the plants and the light warm wind flowing through the leaves. It was altogether unnerving this loud silence.

The second thought was what he remembered when researching the J'ba Fofi spiders online prior to this trip. Everything he had read was only theory, second or third hand accounts of sightings or simply, elaborate stories. Though one bit of information kept nagging at him. It described in detail the spider they had just seen, with pale, yellowish hair in places and a purple body. Though in the text, this description was referring to a juvenile J'ba Fofi.

Lance swallowed and tried to focus rationally, feeling like he was being caught up in Quent's fantasy. The other man was again nowhere to be seen, having pushed through some thick bushes next to the tree line. He was about to follow when he heard the older man cry out.

Tropical Rainforest,
The Democratic Republic of the Congo,
July 21,
5:50pm (Congolese and UK time)

Lance raced towards the sound, unsure if the cry was in fear or excitement. Quent was standing staring up at another enormous tree. He followed his gaze to an astonishing sight. The high canopy of trees were covered with what could only be described as a mass of spider webs. The pale silky strands filled vast spaces above them, so thick in places that they obscured some of the light.

Quent gasped. 'We've found it, mate! We've made it! Check out the size of those webs. Only giant spiders could make something like that!' he proclaimed confidently. Lance studied the vast structure. It certainly did look like web. It was heavy with forest detritus, countless insects and some larger shapes, which could be small animals or birds.

The older man began taking photographs, clearly thinking that this was conclusive proof of the J'ba Fofi. Though Lance knew that spiders much smaller than the one they had just seen could, over time, construct such vast webs. And, he reasoned, if the J'ba Fofi resembled gigantic tarantulas, it would be very unlikely that they would produce such vast webs, as they would more likely to be hunting spiders.

He pushed such outlandish thoughts to the back of his head. Quent, like an excited child, waded on through more trees, though constantly looking up at the colossal web which continued on up ahead. Lance was close behind as both men entered a clearing. It was small, bordered by more large trees. A thick tree stump protruded up from the bushy floor, the rest of the fallen tree lay rotting in the moist ground.

Quent was standing underneath the imposing forest, still fascinated by the vast web above them. Lance now felt even more uneasy. The silence of the place continued to disturb him but now it was accompanied by something else. A sickly smell of something dead. The other man seemed not to notice, but his nostrils were now filled with a nauseating stench, which seemed to be getting stronger the more he thought about it. *This was not good at all*, he thought quickly.

Lance looked over at Quent, who was engrossed in taking photographs in the fading light. The older man was delirious with excitement, as if he had discovered an ancient secret. The thought of turning around and getting out of there was stronger than ever now. He secretly hoped that seeing that spider and these gigantic webs was enough to convince Quent that he had found his J'ba Fofi and would happily head back with his "evidence". Though at the moment, the man was acting like a young child who had just walked into a funfair.

To try and capture the sheer scale of the webs on his camera, Quent edged backwards, clumsily knocking into a thin, gnarled tree causing it to shake. As Lance continued to survey the small clearing, he saw a large shape fall from the branches above Quent. He let out a horrified gasp, as he recognised what it was. The sound of the falling object caused the other man to glance up. And his terrified scream pierced the deathly silent forest.

Tropical Rainforest,
The Democratic Republic of the Congo,
July 21,
5:52pm (Congolese and UK time)

It was Duncan. Or what was left of him, Lance realised in horror. The remains of Rufus's companion fell to the forest floor with a sickening thud. Quent continued to gasp and groaned, as the body came to a stop near his feet.

The older man put a hand to his mouth and turned away making a choking sound. Lance could understand. It was one of the most horrific sights he had ever seen.

Duncan looked as if he had been partially mummified. He was almost a skeleton, his skin a mottled brownish yellow colour, which was tight and shrivelled like thin leather stretched over bone. The poor man's eyes were gone, leaving only deep haunted sockets. It was dreadful to look at. But the most disturbing thing of all was the fact that his body had been wrapped in more of the silky web, which surrounded this whole place.

The pale substance covered his entire body, in fact Lance could only recognise that it was Duncan due to his clothing. He had seen the same clothes on a picture Rufus had sent him at the start of their ill-fated trip. The whole body was secured with this strong looking web, almost resembling a cocoon.

Quent was now throwing up a few feet away and muttering between sobs. Lance had no time to feel any sadness or pity for the man who had only come here to do good and important work. He only felt a rising fear. An uncontrollable feeling that overtook him in a wave of confusion that could lead to an irrational feeling of panic. Duncan had been killed in an unimaginably horrible way by the look of things. But exactly *what* had killed him?

He scanned keenly the small clearing surrounding them. It remained deadly silent apart from Quent retching, which had now lessened. His gaze fell back onto the tragic sight of Duncan. He pushed the overwhelming fear to one side as best he could. He tried to focus. He still knew that the mythical J'ba Fofi could not exist, but perhaps something else had killed him and the local spiders had merely fed on what they had found, which was a grim enough thought.

He found himself imagining large jungle cats, poisonous animals or even still, the warlord's men. Finding Duncan dead was, sadly what he had expected, though as he studied the grisly remains, he saw something protruding through the thick silky strands. A camera, attached to the man's stick-like wrist by a small cord. A nauseating thought came to him. That camera could hold vital evidence of what had occurred here back in May. But he needed to take it from Duncan's shrunken body.

The smell of decay was stronger, as he approached the ghastly sight. Seeing Duncan like this now filled him with pity and sadness. Duncan was here doing good and worthwhile work. He had been a decent and honest man and to end up like this was truly tragic. Quent looked up, his face ashen and was trembling as Lance approached the ravaged body. 'What are you doing?' he asked loudly, sounding terrified. Lance ignored the question and tried to ignore the stench, which he knew was coming from the body. He focused, fighting his feelings of revulsion at the appalling scene, which grew closer with each step. 'Lance, we need to get out of this place! Do you understand? We need to go now!' Quent's voice, filled with desperation, echoed through the place as he backed away towards the area they had entered from. He had no idea how the younger man was even able to get close to such a disturbing find.

Lance sheathed his machete and was now holding his breath as he stood over the emaciated body and without too much thought, grabbed the camera that was still clutched in the man's dead, brittle fingers. With stomach churning snapping sound, he pulled the camera from Duncan's death grip, but the sticky bonds would not let it free so easily. It was stuck to the fine threads and as he tugged harder, to his horror, the skeletal arm lurched forward, as if reluctant to let go of the precious item.

Quent screamed from behind and Lance turned to see him standing there, terror and disgust etched across his pale face. With one final pull, the camera came away, though it was coated in the tacky glue-like substance, which was holding Duncan so firmly in his final state.

He turned and headed towards where Quent was standing, whilst securing the camera in his backpack. The older man looked almost green, as he stood there panting and shaking. As Lance approached him, something caught his eye about forty feet behind the man, which made him stop. It was movement in the thick bushes just past the tree line. He tried to focus his vision in the poor light. Something quite large was steadily making its way through the dense bushes heading directly for Quent. It had to be some sort of animal, he thought. The stealth of its approach made its movements appear threatening. It was now thirty feet behind Quent who was oblivious to what was behind him, even though it was making some subtle noise now.

Lance was about to wave and warn Quent when it suddenly emerged from the bush. His mind went into overdrive due to what he saw, though not able to mentally process it. Lance felt lightheaded and almost faint at what he was seeing. His heart pounded so fast it felt like one continuous beat with small flutters. As his legs began to give way with shock, he managed to remain upright somehow. Quent was now staring at him, confused at this new look of disbelief mixed with pure terror, which was the first time he had seen such a look on Lance's face.

The older man turned gradually around, dreading what he would see. And then, he too saw it. Steadily walking towards him was a spider, but one of impossible size. It had a body the size of a large dog and eight brown hairy legs, which spread out would reach five or six feet at least in diameter. Numerous eyes stared ahead from on top of a hairy dome shaped head. Further down the head were two black fangs, at least six inches long, solid and razor sharp looking.

Neither man could comprehend what they were seeing. The J'ba Fofi, the mythical Congolese giant spider was unbelievably, terrifyingly real. And right now, one of these nightmarish creatures was coming straight towards them.

Tropical Rainforest,
The Democratic Republic of the Congo,
July 21,
5:55pm (Congolese and UK time)

The next few seconds seemed to last for hours. Time had suddenly slowed down. As if in slow motion, the spider, which actually resembled a tarantula, but gigantic in size was crawling steadily towards Quent, who was now facing the colossal creature, though his body visibly sagging.

Lance was transfixed in a dream like state, feeling like he was floating. The brown hairy legs of the enormous arachnid were now raised in a threatening manner, as it continued charging towards Quent who was rooted to the spot in pure terror.

Blinking rapidly then rubbing his eyes to make sure this was not simply a hallucination caused by the heat and stress, Lance was still shocked to see this animal remained real and less than twenty feet away from Quent. Focus rapidly found his senses. Practical thoughts suddenly overtook disbelief and shock. They had to get away from here or else they would be dead in seconds.

Quent remained still with fear, his camera falling limply out of his hands. Lance picked up a number of small rocks and thick branches from the ground and began throwing them towards the charging spider. He knew they would not hit it, but disturb the ground in front of it. The mud, leaves and low bushes shook with the force of the hits and it caused the giant arachnid to slow and raise its thick legs higher and more aggressively.

He heard a whimper from Quent who remained motionless. Lance checked the LANSPEAK. Eleven percent. It could work briefly. As he thought about how the device could help them, more movement in the clearing distracted him. More shapes were moving through the low bushes towards himself and Quent.

One. Two. Moving slower than the first spider but gaining ground steadily. Three. Four. He swallowed hard and looked at the area they had entered from, which was now blocked by the first spider. Five then six, the brown hairy creatures visible through the plants at some points. This was clearly their territory and they seemed to have little fear, though why would they, Lance thought wearily.

Seven. Eight. Nine. They were being surrounded he now knew, pushing sheer panic to the back of his head. If he lost control now, they were dead. Ten, eleven. They were now almost completely circled by twelve enormous carnivorous spiders, in their own forest and it was about to get dark. Lance's dread feeling of panic suddenly returned.

Tropical Rainforest,
The Democratic Republic of the Congo,
July 21,
5:56pm (Congolese and UK time)

Focus. Focus. They are animals, looking for food and protecting themselves. Rationalising them as just another animal helped his mind to clear and control the panic. He looked at the LANSPEK. Unsure if a high-pitched sound would affect them, though glancing up, Lance saw the first spider continue its approach to Quent, now only ten feet from the unmoving man.

The others had picked up speed, causing the bushes to rustle with an ominous sound. One thought flashed though him. The gorillas. There was no sign of the J'ba Fofi spiders on the other side of the bridge, revealing that these massive creatures possibly never ventured into the ape's domain. Lance had no time to ponder this and pushed the LANSPEAK a couple of times.

A loud roar, sounding as similar to an angry gorilla as he hoped, bellowed from the device. All of the arachnids stopped immediately. Quent turned quickly, his face haunted, eyes glazed and staring. The spiders remained motionless, some still hidden in the thick plants.

The LANSPEAK screamed again. More of the spiders now raised their legs in a defensive posture. Seeing numerous brown hairy limbs reaching out like some terrifying spider salute, Lance realised they were afraid of the apes. Though they were making no efforts to retreat and the device was desperately low on power.

Without dwelling on further depressing thoughts, he threw a branch at Quent, which struck him on the arm, momentarily distracting him from his mortal terror. Lance knew the only way out was further into the forest, away from the bridge. He thumbed a direction to the older man, who just stared bewildered. To his horror, this was the similar vacant fear on Quent's face that Rufus had back in London. There was no time to argue, Lance tapped the device and the voice '*Run'* loudly echoed through the silent space.

Thankfully, he began to trudge towards Lance, though as Quent looked back, he saw the nightmarish spider begin to follow him, though much more cautiously. This was a trigger and the older man broke out into a sprint and joined Lance as they ran as fast as they were able to in such a wild environment, towards the edge of the clearing.

The trees looked darker than ever and he knew they could be heading into even greater danger which was yet unseen. Lance glanced back and his worst fears were confirmed. The giant spiders were in pursuit. In the darkening forest, the shapes of the massive arachnids were still clear, the creatures seeming to have lost their fear of the primate roar.

As the two men battled through the dense vegetation, tripping, getting scratched, not knowing their direction, the sound of the scuttling J'ba Fofi remained in their ears, despite the feeling they were making up a considerable distance. How large was their territory, Lance wondered, with a disturbing feeling that these spiders' hunting ground could stretch for many miles.

He glanced at the LANSPEAK. The power was too low to make further sounds. It needed sunlight to re charge. Which would be in about twelve hours. They had no choice but to run until they collapsed. If they stopped anytime soon, they would be literally eaten alive.

Tropical Rainforest,
The Democratic Republic of the Congo,
July 21,
6:01pm (Congolese and UK time)

It felt like his lungs were burning with each step he ran. He had no idea how Quent must be feeling, though he was keeping pace well, but running on pure adrenaline, Lance guessed. The enveloping vegetation was getting darker by the minute and they were running blindly into it. He had a vague idea in which direction they were heading, which was west, towards the edge of this land island.

Quent's gasps and intermittent frightened sobs, along with their feet cutting through the plants were the only sounds he could hear. No other animals, including birds and insects were making any noise. It really felt that this part of the forest was owned and controlled by the colossal spiders.

Glancing around briefly, Lance saw no sign of the giant arachnids. Though somehow, he knew they would be following. They would be virtually invisible in this poor light now, which was just one more terrifying thought. Every inch of his body now ached, which had not had time to recover from his fall from the aeroplane.

The other man's obvious lack of fitness and his own injured body made maintaining a fast pace harder and harder. Gradually slowing to a jog, Quent began to shine his torch around the darkening trees, the beam shaking eerily as they ran. Lance surveyed their surroundings; the shadows dancing with each step they took made the forest appear alive with movement, which made seeing any following spiders even harder to spot.

To hold the light steady would mean them stopping. At this moment, Lance thought that to stand still for more than a few seconds would seal their doom. He continued to search the animated light for any signs of the J'ba Fofi, though seeing none. The men continued their slow run through the darkening wilderness, the torch in Quent's grip wildly scanning every area surrounding them.

It was when Lance thought the other man should shine the light ahead of them that they both crashed into a fallen tree in front of them. It was the same height as their shins, so they both tripped and fell forward, the torch flying out of Quent's grasp, spinning its light around the forest like flashes of lightening.

The older man cried out in fear and pain, as they both tumbled to the bushy ground. The torch, still shining landed a few feet away. Fear and adrenaline made the men stand back up swiftly, any injuries ignored. Quent groaned briefly in pain and then walked towards the torch. As he knelt down and picked it up, the light suddenly shone upwards. What it illuminated made Lance scream silently. The cry caught in his throat and stayed there. The trees were filled with spiders of varying sizes, but all clearly J'ba Fofi. The arachnids blended into the plants seamlessly, though not moving.

Quent did not notice this nightmarish sight, though he did notice when a brown, hairy spider the size of a coffee table dropped from the trees onto his back.

Tropical Rainforest,
The Democratic Republic of the Congo,
July 21,
6:05pm (Congolese and UK time)

The piercing shriek that Quent made would stay with Lance for the rest of his life. It almost did not sound human. A high-pitched scream accompanied by the man leaping into the air, arms thrashing around violently. This action appeared to take the gigantic spider by surprise and it was knocked backwards, falling into a tangle of bushes on the forest floor, its eight thick hairy legs flailing wildly.

The torch fell at Lance's feet and he picked it up, the beam illuminating a petrified Quent running towards him, his screams intensifying. The clutter of huge spiders began to follow keeping a steady pace. The men wasted no time in breaking into a run, the older man making deep guttural groaning noises with each hurried step, overtaking Lance and charging through the forest blindly, the way ahead illuminated only slightly by the torch the younger man now held.

He consciously chose not to look behind now. The forest was getting darker and he knew seeing how many spiders were chasing them hungrily would only lead to him panicking and that would be only hinder their escape. He tried to focus and evaluate the situation, which he knew to be dire.

Time once again seemed to stand still. The forest enclosing around them it seemed as the light beam made the men feel like they were running through a narrow tunnel, surrounded by pure darkness. The torch shone ahead and Lance noticed a light area possibly forty feet ahead of them. Was this a way to more open ground? Possibly an environment, which would be safer for them from the J'ba Fofi.

As they sprinted closer, horror at what he now saw filled him. The light was not light at all but a white silky wall of web, stretching across their path, roughly about eight feet high. Quent continued to charge ahead, making no attempt to slow down, making Lance think the man was running with his eyes closed.

Lance tried to gain ground and grab his collar to stop him crashing into this sticky barrier. He managed to get right behind the man and grasp his shoulder just as Quent ploughed blindly into the dense web. More screams, as he tripped into the net-like substance, pulling Lance down with him.

The web was not as strong as it looked as it felt like they were colliding with thick hanging sheets which tore as they tumbled to the ground and rolled over together, wrapping themselves in the clingy web. It felt like they were rolling for a long time until it occurred to Lance that they were actually tumbling down a slope.

The two men rolled and slid down a leaf-strewn incline, coming to a stop about thirty feet down from the forest floor. Dazed and in pain, the men looked around. They were in a small crater-like area, muddy and filled with vegetation. And something else. The smell hit Lance's nostrils like a physical blow. The same foul stench that poor Duncan's body had given off. The rotten smell of death.

This time, Quent was aware and he began sobbing between gasps. The crater was in a clearing, larger than the one where they had encountered the spiders. The last light of the day revealed that the two men had landed in what could only be described as a bone yard. The entire pit was filled with rotting skeletons of every description. Mostly random bones, covered in slivers of decaying flesh and covered in the same silky web the men were.

Lance noticed small animal remains and numerous skulls, some which looked sadly like baby gorillas. It was like a huge burial pit. And then in the fading light, he noticed them. One or two unmistakably human skulls. He swallowed hard, his throat dry. What Dan had said was true. Other people had come across these massive spiders and not all had lived to tell the tale.

He also noticed, scattered throughout the pit, some dead J'ba Fofi, all of different sizes and at various stages of decomposition. Lance was unsure at what this meant, though right now he had to focus on getting out of there.

Quent continued to sob and breathe raspingly. Lance tried to stand and realised that he and the other man were stuck together tightly. The web had become tangled around them both when they had fallen. It felt like they were wrapped in twisted cling film. Their bonds could be cut, but their movements were very limited. Panic began to rise in his mind and he struggled to push it aside. His right hand was free, still clutching the torch. He put the light down and began pulling at the thick cocoon they were packed in.

Both men's machetes were sheathed, which had probably saved them from serious injury during the fall but now they could do with something sharp to cut these tight gluey restraints. As Lance desperately tried to break free from the silky bonds, he heard Quent go quiet. He glanced at the men whose face was white with shock and staring up at the top of the pit.

One entire edge of the crater was lined with the J'ba Fofi. The terrifying sight looked almost like an army poised for battle. The older man began to struggle violently to try and break free, his panicked movements actually pulling the knotted webs even tighter. Lance placed a hand on the other man's face to try and calm him, though it had little effect.

The line of spiders had still not moved, though that somehow made it feel more frightening, as if they knew their prey were trapped and they could take their time. Lance reached with his free hand onto the ground, searching for anything sharp he could use to cut them free. The torch next to him illuminated the grisly sight of the spider's previous meals. One thing caught his eye. Large fangs staring upwards attached to what appeared to be a spinal column.

Looking closer, Lance saw it was the remains of a huge snake. Whilst trying to get Quent to get stay still, he leaned forward and shuffled them towards the skeleton, which was about five feet away. Crawling over the gruesome remains felt vile, but he knew it had to be done. The older man began to assist with their movement and they quickly reached the serpent's skull, which crumbled like paper when Lance grabbed one of the fangs.

The thin tooth came away in his fingers, though it was thinner and more brittle than he had hoped. But with nothing to lose, he began desperately hacking at the tight web with the point of the fang.

'Lance!' The terrified shout from Quent led Lance to look up, only to see the vast army of arachnids begin their stealthy crawl down the slope towards the trapped men.

'No! No! No!' The other man was crying now, his body shaking with breathless sobs, though he could understand these tears. If they could not get free in the next few seconds, Quent and he would share the same horrific fate as Duncan.

Tropical Rainforest,
The Democratic Republic of the Congo,
July 21,
6:11pm (Congolese and UK time)

As the giant creatures crept closer, Quent's panic intensified and he began shaking the binding webs, pulling them taught. This now actually worked in Lance's favour. The twisted threads now became easier to slice through when they were stretched. The bond around his left arm began to give as the fang picked away at the tacky silk.

'Oh no!' Quent's desperate plea was due to the fact that some of the spiders had reached the foot of the basin and were now creeping over the many remains of their prey to reach them. The closeness of the danger was not lost on Lance as he hacked at the sticky bindings. He was two thirds of the way through the tight bond when, to his horror, the fang crumbled in his hand.

Without thinking, he used his right hand to pull at the webbing, the pain from his previously dislocated shoulder sent painful burning shockwaves through his whole right side. The adrenaline took over and allowed him to pull with all his strength until the sticky ropes snapped and he released his other arm.

It was now easy to pull the remains of the cocoon off them both, Quent frantically tearing off the thick silk and kicking it off him. At least five spiders were about ten feet away and gaining speed rapidly. As Lance looked behind them at a much flatter slope, which was their only way out of this nightmare. Quent had picked up the tattered web and threw it angrily at the closest creature, which scuttled sideways, narrowly avoiding contact.

It was as if a different form of madness had affected the man now. The fear appeared to have temporarily gone, replaced by pure aggression. He began to pick up anything he could find around him and began pelting the gigantic spiders whilst shouting angrily. Rocks, branches but mainly bones and rotting body parts were all being launched towards the attacking arachnids whilst Quent bellowed 'Get back! Get back! Get back, you monsters!' His face red with a look of raw rage etched across it.

This tactic was holding the massive spiders back to a point, though more were approaching from the edge and he knew it was time to retreat. Lance grabbed Quent's shoulder and motioned for him to head up the opposite slope. The man needed no further encouragement and raced up the side of the pit towards the tree line, Lance close behind and not looking back. He had picked up the torch and kept its beam ahead of them.

He could hear the spiders following, their countless legs making a sickening sound as they scuttled over the mass of rotting bones. The sound chilled him deeply. As they pushed through more dense trees and plants, Lance briefly glanced back. The crater was now a black hole in the approaching night. He could hear the countless J'ba Fofi crawling over the mass of carcasses, their black hairy bodies thankfully hiding such a ghastly sight.

As they both desperately tried to put as much distance between themselves and the spiders, Lance began to think about what was written on the sign, which was just before the bridge they crossed. "*If you spend long enough in Hell, even the devil will fear you.'* Lance knew this was to try and warn religious or superstitious people away from the area. He also knew that, everything he had seen in this forest, though horrific, was no more than nature. The J'ba Fofi are merely animals, doing exactly what all animals do. Eat, protect their home and just try to survive. Though as they got further away from the crater, Lance could not shake the feeling that Quent and himself had just narrowly escaped the very pit of Hell.

Tropical Rainforest,
The Democratic Republic of the Congo,
July 21,
6:16pm (Congolese and UK time)

The darkening forest only added to the feeling of impending doom. They had escaped the pit, but had no idea where else these spiders were. If there were any ahead of them, they would have no hope. The silence of the trees made their quick breaths seem much louder. Lance felt like he could hear his actual rapid heartbeat echoing through the area.

Though both men were running on adrenaline, sheer exhaustion would overcome them very soon, Lance knew. And how Quent had not collapsed by now was nothing short of miraculous, he thought. The older man was nowhere as near as fit as Lance, so it was only a matter of time when his body would force itself to shut down and be unable to continue at such a pace, or even continue at all.

He pushed those scenarios to the back of his mind and focused on their current situation. They were both running at a steady speed and Lance wondered how fast the quickest spiders could run and for how long. He almost did not want to find out.

The surroundings continued to dim, the last evidence of a clear day rapidly dwindling, the torch now being the only source of decent light. Their bodies cried out for rest yet the men doggedly continued running, though they had slowed to a jog now. As long as they kept moving, they had a better chance of surviving, he continually reminded himself.

The silence seemed to grow as the forest embraced the night and it was as if the lack of light intensified his other sensory sensations Lance felt. The penetrating silence enabled him to possibly hear for the sounds of the following arachnids, though he was not prepared to stop and listen anytime soon if he could help it.

The sounds of their feet cutting through the thick undergrowth of the forest floor was all he could hear, apart from their loud rapid breathing. They continued to head where they thought was west, though now the sun had disappeared, it was harder to orientate their direction, Lance thought. Heading in the same direction was all that mattered right now. Though a horrible thought came to him. If they became completely disorientated in the darkness with no recognisable landmarks as a guide, they could easily run in a circle and head back directly into the path of the chasing spiders. That thought was too horrible to comprehend, as he led the way in the direction he guessed was west.

The forest became darker by the second, giving Lance the feeling that they were totally lost in an incredibly dangerous, unforgiving place. Such feelings could lead to despair and notions of simply giving up. *Focus. Focus,* he reminded himself. Panic would be the end of them both. And they had survived this far, which was miraculous when he considered it.

Then the torch suddenly flickered out, plunging the two men into a smothering darkness. Quent let out a sob but Lance grabbed his chest forcing them him listen. The forest was silent apart from the noise of their breathing. And the unmistakable sound of hundreds of unseen scuttling legs rapidly approaching them in the dark.

Tropical Rainforest,
The Democratic Republic of the Congo,
July 21,
6:29pm (Congolese and UK time)

'No! No!' Quent screamed, his cry shattering the stillness of the forest. The lack of torchlight made the sudden darkness impenetrable, though a few seconds of adjustment gave Lance some vision in the low light. The last hues of the pink sky were just visible through the trees ahead of them. They were heading in the right direction, he thought, as the sound of the marching arachnids intensified.

Quent was silhouetted in the low light and Lance wasted no time in grabbing his shoulder and pushing him towards the fading western sky. The older man was now making incomprehensible sounds, but complied and began running blindly forward. They stumbled over tree roots, were scratched constantly by branches and leaves but it did not matter. They were moving again.

Lance wondered how good the eyesight was of these determined arachnids, hoping it was no better than their own. Though guessing that these giant spiders were nocturnal and also each of them having eight eyes, the odds were not in their favour, he thought heavily.

The last light of the day was almost gone but both men headed towards it, sensing the presence of the approaching spiders. Lance wondered how much more Quent could take, mentally and physically, as he himself was feeling drained in every sense. His thoughts briefly focused on Rufus. He finally understood how a trip to this place could literally shatter someone's mind. Lance hoped that the other man could keep hold of his sanity for a while longer. Though knowing the near hopeless situation they were in, it was looking increasingly less likely.

The sounds of their own frantic steps through the undergrowth thankfully drowned out the sound of the pursuing J'ba Fofi, though there was no doubt that they were following. It was difficult to tell how fast they were running in the poor light, though it would never feel quick enough. This was the spider's territory and they were at the mercy of these creatures.

Once again, time seemed to slow down. The surreal feeling of running blindly through the unknown, being chased by mythical animals, which should not technically exist felt dream like to Lance. It was if reality had temporarily been put on hold. It was at that point he realised this was how a person could lose their mind. Being in a seemingly impossible but nightmarishly real situation could easily destroy rational thought, leaving only a dark, disturbed mental state.

This was exactly what had happened to poor Rufus. His balanced mind had been shattered. And Lance knew that if they stayed in this place much longer, Quent could suffer the same fate. His own mentality had some level of protection he briefly mused. Lance's mind worked differently to a majority of people. It was closed off in many ways, being extremely selective to what it allowed in, simply to protect itself. Over the years, this had been seen as a weakness or even a disability.

But right now, his mind's self-preserving filter was working in Lance's favour. Only allowing practical, rational and relevant thoughts in was his biggest weapon against the rapid consuming madness which could affect many people who were unfortunate to find themselves in such a place.

Tropical Rainforest,
The Democratic Republic of the Congo,
July 21,
6:40pm (Congolese and UK time)

The light had almost gone but they continued to push through the vast void of the darkened forest. Lance in the lead, Quent's hand on his small backpack. It felt like he was leading a blind man, but in truth his vision was no better than the older man's. It was literally the blind leading the blind now.

It was then he remembered the night vision goggles, which were still in his pack. He cursed himself for not considering them sooner when they still had light. Though since they had crossed the bridge, it had been difficult to think of anything except the dire situation they were constantly in.

Knowing they could not stop, Lance slipped the pack from his back mid run, Quent's hand moving to his arm, his panicked grip firm. It did not take long to locate the goggles and he wasted no time in placing them over his head. He put the torch in the bag, knowing it could still be useful. The forest was then suddenly illuminated in an unnatural green glow. Relief flushed through him. Their route ahead was no longer guesswork now.

As he slung the pack back over his shoulders, Lance dared to stop and glance behind them, much to the sobbing gasps from Quent. His keen new vision scanned the thick forest and at first could see no movement. Before he could feel any form of relief, he spotted them. Stealthily creeping through the trees, though some scuttling along the forest floor.

The sight of these gigantic spiders heading towards them in the artificial green glare looked almost otherworldly. Feelings of being detached from reality would be easy to accept right now. But he focused. Be rational, he told himself. The colossal arachnids were taking their time but making steady progress to where both men were standing, gasping with exhaustion.

It was obvious they were nocturnal and this was their domain. So he was unsure about why they were acting so cautiously. They could either be tiring (which he doubted) or they were entering unfamiliar territory (which he hoped). Standing transfixed, seeing these terrifying but in many ways magnificent creatures slowly stalk them in this almost ethereally lit scene was disturbingly hypnotic.

His semi trance was broken by Quent suddenly gripping his arm. 'We need to keep moving!' he cried despairingly. Lance realised that Quent could not see that the spiders were not right on top of them. He was standing in almost complete darkness and Lance had no way to communicate verbally with him.

Focusing on the way ahead, he led them through the least overgrown section of the plants, though these thinner areas were infrequent. Quent continued his firm grasp on the backpack. The renewed vision enabled the men to navigate through the rough terrain much more efficiently and so moving quicker, much to their relief.

Lance kept the pace at a jog, hoping that the tenacious spiders had not drastically increased their speed. The forest was endless, an eternity of trees spreading out in every direction, looking unnatural through the goggles. His thoughts began to race. What else could he do to help their situation? Nothing immediately came to mind. They were still at a huge disadvantage, their chances of survival still poor. Focus. Stay in control. Panic would finish them. Their pace quickened as a flat area of forest led to a rocky plateau. Trees hugged the edge of what appeared to be a small clearing. They broke into a run but something made them both stop suddenly. It was something that filled Lance with concern but also, strangely, with a surge of hope. It was something they had not encountered since they had crossed the bridge. For the first time in over an hour and a half in this part of the forest, they heard the sound of another animal.

Tropical Rainforest,
The Democratic Republic of the Congo,
July 21,
6:52pm (Congolese and UK time)

It was a low guttural growl, like something a large cat would make. Lance scanned the tree line though could see nothing. He had no idea where the noise had come from, although it was definitely ahead of them. And it was not a sound the spiders had made so far. Looking back, there was no obvious sign of the J'ba Fofi, though he knew they were not far away.

Quent let out a laboured breath and collapsed onto his knees. Exhaustion had finally hit the man. His breathing was rapid and dry. Lance leant down and offered him some water, which he took with a grunt. The sound of him guzzling the water greedily was momentarily the only sound he could hear. Until a loud roar cut through the trees, causing Quent to choke on the last dregs of water as he spluttered and coughed.

Lance scanned the area the noise had come from, as it was much clearer where the sound had come from this time. He still saw nothing but did hear the leaves rustle straight ahead. He focused on the trees and suddenly noticed the branches begin to sway gently, though not caused by the wind. If he had not heard the roar, he would have feared there were more huge arachnids waiting for them in the dense plants.

Then he saw them. A pair of eyes, which seemed to glow in the green forest, neither moving nor blinking. Staring straight at him in the darkness. For what seemed like an eternity, these bright orbs remained still and silent. Quent's breathing was the only sound, except his own pounding heartbeat in his ears.

Then with a stealthy elegance, the eyes floated forward. And the large leopard, which they belonged to, slithered through the trees and out into the clearing. The bright eyes were locked on him, though he strangely felt little fear. The jungle cat stopped and crouched low, its gaze had a hypnotic feel in the unnatural green vision.

Lance was transfixed, temporarily forgetting the threat in the trees behind them. The animal looked huge and muscular, despite it laying low to the ground. Its behaviour seemed more curious than threatening to him, though he was under no illusion that they had wandered in to just another type of danger. The animal then began to growl, a long high-pitched growl, which was definitely threatening.

This noise caused Quent to stand up suddenly, his breathing becoming louder, mixed with groans. 'What is it now?' His voice cracking with fear.

The sudden movement and sound caused the leopard to stir and it leapt forward and began to trot aggressively towards the men. Its teeth were bared and the growling intensified. Before Lance had time to think what to do, the huge cat stopped a few feet in front of him and crouched again. It was no longer staring at him, but focusing on the trees behind him, the low growl intensifying.

Slowly and as quietly as possible, he turned to the trees behind them. It was clear what the leopard was staring it. The leaves and branches were alive with movement. The J'ba Fofi had caught them up.

Tropical Rainforest,
The Democratic Republic of the Congo,
July 21,
6:55pm (Congolese and UK time)

He could not see them, though it was obvious that a significant number of the huge spiders were crawling through the trees just behind them. The sound they made was frightening, though that was almost drowned out by the roar the huge cat made, causing Lance to jump. Right now, he was unsure which direction to go in was the least dangerous.

Then in an almost unnaturally quick motion, the leopard pounced forward and ran fluidly towards the trees, disappearing into them with a final roar. The sounds, which echoed through the trees, were some of the most terrifying he had ever heard in his life. The high-pitched shriek and roars from the cat were mingled with dreadful hissing sounds, presumably made by the threatened spiders. The entire section of forest was suddenly vibrating with movement and noises. It was horrendous to hear, almost like a savage battle between two bloodthirsty armies.

Quent began to groan loudly, this new development seemingly too much to take. He slumped down, cradling his head in his hands, his body trembling with emotion. Lance reassessed the situation practically. Behind them were some of the most dangerous animals on earth fighting to the death in a dark forest. Ahead of them was an equally dark forest, which could have anything hiding in it. It took no time to decide.

He grabbed the sobbing man and led him through the trees. Anything to be away from the brutal sounds pouring out of the forest behind them. They pushed through the trees, his night vision scanning for any movement. It seemed quiet once they were out of range of the disturbing sounds behind them.

Quent's pace was much slower and his grip on Lance's back felt much weaker. Exhaustion had now overwhelmed him. Despite his obvious terror and desperation to escape, his body was trying to force him to stop and rest. Knowing they were still in serious danger, Lance made the decision to stop running. The other man made no protest, as they slowed to an average walking speed. Quent's breathing coming in dry wheezing gasps.

As long as they kept moving, they would still make cover a good distance. As they trudged through the thick plants, a heavy feeling of guilt fell over him. Guilt for the leopard. The sounds coming from the forest earlier had truly been horrific. He knew that the large cat would be no match for the J'ba Fofi, their numbers were too great. It was clear that the animal had rushed boldly into the trees to protect its own territory. It was obvious now that they had reached the edge of the spider's domain, or at the very least the edge of the area where they felt safe.

The clearing felt like the border of their hunting ground. Lance felt that they had lured the spiders to the furthest reach of what would be their comfort zone. They probably would not ordinarily venture this far, but in their pursuit of Quent and himself, had travelled too far into another predator's area. And the resulting fight was inevitable he knew. The leopard should not have had to face such an overwhelming hoard unless it was necessary, he thought grimly.

It suddenly occurred to him that if the leopard had sacrificed itself to protect this place, what exactly was it fighting for? The thought of running into a leap of leopards right now was something he tried not to think about, but searched the green-lit vegetation ahead of them.

Despite the possible threat of a jungle cat family running up to meet them, this part of the forest felt safer somehow. Their pace was steady but not rushed. The new noises all around were reassuring. Often a bid or two could be heard flapping out of the undergrowth near them. A monkey call from a distance cut through the darkness more than once, making the men jump.

After another hour of walking, they decided to stop for five minutes. They drank and ate some rations. A feeling of calm overcame Lance. The forest felt like it had before they encountered the gorillas. It was a dangerous place for certain, but also an unspoiled natural world, containing more wonder than fear. Quent would obviously disagree, as the man was now very subdued. Since they had left the cat and spider fight behind them, he had not spoken one word.

Normally, Lance much preferred this in people. But a man who was normally extremely vocal, this silence was not good. His thoughts once again strayed to Rufus and his mental breakdown. If Quent sank into a similar catatonic state as his friend had… It did not bear thinking about, so he pushed such a dire scenario to the back of his mind. *Only deal with situations when you encounter them*, he told himself firmly.

They stood after an extremely long feeling five minutes. Lance's whole body ached with pain from his fall from the plane and new pains from the gorilla attack. Quent also groaned in pain, though he guessed it was because he was quite unfit and had probably not put his body through such physical strain in his entire adult life.

With a renewed sense of hope, they continued their endless walk. He had no idea where they were headed but if they could reach a place of genuine safety, they could re-evaluate their situation. Though a place of safety felt like a faraway place right now, he thought inwardly.

Tropical Rainforest,
The Democratic Republic of the Congo,
July 21,
10:05pm (Congolese and UK time)

They continued walking into the night, heading west or as west as the terrain would allow. Neither man spoke though Lance guessed Quent's silence could be down to exhaustion as much as anything else. The night vision was the most valued piece of equipment he had right now, he thought. It had most likely saved them numerous times up to this point. Though what lay ahead of them was still uncertain.

He knew it was just after ten pm. The hot sun would rise once more in roughly eight hours. Lance began to think that they should settle down somewhere until the morning. He was unsure how Quent would react to staying in one place for any longer than a few minutes. They desperately needed to rest properly. And the thought of walking until it was light was not an option in his opinion.

As if reading his thoughts, the older man stopped and sunk to his knees, his breathing laboured and rapid. 'I can't go on, man. My whole body's on fire. My legs are like jelly. I have to stop.' His words were slow, as if even speaking took great effort. Lance nodded, though knew the other man could not see the acknowledgement.

Quent half collapsed and curled up into a foetal position, his breathing gradually slowing to its regular rate. He had made no attempt to make the area comfortable or check for any dangers. In less than a minute, the man was asleep.

Lance scanned the area. It was quite open and the trees were spaced more thinly than in other parts of the forest. *This could be advantageous,* he thought. He loosened the LANSPEAK, slipped it off his wrist and placed it in the highest point in the clearing he could reach, which happened to be on the side of a solid tree trunk. He reasoned that the first rays of the sun would shine onto the device giving, thus providing it much needed solar power.

Once it was secured and ready for the morning light, he climbed down the few feet and found a grassy area under a short, stocky tree and closed his eyes, though sleep did not come to him as quickly as to the other man, who was now snoring loudly.

Thoughts and images of the last few hours filled his mind. The gorillas, Duncan, the impossible but very real giant spiders. And the leopard. It had been beyond surreal and once more, he was reminded how easy it was for Rufus to have been mentally broken. And Rufus had been alone. He must have seen Duncan attacked by these gigantic arachnids. It would have been horrific for anyone to witness. But Duncan was more than Rufus's friend. They were soulmates, sharing everything in their lives together.

It was no surprise his friend was a broken man and Lance now wondered just how well Rufus or anyone could recover from such an ordeal. Seeing someone you love die in front of you was the worst thing anyone could ever have to face. And he knew this, knew it all too well. Watching his own mother die that day had killed a part of himself. And he had not uttered a single word since that day.

Focus. Stay focused and in control, he told himself over and over until he too fell into a deep exhausted sleep.

Tropical Rainforest,
The Democratic Republic of the Congo,
July 22,
8:12am (Congolese and UK time)

Both men slept deeply through the night. Lance had dreamed many things but fortunately, they had not descended into nightmares. His subconscious mind had played the previous day's experiences over and over, in no particular order. At times, the dreams were outlandish, as they often were. At one point, the giant spiders were able to talk. In the dream, he was having a conversation with the king of spiders and was trying to bargain for their lives. Though the entire dream was absurd, the spider king's voice was familiar. It was identical to the warlord's, the self-proclaimed "J'ba Fofi". Which felt quite apt somehow.

Lance was still in a deep slumber. His subconscious thoughts had him floating through the sky towards the river when the screams overtook everything. The piercing shrieks cut through his mind and forced him awake, his heart pounding. Blinking in the morning light, his body racked with pain when he sat up too quickly, searching for the source of the horrendous cries.

It was Quent. The man was still asleep, but in the middle of what appeared to be a terrible nightmare. 'No! No! Get off! Get away! Get off!' His cries were loud but still had an unfocused unaware sound to them. His body was twitching, both arms flaying around at an unseen menace.

Lance strode over and knelt beside the terrified man. His eyes were closed but beneath the lids were rapid movements, almost like he was trying to blink but they were glued shut. Grabbing the man's shoulders attempting to shake him awake, he knew was an instant mistake.

The physical touch sent the older man into a frenzy. He screamed so hard Quent's face reddened and his whole body began writhing in panic. 'No! Nooooo!' The last word was accompanied by a swift punch to Lance's face. The fist connected with his jaw, thrusting his head back and forcing his whole body backwards causing the man to land on his back.

Thankfully, the ground was quite soft and he was grateful there were no protruding rocks behind him. More stunned than hurt, Lance sat up just in time to see the thrashing man suddenly wake up, his eyes suddenly wide, though the screaming still continued. Quent's head jerked quickly in every direction, the cries replaced by confused sobs.

Though awake, he was still not aware. Reality was slow in registering. The younger man stood and Quent had something to focus on. His tear-filled eyes looked up and down at Lance as if trying to establish if he was real or not. After what seemed like ages, though was in fact a few seconds, Quent sagged and began crying quietly.

Clearly, he had not escaped the nightmares, he thought grimly. As the man's body shook with emotion, Lance scanned the area quickly. It was light and very warm already. He wasted no time in climbing the tree to retrieve the LANSPEAK. Strapping it to his arm, he checked the power. The two hours of sun had given it the power boost he had hoped. It was at twenty-three percent. Lance had his voice back.

Tropical Rainforest,
The Democratic Republic of the Congo,
July 22,
8:15am (Congolese and UK time)

The device needed much more sun, which fortunately they had if they remained out of the shade as much as possible. He glanced over at the older man. The sobbing had ceased, though he remained slouched on the ground breathing heavily. Lance cautiously walked over, conscious of not upsetting him again. Quent slowly raised his head as he approached, though he did not seem to register his arrival at first.

Bloodshot eyes stared up, a glazed look not focusing on anything. Lance's heart suddenly thudded quickly. Had it happened? Had Quent finally descended into a maddened state like Rufus had? This would be disastrous for them both. He found it easier looking at the older man's eyes because they were not looking into his. They were elsewhere. It was as if Lance was not there and he was vaguely searching for something, anything to concentrate on.

He pressed the LANSPEAK a couple of times. '*Quent. Can you hear me?*'

The artificial voice seemed to register in the puzzled face and his eyes gradually focused on Lance, causing him to eventually look away as the stare intensified threatening to bore into him. A vague half smile slowly spread along the man's face. 'What a nightmare,' was all he could say, his voice cracking with emotion and fatigue and shaking his head wearily.

Relief flooded though Lance. Quent's sanity had been preserved for another day he gratefully told himself. Though it was obvious that the older man was mentally and physically worn out. He was unsure how much more the man could take. Lance was quietly that Quent had made it this far, though he knew that fear and adrenaline had played a large part.

Once the older man had regained some of his composure, they had more rations, which were running thin now, though he guessed they had a few days' supply left. Quent remained silent, as they prepared to set off again. His personality had changed since they encountered the spiders, which was hardly surprising, seeing them would affect anyone. Lance just hoped that the other man could stay mentally strong until they were out of immediate danger.

With the sun behind them, they continued their journey into the unknown. This time, Lance held the LANSPEAK in the full glare of the rising sun, determined to charge it as much as possible whenever possible. They both did feel the benefit of more than ten hours sleep. The fact that they were not attacked by anything in the night was also a positive thing. It did feel that they were away from the J'ba Fofi, though what new dangers lay ahead they could not know as they headed west once more.

Tropical Rainforest,
The Democratic Republic of the Congo,
July 22,
11:01am (Congolese and UK time)

Despite the heat, they made good progress. Stopping only for toilet and ration breaks. The rations were running low but Lance guessed they could keep them going for a couple of days longer if they used them sparingly, which they were. He checked the LANSPEAK. Fifty-eight percent power. The hot sun was working wonders on the device.

Even though Lance was able to communicate freely again, Quent was making no effort to converse. The older man seemed quite withdrawn now, though it could largely be due to physical exhaustion, he guessed. The pale complexion of the man was not suited to such extreme heat either, so he kept himself in the shade as much as possible.

Lance had to stay in the direct sunlight to charge his communication device. To minimise overheating, he also sought shade regularly.

The edge of the J'ba Fofi's territory was now six hours' walk behind them. He felt like they were a safe distance away from them now, though what other dangers lay ahead of them could only be imagined. Their pace was steady, though the intense heat of the relentless sun did drain their energy considerably.

Silently, the men traversed the dense forest, unsure of what lay ahead. It was around noon when they stopped to rest and take refreshment. The LANSPEAK was at seventy percent power. This was a relief as the device had come in useful numerous times on this journey and not just as a communication aid.

Lance lay down in the shade, which did not offer much relief from the oppressive heat but was grateful to be out of the direct sunlight. Taking a well-earned drink, he felt his body ache once more. The pause in walking always highlighted the punishment his body had gone through over the past few days. Though Lance was an extremely fit man, it was impossible not to notice the damage he had inflicted upon himself. The pain in some areas made him wonder if he had sustained more serious or permanent injuries. His train of thought was suddenly interrupted by excited cried from Quent.

'Lance! Lance, come and see this! We're saved! We're going to be okay!' The man emerged from a thick tree line to the west. Lance had assumed the man had wondered off to be alone for some reason. The older man had an almost manic look of delight on his face, one he had not seen since they were reunited in Rivertown.

'Ah, mate, we've made it! Civilisation! We've made it! Woohoo!' The man's sudden elation puzzled Lance, who was now rising wearily and heading to where Quent was standing and pointing animatedly at what he had discovered a few feet away. As the younger man approached, Quent darted back through the trees like an excited child showing their parent a wonderful new discovery.

He waded through the mass of leaves and small branches to find what the other man had been so thrilled by. When Lance saw it, his blood ran cold. He was staring up at something, which now filled him with possibly more fear than the giant spiders. It was a fence. The same fence he had seen from the river. The tall, crude, makeshift structure that was the border of the warlord's territory. Quent and he were right at the edge of J'ba Fofi's domain.

J'ba Fofi's Territory,
The Salonga National Park,
The Democratic Republic of the Congo,
July 22,
12:00 noon (Congolese and UK time)

The metal and wood barrier looked even more thrown together when examined up close. Detritus from the forest littered the fence, mixed with rubbish from the men camped on the other side of the flimsy barrier. And a narrow but not very steep gorge ran parallel to the manmade structure. The third land island lay on the other side of the gorge. Lance scanned the area past the fence. It was as barren and damaged as he had remembered.

Quent was standing next to the structure, staring up in awe. It was obvious that the older man saw the fence as a sign that they had reached somewhere safe. He could not have been more wrong as Lance approached him from behind and pushed at his shoulders, forcing the older man low to the ground.

'What're you doing?' Quent asked irritably, though actually letting the young man steer him into a crouching position. Lance looked closely at the vista before them. The river was to the left and seemed much further away than he recalled. The camp was much larger when right next to it. The low bushes gave the men some cover but Lance would have preferred to be out of sight completely.

He could see a small number of men spread about the area, though none appeared to have noticed them, which was pure luck, he reasoned. Quent had obviously made no attempt to conceal himself when he had first wandered up to the fence, in fact he probably wanted to be noticed. Lance knew they had to head back to behind the tree line if they were to avoid being seen.

As he was preparing to stealthily creep back to a less visible position, enabling him to reassess their current situation, which was dire he grimly realised, a shout echoed through the area. A shout accompanied by more shouts and then many raised urgent voices.

Trying to stay as low as possible, he looked ahead. Many men were now coming out of their huts, some half-dressed and clumsily picking up their nearby weapons. The men began to gather around one man who was about eighty feet away but was screaming something unintelligible whilst pointing excitedly to where Quent and he were attempting to hide. A number of men then began running directly towards them, yelling angrily and pointing their guns ahead. *We have been seen,* he wearily told himself.

J'ba Fofi's Territory,
The Salonga National Park,
The Democratic Republic of the Congo,
July 22,
12:02pm (Congolese and UK time)

'Oh no!' Quent whimpered at the sight of the approaching men.

'*Move.*' The LANSPEAK spoke the simple instruction, as Lance stood to a hunched position and swiftly headed towards the thick trees. He felt relief as Quent followed without objection.

As the men entered the relative seclusion of the forest, a gunshot echoed around them, causing many birds to take flight. The older man made a sobbing sound. His wheezing gasps became louder as Lance crouched low at the base of a thick trunk and stared through the leaves and branches, confident that they could not be seen easily from this position.

Through the undergrowth, he had a decent view of the camp. The men had slowed to a walk but had grown in number and were steadily walking towards where they were hiding. As Lance tried to focus on the current situation, he noticed someone who suddenly sent a chill down his spine. The warlord J'ba Fofi was amongst the men who were heading their way.

Although he was a considerable distance away, there was no way of mistaking the man. His distinctive clothing, complete with an animal skin draped over his shoulder and the way he held himself. It was obviously the same man who had interrogated him, so long ago it now seemed.

Lance took out the small binoculars and tried to have a closer look. His enhanced vision found the warlord. He was marching determinedly towards them, something held in his left hand, accompanied by more and more armed men. What he did notice was that the man was no longer wearing sunglasses. Which was puzzling as he was now actually walking in bright sunlight, not sitting in a darkened hut.

As the man got closer, Lance was able to study his face clearly for the first time. The warlord could not make eye contact so he had an uninterrupted view of this evil man's face. And he noticed something quite alarming. J'ba Fofi's face had a familiarity about it. Lance felt that he had seen this face somewhere before. Although he had an excellent, almost photographic memory, faces were much harder for Lance to mentally recall. Due to the fact that he found direct eye contact so difficult.

But seeing this face without sunglasses gave Lance the chilling feeling that he was known to him. Before he could dwell on this strange recognition, the warlord waved a hand and motioned for a man who was jogging alongside him to head towards the tree-line. The man, who looked very young, had a bulky pack strapped to his back, which had a tube running from it, which was attached to what looked like a rifle in his arms. J'ba Fofi then lifted his left hand and raised to his mouth what he was holding.

The megaphone roared to life with the resounding deep voice of the man. 'Rich man! Hey, rich man! I know it's you! I saw you, man!'

'What's he saying?' Quent's desperate voice croaked from behind him. Lance raised a hand to pause the man from speaking again.

'You don't need to hide, man! You're safe from me! As I know you can help me!' The man's rasping sinister laugh finished the statement.

'Who is he? What's he saying? Do you know him?' Quent's questions sounded like pleading.

Lance sighed. '*I know who he is.*'

'Well, can he help us? Is he friendly?' Lance was aghast at the naivety of the man's questions. The warlord was marching towards them with about fifty armed men, one of whom had just fired his weapon and Quent was asking if he was friendly. But then, it was no surprise because of what they had just been through, the man was desperate to find safety at whatever cost.

Once more, time seemed to stand still for Lance. They had escaped near death by sheer luck and now faced an equally dangerous threat. His mind swam at the thought of their current situation. The phrase "stuck between a rock and a hard place" was so true right now.

Focus. Focus, he told himself. The river? Could they make it through the forest and somehow cross the river or make their way to Rivertown? No, impossible he knew. The warlord controlled this whole area, including the river. And there was no well-timed helicopter coming to rescue them this time. It felt hopeless.

A scream from Quent shook him from his thoughts. Looking up, Lance saw and felt, a thick line of fire shoot through the trees near them, scorching the vegetation, the smell of burning plants reaching his nostrils. Quent began to sob desperately. Another fierce jet shot even closer to them, the intense heat could be felt much easier now.

Without another thought, Lance grabbed Quent, pulled him up and ran, half dragging the man deeper into the trees. He could scarcely believe the horror the warlord was capable of. It was a flamethrower. An evil invention, but one J'ba Fofi had no qualms about using. They headed deeper into the shaded forest. Another blast of flame engulfed the area where they had been crouching only seconds before.

Lance was still shocked at this new level of brutality from the warlord. It seemed the man was no longer interested in keeping him alive. Quent continued to sob weakly. Then a deep rasping voice echoed through the trees. 'Hey, rich man! Rich man! How you feeling? You feeling warm?' The warlord laughed, which was accompanied by further laughter from the other men. 'What should I do, man? Cook you and feed you to my men! Should I do that rich man? Make some use of you!' More laughter and whoops of delight from the men could be heard just beyond the tree line.

Lance sighed wearily. The wretched truth of their situation had suddenly been made clear by the warlord's sickening words and actions. As the cruel laughter died down to be replaced by the continuing whimpers from Quent, he knew what they had to do. Lance stared solemnly into the vast endless forest behind them and admitted the truth to himself. The only way to survive was to go back the way they came from.

J'ba Fofi's Territory,
The Salonga National park,
The Democratic Republic of the Congo,
July 22,
12:04pm (Congolese and UK time)

'No way! No! No!' Quent's anguished cries were totally expected. Having dragged the man further away from the warlord and his men, Lance had to put to the older man their only option for survival.

'It is the only option. The warlord will kill us as soon as he finds us.'

'No! No, I can't! I can't go back there!' Tears streamed down the older man's face. His body wracked with sobs. Lance felt real pity for him, as he was terrified himself.

'*We cannot stay here.*' Lance could only repeat what he said. Quent looked up, his eyes red and fearful. He was about to speak when another red-hot spurt of flame burst through the trees behind them, igniting the dry branches and leaves. Then a sinister voice, amplified by the loudspeaker, boomed through the trees.

'We are coming for you, rich men! You can't hide from me! Nobody gets away from me!' The warlord sounded angry now. Quent blinked, as if starting to register the imminent threat. Lance crouched in front of him and stared at his face but avoided his eyes.

'*Listen to me. If we stay here, that man will kill us. Without a doubt. We stand a better chance of survival going back.*' Quent moaned in fear and tried to stand, his face frantically looking around.

'*Listen. Listen. We will be more prepared when we return. I have the LANSPEAK at full power. It will help. We will rest a few hours before we reach their area. We will get there in the morning. They are nocturnal. We will creep through the area and head for the bridge. We will be fine.*' As Lance typed the plan, he was actually struggling to believe one word of it. Their chances of surviving a return journey to the centre of the gigantic spiders' domain were virtually nil. But still, better odds than what the warlord was offering.

Gunshots now cracked overhead, followed by a collective roar from the warlord's men. He had clearly worked them up into a violent frenzy. If they stayed where they were, they would be dead in less than a minute, he guessed. The warlord had clearly realised Lance could be of no use to him now. 'We're coming for you, thief! Nobody betrays me!' The use of the word thief was new to Lance. Though it did not matter right now. Without another word, Lance guided Quent up and the two men headed back into the forest. The older man seemed too tired to argue. Lance hoped that he could hold his mind together long enough to get them through this. Though thoughts of Rufus and his shattered mind were never far from his thoughts.

More gunshots rang out through the trees, some hitting objects in front of them. They were not warning shots, they were aimed to kill. Both men broke into a run and swiftly retraced their steps back through the dense vegetation. The sound of the gunshots faded with each step. They were leaving J'ba Fofi's territory and heading back to another extremely dangerous part of the forest. Lance began to wonder if they had any luck left to get them through the next deadly place.

Tropical Rainforest,
The Democratic Republic of the Congo,
July 22,
12:15pm (Congolese and UK time)

They ran until they could run no more. Or more accurately, until Quent could run no more, Lance knew. The man was permanently exhausted now. The gunshots could not be heard anymore, though he wondered how far the warlord or his men would follow them. It was reasonable to believe that J'ba Fofi and his personal army were aware of what was living in this forest. Perhaps that was how Dan seemed to know that the warlord's territory had not reached this far into the forest.

Had he lost men to the spiders? Or were Dan's superstitious warnings enough to keep them away. Both were probably the correct answer. Right now, all he wanted to know was that whether they were being followed or not. At the moment, the sounds of the forest was all that could be heard over the noise of them traipsing through the thick undergrowth. The birdsong and other natural sounds were comforting to Lance for some reason. Though he was concerned how Quent would act when they returned to the "silent" part of the forest.

Once again, worrying thoughts were pushed to the back of his mind. He had to focus on the here and now. The midday sun was fiercely hot and Lance was alternating his journey by staying in the shade and recharging the LANSPEAK as much as possible. Keeping a steady pace, the men made good progress, as they continued through the wilderness. Lance ensured they rested regularly and took food and hydrated. Though the rations were now running low.

They walked in silence but after a few hours, Quent broke the silence as they took rest.

'I want to thank you for getting us through this so far.' His voice was croaky and weary. Lance looked his way but made no eye contact and nodded whilst raising a hand in acknowledgement.

'I know I was unprepared. But I had no idea we'd find those…things.' The last word was spoken in a quivering voice. Lance was now intrigued. This was a man who had devoted a large part of his adult life to try and prove the very existence of these colossal spiders but was as surprised and horrified as he was when they actually discovered them.

'I thought that you wanted to find them. To prove to everyone that you were right.'

'I did. I do. People won't think I'm crazy now. Once I show them proof.' He smiled weakly when he talked of exposing these creatures to the outside world.

'But…I…I didn't think they would be so big. So huge. And so many of them. I figured they would be shy and we would have to seek them out. Maybe get one or two photos of them from a distance. I thought they were the size of a small dog or maybe a monkey. And only see a couple of them. But, mate, they were gigantic! And there were hundreds of them! Hundreds!' His voice began to rise and became more and more panicked.

Lance could only shake his head. What Quent had just said came as no surprise to him. He was desperate to prove he was right. To be recognised and praised by the very people who have mocked and ridiculed him over the years. But Lance knew in his heart that if they made it out of here alive, which was looking unlikely, he could not allow Quent to reveal the truth about the spiders to the public. If the world knew about the existence of such animals, this entire area would be put into jeopardy.

Tropical Rainforest,
The Democratic Republic of the Congo,
July 22,
2:22pm (Congolese and UK time)

They said no more and resumed their journey. Lance knew that Quent's sudden realisation of the enormity of their discovery had given the man a renewed sense of purpose. This new determination could possibly boost their chances of surviving this situation.

Lance knew if Quent held out hope that the fame and fortune he so was desperately seeking would make this trip worthwhile, then he had to go along with it. It was preferable to accompanying a man who had given up and descended into a state of madness as Rufus had done.

They continued their trek, Quent having found a new level of energy kept a good pace as they came to roughly half way between the warlord's territory and the spiders'. There had been no further signs of J'ba Fofi or his men since their escape. It really did seem that Dan was right and that the warlord had no control over this part of the forest. It was unclear why. Though perhaps his men had encountered the giant spiders and decided to permanently give this whole place a wide berth.

That theory did not sit comfortably with Lance. As terrifying and dangerous the spiders were, he guessed that the brutal machine-gun and flamethrower-wielding soldiers of the warlord would easily be able to defend themselves against such creatures.

The thought of heavily armed men storming the spiders' home and indiscriminately slaughtering anything that moved there was a sickening notion. These animals were rare, if not rarer than the gorillas they had encountered. And they too needed protecting. Which would seem an absurd thought to many, knowing how dangerous and aggressive they were. Though the same could be said for the gorillas, he mused.

Lance knew that this was a unique and fragile place. He already felt honour bound to protect it, if they were able to survive of course. Which he knew was a very slim chance indeed. He was unsure how long Quent's newly discovered nerve would last, especially as they got closer to the border of the arachnids territory with every step. In fact, he wondered how long his own nerve would last for that matter.

The sun remained mercilessly hot, though the LANSPEAK was well charged now. He stopped in the shade and sat, grateful for a slight relief from the heat. Quent walked up and stared down. 'So, you think we wait here? Start again in the morning?'

The younger man nodded. Quent sighed wearily and sat underneath a nearby tree. 'Good plan. Our only choice of action to be fair.' Lance turned looked the other man up and down. He looked hot and exhausted. It was indeed the right decision to rest and regain as much energy as possible.

It was difficult to rest in the uncomfortable heat. The constant attack from flies did nothing to help either. Quent attempted to start up a conversation with Lance but he simply replied, '*The Lanspeak has to keep as much charge as possible. I must speak as little as possible. I am sorry.*' Quent merely shrugged, accepting this, as he too knew that the LANSPEAK could make the difference between them surviving and not. Lance also did not want to engage in lengthy conversations about what would happen if they did make it out alive and return to the UK.

He had visions in his head of Quent getting paid vast sums of money by giving lectures to captivated audiences all over the world. And exposing this entire place to greedy or even just curious eyes would only end in utter destruction. We might as well allow CES full access, so they can come in and destroy anything in their way. No. He would never let that happen. This place must be protected at all costs.

The remainder of the afternoon and into the evening, Quent attempted to make conversations, which Lance mostly answered with a nod or shake of his head. As darkness descended on the forest the two men retreated into their own thoughts. It was not long into the night that Quent could be heard snoring. Hoping the man would have no more nightmares, Lance settled on the soft ground and listened to the peaceful sounds of the forest going to sleep.

Nature was calming to him, it always had been. The solitude he felt, even though only a few feet away from the snoring man, was therapeutic. Lance was grateful for this relaxing sensation, as it was the tonic his mind needed. Tomorrow he needed his head to be clear and focused, as they were walking straight back into extreme danger.

If he panicked or made irrational decisions, they would both be dead without a doubt. He closed his eyes and joined the natural world in all its glory. He went into an almost meditative state. The forest no longer seemed threatening but protecting. It was alive and in harmony with itself. His subconscious mind found a renewed sense of positivity, enabling to slip into a peaceful and undisturbed sleep.

Tropical Rainforest,
The Democratic Republic of the Congo,
July 23,
06:15am (Congolese and UK time)

He was unsure if it was the early morning heat or the cries from Quent, which shook him from his undisturbed sleep. Blinking furiously to focus his vision, Lance looked over at the sleeping man. He was laid on his back, hands drawn up to his face and occasionally lashing out at an unseen foe. If he were standing, it would look like he was boxing.

'No! Get away! No! No!' His words came in small sudden bursts, alongside gasps and grunts. The younger man approached, his body still aching and knelt beside him. He was about to place a hand on his shoulder when Quent's eyes flicked open a look of sheer terror was etched across his face. Unable to focus on Lance, who was unable to make eye contact, the man looked around as if in a panicked state.

'*Quent. It is okay. You were having a nightmare.*' Lance wished his LANSPEAK could convey some emotion at times. The man sat bolt upright causing the younger man to topple back. His sight managed to focus and he stared directly at Lance, forcing him to look aware from the penetrating glare.

'Having a nightmare? Mate, we're in the middle of a nightmare,' he said darkly. Lance could only nod as the man was speaking the truth. They were roughly a three-hour walk away from mortal danger. To reach safety, they had to go directly through one of the most hostile places on earth, which it undoubtedly was.

They took refreshments in silence and reluctantly headed towards the perilous area they could not avoid. The calming effect his restful sleep had given him was rapidly disappearing with each step closer to the unreal spiders. He concentrated his mind, trying to focus.

Lance was unsure if it was returning to such a place that was causing his renewed anxiety or if it was Quent. He was unsure how the man would behave once they got back to the arachnid territory. The man was boldly heading forward with fresh vigour, thoughts of fame and fortune spurring him on. But what if Quent begins to have a breakdown when they get nearer to the place? His sanity appeared to be on a knife-edge the last time they were here, which was totally understandable. Lance knew that if he remained focused he could get them both through the place alive. But if Quent's behaviour became irrational, it would lead to both of them being killed.

Another uncomfortable thought slid into his head. He knew he would stand a better chance of survival if Quent were not with him. Alone, he could get through the territory swiftly and possibly unseen. He knew the older man would slow him down, even if he did not have a mental breakdown. He pushed that train of thought away. He would, nor ever could, abandon Quent to such a grisly fate. It had always been in Lance's nature to protect and support people more vulnerable than himself. His mother had taught him this from an early age to instil a sense of purpose and self-worth. Tristan had also nurtured this strong morality in Lance over the years, though in a subtler, more structured way, as the man was a soldier.

He felt ashamed that his mind had entertained such a notion of leaving Quent to his fate. But that was how his mind worked. It had to think rationally and process all scenarios practically. He had to weigh up all their possibilities if they were to survive. Fortunately, for the older man, Lance's moral code was strong and unwavering. They would get through this together or not at all.

He focused and tried to regain the inner peace his sleep had afforded him. Knowing there was no going back, the men silently and cautiously made their way towards the territory of the gigantic spiders.

Tropical Rainforest,
The Democratic Republic of the Congo,
July 23,
09:00am (Congolese and UK time)

As they made their way closer to the arachnid's territory, Lance suddenly found himself overwhelmed with thoughts and feelings about what they were about to face. He felt he had to have numerous plans of escape ready in his mind and the ability to implement any of them at a second's notice. The reality was that he would assess each situation as it arose.

Making plans in a place such as this was futile at the moment. And he admitted to himself that he was unsure of what they would find. He was only assuming that the spiders were nocturnal, judging by their behaviour when they had entered their domain. The truth was Quent and he could be walking straight towards certain doom.

Thankfully, the other man's emotional state had remained constant. That could change in a heartbeat of course but for now, they were doing well. Lance's memory and keen sense of direction had led them back along the route they had taken only the day before yesterday. He had not needed the map or the LANSPEAK, which was thankfully still well charged.

The familiar terrain led them to the small clearing, where they had encountered the leopard, so long ago it seemed. So here they were, the boundary between the spider's domain and the rest of the forest. The trees were alive with the sounds of nature. Animals and insects made up a constant humming of life.

It was a welcome and reassuring sound. Lance wondered how he would feel when they entered the "silent place", or more concerning, how Quent would feel.

They paused in their walking when they were in the clearing. He half expected the leopard to pounce from the trees at any moment but the place was deserted. Lance assessed the distance they needed to travel to get to safety. And when he thought of safety, he thought of the rope bridge, which had given them access to the spiders' territory. What was beyond the bridge was not particularly safe either. The rare gorillas were not exactly friendly but he would rather face them than the J'ba Fofi. In fact, they were going to *have* to face them if they survived the J'ba Fofi. He has had less stressful journeys he told himself humourlessly.

It had taken them less than two hours to previously get from the bridge to where they were standing. But Lance had to factor in that they were running for a good part of the journey. He figured that if they were to have the optimum chance of survival, stealth would be called for. Lance thought that the approach to the heart of the arachnid's lair should be done as quietly as possible. If they crept in, there was a chance the spiders would not even notice them. It was a slim chance, but the best chance they had. Running as fast as possible would be the wiser option once they were heading away from the lair and towards the bridge.

They took refreshments and then without a word to each other, gingerly returned to the domain of some of the biggest and most dangerous predators on earth.

Tropical Rainforest,
The Democratic Republic of the Congo,
July 23,
9:05am (Congolese and UK time)

They entered the tree line. Both men breathed a sigh of relief that there was not a huge mass of giant spiders waiting for them. He scanned the trees looking for any signs of the creatures and thankfully saw none. This part of the forest was still alive with sound. *Another thing to be grateful for,* Lance thought. He had guessed that their previous visit had lured the spiders out of their territory, out of their comfort zone in their pursuit of them. Lance also began wondering what actually had happened to the leopard they had encountered.

His thoughts returned to the sounds he heard from this very section of forest when the huge jungle cat had charged in. The disturbing noises of the vicious feline/arachnid fight sent a shiver up his spine. The cat could have made the spider's retreat to where they felt safer and had greater numbers. He dared not imagine that they were about to discover a cluster of J'ba Fofi poised for attack behind the next tree. *Focus*, he told himself. A runaway imagination was not helpful in this situation. *Focus*.

They traipsed through the thick vegetation, a journey in which they had previously made in almost total darkness. Though making the return journey in clear daylight made the place no less foreboding. Grateful for the continuing sounds of the wildlife, they steadily made their way through the trees and bushes. Lance had his keen eyes focus on every movement, any sudden noise. He was mentally on high alert and was once again grateful for the adequate rest he had gotten the previous night.

It was almost easy to imagine that they were not in any imminent danger, but were in fact just two men enjoying a brisk stroll through an unspoiled wilderness. He had to push such complacent thoughts away. They were heading into one of the most hostile places on the face of the earth. It was no exaggeration that this was as deadly a place as anyone could be. *Focus*.

They walked for another half an hour and still no sign of the spiders. He wondered if they were being secretly watched by them, possibly from some distance away, their previous boldness having temporarily left them since the leopard attack. He dismissed that notion. These spiders were aggressive and unafraid. They were well aware, he was sure, that they were in total control of this entire area. *These creatures are in charge, make no mistake*, he mused.

Their journey through the forest was steady, as they felt caution could be their best defence at the moment, if not their only defence. Both men were mindful to minimise the noise they made, which was not easy in such an overgrown environment. Lance was also looking out for any sign of webs. The previous encounter with the creatures had shown how vast their web structures were. If the J'bs Fofi were anything like their much smaller relatives, the slightest vibration on the thick silk would bring them scuttling directly to the source.

It felt like every step had to be carefully worked out to reduce the risk of being discovered. He was grateful that Quent was taking this slow and steady progress seriously. Though he doubted there was anyone on earth who would rush into this place willingly. The lack of webs also indicated that this was still not arachnid territory but merely a section of the forest they are forced to enter only if they must.

Step by careful step, the men made steady progress through the foreboding forest. Lance was acutely aware of not letting the relative tranquillity of such a place lull in him into a false sense of safety. Though it almost felt like he was walking through a minefield at times, such was the overwhelming feeling of dread with each step.

Heading east, the men covered large amounts of ground, despite their unhurried pace. Lance continued to scan everything in his field of vision. It was then that he noticed something up ahead. In a patch of recently flattened grass and bushes were what appeared to be a pile of burnt branches. The black twisted objects were visible just above the disturbed plants. As he slowly crept forward, he realised suddenly at what he was looking at. His heart jumped into his throat as he stared at three very large J'ba Fofi.

Tropical Rainforest,
The Democratic Republic of the Congo,
July 23,
9:48am (Congolese and UK time)

His mind swam as he gazed in horror at the gigantic spiders. Quent was following and had not seen until he was just behind Lance. 'Why have you stopped? We need to…'

His low voice ended with a sudden gasp of alarm. He grabbed the younger man's shoulder and began to hyperventilate. Between gasps, the occasional word burst out. 'No…no…we can't…must go back…' Lance turned his head so the man could see his face but did not look him in the eyes. He simply put his index finger to his mouth to tell Quent to be quiet. The man nodded quickly but his body began to shake with terror.

On looking closer, Lance noticed more. He tapped the LANSPEAK. '*I think they are all dead.*' Quent stopped shaking and stared past the other man's shoulder, staring intently. His breathing slowed put he was still panicked. 'Are you, are you sure? How can you tell?' His voice was strained. Lance wondered why the man seemed not to see what he could. The huge spiders were stacked on top of one another in a gruesome tangled pile. Many of their legs were twisted, some were missing and there were obvious wounds visible in places. Gouges made by powerful claws could be seen. The work of the leopard, he guessed.

He took a couple of steps closer and then suddenly gagged at the stench. Flies were loudly buzzing around the grisly sight. There was no sign of the jungle cat but he was in no doubt that these huge arachnids had lost the fight when the leopard attacked. Quent remained where he was, whimpering at the hideous sight in front of them.

Lance did not want to move any closer, the rancid smell of the already rotting spiders made him feel nauseous. Though seeing these creatures in such a state stirred up feelings of pity in him, he admitted to himself that he was grateful they had not met some living J'ba Fofi yet. But to see such magnificent animals like this was sad. He knew it was nature and nature could be cruel. But it was still a sorrowful sight. These spiders, like every other creature to walk this earth, wanted only to live, to survive. His thoughts once again returned the possibility that it was Quent and himself who had drawn the spiders out further than they normally would and into the domain of the leopard. Their unwanted presence here could have caused this.

The sounds of sobbing shook him out of his guilty thoughts. Lance sighed and motioned for Quent to follow him, giving the ghastly discovery a wide berth. 'Are we sure we should go on?' Quent's desperate question was one that Lance had feared. The first sign of potential danger and the man would fall to pieces. He had done well up until now. Though seeing the spiders, even dead ones, had obviously been a stark reminder to the man that these animals were not some glorious prize to make him famous, but deadly creatures who would kill them immediately the first chance they get.

It was right that Quent had been reminded of this fact. But if getting any closer to these creatures would cause him to spiral into a state of despair like Rufus, then their chances of surviving this were a whole lot slimmer, Lance grimly told himself.

Tropical Rainforest,
The Democratic Republic of the Congo,
July 23,
10:05am (Congolese and UK time)

Their pace remained as cautious as ever, the dreadful sight they had encountered was a harsh reminder that they were in the middle of extremely hostile territory. Manoeuvring through the dense trees and plants, Lance noticed that Quent had armed himself with the machete. Holding the large blade like a sword, he wondered if he should tell him to re-sheath it. He knew that if they were faced with a large cluster of the gigantic arachnids, that single blade would be virtually of no use. In fact, it could actually be more dangerous to have it out if attacked. He quickly decided not to say anything, as clearly feeling like he was armed gave the man a much needed (though false) feeling of protection, if only slightly. Lance knew that their best, in fact their only way of escaping these creatures was avoidance. To pass unseen or even heard was the only way they could survive this place.

The sun beat down hard though the vast canopy of leaves and branches offered some relief, but not much. The forest was still humming with life, which was a constant reassurance. He wondered if this section was much quieter last time they were here due to it being almost night. This was another comforting thought, knowing that the spider's domain could actually be a lot smaller than he first believed. Though it was no reason to lower his guard. In fact, this could also mean that the arachnids will be more condensed into one area, to practice safety in numbers, he thought gloomily.

Lance did not convey any of these scenarios or theories to Quent. It was clear that the man's head could not cope with even one more brutally realistic thought. His tension was almost at breaking point, so no use in bombarding him with his mental assessments of what they may be facing at any moment. He needed the man to be as clear and focused as he was able to be. A fit of panic now would doom them both.

The air of the forest was foreboding, but only due to the fact that he knew what was living in this part of it. The place itself had an unspoiled beauty Lance had not seen in a long time. A lot of the places he wrote about were often anything but unspoiled. A majority of his reports were from locations, which had been destroyed by mankind's greed and corruption.

The thought of this wilderness suffering the same fate as so many other natural habitats was unbearable. That monstrous thought strengthened his resolve to get out of this place alive to help ensure its very survival. He glanced back at Quent. The man was red faced and sweating. Lance again felt pity mixed with some guilt now. If they survive, the other man would immediately want to go public about the giant spiders. And that is something he could never ever allow. The secret of this unbelievable place must forever remain just that. Secret.

Tropical Rainforest,
The Democratic Republic of the Congo,
July 23,
11:57am (Congolese and UK time)

Their cautious steps made good progress. As midday approached, they were both very grateful not to come across any further evidence of the J'ba Fofi. *This could be either good or bad,* Lance pondered. The heat was now quite fierce, despite the shade. They rested and hydrated. They were low on water until a stream they came across gave them a welcome top up. Lance knew that the rainy season had ended about two months ago, so any water was precious.

After walking for roughly an hour and a half, their route became less familiar to him. Possibly due to the fact that they had previously passed this way in a panicked exhausted run in poor light. Lance tried to re-orientate himself. He knew they were heading east, though he wanted to be sure that they were not going to find themselves in an (if possible) even more dangerous location. He had visions of them falling down a steep cliff edge or entering a dead end and being cut off by the spiders.

Calming his mind and focusing, Lance began to notice a familiarity about the place. They had passed this way at a run. Their slower return had taken twice as long. If what he remembered, they were about to enter a crucial part of the journey. He glanced back at Quent. The older man was sitting in the soft grass, machete in hand, panting like an overheating dog. This trip was having a punishing effect on the older, unfit man. He was grateful he had made it this far. Though the next level was going to seriously challenge Quent's fragile mental state.

He did not say anything, as it was pointless at this stage. Instead, the younger man waited until the other man felt ready to continue. After a few minutes, he stood and nodded wearily. They set off through more thick trees, constantly on the lookout for danger in any form. Lance was unsure if it was his imagination playing tricks, but this section of forest *did* seem quieter, though the hum of insects remained constant. Thankfully, Quent did not seem to notice this sudden change in the forest's atmosphere.

Lance kept their pace slow and as light as possible. An unwelcome feeling of dread threatened to overwhelm him. He pushed it away. *Focus. Focus.* They crept deeper into the undergrowth. Lance ignored feelings of being watched. Panic would be disastrous now. It was not long before they came across what he was expecting to find. 'Oh no. Oh, please no. We have to go back. We can't…' Quent's desperate voice from behind quickly descended into gasps and sobs. Lance held up a hand to silence the man but did not look round. His vision was focused on what had panicked the older man. They were staring down at what he remembered as a crater. A bone yard filled with countless skeletal remains of every kind of animal, including human. *Where do we go from here,* a dejected voice in his head asked.

Tropical Rainforest,
The Democratic Republic of the Congo,
July 22,
12:12pm (Congolese and UK time)

He surveyed the entire area with a fresh set of eyes. Last time they had been here had been in poor light and they had wasted no time to get out of there. It was now spread before him in all its horrific glory. Lance had possibly never seen such a ghastly sight in his life. The stench rising up in the midday heat was nauseating. The hum of flies was louder here for obvious reasons. He tried to focus and look at the place in a practical way.

The first thing that struck him was that it was not a crater at all but a wide section, which resembled a dry riverbed. The crater narrowed at the southern aspect and led into what was unmistakably a dry river, though a much smaller one than the Congo River itself. His gaze turned to the north. The entry to this dry bed was also narrow, but he could not see too far up as it disappeared over a brow in the hill.

It was rocky and Lance could see that this would be a wild rapid flowing river if it had was ever filled with water. Quent was still whimpering in the background when curiosity got the better of him and he decided to climb the steep edge to see beyond the brow. The older man mumbled something incomprehensible as Lance swiftly strode up the tree line to see what was beyond.

His heart skipped a beat as he saw more rocky tracks, which when flooded would have formed a series of waterfalls. It was what was beyond this which surprised him. There was water here and plenty of it. In the flat plateau behind the dry bed was what appeared to be a small lake. But it was actually a flooded part of the river, as the flow had been stopped by what could only be described as a dam. A huge mix of dead trees, branches, mud and various sorts of forest detritus all clumped together to form a watertight barrier.

But what was even more fascinating and at the same time alarming was the vast areas of the "dam" had large chunks of thick webs interweaved into it. On looking closer, there were also some animal remains mixed into the structure. A disturbing thought struck him. Had these giant arachnids built a dam? He shook his head at the absurdity of the very idea. They were spiders not beavers. Plus, it was too tangled and random looking to have been anything but a natural phenomenon.

He wondered how long this structure had existed. Probably only since the previous monsoon season. And the following rains would surely produce enough water to overwhelm the dam and let the small river flow once more. Somehow, this dry river felt like the real boundary of the J'ba Fofi's domain. He guessed they would not be able to cross this place if it were in full flow. In fact, it would form a true impassable border.

Part of him wished he could break the dam and allow the river to take its natural course. That was impossible of course. Though he thought he should be grateful for this river being dry at this stage. If it was a fast-flowing torrent when he and Quent were running from the chasing arachnids, they would have either drowned or been eaten. Another fluke, which had saved them on this insanely dangerous journey, he mused.

Lance looked down at Quent and gave a short wave to try and reassure the distressed man. His gaze then looked south, following what would be the obvious course of the small river. His mind raced. Could this be an escape route? Could they walk along this dry bed all the way to the river? Then perhaps keep to the water's edge, as they made their way back to Rivertown. He shook his head. No. The arachnids could possibly be in every corner of this land island. If they made it to the river, it would become an instant trap. Also, the warlord's men were patrolling that section of river he was sure. It was preferable to face one foe rather than two.

Another thought, which had been nagging him ever since he had ran from the warlord and his guns began to nag louder. It was the idea of heading in a different direction. Lance had assumed that the only way back to safety was the return journey to Rivertown and wondered if their chances of survival would be higher if they headed north, further into the jungle. No. The nearest settlement could be up to one hundred miles away. One hundred miles through a wild forest would spell the end of his companion. Lance knew *he* could possibly survive such a journey. Quent could not. There was no chance of the older man finishing such an arduous journey. Taking him blindly north would be as good as killing him. Their only, very slim chance was back through the spider's territory.

They had no time to waste. He headed back to where Quent was standing. The man's face remained ashen. The foetid smell from the bone yard was stronger here. Lance turned to the other man but did not make eye contact. '*We have to cross now.*' The older man screwed up his face in a combination of fear and disgust.

Tropical Rainforest,
The Democratic Republic of the Congo,
July 22,
12:20pm (Congolese and UK time)

He gave Quent no time to argue or even think about what they had to do. He strode down the slope towards the mass of remains. '*Try breathing through your mouth,*' he said without turning around. *'But keep your eyes open. You do not want to fall over in here.'* His last comment was met with more whimpers from the man.

Lance took his first steps into the rancid pit. He tried to walk on the dry mud as much as possible, but shivered inwardly at the horrible crunching sound he made each time he trod on some brittle bones. Quent could be heard walking just behind, trying to remain calm, as they walked through the lake of cadavers.

The flies were thick in the air, but this time, nature's sounds were offering no comfort. They had entered "no man's land" if it needed a title. *Back into Hell,* he thought. *Focus*. He tried to push negative thoughts aside, though it was almost impossible to have positive thoughts in such a place. He wondered about Quent's state of mind. The man could have a full panic attack at any time. The thought of having to support someone who could end up in the same state as Rufus did not bear thinking about.

Although they had made cautious steps up to this point, both men were now striding through the foul riverbed with real haste. Neither man wanted to spend a second longer here but also it felt very exposed. If they were suddenly attacked by the spiders, or any other animal for that matter, escape would be near impossible. The tree line on the far side looked almost inviting, though he knew it could be swarming with giant spiders. But to be out of this hot, stinking death trap was more important right now.

They made their way across the bed and into the slightly cooler forest. The trees felt threateningly dark after the glare of the midday sun. He waited for his eyes to adjust for a moment, though the exposed feeling remained with him. Once his vision got used to the new low light, he immediately scanned everywhere for movement or sounds. The lack of movement (and huge spiders) was a brief relief. But what was not so reassuring was the lack of sound. The light breeze rustled the leaves and the hum of bloated insects could still be heard from behind them. But he was in no doubt about where they were now. Quent and himself had re-entered the "silent place". They had returned to the territory controlled completely by an unknown number of gigantic carnivorous spiders.

Tropical Rainforest,
The Democratic Republic of the Congo,
July 22,
12:25pm (Congolese and UK time)

Quent could already sense the change in atmosphere and began to hyperventilate, though also tried to speak between breaths. 'No. No! We can't… No. We just can't… Hopeless… Those things, those creatures. They'll get us! They'll…' His words merged into frightened gasps. Lance put a hand on the man's shoulder, which caused him to jump slightly, his body shuddering. '*You have to stay calm. We are more in control this time. We know what to expect. We have the benefit of daylight. And we have the LANSPEAK.*' The man seemed to calm slightly, his breathing slowed but was still rapid. He noticed that Quent had re sheathed the machete. He had only done this so he was able to climb the slope leading to the trees much faster. Lance did not remind him to take the blade out again. The man's mental state was clearly deteriorating by the minute. He was afraid of this. Quent was beginning to lose what nerve he had left and they had not even seen any spiders yet, at least not alive anyway.

He kept a hand on his shoulder but did not make eye contact. He tried to calm and focus his own mind. If he were also stressed, Quent could quickly become worse. Lance controlled his breathing and motioned for the older man to take longer deeper breaths. After a minute, the man seemed to regain his composure, though he was still clearly on edge. This was the best Lance could hope for right now. After another minute, he tried to reassure the man as much as possible. '*I do think they are nocturnal. We could walk right through and not be noticed. If we are quiet and avoid those webs.*' Quent's body stiffened and he screwed his eyes up and nodded vigorously. '*If we are careful and quiet, we will survive this. Okay?*' The man opened his eyes and nodded, but slower this time.

Once he was satisfied the man was at least compliant, they set off through the dense trees. Lance thought back to the last time they were here. It had taken them roughly fifteen minutes to run from the place where they had first encountered the spiders, to here. So at a steady walk, it would be no more than thirty to forty minutes until they arrived at the clearing. The very clearing that was surrounded by huge thick webs and massive spiders.

For all he knew, they were walking right into their lair. The very heart of the J'ba Fofi's domain. *Well, we cannot make it too difficult for this nest of gigantic spiders,* Lance thought humourlessly.

It was not long before the men came across their first web. Great silky strands were weaved in between various branches. If he did not know they were in such danger, Lance would have found these sticky webs quite beautiful. They had a graceful purity to them. Shining like lines of mist in what sunlight reflected on them, it was almost difficult to think of these almost ethereal structures as anything but what they actually were. Sticky, invisible traps to snare any living creature unfortunate enough to not see them, to then be cocooned as soon as they were caught, only to be consumed later. Such was the harsh reality of nature, he mused.

The sight of the deadly wisps caused Quent to stop, his breathing and gasping becoming faster and louder. Lance also stopped and turned around, raising a finger to his lips. Urging, in fact pleading to the man to be quiet. He tried to calm himself but he was clearly terrified. Quent put a hand to his mouth and tried to control his gasps. The sobbing sounds of the man resonated much louder in the silence of the forest. Lance began to wonder how good the hearing was of the J'ba Fofi.

Tropical Rainforest,
The Democratic Republic of the Congo,
July 22,
12:35pm (Congolese and UK time)

Quent's whimpering breaths continued as the two men walked, ducked and avoided the vast webs which were sporadically woven between the dense trees and undergrowth. The other man was thankfully quite quiet as they navigated a path through the jungle, which would cause the least disruption.

The presence of the webs only confirmed that they were closing in on the centre of the J'ba Fofi territory. He only hoped that this obvious fact would not send Quent's sanity over the edge and expose their presence here. The last time they were here the place was alive with the huge spiders. Lance wondered if the absence of their presence this time was good or bad. Though it made no difference really. This was the arachnid's home turf and they were trespassing.

It was after only a few more minutes that they came across something that was to potentially send the rest of their trip back to Rivertown into chaos. It was the moment that their path ahead was blocked by the largest spider they had ever seen. Lance had pushed aside a particularly dense bush when they both saw the creature at the same time.

Ten feet away, the impossible animal was waiting. Brown, hairy, gigantic, with a leg span over six feet, this surreal beast in which nightmares were made from was neither moving nor making a sound. His heart jumped into his dry throat as he stopped, Quent's quivering hand gripping his shoulder so hard it almost hurt.

'No. No. I can't do this. No, I can't. I can't! No! No!' His voice became louder and higher pitched until his final words were no more than a shriek. 'Ah no! Ah no!' He had finally broken. The man's last ounce of rational thought or behaviour had suddenly vanished at the sight of this colossal spider. Quent turned and ran wildly back through the forest. He did not follow the route they had entered but in more of a random north-westerly direction.

Lance watched as the man ran, stumbled half crawled through the undergrowth with no thought of where he was going. He looked at the massive creature blocking the path. On a brief closer inspection, he noticed that it was not particularly solid looking. The structure of the animal looked brittle and fragile and almost transparent at the edges. Was it dead? On closer inspection, he realised what had cause Quent to shoot off in a panic. It was not a dead spider. It was not even a spider at all.

It was the shed skin of a large J'ba Fofi. That was why it appeared so big. It was the exoskeleton of one of the spiders. A harmless shell, though still quite terrifying to look at. He had no time to gaze in wonder at such a sight. Quent's outburst had created so much noise that the notion of creeping through this area unnoticed was now gone. The panicked man had also cut through numerous sticky strands of web, so if the noise had not alerted the spiders to their presence, his blind dash through the place certainly would have.

As if right on cue, the forest began to rustle with individual noises of things moving in various parts and in all directions. His heart sank as he realised what he was hoping to avoid was now happening. The J'ba Fofi, whether they had been sleeping or simply waiting, were now suddenly aware that the two men had re-entered their domain.

Tropical Rainforest,
The Democratic Republic of the Congo,
July 22,
12:40pm (Congolese and UK time)

He glanced around frantically, trying his best to remain calm and in control. He could hear them but could not see them, which in some ways was more frightening. There was no point in staying there and he quickly broke into a run and followed Quent. It did not take long to catch up with the man, who was clumsily wading through the thick plants, clearly having no idea where he was headed. Though in truth, neither did he. The phrase stuck between a rock and a hard place once again sprang to mind.

The man heard the younger man approach and turned his head, through still wildly running through the trees. His face was deathly white and etched in pure terror. 'I can't go back there! There's no way! I just can't!' His voice came out between gasps and dry sobs. Lance had no idea what to say to him. He merely followed trying to focus and decide their next course of action. Of course he had no idea where they possibly could go from here.

The noises coming from the forest behind literally felt like approaching doom. Before he could process another thought, the sunlight hit them and they burst out of the tree line right to the edge of the dam he had examined earlier. It looked even more tangled and unsteady up close. He stopped but Quent continued his manic run right onto the floating mass of detritus. The whole structure sunk and creaked as the man scrambled over it. It was extremely unstable Lance could see. '*Quent. Do not move. It could give way any moment.*' The older man seemed to neither hear nor care. His tear-filled face was desperate. 'I can't go back through there! I can't! I'm going back! I'll take my chances with that man and his army!' His voice cracked with fear.

'*Quent. Come back. That thing is collapsing. The LANSPEAK will get us through them. If we run, the rope bridge is not far away. We can make it.*' It felt his pleas were falling on very deaf ears now.

'I can't go back! I'd rather be shot than be…than be…' His voice trailed off into wracking sobs. Lance was about to type again when an ear-piecing scream erupted from the terrified man. The look on the man's face was truly horrific to behold. With a renewed fear, he turned his head to look at what Quent was seeing. And immediately wished he had not. The trees were filled with J'ba Fofi. Smaller than the ones they had first seen on this journey but it was still a horrendous sightseeing so many of these huge arachnids scuttling swiftly through the branches like eight-legged monkeys.

Panic now gripped him and he too jumped onto the dam. His added weight caused the structure to shift and buckle. He could hear water begin to gush through new openings their actions had caused. Quent tried to run on the hazardous mass of debris but the sudden movements of both men caused the structure to come apart. Lance watched helplessly as the older man fell forward, towards the gradually flooding riverbed. His full weight crashed onto the bough of the dead tree, which had become the base of the dam.

The vast wooden truck shifted in the water, dislodging leaves, mud, webbing, animal bones and anything else which had floated down to settle here. More water began to rush through the swiftly widening gap. It reminded Lance of a canal lock being opened to allow boats through. The water continued to find any access point to flow through.

He glanced behind briefly. The cluster of spiders were watching and waiting intently from the safety of the trees. They were clearly not stupid, he thought. Looking towards the riverbed which now had a fast-flowing stream cutting through it, he saw Quent. The man had fallen from the tree and was now running through the flowing water and down the rocks, which were quickly forming a waterfall.

Knowing there was no choice now as the dam began to break apart beneath him, Lance leapt from his position and onto the dead tree. The tree was certainly dead he discovered as his whole body crashed through the rotten crumbling wood. His mouth filled with dust, dirt and many other tiny objects he did not want to imagine as he fell with a painful thud onto the riverbed which was now almost full with over a foot of water which was rapidly rising.

Lifting his aching body up, he ran painfully slowly through the rising tide, knowing what he was racing against. The rocks were now slippery beneath his feet as he ungracefully manoeuvred his body down the newly formed waterfall and down to the wide riverbed. The water was already churning the vast amount of skeletal remains, forming a grotesque sight. Many parts of numerous animals bobbed and floated in the swirling foaming mass like a giant putrid soup.

The thought of entering such a foetid pool was horrible, though he knew had no choice. He saw Quent at the edge of the tree line, gripping onto the roots of some of the thick plants. He was clearly reluctant to re-enter the forest but had no other option as the rapidly rising water gathered momentum. It was too rapid now to traverse to the other side of the river.

Lance was slowly making his way towards where the man was when he heard the crash of the dam bursting open. A wall of water crashed down the rocks and sent a torrent of foaming forest debris right at him. He was about twenty feet away from Quent when the water smashed into him. The immense weight of the surging flow ripped his feet from under him and he was also winded.

Lance was powerless to control where the rapid water was taking him, though it was only a matter of seconds until he was sucked beneath the surface. What breath he had, had been knocked out of him. He had literally no air as the undercurrent dragged him through the foul water until he crashed into the bank.

His whole body was suddenly wedged into some thick tree roots as the endless torrent physically held him in place unable to move. He had no air and no way of reaching the surface. Focus. He tried to calm his mind. His eyes and mouth were clenched tightly shut, protection from the putrid water. His arms grasped above him and one hand found a solid root. He gripped it and using what strength he had, attempted to pull his body up.

The power of the newly released water was incredible but with one last effort, he managed to lever his body up and gasped desperately when his head broke the surface. Gulping lungful of air before the full weight of the river pulled him under again Lance tried to relax and conserve energy. As a keen swimmer, he was able to hold his breath for up to four minutes if required. Though in this situation, he doubted he could stay submerged for much more than a minute.

He let the new river flow over him. The water was quire cooling after the stifling heat of the forest. The water also felt clearer with each wave. The fast flow of the current was making swift work of flushing the mass of debris, which had built up here, a fact he was grateful for. As the seconds rolled by, Lance felt his body and mind relax. The water cancelled out most of the sounds in the world. All he could hear was the flow of the water churning around him. It had an almost hypnotic quality to it. It felt like he was being cleansed somehow, at least if the water had felt less dirty.

Then the chance he was waiting for happened. The initial surge from the dam breaking had slowly subsided into the normal flow of this small river. It was still a rapid and dangerous current, but he felt confident he could pull himself out. Which he did, without too much effort.

His breathing was rapid as he crouched on the muddy bank. He wasted no time in looking around and listening. There were no signs of the spiders but it was difficult to hear anything whilst being so close to the flowing river. Lance looked at the newly formed body of water. The grim sight of the bone yard was thankfully nowhere to be seen now. He guessed that the water was up to eight or nine feet deep in places. It would be suicide to attempt to cross it. So one thing was for certain, there was only one direction to head in now.

Tropical Rainforest,
The Democratic Republic of the Congo,
July 22,
12:45pm (Congolese and UK time)

Lance hurriedly did a check of himself and his equipment. He had stored everything in his backpack. He hoped nothing was broken from his unplanned swim. The LANSPEAK was intact and well charged. The machete was still secured safely in its sheath. He was wet and covered in mud and other things he would rather not think about. Otherwise, he had sustained no real injuries apart from a few cuts and bruises. He took a moment to catch his breath.

Looking around, there appeared to be no immediate sign of the spiders. Nor any sign of Quent for that matter. His body ached as he stood and intently examined his surroundings. It was then that he heard them. Quent's screams in the distance, the sound getting fainter with each second. The man was moving at least, he thought. Instinctively, Lance set off at a brisk run towards the terrified screams.

It did not take long to orientate himself to the growing desperate cries. Following the screams, he quickly caught sight of the man. Running wildly through the dense undergrowth, the older man was heading in a south-easterly direction. His hands were raised above his head in what appeared to be a blind panic. Lance was unable to type any words due to the fast pace of his run through the uneven ground.

There were no obvious signs of any spiders, but he was in no doubt that many of them were close by. Quent continued to stumble and run towards a dense group of very tall mature looking trees. It was then that he heard a new sound. Over the noise of his running and tired breaths, he heard water. Not as loud as the new river he had just emerged from, this was more a stream in full flow.

He saw the source of the sound, as he got closer. Clearly, the release of the water from the dam had fed into more than one outlet. This had definitely not existed the last time they were here. A mini river, heading towards the steep slope of the trees in which Quent was heading. About three feet across, it formed a divide in the forest floor and Lance found himself running alongside it towards his panicked companion.

The huge trees up ahead were clinging onto a steep slope, he began to notice. The edge of this dip in the land became more obvious the closer he got to it. Quent had stopped running and had also stopped screaming. Lance was looking at the man whose face was etched in silent terror, as he looked at his surroundings. The man appeared to be standing on the crest of the steep ground from which the huge trees were elegantly protruding. It was impossible to see how steep the incline was, though it could not be too severe, he reasoned, judging by the trees growing from it.

His pace quickened as he approached Quent. It was then that the man suddenly disappeared from view. Almost as if the man was playing a practical joke, one minute he was there, the next he was not. He had been standing on the bank of the fast stream when he vanished. Lance had briefly looked behind to check for any chasing spiders and when he glanced back, Quent was gone.

Approaching the spot where the man had been standing, the mystery was quickly solved. The stream led into a small waterfall, which then fed into a muddy water chute. It resembled a waterslide in a swimming pool. Clearly, this small stream of water was regularly flooded with each heavy rainfall. The flow went around a bend in the landscape. Quent must have fallen into this small but strong torrent and been dragged down hill. The solid trees clung to the steep earth, which ran alongside the water, their gnarly roots tenaciously gripping to the side of the slope. The land dipped at roughly forty-five degrees, he guessed, though the flowing water looked steeper in parts as it sliced through the ground.

Whilst he was considering what to do, whether to follow the man or search out an alternate route, a sudden tugging sensation at the water bottle strapped to his belt forced him to turn and look down. His heart momentarily stopped beating it felt like as he gazed in horror at the huge fangs of the gigantic, brown hairy spider tugging at his belt.

Tropical Rainforest,
The Democratic Republic of the Congo,
July 22,
12:47pm (Congolese and UK time)

Lance's mind went into overdrive. The spider was not as large as some of the others, being roughly as big as a medium sized dog. Its two front legs were raised and resting on his leg. He did not notice the touch of both hairy limbs, as it was the pulling of his belt that he could feel. He instinctively recoiled in horror and jerked his whole body away so hard he stumbled back. The huge arachnid let go easily, its initial grip having obviously been quite weak. The creature regained its balance and remained motionless for a moment, its eight dark eyes fixed on him.

Lance was about to press the LANSPEAK to mimic a gorilla's roar when the ground gave way beneath him. Unable to control himself, he tumbled a few feet down the relatively gentle slope, though the loose ground made it impossible to get a grip on anything, until his body suddenly jarred in pain, as he crashed into the trunk of one of the larger trees.

Momentarily dazed, he glanced around frantically, whilst lifting his increasingly painful body up and leaning against the dry bark. The spiders were scuttling towards him en masse, at least ten or more of varying sizes. Lance punched the LANSPEAK and seconds later, a loud primal roar echoed around the area. Like before, the sound of an angry primate stopped the arachnids in their tracks, their front legs aggressively raised in a defensive move.

Whilst thinking that the LANSPEAK was just a short-term fix, a hissing noise from behind made him turn quickly. Coming up the incline between the trees were even more spiders. Some were truly gigantic and approaching at an alarming speed, he was shocked to see. They had cut him off. Had this been planned, he briefly wondered? He doubted these creatures had formed any strategic plan on seeing him. It was simpler than that he knew. The men had wandered freely into their territory and there were just more of them. A lot more, he was now discovering to his horror.

A singular thought entered his head. The only way is up. Making the LANSPEAK roar one more time, Lance quickly began to climb the huge tree. Not glancing back, he scrambled as high as he could and as quickly as he could, in the general direction of the small waterfall. Noticing that large parts of the tree appeared to be dead, he was cautious to hold onto the most solid branches.

It took no time to get over twenty feet off the ground, though he felt anything but safe. The spiders were swarming around the base of the tree, the ground now a mass of brown hair. If he fell now, it would be instant death as soon as he touched the ground. This was not the reason for his renewed feeling of danger though. This feeling was due to the numerous smaller J'ba Fofi, who were now skilfully scuttling up the stiff branches towards him.

Tropical Rainforest,
The Democratic Republic of the Congo,
July 22,
12:50pm (Congolese and UK time)

Lance guessed he had only seconds before the climbing spiders reached him. The LANSPEAK roared like a huge ape once more. The pursuing arachnids stopped briefly at the sound, but continued their chase when they had obviously figured out that there was no strong gorilla sitting in this tree. He had overestimated the usefulness of the LANSPEAK, he thought grimly.

Trying another tactic, Lance set an alternative sound. As the spiders were rapidly approaching, the device roared with a sound as much like a leopard as he could create. This had more of the effect he was hoping for. Some of the creatures stopped and tried to retreat. Some of the arachnids, mostly the smaller ones, dropped from the branches in fear. This was much more effective and he regretted not using this sound first.

Though the noise had worked to some degree, a couple of larger spiders were still continuing their approach, though now much more cautiously. Lance did not want to overuse the LANSPEAK and continued to put as much distance between himself and the J'ba Fofi. Climbing higher and further out, the branches became thinner. The waterfall was almost below him now. He wondered if this strong stream was his only way of escape. Though looking at it, the rocks in which the water was surging over could cause serious injury if he fell from this height.

An unnerving cracking sound caused him to stop and assess his surroundings. This section of the tree so was dry and brittle and further creaking sounds were caused by the largest spider scuttling clumsily onto the branch he was on. Lance made up his mind; he was going to risk the water frothing beneath him. He stood as well as he could, grabbed the thickest branch above him and lifted himself to the next level.

His body was gripping the fragile bough when it suddenly cracked and he found himself slowly dropping, as the broken branch was still loosely attached to the rest of the tree by some fibrous strands of dead wood. Hanging on with his right hand, he was precariously lowered towards the branch below, which now supported one of the spiders.

His left arm dangled down, as the breaking branch knocked him off balance meaning he was unable to press the LANSPEAK. Just as he was about to lift his left arm, the huge spider lunged up, its hairy front legs desperately trying to get hold of his arm. Lance tried to pull away, but the arachnid's weight only caused him to fall further, the branch above him tearing away from the trunk.

A renewed fear gripped him and he desperately tried to stifle a feeling of panic, as he was literally being pulled into the jaws of death. Lance risked a glance down. The massive spider was using its front legs to pull him towards its waiting fangs.

He had never felt so close to death as he did in that moment. The fangs, six inches long and looked as sharp as blades. But it was the gaze of the eight dark eyes that disturbed him the most. They bore into him as if they knew that they had triumphed. It was as if the spider was saying “give it up, you have lost”. As if to confirm that, those powerful fangs closed around his arm and cut deeply into his device. He pulled his left arm up despairingly. The LANSPEAK had been completely destroyed.

Tropical Rainforest,
The Democratic Republic of the Congo,
July 22,
12:51pm (Congolese and UK time)

The action of biting through the LANSPEAK had caused the spider to lose its balance. It was struggling to keep all its remaining six legs gripped to the thinning branch anyway. The creature fell back and futilely attempted to remain on the fragile wood, its focus on Lance momentarily forgotten. The scrambling of all desperate eight legs caused the tree to vibrate. This was all that the delicate bough he was clinging onto required to finally snap completely.

With a loud crack, Lance fell straight down, still grasping the rotten wood. His body crashed into the lower branch, breaking his fall, but only slightly as this too broke cleanly as if it had been sawed through. Both spiders fell at the same time, still trying to hold on to the tree. Their bodies dropped from the falling branch and landed with a sickening thud on the soft earth below.

Lance, still clinging to the dry wood, briefly saw the creatures land on their backs, all eight thick legs thrashing wildly in the air, attempting to flip themselves over. It was a terrifying sight to be falling into. His body crashed into the soft mud at the edge of the water, the branch he was holding, along with the one which had broken his fall cracked loudly and shattered into sharp fragments, some which hit the spiders, causing their bodies to spin around, whilst still on their backs, their legs still thrashing frustratingly.

He had only one second to consider his next move when it was decided for him. The damp ground at the edge of the flowing water suddenly gave way and he, along with large sections of the broken branch and various rocks and leaves were all plunged into the water with the collapsing bank. The last section of the small rocky waterfall made the descent steep, but thankfully, there were no more rocks as his body and the rest of the heavy detritus were quickly caught up in the smooth flow through the muddy chute.

The swift flow of water made sure Lance had absolutely no control of his sudden unexpected journey. His breath had been knocked out of him when he landed and though he was not submerged in the shallow water, his body felt like it was in a washing machine on fast spin. The speed of the flow, whilst also being tangled in what felt like half of the tree he had just fallen out of, caused his body to be pulled in all directions.

It felt like he was plunging through the churning half tunnel for hours, though it was only in fact thirty seconds before the journey came to an abrupt stop. The little river was only about four feet in width, but the sides were steep, smooth and unstable. Lance had managed to steady himself as best he could by using the largest section of branch as a sort of anchor. He was shooting headfirst through the water whilst gripping the log with both arms when he saw ahead that the water was suddenly being forced through a much narrower section.

Two large rocks formed a narrow but open gateway, with a gap of only about two feet wide. The bough crashed into it, wedging itself tight, forcing Lance's body to thrust forward, almost all the way through the tight gap. He managed to hold on to the firm edges, which he was grateful for, as it appeared that another, much steeper waterfall was immediately beyond this precarious gap.

He briefly wondered if this deadly part of the mini river had been Quent's final fate. Without having time to think further, the rest of the debris he had brought with him began crashing into the jammed log. The rest of the fragmented wood all smashed into the new barrier, suddenly restricting the water flow, causing the level to immediately rise. The remaining earth and forest detritus now continued to gush into the new structure. A mini dam was suddenly forming, causing the water to rapidly rise.

He pushed his body away and backed into what he thought was the steep bank, though he suddenly found himself shuffling backwards into a small, enclosed space. Lance looked to his side and saw he had entered an inlet, with much higher sides. The leafy bank to his left had a gentler incline and was only about six feet high in total. It was then that he noticed footprints in the moist soil. Quent. He must obviously have gotten out at this point. Finding himself more relieved, even more than he would have guessed he would be, Lance attempted to stand, but stopped suddenly when he heard a loud hissing from behind.

Not wanting to turn around but knowing he must, Lance slowly turned his body around whilst gently rising to a stand. Not thinking he could see anything more on this trip that could shock or terrify him further, his reluctant gaze settled on a sight, which suddenly, horribly, proved him wrong.

Tropical Rainforest,
The Democratic Republic of the Congo,
July 22,
12:52 pm (Congolese and UK time)

What Lance now saw caused his mind to feel detached from reality. At first, he did not feel fear, more a sense of awe. Then an absurd notion filled his mind. It felt as if he was in a computer game. A realistic, complicated adventure and that he had almost completed this level. All he had to do to win was defeat the big boss. Yes, the big boss, that was what it felt like. The final challenge. Though this particular big boss that Lance was now facing at was not a villain in a game. It was a spider.

But it was the biggest spider he had seen on this trip. His mind tried to focus and grasp the reality of the current situation. Focus. He mentally floated back into rational thinking. Yes, a spider. A female spider was the obvious guess. Set back in a rocky cave was the brown-haired spider queen. The phrase spider queen entered his conscious thoughts easily and found he could not describe her in any other way. He was staring at the J'ba Fofi spider queen.

Her vast body looked bloated, particularly the rear abdominal area. Coarse brown hair sparsely covered the swollen hind section of the gigantic creature. The entire cave had a thick layer of web coating every inch of rock. Her eight legs must have been five feet in length at least. Fully extended her body would be eight feet in diameter at the very least.

Whilst he wondered how her legs were able to support such a solid body, his own question was answered when he spotted the vast thick strands of web, extending from the dense cave wall coverings and wrapped around each vast limb. Her body was literally being supported, almost held up by these silky ropes.

Her head was similar to the rest of the arachnids he had encountered in this place. A brown-haired dome with eight black eyes staring intently, though her fangs were considerably smaller considering her immense size.

The reason, or reasons he knew she was female were scattered around this small inlet. Small yellowish round shapes, roughly the size of golf balls and coated in silky layers of web were randomly spaced throughout the entire area, though they were more numerous closer to the enormous animal. Eggs he guessed, though in fairness he did not know what J'ba Fofi eggs would look like.

He remained as still as possible, half rooted to the spot in terror, half mesmerised at such an incredible sight. The spider queen hissed loudly, her whole body trembling, but unable to move. Lance had an irrational thought, that if he took one-step closer, the gigantic arachnid would break free from her restraints and charge straight at him. He pushed such idiotic thoughts away. Despite her fearsome size and appearance, this was the least dangerous J'ba Fofi he had encountered on this trip, as long as he was out of reach of her legs.

The spider queen continued to hiss and shake her colossal body. It occurred to him that she was afraid. Not for herself but her eggs. She would be powerless if had decided to steal or destroy her unborn babies. Suddenly, he found himself pitying this huge animal. She was simply a mother desperate to protect her young. Like most mothers in the entire animal kingdom. All mothers would die to protect their young, he thought sadly, as his thoughts surprisingly drifted towards his own mother and what she had sacrificed for him.

Lance shook these sentimental thoughts away as they would not get him out of this situation, only his focused wits would. It was clear the easiest way out was the route Quent had taken. Just as he was about to head towards the damp slope, he heard a shout in the distance. 'No! No! Get away! Get away, you devils!' Quent's terrified screams echoed loudly through the relatively silent forest. The man was in trouble. He took a couple of steps towards the incline when the massive spider hissed even more loudly.

Looking at the flowing water, he realised it was not *him* that she was frightened of, it was the rapidly rising water which his dam had caused, which was now quickly filling the inlet, that he now knew was a nest. He cursed himself. The current flow of water was his fault, well his and Quent's to be specific. But the dam *was* his fault. His mind raced. He needed to head towards Quent's cries, as it sounded like the man was in mortal danger. Lance also guessed that the spider queen's apparent helpless state meant that she would not be left alone for long. He suddenly had horrifying visions of some powerful spider sentries appear from nowhere, prepared to aggressively defend their queen to the death.

As if to confirm that dreadful notion, he heard the unmistakable sounds of numerous J'ba Fofi approaching the nest, their multiple legs cutting through the grass, the sounds getting closer. The hissing from the queen became more high pitched, a disturbing shrill sound and one which would attract more protective arachnids to the place. But the piercing sound had been produced out of fear. The water was now leaking into the nest, towards the first batch of eggs, which were secured to the ground. It was clear that the nest would soon be filled with water and that the queen's offspring would not survive. Neither would the queen if it got too high, which Lance guessed could be the case knowing how much water was heading this way.

He knew what he had to do. Something he was certain was suicidal but felt there was no choice. Pushing all rational, practical and sane thoughts to one side, Lance drew his machete, leapt at the small dam and began hacking and kicking at the structure. Most of the debris fell away and was quickly swept of the edge with the powerful flow. The wooden branches were stubbornly wedged between the tight gap. One thing he was grateful for was that the wood was largely rotten and now damp, making it weak. The logs and branches began to break apart with a few kicks, sending them hurtling over the blind ledge.

He heard Quent scream again, though he sounded further away now and his words were unintelligible. At least he was still alive, Lance thought optimistically. The last log, which he had floated in on, was the last obstacle to the flow of water. He kicked it a couple of times but refused to move. Lance began to hack at the soft wood, hoping to weaken it enough to break it. As he was slicing into the bough, he heard a noise behind him. Over the sounds of the running water and his powerful cuts into the wood, Lance heard something large slide down the muddy bank into the nest just behind him.

It was pointless turning around; he could not be distracted from this current task, though his blood suddenly ran cold as he heard eight distinctive steps approach him slowly from the rear.

Tropical Rainforest,
The Democratic Republic of the Congo,
July 22,
12:53pm (Congolese and UK time)

The steps were drowned out by the loud crack of the log, as Lance was able to kick it in half and send it hurtling through the gap and over the edge. Turning around, he was now face to face with a large J'ba Fofi. Its brown hairy body poised aggressively as if ready to attack. He wished he had the LANSPEAK right now but he quickly had to improvise.

The arachnid was between him and the queen, very much like the sentry he had imagined, though at least there was only one of them, he thought humourlessly. The muddy bank was about five feet to the left of the creature. There was no way he could reach it before the spider could. Without thinking, he waved the machete above his head in as threatening an action as he could. The J'ba Fofi remained motionless and it looked like the animal was sizing Lance up as an opponent, wondering how easily it could overcome the man. Pretty easily, Lance guessed.

He glanced around the ground looking for anything to distract the spider. There were only a few rocks scattered about. Lance picked one up and began smashing it against the blade whilst waving both objects around as wildly as he could. The loud chinking sound reverberated around the nest louder than he thought.

The spider raised its two huge front legs, clearly more intimidated by this new sound. Without a second thought, he threw the rock at the defensive arachnid, the missile hitting one of the raised legs, causing the creature's body to lose balance and shift to the right and Lance took his chance and sprinted to the slope leading out of the nest, whilst all the time waving the machete above his head.

He leapt at the bank and used every muscle in his body to pull himself to the top and out of the nest. Just as he was nearly free, he felt a sudden pressure on his right boot and looked down in horror as he saw the huge spider desperately trying to grip his foot with its large front legs. Lance's clothes were soaking wet and his boots were slick with mud and the massive hairy legs failed to get any grip and with a firm shake of his leg, Lance was able to push the creature back and it tumbled clumsily down the bank back into the nest.

As the spider tried to hurriedly re-orientate itself, Lance was now standing and backing away from the nest, slowly re-sheathing the machete. He glanced briefly at the spider queen, which was now glaring up at him, still hissing angrily. Oh, you are welcome, your majesty, he said inwardly, almost allowing himself a small but brief smile.

Tropical Rainforest,
The Democratic Republic of the Congo,
July 22,
1:25pm (Congolese and UK time)

Lance wasted no time in getting away from the nest and ran in a north-easterly direction, knowing that the bridge should be nearby and that hopefully, Quent was heading there too. It had taken them almost an hour to get from the bridge to roughly where the river was, but at a steady jog, it had taken him less time to cover a similar amount of ground. The forest echoed with sounds coming from every direction. This could only indicate that the J'ba Fofi were now on full alert to the men trespassing in their domain.

The steep terrain was uneven but he made good progress heading up the sloping ground towards the general direction of the bridge. It was also a relief not actually seeing any huge spiders, though he knew they were out there, in the trees, in the grass. Lance also assumed that the spiders would be even more hostile now, knowing that the very heart of their territory and been compromised.

Listening intently for any further sounds from Quent, he found himself approaching a clearing. He knew it could not be the same location in which they had first encountered the spiders and the unfortunate Duncan. That area should be behind them he had worked out, although he was not surprised to find himself quite disorientated at this point.

The light became sharper as the trees thinned out and Lance was now running through low bushes but with open sky above him. The heat hit him, but he welcomed the relief to be out of the forest, which had become to feel quite overbearing, though he knew that the local inhabitants had something to do with that.

After running through the break in the trees, he suddenly found himself in familiar territory. This was the way they had come and found the clearing. He knew for sure that the place where Rufus and Duncan's journey had been tragically cut short was behind him. This meant that the bridge was not far ahead of him. Lance increased his speed, as this sudden realisation had given him renewed energy.

His thoughts then focused on Quent. If the man had not made it to the bridge, what would he do? Go back and try to find him. That would be a fatal decision he knew. As if to halt his train of thought, Lance caught a glimpse of the bridge straight ahead. It was beyond some thick trees about one hundred feet away. It was a vague outline, but unmistakably the rope bridge, which had been their gateway into this deadly place.

He entered the trees and swiftly sped through them. It was then that he caught a glimpse of the far end of the bridge. On the opposite side, at the edge of the gorilla's domain was Quent.

Relief swept through him. The man had made it despite everything. This meant they had both made it as the bridge was a mere fifty feet away now. He increased his speed and powered towards the wood and rope structure, which was his exit from this place. As Lance got closer, he wondered what the man was doing. Quent was standing still and crouching toward the ropes, which were secured to the supports. Was he injured? Exhausted? Overcome with terror like Rufus? Probably all three. It was then that the horrifying reality dawned on him as he saw him lift both arms above his head and, with machete in hand, brought it down onto the fragile ropes.

Lance could only gasp in horror as he saw the man feverishly hack at the bridge in an attempt to sever Lance's only link between safety and certain death. He was emerging from the trees now, wishing that he could warn the man of his approach. He waved his arms frantically, and tried to make as much noise as possible whilst running through the forest.

The bridge began to shake and sway as piece by piece its supports were severed. Clouds of dust burst from the old structure as it began to sway as if caught in a strong wind.

He burst through the tree line and hoped it was not too late as he sprinted towards the ancient link between two very different parts of the jungle. Lance was ten feet away from the bridge when Quent suddenly looked up instinctively, just as his machete smashed into the last frayed binding rope. He gazed up at Lance who had just run onto the bridge now. The older man looked at him, though he seemed not to recognise his companion. His eyes had a glazed faraway look, but as soon as Lance's weight hit the bridge, causing it to fall away, the man seemed to briefly recognise him and weakly held out his hand whilst mouthing something incoherent.

The whole bridge dropped suddenly and Lance found himself momentarily in mid-air before he helplessly fell forward. His body crashed into the mossy slats of the falling walkway. He desperately tried to keep hold of the structure as it continued its descent before the whole thing violently jerked as it was pulled into the steep rocky wall, which led back up to the J'ba Fofi's domain.

His body was wracked with pain as the section of bridge he was clinging to, crashed into the jagged rock of the steep gorge. Momentarily stunned, he let go but was shocked to find himself still suspended in the air, his body upside down. One of his feet had become entangled in the ropes and was preventing him from falling. Lance's relief was short lived, for when he rubbed and blinked the thick dirt and grit from his eyes, he was able to see what was beneath him.

The base of the gorge was roughly twenty feet below him, as he was tangled in the centre of the bridge. Staring below, he rubbed his eyes once more, wondering if he was concussed. The dusty ground seemed to be moving. The whole area, starting at the foot of the rocky wall appeared to be swirling, as if it was comprised of mist or smoke. Suddenly, the awful truth dawned. The entire base of the gorge was filled with J'ba Fofi. The brown furry bodies of the gigantic spiders were packed literally wall to wall.

It was no wonder that Quent was desperate to cut the bridge; it was as if the spiders were waiting for him. Like they knew he would be leaving by this route and they lay in wait. Lance pushed that absurd thought away. He needed to focus. Whilst staring down at a carpet of giant spiders, the bridge suddenly lurched and dropped a couple of feet. *This thing will break any second*, he knew and the thought of falling headfirst into that sprawling nightmare was too horrible to contemplate.

Though his entire body ached, Lance used every ounce of strength left to lift his head and twisted his body upright. His hands gripped the ropes that were wrapped around his feet and tried to release himself. Despite the ropes being old and weather worn, they were still intact enough to bind tightly. He looked down reluctantly. The river of arachnids was massing directly underneath him, the smaller ones scuttling over the bodies of the larger creatures. To renewed horror, Lance could see that they were forming a wall of spiders to climb up to reach him.

He managed to free one leg but the other was still trapped. With renewed vigour, spurred on by the terror beneath, Lance reached for the machete, almost slicing into his arm whilst withdrawing the blade and began sawing at the tight rope. It did not take long to cut through, which caused both legs to drop beneath him, leaving him dangling from one arm for a moment.

He gripped the machete between his teeth, re-sheathing it would take too long and began to scramble up the last section of the bridge. Almost losing his grip a few times on the mossy wood, it was a relief to feel solid ground under him once more. But that relief was short lived. He glanced down and saw that the mass of spiders were at the bottom of the broken structure. The climbing creatures were having trouble securing their numerous legs onto the thin slippery slats, though it would not be long before they would reach him.

Think, focus, he told himself. Looking over to the opposite side, over thirty feet away, there was no sign of the other man, though he was not surprised. Knowing he could not survive more than a few minutes on this side of the gorge, he looked up at the vast mature trees bordering the edge of the rocky ravine. If their branches were longer, he could climb across them and jump the rest of the way. Unfortunately, they were not. A sudden thought struck him.

With the machete still in his mouth, he began to pull at what he could see was the longest singular rope, which had previously formed the rail of the bridge. Tugging at the ancient woven cable, he managed to tear free a section of roughly twenty feet in length. The rope was so worn he had not needed the blade, which was quite concerning. Lance re-sheathed the machete then attempted to throw the rope over what looked like the most solid branch, which was protruding out the closest to the opposite side.

Whilst looping the rope over the branch, a sickening cracking sound echoed up from the gorge, accompanied by numerous hissing sounds. Daring to glance down Lance saw that the remainder of the bridge had collapsed under the sheer weight of the arachnid horde. Despite this setback, they immediately continued their desperate plan to reach him, though it had given him a few more vital seconds.

He pulled on the rope with his full weight. The sturdy bough overhead did bend but not break. Wasting no more time, he gripped the rope as high as he could whilst keeping both feet flat on the ground began to run towards the edge swung out as far as his strength would allow. As he swung back, he kicked at the earth, trying to build up momentum for the next swing. Each swing over the gorge became longer, but it was still a considerable distance to the opposite side.

Every time Lance swung closer to the edge, he caught a terrifying glimpse of the amassing J'ba Fofi, their huge hairy bodies reaching ever higher. They would very soon reach the edge he was on. The old rope creaked worryingly with each swing, though the tree above appeared to be supporting his weight adequately.

The swings became longer and Lance wondered at what point he should just make the jump, as he was unsure he was able to gain much more height with each swing. The opposite side was temptingly close when he swung towards it. The tree line, which was the entrance to the gorilla's territory, had never seemed more inviting. Quent remained nowhere to be seen.

The first of the spiders were attempting to crawl their way over the rocky edge of the crevice. He had run out of time. Using all his strength, he swung towards the opposite side of the deadly gorge. He was about to let go, hoping that his height and falling speed would take him across. Then the rope snapped.

Tropical Rainforest,
The Democratic Republic of the Congo,
July 22,
1:29pm (Congolese and UK time)

Once again, he was falling. He was not high enough to reach the solid edge of rock, but his body was travelling through the air quite fast, though heading rapidly downwards. He had no time to think as his sprawling body hurtled towards the solid rock face. In desperation, he reached out his right arm as he smashed into the jagged rocks, slightly relieved, Lance realised that he was gripping firmly onto a dry section of rope, which was left over from Quent's severing of the bridge.

His mild relief was short lived as an intense, sharp pain shot through the right arm forcing him to release his desperate hold. His left arm instinctively grasped at anything solid, as he fell about two feet down the rock face. He managed to grab the last section of rope, the dry brittle strands burning into his hand as he slid down and was dangling helplessly over the death pit beneath.

The pain surged through his right arm like electrical bolts, the limb limply swinging by his side, now useless. Lance's entire body ached and he felt his strength leaving him. Not wanting to look down but unable to lift his head, he saw the mass of spiders begin to scuttle across to his side of the gorge, repeating what they were doing before. As if sensing their prey was now much more vulnerable, they aggressively tried to scale the sheer rock face with renewed determination.

His thoughts began to fade, as he knew escape was now impossible. He had gotten so close to making it out alive, but deep down, he had known that his chances of surviving this place were minute. It was unlikely Quent would be able to survive the remainder of the trip alone now, with his limited resources and no apparent survival skills. He had failed. Tristan, Ezzy and various other faces and memories began to form in his now quite sedate mind. Lance imagined Tristan angry with him and Ezzy very upset.

Finally, the serene face of his long dead mother swam before him. His beautiful, kind mother, Anaisha Knightly believed in reincarnation, which right now seemed very important. Lance suddenly found himself at peace. As if his mother's love was now protecting him somehow. The physical pain lessened and his fears were lessening, even though he could feel a huge hairy leg attempting to grip his boots as he hung suspended above the arachnids.

'Lance! Lance!' the voice cut through him like blow to the head. His pain suddenly returned, as he found himself becoming increasingly aware of his situation.

'Lance! Grab the rope! Grab it!' He still could not understand where the voice was coming from. It felt far away, but bizarrely also inside his head. Was it Tristan? How was he here? In fact where was "here"?

A rough heavy object rubbed against his cheek and he found himself looking at a thick rope scratching his face. Suddenly, his senses began to normalise. He shook his head and stared down at the gigantic spider, which was crawling up his knee, the enormous fangs about to sink into his leg until he quickly shook the limb, causing the arachnid to fall back onto the numerous hairy bodies beneath it.

'Grab it and I'll pull you up!' The voice came from above and Lance lifted his heavy head and stared up at Quent, both hands gripping the rope, which now brushed against his chin. The other man had no idea that Lance had only one useful arm, but he had been given an unexpected lifeline. Without another thought, he quickly grabbed the rope between his teeth, ignoring the foul-tasting dirt, which caused him to cough. Letting his mouth briefly take the strain, Lance let go of the frayed rope he was clinging to and grabbed the offered line as firmly as possible.

His body dropped briefly as Quent took the strain and, very slowly, Lance felt his body being pulled up the rough rock wall. He hoped this rope would hold this time. The J'ba Fofi were still angrily trying to reach him but he was gradually putting a good distance between himself and the massive creatures.

His ascent remained slow, with numerous pauses, for Quent to catch his breath, he imagined. Lance wished he could help but he was incapacitated with his injured arm, which now was throbbing painfully. It did not take long for him to reach the edge of the gorge. He stared up at Quent's red, sweating face. The man looked as if he was about to pass out.

Lance shuffled his aching body onto the flat, solid ground away from the gorge and sat, regaining his breath. Quent let the rope slide away and knelt towards the younger man, his body shaking with exhaustion. 'You okay, man? We need to move right now,' he asked between gasps. Lance shook his head wearily and raised his left arm, showing the man the broken LANSPEAK. 'Terrific,' was all he could say. Lance then painfully pulled down his shirt, far enough to reveal his dislocated shoulder. The older man's face suddenly went white as he gazed upon the severely bruised and misshapen joint and he put a hand to his mouth. 'Oh no. That's…that's just… What're you going to do?' His face looked quite revolted.

As if to reply immediately, Lance stood gently and shuffled over to the nearest large tree and gritted his teeth. From behind, he heard Quent's voice 'No way, you can't…' His protest was cut short as Lance rammed his shoulder into the solid trunk and winced, as the pain shot through him like internal lightning. The sickening sound of the head of his humerus violently being snapped back into place caused the older man to make a retching noise.

The pain caused Lance to fall to his knees, his entire body now shaking with pain. 'Get moving!' The sudden shout from Quent forced him to turn and see the older man run towards him. Just behind, a couple of smaller J'ba Fofi could be seen scuttling over the top of the rocky edge and were now stealthily creeping their way. Lance needed no further incentive to move his tortured body, stood as fast as possible and joined the older man in a run to get as far away from the gorge as possible.

They manoeuvred through the dense trees and he allowed himself a final glance back and could see there were now three huge spiders, though none had made up much distance. Lance secretly hoped that their interference here had not been too damaging. His thoughts went back to the leopard and the fact that they had drawn the arachnids into its territory, which had probably cost the great cat its life.

Looking back, he managed to get one last sight of the unreal spiders before the forest blocked his view. The creatures had now stopped. Please go back he said to himself. Please do not force a confrontation between spiders and apes. The last now stationary arachnid disappeared behind thick leaves and he sincerely hoped that would be the last time he ever set eyes on a J'ba Fofi.

Tropical Rainforest,
The Democratic Republic of the Congo,
July 22,
1:40pm (Congolese and UK time)

They had been jogging at a steady pace for about ten minutes when Lance stopped suddenly, grabbing Quent by the arm. The older man looked puzzled as his companion put a finger up to his mouth, indicating him to be quiet. The area was suddenly very familiar to him. The forest was now alive with birdsong, which was reassuring, although last time they were here, an alpha male gorilla had chased them to the bridge.

Lance crouched down low and motioned for the other man to do likewise. It had taken roughly ten minutes, at a run, from their first encounter with the apes, to get to the bridge. Which was almost exactly the time it had taken them to jog from the bridge to this point. They had thoughtlessly wandered into the heart of the primate's territory. Both men had been so desperate to be far away from the arachnid's domain that they had almost forgotten this new danger.

There were no obvious signs or sounds of the primates but he knew they were close by. This was their home. He sat down in a patch of soft grass and rested his aching body. There were very parts of him that did not hurt and he knew that if the angry male gorilla spotted them, there would be no escape. His body was too weak and the LANSPEAK was useless now.

The other man seemed to sense Lance's overall fatigue and slumped his shattered body down beside him. The younger man rummaged in his bag and checked all its contents. Despite what his body had been through, such as near drowning and being eaten alive, his equipment was remarkably intact. The night vision goggles were thankfully still working, even though it was as saturated as his other belongings. He took out his notepad and pen, grateful that he had kept them in a waterproof bag. He scribbled a few words down and showed them to Quent. *I think we should stay here until it is dark.*

The older man read the suggestion with a bemused look on his face. 'Really?' his voice cut loudly through the forest, forcing Lance to raise his index finger to his mouth.

'Sorry,' Quent said in a whispered voice. 'Do you think that's wise? Last time we were here, King Kong nearly killed us. And we don't even have your gadget to help us this time.' His voice remained hush but it gradually became louder as he continued. The younger man wrote more.

'*We startled them. It was natural for head of the family to want to protect his own. If we stay here out of sight until we have darkness cover, we should be able to walk out unseen.*'

Quent shook his head as he read. 'Out of sight? How do we do that?' the man enquired with renewed concern. Lance nodded his head to a huge fallen tree a few feet away from them. Its vast thick roots had pulled a section of earth up, creating a small basin, complete with the base of the fallen tree as a solid edge to it. He wrote more. '*That is deep enough to hide us if we place a few branches over us. It will be dark in about four and a half hours.*'

Quent read the next part of the plan. Lance was grateful when the man actually nodded wearily. 'Why not?' he replied with a sigh. Both men knew they were exhausted and that this was possibly the best idea to staying safe, or as safe as they could be in such a place.

As quietly as possible, the men used their machetes to cut away the thickest branches from the fallen tree and soon had constructed a crude cover to the basin. Some large leaves were placed over the stacked wood and it produced a remarkably effective covering. Tristan would be proud Lance smiled inwardly. Without delay, they both climbed into the small opening at one edge and pulled as much stacked wood and dead plants as they could to form a seal.

The heat was still intense but the shade was welcome. Lance wrote more and handed the final instructions to his companion. '*We stay here until it is fully dark. Which will be at about 6:30. Until then, stay as quiet and still as possible. When it is dark, I will wear the night goggles and lead us both out of here.*'

Quent took longer to read the message in the poor light. He merely nodded in compliance. With that, both men tried to find a comfortable spot in the knotty earth and wait patiently.

Tropical Rainforest,
The Democratic Republic of the Congo,
July 22,
10:58pm (Congolese and UK time)

Lance woke up suddenly in total darkness. His entire body was aching; the right shoulder feeling like it was on fire. His sudden movement also stirred Quent into waking, who coughed, then yawned loudly, causing the younger man to jab him with a finger to be quiet. Not allowing for the sheer exhaustion of them both to be a factor, Lance realised that they had slept and for a considerable time. They both had needed it, he guessed.

It was still warm, but the forest was much quieter now. Lance had no idea when sleep had overcome him. He remembers hearing many noises as the afternoon slowly drifted by. Some sounds were clearly the apes, though none of them had seemed too close by though that was only whilst he was awake. Pushing "what if" thoughts to the back of his mind, where they belonged, he searched in the darkness for the night vision goggles.

All that mattered now was that although both men had slept for a considerable time surrounded by imminent danger; they had survived unharmed and now had the cover of darkness and the advantage of being more prepared this time. The goggles fitted over his face and once again, the world was transformed into an ethereal low-lit green environment.

Quent had wasted no time in gathering his things and stealthily looked for the small exit of their temporary den. Lance put a hand on his shoulder and quietly crawled past the older man and crept slowly into the inky black forest, which looked an unnatural green to him. The older man followed closely behind, his hand holding Lance's backpack loosely.

There was no way to communicate between the two men now and Lance hoped that his companion would trust him to lead the way as quickly and quietly as they could away from the reach of the gorillas. He knew the forest was much more intimidating for the other man, as the darkness was almost total. There was no moonlight and the trees were thick with leaves. Quent could not see his hand if he held it to his nose, so he was now totally reliant on the younger man for his very survival.

Lance was grateful that the man was being quiet and compliant. Their near impossible escape from the J'ba Fofi must have made Quent realise that Lance knew what he was doing when it came to staying alive in such a hostile environment. This renewed respect, along with putting the arachnids firmly behind them had given the man a much-needed boost in energy and optimism. He one hundred percent believed that this remarkable young man was more than capable of getting them safely back to Rivertown unharmed.

They slowly waded through the long grass, knotty roots, mud and small bushes, Lance looking in all directions when able. An uncomfortable thought at the back of his mind regularly reminded him that the J'ba Fofi were likely to be nocturnal. Though he was reassured by the fact that there had been no sign of them since they had fled from the wrecked bridge, it was as if their presence could no longer be felt. It did not stop him being on high alert though.

Making slow and steady progress in an easterly direction, he was confident that their exit from the ape's domain would be a lot smoother than their escape from the spiders. His optimism may have been premature, he thought suddenly when out of nowhere, a huge male gorilla casually strode right across their path, stopped and faced them.

Tropical Rainforest,
The Democratic Republic of the Congo,
July 22,
11:12pm (Congolese and UK time)

Lance stopped immediately, causing Quent to momentarily stumble into the man's back, though thankfully he made minimal noise. The great ape, Lance was unsure if this was the alpha male, though he was big enough, stared curiously in the direction of the two men.

They tried to stay as still and silent as possible, even attempting to control their breath sounds. Lance's heart was pounding so loudly in his chest he was surprised the gorilla could not hear it. The huge primate made no attempt to approach and this absence of aggressive behaviour was reassuring. He was unsure how good a gorilla's eyesight was in total darkness. Though this was his natural habitat and if his eyesight was poor in such conditions, he assumed all the animal's other senses were well attuned to this environment.

The massive primate then sat down and began to scratch himself, almost as if he was toying with them. Lance and Quent did their best to become invisible as the seconds turned into minutes, though they felt like hours. It was almost as if the ape was waiting for them to make the first move. It was difficult to know if he could sense them on some level or he was merely just sitting in their way.

Attempting to walk around the animal would certainly alert him to their presence. The gorilla appeared very relaxed as he continued to scratch and grunt lightly a couple of time, causing Quent to involuntarily squeeze Lance's backpack. He realised that the older man had no idea what had caused them both to stop but again he hoped the man trusted Lance's judgement. The younger man was also grateful that the ape had grunted a few times, as it revealed to Quent that it was indeed a gorilla in their path, not a giant hissing spider.

After what seemed like hours but was no more than three or four minutes, the massive ape stood back up on both arms and legs and slowly began to trek back to the dense trees. Momentarily stopping and sniffing the air, the primate had soon disappeared into the bush. Lance waited a further two minutes to make sure he would not be returning imminently and then he gradually took a few furtive steps in the direction which they were heading.

Both men managed to keep their noises to a minimum. There was no sound coming from the area in which the gorilla had entered. It was a good sign. They gently increased their pace, eager to put distance between themselves and the ape but not wanting to rush and make unnecessary noise. They were not out of danger yet. They would probably not be out of danger until they reached Rivertown, he thought realistically.

The minutes rolled past and still no sign of the ape or any of his family, but he knew he could not be complacent. Their journey through the dark forest was slow but constant. After twenty minutes, Lance picked up the pace and they were now confidently strolling through a pitch-black unspoiled wilderness. And for the first time on this trip, he felt an unburdening sense of genuine relief. And most importantly, he managed to smile to himself as a powerful sense of hope warmly overcame him.

Tropical Rainforest,
The Democratic Republic of the Congo,
July 23,
3:14am (Congolese and UK time)

They walked through the night, their speed gradually increasing until they were vigorously striding through the pitch-black forest. Stopping for refreshments only sparingly, they were making remarkably good progress. Lance worked out that they roughly had a twenty-two or twenty-three hour walk back to Rivertown. Each step felt closer to safety and further from danger.

Having slept for most of the previous day, they were both wide awake and Lance took the decision to make up as much ground as possible whilst the forest was sleeping. Though as if to go against that decision, Quent suddenly slowed his pace right down until Lance could hear the man panting in behind him.

In the surreal green light, he saw the older man crouch down with his head in his hands. The man's whole body was trembling and looked as if he was struggling to stand as he took his rucksack off, letting it fall to the ground. 'Mate, I don't feel too good. Not good at all.' His voice sounded strained and suddenly he slumped down to a sitting position, his shaking hands cradling his head. Lance knelt beside him and took the torch from his backpack, relived it was still working.

Quent's face was shocking to look at. His skin was deathly pale but was also dripping with sweat. Huge beads of water covered his face and neck, giving him the appearance of someone who had just climbed out of a shower. Lance placed a hand on his wet forehead and was startled to feel how hot he was. The man possibly had a fever. 'I feel cold,' he croaked, as his body shivered uncontrollably.

Lance sighed silently to himself. This was all they needed. The older man has become acutely unwell. He should not have been surprised, knowing how incredibly unprepared Quent had been for this trip. Though most diseases, which were well known in this part of the world usually took much longer to show symptoms. He had no way of knowing what the man had contracted, how he had gotten it and had no way of treating him.

His overconfidence had been premature, he miserably thought. 'My head's pounding.' Quent's voice sounded weaker each time he spoke. 'I reckon it might be this.' He continued wearily, as he pulled up the left leg of his trousers to reveal a thin cut to the skin, which was already looking red, swollen and painful. A glazed smile spread across his sweating face. 'They got me. I needed proof and they happily obliged.' He smirked briefly then slumped back into the long grass.

Lance quickly checked the man, but he appeared to have passed out. He felt his pulse and it was rapid. His breathing seemed laboured and the feverish chills were still causing his body to tremble. There was absolutely nothing Lance could do and he hated feeling so helpless. He poured some water on the wound to try and clean it, though knowing it was a useless gesture. The infection was deep within his body. *Had a J'ba Fofi really bitten him?* He wondered. How did he escape if they had gotten so close to him? Though he reminded himself that he too had been bitten and it was thanks to the LANSPEAK that he too was not injured.

Gazing down at the desperately ill man, he knew there was nothing to do right now but wait. Wait and see if Quent would still be alive by the morning.

Tropical Rainforest,
The Democratic Republic of the Congo,
July 23,
6:12am (Congolese and UK time)

The dawn sun cutting through the trees was already warm. Lance had not slept at all, as he was constantly checking on any changes to Quent. After about an hour, his breathing had become less laboured and rapid and he seemed to have rested properly. His body was still sweating and he looked pale. The wound looked even angrier in the daylight.

As soon as it was light, Lance had sorted out the final rations he had left, which were not a great deal. The water was still full and clean enough, he hoped. Gently squeezing the older man's shoulder, he wondered how unwell he had become overnight. The fever could have made him delirious. Either way, Lance needed to find out. Increasing the pressure on the man's shoulder, Quent's eyes began to blink open. They were bloodshot and looked even redder against his deathly pale skin.

Struggling to focus, the older man seemed to mouth something but no sound came out. His eyes quickly shut again and Lance wondered if he had drifted out of consciousness once more. After an endless amount of seconds, the tired eyes blinked open again and managed to focus on his companion's face. A vague recognition seemed to register and he once more moved his mouth, this time a croaky voice whispered. 'What? Where?' His head shaking in confusion.

Lance's body ached as he used his full strength to sit Quent up. The older man's body was a dead weight but he also did not resist. He sat, or rather slumped on the dry ground. Before he could attempt to say more, Lance raised the water container to the man's lips and he began to drink ravenously. He drained the bottle and began gasping heavily once finished.

Lance was momentarily alarmed, thinking that the man was choking, but after a minute, his breathing slowed and he gradually calmed down, though his body still trembled slightly. He felt his head, and it did feel cooler since last night. The older man gazed up at him, a glazed almost dreamy look on his flushed face.

'What a night.' He sighed heavily, his eyes trying to focus on the concerned face staring down at him, though not making eye contact.

'I feel wasted,' he said, shaking his head weakly. Lance took out some of the last remaining food rations and handed it to him. Quent ate the food gratefully, the urgency in which he downed the water no longer present. The younger man took out his pad and pen and began to scribble a question.

'Are you able to walk?'

The man initially looked at the paper as if he could not understand the writing, though eventually he slowly nodded his head.

'We need to get out of this place, mate. It's killing me.' He smiled thinly as he spoke.

After a few more minutes, the older man stood up shakily and took in some deep breaths whilst stretching his limbs. Lance hoped that the infection Quent's bite had caused was only mild and that he had come through the worst of it overnight. Though when he took his first cautious steps, he now had a significant limp. A couple more steps and the limp seemed to lessen. He gingerly began to put all his weight through the injured limb, confident that he was not causing further harm. Once he was sure, the man put his backpack on, and began to bend both knees a couple of times, checking if he could bear the extra weight. He felt satisfied he could.

Lance watched this positive progress with enormous relief. If Quent were unable to walk, then the twenty-three-hour trek, which lay ahead of them, would have been near impossible. He began to gather his things together and was already thinking ahead. It had been an uneventful journey when they had first travelled through this part of the forest. His only concern, apart from Quent's state of health, were their desperate lack of provisions. The man had finished off all the food that they had, though he had needed it. Lance could not remember if they passed any flowing water on their way up to this point. If he were unable to find some fresh water quite soon, dehydration would be a serious problem for them both.

As the older man slowly but confidently walked up to him, Lance knew that they had no choice but to proceed and just hope that they found water sooner rather than later. Together, the two weary companions began what they hoped to be their final part of this unreal journey.

Tropical Rainforest,
The Democratic Republic of the Congo,
July 23,
9:58am (Congolese and UK time)

After walking for less than four hours, Lance was concerned at how fatigued *he* felt. They had walked in the shade the entire time, as the trees were dense. Though they did prevent the fierce direct sunlight reaching them, the huge plants did not do much against the oppressive heat. It felt like walking through a sauna. There had been no sources of water so far and he could feel himself getting more dehydrated with each passing hour. Quent was keeping up, but he wondered how much farther the older man could go in such a weakened state in this heat and not hydrating.

Stopping regularly to rest did little to help, as they had nothing to drink. Lance did not feel thirsty, though his mouth was dry and his tongue felt like sandpaper. He had to conceal feelings of panic as the seriousness of their current situation became more and more apparent.

He almost laughed to himself. On this trip, he had survived falling from an aeroplane, escaped from a ruthless warlord twice and, more amazingly, had not been killed by giant spiders or angry gorillas. But the way he was feeling now, they could ultimately be defeated by dehydration. That thought almost seemed ludicrous to him. Pushing negative scenarios aside, he continued heading east at a pace, which he knew Quent could keep up with.

Another hour passed and the heat seemed to intensify. Lance began to curse himself for not being prepared enough for the entirety of this trip. He had not factored the older man's needs into his planning. His personal quest to discover the truth of what happened to Rufus and Duncan should have been his alone. He knew he was probably fit enough, rational enough and focused enough to have endured this journey as quickly and as safely as possible. Though he knew the discovery of the J'ba Fofi, which he previously was certain only existed in local folklore, was an unexpected surprise.

Lance put this train of thoughts out of his head. It was pointless to dwell on what could or should have been. This was the current situation they were in. It was the only thing that mattered right now and the only thing worthy of his current thoughts. Though right now, he had no idea how he was going to get Quent and himself through the next eighteen hours of forest with nothing to sustain them. The only way was east, he doggedly told himself and continued to head in the direction of Rivertown.

Two more hours passed and Quent's pace was slowing by the minute. The man had nothing left physically. It was surprising that he had made it this far. When they took another rest break in the coolest area they could find, which was still uncomfortably humid, the weakened man slumped against a tree and closed his eyes. His exhaustion was complete. He fell into a deep sleep, his body clearly craving rest. It was also craving fluids, which unfortunately were in short supply right now.

Lance looked at the man. It was impossible to hope Quent could muster any more strength to continue the journey. He wondered how much energy he had himself. It was then that he decided that he must leave his sick companion and go in search of water. Both their lives now depended on it.

Tropical Rainforest,
The Democratic Republic of the Congo,
July 23,
1:11pm (Congolese and UK time)

He made a circular walk around the entire area for over three hours. No water was to be found. He cursed himself inwardly, as he felt like this should not be a problem for him. He had learned his outdoor survival skills from Tristan, who was a seasoned, senior member of the SAS. But as hard as he searched, there was no water here. A few times, he used his machete to hack at some plants or vines to try and source some precious life-giving fluid. The most he found were a few moist areas inside the vegetation, though not enough water to drink, let alone collect.

With a helpless feeling of despair, he reluctantly decided to return to the area in which he had left Quent. It was another two hours walk in the fierce early afternoon sun. The merciless heat seemed to absorb every ounce of energy he had left which each step he took. There were unnerving times when he became disorientated and found it a struggle to concentrate and remember the route back to Quent.

Concentration became increasingly difficult for Lance, as he walked towards the area the older man was laying. The forest began to look the same as he neared the spot which he thought he had left his weakened companion. Normally, Lance was excellent at navigating his way through even the wildest and harshest terrain. Right now, it felt as if he had never been anywhere near here before.

Subduing a mild feeling of panic, he continued in the direction he guessed was the correct one. Lance shook his head. Locating Quent had suddenly become guesswork. This was not how he operated. Something was wrong. He had intermittent periods of light-headedness, coupled with thudding headaches. Never feeling so physically weak, it required every remaining part of strength he had to push his fatigued body forward. Through a fuzzy haze, he vaguely remembered the tree Quent was resting beneath, though he was really struggling now to familiarise himself with any part of his surroundings.

Then, as if his memories had become suddenly clearer, he saw the tree and the man slumped beneath it. He was too exhausted to feel relief. It felt like he was sleep walking with his eyes open. Seemingly taking hours to walk the fifty feet towards the man, Lance felt his legs give way. As if the nerves had been switched off, his legs collapsed beneath him a few feet away from Quent.

He lay on his back and gulped in deep dry breaths in an attempt to stay conscious. His last thoughts swam in his head. He could hear the older man breathing shallowly nearby. He was still alive, he thought vaguely. Three words kept swirling through his fevered, sleepy mind. I have failed. The phrase kept repeating itself as clouded memories from his life tried to rationalise his situation. His few friends and family floated into his darkening vision. I have failed. I have failed Quent. He will die out here when I should have saved him. I have failed Dan and Fim. The precious information I was to bring back to them will forever be lost with me. I have failed Tristan and Blake. They warned me this place was too dangerous to come to. I have failed Ezzy. She never wanted me to risk my life for a story. I have failed myself. I wanted to make a difference. I wanted to help. But now, I just need to rest. The thought of rest was Lance's final thought, as he slipped into unconsciousness.

Tropical Rainforest,
The Democratic Republic of the Congo,
July 23,
8:20pm (Congolese and UK time)

'Lancelot! Lancelot!' The voice sounded far away, like it was being shouted from the other side of a long tunnel. 'Lancelot, my friend! Wake up!' The distant voice became louder. Clearer. What was being said? The voice was French, which only added to Lance's confusion. He had no concept of time or place. His body felt like it was floating in a pool, completely submerged and shut off from the outside world. It was a comforting place to be.

'Lancelot!' This time, the voice was louder, directly in his ear. Lance felt the warm breath of the voice on his skin. It awakened his senses slightly. Someone was shouting at him. His eyes were closed and the darkness was welcoming, but this peaceful state was then disturbed by a light shining on his face, causing his closed eyes to automatically clench at the sudden brightness.

'Wake up, my friend.' The voice seemed closer now. Lance then heard other sounds, possibly other voices close by, which all merged into one low hum. He felt no fear. In fact, he felt very little of anything. All he wanted to do was fall back to sleep and forget everything. The voice (or voices) began to drift away as oblivion held out its arms to welcome him back. He was fading away to the jumble of voices getting fainter and less understandable.

'Lancelot, don't die!'

'They're both in bad shape.'

'The other one has a nasty wound.'

'Probably heat exhaustion.'

'Can't believe they're both alive.'

'We need to get them back before it's too late.'

He knew these words should mean something, but they did not. They were irrelevant. Everything was irrelevant. Nothing mattered now, nothing was important. This was peace. Pure peace. Something he had rarely, if ever known in his entire life. Why should he fight it? He belonged here. It felt right. Nothing should disturb this wonderful state of contentment.

This blissful state was, unfortunately, Lance thought, not to become a permanent feeling, as he felt his entire body suddenly being pulled up by strong arms. Searing pain flashed through his muscles and as he vaguely felt himself roughly slung over something very uncomfortable, then the darkness overcame him fully as he finally blacked out.

Rivertown,
The Democratic Republic of the Congo,
July 25,
8:07am (Congolese and UK time)

Lance's first conscious thought in roughly thirty-six hours was one of curiosity. What was this itchy thing stuck to his right arm. On movement, his second thought was pain, extreme pain in his right shoulder and back. He opened his eyes and found himself staring at a light-brown wall. On attempting to sit up, the pain intensified, but he pushed through it and was able to raise the top half of his body to a sitting position. He was in one of six beds, which were inside a small mud-brick building. On closer inspection, it was obvious it was some form of medical facility. Some basic medical devices were scattered around the room.

The thing causing the irritation in his right arm was an intravenous drip. A clear tube led from the cannula in his arm up to an almost empty bag of saline, which was slowly dropping the hydrating fluid into his vein. It was not the only drip in use in the room. In the bed opposite, a similar device was hydrating the person who lay there. Quent looked to be in a deep sleep. His breaths were deep and loud at times. His face was an alarming colour. Lance could not recall seeing anybody's skin so red. It looked as if the man had been boiled. It did not help that he was lay on brilliant white pillow, the contrast in colours making the redness even more vibrant.

A feeling of relief overcame him. They had been saved. Saved by good people from this village. Probably the same people who had begged him not to attempt the dangerous journey in the first place. Strong emotions overcame him, which he tried in vain to subdue. And before long tears began to fill his eyes, blurring his vision. His breathing became painful as his throat tightened with the uncontrollable sobs, which suddenly welled up from within.

Lance was still slowly crying when a woman entered the room and approached him. She was a middle-aged woman wearing a white apron over a long colourful dress. Her silvery hair was tied neatly in a bun on the top of her head. Lance tried to control his emotional outburst as the woman approached him. Her smile was kind and warm as she placed a jug of water and a plastic cup on to the small table next to his bed.

'Drink. Drink lots.' Her warm and soothing voice was French. Lance felt quickly reassured in her presence. Without another word, the woman, who he presumed was a nurse, clamped the drip and skilfully removed the cannula from his arm. She continued to smile, as she applied gentle pressure to the site. Once satisfied it was not bleeding, she placed a small plaster over the area and nodded, pointing to the jug of water.

'Drink, please. You need to stay hydrated.' With that, she walked over to Quent's bed and began to check his drip. The man did not stir as the woman checked his pulse and wiped a damp cloth across his burnt forehead. He had to stifle feelings of guilt. Both Quent and himself had put themselves in danger on a foolhardy trip. And it seemed to him that medical resources in this village were probably expensive and precious. And here he was taking up a bed and using supplies that these people can ill afford to spare.

It was pointless overthinking such things now, he thought. Getting his strength back was his current priority. Lance poured himself some water and drank the cool liquid with sudden urgency. It was like drinking nectar. His mouth and throat were so dry and the quenching drink was a soothing tonic. As he almost finished the jug, Lance looked up to see the nurse leave the small building. On exiting, she passed two figures, who had appeared in the doorway, both who were now looking directly at him.

Rivertown,
The Democratic Republic of the Congo,
July 25,
8:14am (Congolese and UK time)

'Lancelot!' The unmistakable shout from Pod echoed through the room, just as the child ran towards Lance's bed and placed a hand at his feet, slapping it up and down excitedly.

'Pod. He's still weak.' The deep voice, which came from the doorway, was equally as recognisable. Dan was standing in the entrance, his huge frame silhouetted against the brightness of the morning sun outside. Lance managed a faint smile, as he looked towards the doctor. Pod had stopped banging on the bed as soon as Dan had spoken, but then held up in his left hand something Lance recognised. The LANSPEAK, or what was left of it.

'This thing did not seem to help you much, Lancelot,' he said in as stern a tone as he could manage, though a cheeky smirk managed to spread across his young face. Lance raised a hand in appreciation and nodded weakly. He really was drained of strength. As if realising this, Pod smiled warmly and gave a short wave, as he headed towards the door. 'We will speak when you are better, my good friend,' he hurriedly said, as he slipped past Dan who was now slowly walking towards him.

He nodded towards Quent, as he approached.

'Heat exhaustion definitely, the same as you. Though he could be suffering from heatstroke. He's not woken since we found you both the day before yesterday. The wound on his leg has been cleaned and dressed. Despite the size of their fangs, a single bite is not directly fatal to humans we've discovered. A strange quirk of evolution it would seem.' Dan's deep voice stirred some memories in him.

Lance suddenly recalled the voices of those who had come to his aid when he was slipping into unconsciousness. Pod had been there, Dan too by the sound of it. Feelings of guilt, almost shame overwhelmed him. Dan, Pod and others had pleaded with him not to go on this foolhardy personal quest, but he had gone anyway. His confidence and dogged determination had put himself and Quent in danger. Though in fairness, it was Quent's choice to accompany him.

Even so, he had stubbornly set off against the good advice from people who knew the local area a lot better than he ever could and those same people had put themselves in danger to save Quent and himself. Lance hated that they felt compelled to act in such a way, especially Pod, who he had tried so hard to protect up until now.

The weight of the guilt added to his physical fatigue and he slumped back onto the firm pillow. Dan was suddenly by his bed staring down, once again avoiding eye contact, which made it easier for Lance to look at him.

'You're still tired. I'll come back later,' he said gently. Lance shook his head vigorously. He had rested enough and was keen to talk with Dan about what he had experienced. The doctor nodded and smiled. It was when he smiled that a sudden recognition dawned. It was Dan's face. It had a familiarity about it. Lance had an excellent, almost photographic memory, though facial recognition was his weakness. Simply due to the fact that he could never look someone in the eye or even look at a face for an extended period.

Even though he had met Dan very recently, an overwhelming feeling of familiarity surged through him. He was tired and his thinking was not as sharp as usual. Dan pulled up a chair, which was nearby and sat down, his eyes fixed on Lance. It was as if the older man could read his exact thoughts, though what he began to explain was still a shock.

'Yes. You see the resemblance? It's not even subtle when you realise. The warlord J'ba Fofi's real name is Idrissa. Idrissa Santu. He's my twin brother.'

Lance found it difficult to comprehend how two extremely different people could be related, let alone twins. It was seeing the warlord without his sunglasses when the realisation had occurred. Though he still struggled to accept the connection. The self-titled J'ba Fofi was one of the most evil men Lance had met. Dan was the polar opposite of the warlord.

Dan lowered his head as if being related to such a man was a burden. Without saying more, the doctor reached into a pocket in his shorts and pulled out a small note pad and pen and handed them to the younger man.

'For later questions,' he said with a slight smile.

'Yes. It's very difficult to take in, but Idrissa is my own flesh and blood. It's hard to believe that we are actually identical twins. We share parents, blood and birthdays. And that's all.' It felt as if the man was trying to explain that his brother was nothing like him, though Lance knew this already, but he let Dan continue in his own time.

'We were born in a small village which doesn't even exist anymore. Our mother died giving birth to us.' Lance felt a pang of pain for Dan but merely nodded slowly.

'Back then, if a mother had complications during childbirth, there was little anyone could do. Our father was called Vak and he was the head of the village. We had no other siblings and my father's grief quickly turned to bitterness and anger. My very first memories of him were of a cold, angry man.' Dan sighed but showed little emotion, as he relayed the sad story.

'We only spoke the local language and from an early age, we were taught to be tough, to instil fear in people. Vak felt that fear brought respect.' Lance found himself unsurprised that the man referred to his father by his name only.

'He became increasingly ruthless in his actions. He had a notion of defeat your enemy before they defeat you. And in his eyes, everyone was the enemy.

He gradually forced our village to become more war-like. Forcing many of the young men to attack our neighbours, people we had traditionally been friendly with. And as Idrissa and I grew, we knew nothing of love or even peace. It was Vak who taught us the phrase if you spend long enough in Hell, even the devil will fear you. That was his way of toughening us up and moulding us both into violent, viscous versions of himself.' The doctor looked down, any hint of sadness seemed to be absent. It was as if this cruel life had been accepted years ago. Now it was all just a normal memory.

'Idrissa seemed to adapt well to this upbringing. He readily accepted the way things were. Perhaps even enjoyed it, but I'm not entirely sure. We never, ever, felt safe you see? Our lives were lived in constant fear. Maybe my brother could never see a way out. But I could. By the time I was twelve, Vak was a feared warlord, controlling vast areas with violence and fear. Guns were thrust into our hands and we were expected to join him in his terrors. Idrissa seemed to relish the idea of following in Vak's footsteps. I wanted to follow a different path.' Dan gazed over Lance's head, as he recalled the moment his life changed forever.

'During a more daring attack, Vak attempted to hijack a convoy of trucks. What he didn't know was that the trucks were under armed guard. Government soldiers and lots of them.' The man shook his head bitterly at this memory.

'There was a shootout. Men died on both sides. Some of Vak's men were not men at all. They were boys like us. It did not take Vak long to realise he had made a mistake and retreated. He didn't care who he left behind, probably didn't even care about his sons.' Lance listened intently at Dan's shocking history.

'I knew that even though I was young, my involvement in the attempted robbery would have resulted in severe punishment. But I was anxious to escape this life. During the chaos, I risked my life by hiding in one of the trucks. They were crates filled with uniforms and guns. I hid between them as best I could and waited for two days until we reached the outskirts of Kinshasa. I fortunately had a little food and water to keep me going.' Dan then stood and began to pace near the foot of Lance's bed.

'I was totally alone in a city I didn't know. I couldn't even speak French. But after a few months living rough, I managed to find casual work in a big hotel. I was paid almost nothing but I got a bed and sometimes food. But more importantly I got to meet many interesting people.' The doctor smiled as he recalled this obvious turning point in his life. Lance could not even imagine the hardships Dan and millions of others like him have had to endure throughout their lives. His own privileged upbringing could simply not compare, nor could he try to understand. Dan continued, clearly feeling that he was relieving some mental burden by relaying his story to Lance.

'As I was young, I managed to pick up the French language quite quickly. Largely out of necessity, as most people I worked alongside only spoke French. I did not learn English for a number of years. Not until I met Fim did I actually begin to practice speaking English.' Dan smiled warmly at the mention of Fim's name.

'My English is still not as good as my French I believe.' Lance shook his head. The doctor's spoken English was exceptional.

'It is incredible how one person can save someone so completely. But the incredible Doctor Kazadi did just that. As an incredible person that anyone could wish to meet. Her native tongue was French but her father had ensured she received the best education in his opinion. At an early age, Fim was sent to Cambridge University to study business. Her father was very wealthy.' The doctor noticed Lance's surprise at this revelation and smiled broadly.

'I know, you would not think such a kind, humble and down to earth lady could be sitting on a fortune. She could even be richer than you, my friend.' Lance nodded, eager to now hear more of this fascinating information.

'The DRC is rich in natural resources and Fim's father was a shrewd businessman by all accounts. After his wife died, he doted on his only daughter. He sent her to study overseas to try and train her up to one day, take over his business. Fim had other ideas. It was not long after she arrived at university that she decided to take a different direction in her studies. She abandoned the business degree and began a course in zoology. Of course being as dedicated and focused as she was, she gained her degree in zoology and began in depth studies of primatology. That was where her passions lay. In the natural world of her home country.' Dan sat down in the chair once more and sighed. It was if he had offloaded the hardest part of his story. The rest, Lance hoped, was only a positive tale.

'Well, to cut a long story short, Fim and I became friendly with each time she visited the hotel. She saw something in me, which I couldn't see myself. A desire to do something good in the world, I guess. Lord knows I had seen enough evil in my youth to last a thousand lifetimes. Although she was younger than me, she became a teacher, a mentor. I was reluctant to accept such kindness at first. Being a proud man, I always felt in her debt. But we compromised when we agreed that I would be able to help her with the right guidance and learning.' The doctor leaned back in the chair and closed his eyes, the memory of Fim's incredible kindness still made him grin. A genuine smile spread across his face as he opened his eyes. The white toothy beam could not be more different from the warlord's. Lance had only ever seen a cruel, covetous grin, filled with gold when J'ba Fofi smiled. How different these two brothers were, he mused.

'Fim arranged for me to have a passport and also a study visa, so I could also travel overseas. I studied zoology at the University of Paris. My French was far better than my English at that point. I enjoyed it and couldn't get enough of learning. Fim's faith in me was proven. With my degree, I returned home and Fim and I have been working together ever since. Although she is based in London for long periods, I'm her man here. I will be forever in her debt so I pretty much devote myself to doing what I can at this end.' Dan then leaned forward and sighed heavily. Lance leaned his aching body forwards, listening intently at what was going to sound like less positive information.

'The struggles of this country however, are as real as ever. Civil unrest, even war is always looming. Our government can never agree on anything, as corruption is rife in all areas of it. Much like most governments I think.' Lance found it easy to agree with that statement.

'Fim's money goes a long way in what we're trying to do. As you may know, the DRC contains five UNESCO world heritage sites. One of which we're in right now. The Salonga National Park. I wish more areas of the country were classed as such. But what's more important is what we've discovered here recently. There were reports of apes in this section of forest, but it was only local rumour and nothing official or documented. That was where Rufus and Duncan came in. Fim knew Rufus and, most importantly, believed him fit enough to undertake a fact-finding mission. To document and record concrete evidence of these extremely rare gorillas.' The doctor sighed again, the memory of what happened to Rufus and Duncan still weighed heavily on him. Lance knew what happened was nobody's fault. After a long pause, Dan continued.

'I met Rufus and Duncan here and gave them what little information we had. I knew they would be able to locate the gorillas and more importantly, to keep at a safe distance from them.' Lance was about to write something when Dan held a hand up, guessing what it was.

'No, I didn't tell them about the spiders, for a couple of reasons. One being that they wouldn't believe it and so not take the threat seriously. Two, I thought that if I explained that a ruthless warlord was based in the forest on the other side of the bridge would be warning enough to ensure they steered well clear of that part of the jungle. It was much more feasible and not entirely untrue.' Dan sighed again at the memory of Rufus's return from his nightmarish experience.

'And a part of me knew that Duncan had expressed an interest in the existence of the giant spiders, so I worried that curiosity could possibly get the better of him. I fear this is what happened anyway. Duncan always came across as the most reckless of the two.' What Dan was saying made sense to Lance. It did seem that it was Duncan's curiosity that may have put both of them in the path of the huge spiders. Dan paused again before he continued.

'It was also unfortunate that we were, in fact still are on a limited timeframe. Fim knew that your old friends at CES were making plans to begin mining in this area. Even though this place is a UNSESCO site, if you put enough money in enough pockets, you can make pretty much anything happen.' Lance felt a surge of anger at this unfortunate truth. He took the pad up and began writing. Though the first thing he wrote was a formal question.

Anglais ou français? He handed the pad to Dan, who laughed heartily.

'Oh English please! Fim says my written English always needs some work!'

Lance managed a slight smile as he continued to write hurriedly.

Are CES financing a lot in Rivertown? It seemed to me they are. Including Quent's helicopter trip here.

'That's what many believe. Rivertown has been here for generations. But the new additions are part of Fim's incredibly complex plans regarding this place.' Lance leaned forward, intrigued as much as he was confused.

'Well, as you know, CES were going to use that drone which you managed to crash as surveillance of this place. To have a close look and to evaluate precisely how little disruption their mining operations would cause. It was all propaganda in many ways. They knew exactly the irreversible damage their mining would do to this area. And as you know the drone itself was fitted with some form of explosive devices to make a brutal start on the mining, regardless of any permission given.' Lance knew how ruthless CES were but it still disturbed him to hear such horrendous plans explained.

'As I mentioned, the corruption inside the DRC's government runs very deep. But Fim has used this to her advantage. She knew that CES had bribed some government officials a few years ago to allow them free access to this protected place. So Fim, at the same time, pretended that another company had been given equal access by a different government official. And quickly began building some of the crude buildings you may have seen when you arrived. She's even managed to supply us with limited Internet access. It was a shame to have to do this, but a necessary evil. CES were, as always, occupied with their dirty fingers dipped into many other places in the world. Fim's sudden apparent takeover of Rivertown looked, to CES like an equally unscrupulous company had used bribes to be the first company to stake a claim here.' Lance stared at Dan aghast. This audacious plan of Fim's was inspired. Dan proudly continued to explain Fim's detailed and extremely cunning plan.

'Fim left no detail to chance. She set up a fake business name and corresponded through e-mails various transactions and deals, knowing they would be hacked and intercepted. To anyone but a select few, this area was being prepped for mining and anything else they could find. It worked pretty well. Until…' Dan's words trailed off as his confident demeanour changed to a more subdued one. He sighed and continued.

'Of course, when a company like CES have invested time and money into something, they'll stop at nothing to achieve their aims. It turned out that it wasn't just the fake e-mails that were being hacked. Fim's secret and unofficial communications were also exposed. Oh, Fim herself was safe, as in the cyberspace world she goes to extreme lengths to remain anonymous.' Lance's thoughts led to him thinking of his own secret identity, Black Eyed Boy. And he was also uncomfortably reminded of the technological skills of TEX, who had admitted to working for CES at some point. He decided not to mention this at present. Dan stood once more and continued talking.

'So very quickly, it became clear that CES were no longer fooled by the clever deception. That was when Fim's last chance had to be hurriedly used.' Lance nodded solemnly, as Dan confirmed what he knew.

'Yes. It was only a matter of time before CES simply moved in and started stripping the place, endangering the gorillas and anything else which got in their way,' Dan said heavily.

'Rufus and Duncan were Fim's last chance and her only weapons against CES. It's because Fim's public profile is of a conservationist, based between here and London. He voice and position are well respected globally, in the protection of primates in particular. And publicly, Rufus is respected in his own right as a trusted colleague of hers. She knew that if he and Duncan could bring back solid evidence of some of the rarest gorillas in the world, to present to UNESCO, then CES would be forced to abandon their nefarious plans. What Fim really wants to do is put the evidence out there for the public to see. Twitter, Facebook, YouTube, anything. If the proof of the gorillas living in the exact spot that CES want to mine goes viral, CES wouldn't have a leg to stand on. They would have to walk away if international pressure were put on them. Companies like CES operate in secret as much as possible, only revealing to the public what they want them to know. Their lies basically.' Finally, after many months, it was clear to Lance why Rufus had been so important to Stanmer. If Rufus had provided evidence of the gorillas, CES's illegal activities would have been exposed. Lance scribbled down a blunt question.

'If CES are as powerful and evil as we know, why not simply kill Rufus? Why the elaborate plan to bring him home and try and interrogate him?'

Dan paced for a few seconds before sitting down once more. He shrugged and answered as best he knew.

'Rufus's professional reputation was highly respected within the zoological community. Yes, a company like CES could have made him and Duncan disappear. It would be easy to do in such a place as this. But I believe CES were as eager to discover his findings as much as Fim and her team were. I think they figured that if he hadn't found any evidence of the rare gorillas and admitted it publicly, that would be a green light for them to proceed with their mining.' Lance nodded; it did make sense.

'Of course, neither Fim, CES nor anybody had counted on the two men coming face to face with the even bigger secret of this place. Myself included. Though when Rufus did crawl out of the forest barely alive and having lost his mind, that's when things became complicated. I e-mailed Fim and informed her of Rufus's condition. She was devastated to hear about what had happened to him. And crushed that he was unable to provide the proof needed to protect this place. It was then that we realised how easy it had been for CES to intercept our communications. Before we could act, CES, who already had people in the local area, sent a bogus Red Cross helicopter and whisked Rufus back to London. They wasted no time in capturing him. What they weren't counting on was his fragile mental state. But they obviously figured that with time, he could regain some of his memories. And probably even coerce him into saying things in *their* favour. These people have no soul, my young friend.' Lance nodded. The whole elaborate scam of pretending Rufus had an infectious disease, to moving him around to conceal his location only confirmed to him what CES stood for. There were literally no limits to how far they would go to get what they wanted. Dan was about to continue but Lance quickly wrote another question.

Does Fim know about the spiders? The doctor sighed and slowly shook his head.

'No. No, she doesn't. Oh I've wanted to tell her about them. I almost have numerous times. I trust Fim with my life. But I don't one hundred percent trust everyone around her. And I certainly don't trust our e-mails anymore. I could tell her about the spiders. But being a scientist, she'd want proof. And if I couldn't offer her any, which I couldn't, she'd quickly lose respect for me as a professional, and probably as a friend. I mean I very quickly lost my credibility in your eyes once I told you I believed the J'ba Fofi were real.' Lance nodded, feeling quite sheepish.

'Fim would be the same. I'd become a sort of fraud in her eyes. And I don't want that. In fact, as far as I'm concerned, the fewer outsiders know the truth of the J'ba Fofi, the better. I trust you, Lance. I'm not sure why but I do. And it's not due to the fact that you already have money and would clearly never want fame of any sort.' Lance was impressed by Dan's accurate appraisal of him.

'Of course, others, I'm afraid will obviously not be as discreet as you are about what you discovered on this trip,' Dan said whilst nodding towards the sleeping Quent. Lance wrote quickly.

'Don't worry about him. I'll ensure the secret won't ever be proven.'

Dan nodded, knowing that Lance meant what he said. After a long pause, he began to pace nervously. When he spoke, his voice was full of concern.

'What Quent will or won't say has never bothered me. He's, dare I say it, easy to discredit without hard evidence. No, my concern now is you.' Lance raised a puzzled head a stared towards the tall man.

'All this time, since the day you discovered Rufus had run into serious danger, you've been doing everything to protect him in some way and to find out the truth of what happened to him and Duncan. Which has been loyal and brave of you. In fact, I've rarely met anyone with as much raw courage as you.' Lance turned his head. He hated receiving compliments, no matter how sincere they were meant. But he was now beginning to wonder what Dan was leading up to.

‘But you see what’s happened. CES no longer have Rufus. Thanks to you, he’s in a secure location. Not that that matters to them anymore. They knew his mind was lost. And they didn’t know if he would ever recover from such an ordeal. Nobody can know that. But what they will find out, as finding things out is what they’re very good at, is that you’ve taken his place.’ Lance stared at the doctor, realising what he was saying was unfortunately true.

‘It’s now you, who is holding all the vital information about this place. I mean I’ve seen the evidence you’ve got. Good clear recordings of those rare apes. The e-mail of your findings has already been sent to Fim. But it’s you that is the key now. You don’t hold the same public respect scientifically as Rufus, but if you publicly back up the recorded evidence, that should be enough. But Lance, CES will know this. They will try anything to get to you before you meet up with Fim. From this moment on, my friend, in the eyes of CES, you’re one of the most wanted men on earth.’

Dan’s words momentarily stunned Lance. Though when he began to mentally process it, he found himself not surprised by the statement. As Lance began to think ahead about his next course of action, Quent began to murmur something. Both he and Dan looked over as the man began twitching as his breathing increased.

‘Go… Got. Say… I escay… The queen. The queen!’ Only the last couple of words made any sense. Dan looked back towards Lance, a puzzled look on his face.

‘Did he just say God save the queen?’

Lance shook his head. He had an idea of what Quent was trying to say and it was nothing patriotic he was sure. Lance took a glass of water and decided he needed to speak to Dan in a more private setting. He wrote something down quickly before he slowly dragged his legs out of the bed, placing them on the cool earth floor. Every joint in his body burned with pain. His previously dislocated shoulder was on fire but he pushed past that and stood, feeling dizzy for a moment, then held up the pad to Dan.

‘We need to talk somewhere the walls do not have ears.’

Rivertown School,
Rivertown,
The Democratic Republic of the Congo,
July 25,
8:36am (Congolese and UK time)

Lance held a hand up to Dan who moved forwards to steady him as he lost balance for a moment. The light-headedness did not last, the pain, however was still considerable. After a minute, Lance nodded and waved a hand to Dan, indicating that he was ready for him to lead the way.

Both men walked out into the warm sunshine, causing Lance to shield his eyes. They walked for only a couple of minutes until they arrived at another building. It was another modern structure, similar to the others which were dotted around in between the much more visually pleasing mud brick buildings. This building had a generator outside, the machine's noise getting louder as they approached.

Lance followed Dan into what was unmistakably a large classroom. The rectangular room was sparsely furnished, though numerous windows gave it ample natural light. He counted sixteen traditional wooden school desks, complete with chairs, neatly arranged facing a larger desk and chair. Behind the main desk was a whiteboard. Two small bookshelves leaned against two of the walls, both filled with textbooks. On the desk at the front was a laptop, which appeared to be connected to some sort of projector. Dan closed the door through which they had entered, the only way in or out of the building.

'Come in, young man, and let me educate you further,' Dan said smiling broadly, as he motioned Lance to sit at the large desk, which he did, gratefully lowering his aching body onto the chair. It was a relief to be sitting again, he thought wearily. Dan sat on one of the smaller desks behind him. Lance was facing the whiteboard. He was about to turn to face the doctor when Dan's deep voice echoed through the room.

'Stay as you are, Lance. Just press one of the keys, it should still be on.'

Lance pressed randomly at the keyboard and immediately the small screen was suddenly illuminated. Though not just the screen was online. On the whiteboard just in front of him was the computer screen, projected onto the board. He heard Dan chuckle. 'An invaluable teaching aid I must say. I teach here most days, if I'm not too busy with my other work. A few other volunteers help out, though we don't have enough room for all the children at once. They have to take turns when they come in. But they're all keen and it gives them some purpose.' Dan was clearly proud to be offering these children opportunities, which were denied him. Lance was eager to discuss Quent, but the mention of children made him think of Pod and the other boys. He typed quickly and the words appeared on the whiteboards, large enough for Dan to read.

'Have you learned anything about Pod and the others?'

Dan sighed as he read. 'Yes, quite a bit. And it's not all bad. The boys were all taken when Idrissa's men attacked their local villages, no more than four months ago. Doz, Am and Pod were roughly from the same district. Car as you may know was from further away. They were vague about how they were taken, but if what I know about my brother, those boys almost certainly had family killed by them. But again, they have not said.' Lance closed his eyes, unable to comprehend such evil. He heard Dan sigh deeply, it was clear that every reminder of his brother's brutality was painful to him. He continued. 'That's the worst part. The more positive part, if it can be called that, is that fortunately, not long after the boys were taken, Idrissa's bloody campaign hit a quiet period. Whether he had run out of money, or didn't have enough men to continue, or possibly rival warlords or government soldiers forced him to be cautious. I don't know, but what the boys have told me, that since they were abducted, they have thankfully not seen any real violence. Simply because Idrissa's plans have been put on hold, though not by choice I imagine. Oh I've no illusions of the cruel inhuman conditions in which the boys have been held. But I'm grateful that they were predominantly used as guards and parts of patrols. In fact, finding you was probably the most action they had seen since their kidnappings. And it's clear in their behaviour. Yes, they're traumatised, but I have, sadly seen much worse. I have met children their age who have actually been into a war zone and forced to fight and Lance, children like that are truly damaged. Their innocence has been systematically destroyed.' Dan's voice was sombre again. Lance could not imagine what it must be like knowing your own brother is capable of such horrors. He paused for a moment to let him compose himself before typing.

'I want to help them. The boys. I want to help them get a new start in life. I want to be their sponsor.' Lance never felt comfortable offering his money to try and help or solve a problem. He would, given the choice, always prefer to offer his time. But the boys, Pod in particular, had helped him get here. And Pod had

been there when he had needed help the most. Dan's voice boomed through the room once more.

'Ah, my friend, that is incredibly generous and I would expect nothing less from you. But right now, the boys have all they need. Food, shelter and most importantly, safety. And once they're ready, education too. They will have all that here, largely thanks to Fim and others who contribute. I know you mean well and sincerely wish to help, but there are many people here who simply don't trust outsiders. Particularly, if I may say, white western men. People here aren't stupid and many know about CES and vile people such as Stanmer. And the people here are proud, Lance. They don't have much but what they do have they have earned themselves. Fim doesn't offer them charity, she offers them work and self-reliance. If you suddenly began offering money to help, it could be seen as a bribe. Please don't take offence but CES have been presenting themselves as saviours in this place. And we all know they're anything but. It would be hard for the local people to accept anything from you. And Fim I know would agree.'

Lance turned his stiff neck and nodded an understanding. He completely understood and respected this decision.

'Please don't think we're ungrateful, Lance, but this community runs very well without outside interference. And Fim is so grateful for what you've done for her and her team so far. Pod and the boys will do just fine here. Pod even told me he wishes to become a doctor. And I think he's smart enough. We'll be fine.'

Lance nodded and wished to change the subject as he was beginning to feel awkward. He quickly decided to change the subject to Quent.

'How much do you know about Quent?'

Dan sighed slightly and shook his head.

'I know more than I would like to, as I spoke to him at length the day you arrived here. As you've probably guessed, Quentin Roth has been used from the very start of this complex tale. He's been following your stories for a few years. I think he sees you as some sort of adventurer, which is how he probably sees himself. And somehow he managed to work out that your alias, black eyed boy, was actually you.'

This was a disturbing revelation to Lance. As far as he knew only Blake, the editor of the magazine he wrote articles for knew his pseudonym. Dan noticed that this had come as a surprise.

'Don't ask me how he found out, but I figure he can be ruthlessly resourceful when he wants to be. That's pretty much how he managed to convince Stanmer that he could help them. He basically followed you. And because he knows how you operate, figured you would be heading here straight away. That was all Stanmer really needed from him. They had the technology and financing to track your route to Kinshasa and wait for you there. Quent's reward was of course money, which he used to buy his fancy equipment and the helicopter ride here to continue his personal mission.'

'Quent was under the impression that CES had sent him here as some sort of location scout to assess the area. To check it was suitable.' As Lance typed, he suddenly became aware of how absurd that now sounded. The absurdity was backed up by a quick deep laugh from Dan.

'Ha! Like I say, he's been used. Stanmer kept him in the dark about the reasons CES were here until he was on the plane. Once you bailed out, they continued to Kisangani. Quent said Stanmer was met by some angry senior CES staff and had some explaining to do. They knew Quent was planning to go into the forest anyway, so they simply allowed him to continue his wild adventure here. And of course at that time they thought you were dead. I don't actually believe they sent Quent here for any sort of surveillance at all. They have trained professionals to do that. In fact, they already had. CES know what's hidden in the ground not far from here. They didn't need Quent to have a second look. And of course, thinking you were permanently out of the way, they could proceed with their mining freely. The cynical part of me thinks they sent him here with another plan in mind.'

This intrigued Lance, as he had thought as much at the start of the journey. He typed quickly.

'You think that if they sent Quent alone into the forest, he would conveniently disappear?'

'I'd put nothing past a company such as CES. They thought you were dead, Quent could simply have been the final loose end which needed tying up.' Dan's sombre words were difficult to hear, even though he had also considered such a possibility.

'All he's ever been interested in has been proving the existence of the J'ba Fofi. And I hate to admit it, he wasn't wrong about the spiders.' Dan admitted begrudgingly.

'They were bigger and more numerous than he thought they would be.' Lance paused before writing again.

'And he was not saying God save the Queen earlier. I think he was saying "gotta escape the queen".'

Dan said nothing for over a minute before he spoke.

'You're not saying?' he asked incredulously. Lance nodded slowly and said nothing.

'You came across… What? A queen? A spider queen?' His voice rose with excited wonder. Lance glanced at the door to check it was still closed and wrote some more.

'That was the only way to describe her. She was so huge, she was being held up by webs. What appeared to be egg sacs surrounded her. And I know Quent also encountered her.' Dan stood and began to pace the room.

'This is insane. Spiders aren't eusocial creatures like bees or ants. This opens up even more questions about them. Are they even spiders at all?' Dan's voice was rising with excitement.

'Oh, they are spiders all right. No question. They had the legs and fangs to prove it. How we managed to escape I will never know.'

Dan paused and sat down once more. It was a minute before he spoke.

'You both survived the spiders thanks to you. You have a level head and seemingly endless courage. You viewed the spiders as animals, not monsters and acted accordingly. Very few men on earth could have survived such a place.' Lance squirmed uncomfortably at the praise lavished upon him and quickly steered the conversation in a different direction.

'The bridge which led to their territory has been destroyed. We saw the warning just before the bridge. I am guessing it was not written by you. But by who?'

Dan shook his head. 'No. I've never been that far into the forest. Not even close to it. I'm not a field man. It was actually put there by one of Idrissa's men. Well I say men, though boy would be more accurate. It was during Idrissa's quiet period, he didn't have the men or money to maintain control in certain areas so he resorted to using fear as much as possible. One such method was placing warning signs in places he wished to control, but couldn't. He thought that if he made people believe certain areas were under his control, then he still had control. His phrase is well known to anyone who knows his reputation. So one day, he orders a sixteen-year old boy to take a boat to the edge of the gorge, which ran through the forest. The boy's name was Hursan. Hursan did as he was told and dutifully walked up the gorge until he came to the bridge. The sign was already written, so he simply nailed it to the bridge post. It was a dangerous task for anyone, let alone a child. Though that didn't concern my brother. Though Hursan being a curious boy decided to cross the bridge and do a bit of exploring, part of him wondered if he could even escape from Idrissa. Of course it wasn't long before he saw one of the spiders. One of the younger ones I think, but still gigantic. Luckily for Hursan, the spider was alone, though it began to slowly follow him. He needed no convincing to turn around and run. Though once he crossed the bridge, he decided to take a different route. He entered the gorilla's territory. Once again, he was lucky. Only a young female saw him. And he followed the forest all the way to Rivertown. He was one the first people to have witnessed seeing the gorillas. Well one of the few to return alive that is. He made no secret that he was one of Idrissa's men. Many in the village didn't trust him, believing him to be a spy. But I trusted him. And eventually, he became accepted here.' Dan nodded his head slowly. 'I'm glad the bridge is destroyed. The warning not to cross should've been warning enough to stop the inquisitive from doing so. It didn't work on curious Englishmen very well though, did it?' Dan said, unable to contain a smile. Lance nodded. He looked back at Dan as much as his aching body would allow.

'I am very grateful you came to rescue us. I am forever in your debt.'

Dan smiled warmly and lifted both hands as if in surrender.

'When you didn't return, I asked some villagers if they would accompany me, at least at little way into the forest. Pod was the first to volunteer. I wasn't happy with him coming along but I couldn't really stop him. It was an easy decision to make on my part. After seeing the state Rufus was in when he returned from there, I had to see if I could help. A few men came with me, along with Pod. Hursan actually led the trip, as his knowledge of this area is unquestionable. Though he admitted he would not go any further than the gorilla's territory. We agreed that if we didn't find you before then, you were sadly on your own. You fortunately weren't hard to find. And, no, you're not in my debt. Fim, myself and everyone else in Rivertown and the surrounding areas are in *your* debt. You've hopefully saved this area from CES and others like them with the information on the gorillas.'

Lance nodded and shrugged, then turned to the computer screen. He felt tired but also glad he had spoken at length to Dan. Though what the doctor had said only confirmed his next course of action. He knew he needed to return to London as soon as possible. He began to type.

'You know I have to return to London immediately. But I cannot take a direct route. Can you help me?'

Dan could not contain his surprise at Lance's unexpected announcement.

'Well, are you sure you're up to it? You're weak and still recovering.' Dan asked with genuine concern.

'If I rest today, I think I will be okay by tomorrow. That is, if you can help me.'

'Help in what way?'

'Help me head south.'

'How far south?'

'As far south as I can on this continent.'

'You mean South Africa?' Dan asked incredulously.

Lance nodded. '*It is the only place I can leave quickly, directly and undetected. I could easily sneak out via various routes. But that would take far too long and time is not on my side. Can you help me? I need to get to Cape Town.'*

Dan slumped in the chair and shook his head. 'Lance, do you realise that Cape Town is almost three and a half thousand miles from here?'

Lance nodded; he had already worked it out in his head. He knew this was his only way getting back to London in the shortest time possible. Time was now running out.

'I think the quickest way is to head to Kisangani and catch a flight from there.'

Dan nodded. 'It's short notice, but there are flights, though not directly to South Africa,' he said putting his hands to his face, thinking for a moment. 'If you can get down to Lubumbashi, I know a man who could help you.'

'Lubumbashi, in the far south?'

'The very same. It's a big city and it's close to the border with Zambia. It's the mining capital of the country, which will put you at an advantage if you can get there.' Lance turned to face Dan a questioning look on his face.

'The exports into Zambia are frequent. And I know someone there…' Dan's voice trailed off and he looked around uncomfortably, as if checking they were still alone. Once satisfied, he continued.

'An old friend of mine, Leopold Faida. He's based in Lubumbashi where he works for some of the mining companies. He drives trucks to Zambia and, well beyond.' Dan stated, looking like he had just revealed something top secret.

'Beyond? What do you mean?' Lance asked, though he had an idea at what Dan was talking about.

'Leo and I go way back. In fact, back when I had nothing, he found me work. And no, it wasn't always legal. But compared to the life Vak was offering, it was honest work. Leo is a smuggler. And believe it or not, his services are in high demand from people at all levels.' Dan looked at Lance, trying to work out what the younger man was thinking. Lance merely shrugged and nodded, much to Dan's relief.

'It's not as underhand as it sounds. Leo's not a thief. He just transports goods for people who don't want to go through the proper channels. And in a lot of places, the proper channels are corrupt and quite illegal themselves. Yes, he does it for money, but he is a moral man. And in the past, he has even transported people out of war zones. And not taken money, I might add.' Dan clearly thought very highly of his friend and that was good enough for Lance. He had realised quite early on that when dealing with companies like CES, who operated outside of the law, he would have to fight equally as dirty. Lance turned again to Dan and nodded confidently.

'I will be grateful for his help.'

Dan smiled and he too nodded. 'Okay, how're you planning on getting to Lubumbashi?'

'Are there flights there from Kisangani?'

Dan grimaced. 'Well yes. But the route is via Uganda and Ethiopia.'

Lance shook his head. '*That is no good. I need an internal flight only. I need to stay off the grid as much as possible. It could be okay but it feels too risky to use an international flight. Not before I get to Cape Town. Could I get to Lubumbashi by road?'*

Dan shook his head. 'The roads between Kisangani and Lubumbashi are unreliable to say the least. It could take you weeks to get there.' Lance lowered his head. There must be another way. He had come too far to now be defeated by delays in transport. Dan stood and walked up to Lance so he was facing him.

'Well, how did you get here in the first place?' It was a question Dan knew the answer to, but asked anyway. Lance shook his head, knowing what the other man was suggesting.

'I came here onboard The Monsoon. A jet owned by CES and controlled by Stanmer.'

'Wrong,' said Dan excitedly. 'You came here onboard The Monsoon. Which is a private jet, which is for hire to anyone who can afford it.' Lance looked up, mildly confused.

'What are you saying?'

'I'm saying that neither CES nor the DRC government own or control The Monsoon. Anyone can hire it. In fact, Fim once used it when she was stranded. Stanmer certainly doesn't control it.'

Lance was genuinely surprised.

'Oh the government use it all the time. But they only hire it. As did Stanmer.' Lance thought back to when he had met Stanmer once the jet had taken off. Quent and Stanmer were hiding inside. He knew now the reason for such secrecy was that the jet was not CES property. If Stanmer had presented himself to Lance before boarding the aeroplane, Lance would not have even considered boarding. This new information was very welcome. He remembered his utter shock at seeing that Stanmer and Quent were already on board, despite him going to such lengths to travel undetected. It was obvious that both men had been on the same flights as him, and had simply kept out of sight. They had boarded The Monsoon right before him, giving the impression that they had eyes everywhere. The truth was much simpler. It seemed that CES did not have as much power in this country as they made out. Lance began to type.

'So if the price is right, I could hire The Monsoon to fly me down to Lubumbashi?'

Dan smiled and nodded. 'Now that sounds like a plan.'

Rivertown,
The Democratic Republic of the Congo,
July 25,
1:16pm (Congolese and UK time)

Lance's conversation with Dan had given him a much-needed boost of energy. His mind was running on overdrive since it had been bombarded with information. He was not complaining though, these facts needed to be heard. And they strengthened his resolve to return to London as quickly and discreetly as possible.

The two men had spent the rest of the morning planning Lance's next journey. Between them, they believed they had formed a solid plan. Lance went online and booked two tickets on a commercial flight out of Kinshasa on July 30. They were booked in his own name for Quent and himself. He was relying on Dan to ensure Quent would make that flight, as long as he was fit enough. His own journey would not take him anywhere near the capital city.

Dan had messaged his friend Leopold in Lubumbashi, checking that the man was able to meet Lance as soon as he arrived in the city. The doctor had also arranged Lance's journey to Kisangani. It involved travelling by river, then road. And the earlier start, the better. Dan was still trying to convince Lance to rest for a few more days, but the younger man had made up his mind. He was adamant the journey would begin tomorrow.

He managed to rest throughout the day and when not resting, Lance was planning his journey. He dried out his backpack and cleaned what clothes he had as best he could. Intending on travelling as light as possible, Lance packed the bare essentials. Dan had supplied some food and water which should be enough for the journey, though he no plans to trek through any more forests. The pack now contained the note pad and pencil, the GoPro, the binoculars, the compass and his spare clothes. He decided to leave the night vision goggles here. They would be more useful to Dan and his team than they would to him right now. Lance also returned Dan's torch and machete, grateful that he only had to use the blade on plants.

It was when he was busy packing that Lance began to think of ways to fund his trip home. His money had gone as he met the warlord. He had plenty of money in numerous bank accounts throughout the world. It was accessing the funds that might prove to be difficult. Companies like CES could possibly track his movements if he used a well-known bank to withdraw large sums of money.

It was as he was considering his options that Dan approached him with yet another solution. The older man grinned and winked as he handed Lance a large brown envelope.

'Before you protest, it's not a gift. It's an interest free loan from Fim.' Lance was slightly puzzled until he opened the envelope to find it was stashed full of money. American one hundred-dollar bills. He looked up, shaking his head.

'Fifty thousand US dollars, cash and it's not up for negotiation. You, me and Fim know that using a bank could give away your location. We keep cash here for emergencies, which includes bribes, possibly even ransom money when Fim is here. This isn't all of it, so don't worry, you're not clearing us out.' He informed him.

Lance knew this was the most decision, but he felt uncomfortable taking such a large amount of cash from this place. He wrote down quickly.

'I will pay Fim back as soon as I return to London.'

'We know you will; it's all good. Right now, your need is greater. And you're right, we need to get you back to the UK as soon as possible. Keep a few notes within easy reach for quick use.' Dan grinned, as the younger man gratefully took the money. He wrote quickly once more.

'How well does Pod read?'

Dan raised his eyebrows and he continued to smile and nod. 'Oh, he's good. We've encouraged him to take lessons at the school, which he's eager to do. He's a bright young man and with a good education he could have an even brighter future.' This was music to Lance's ears. He wrote more.

'Could he meet me at the school anytime soon?'

Dan nodded. 'I'll get him to meet you there right away.'

Lance nodded gratefully and headed towards the school building.

Rivertown School,
Rivertown,
The Democratic Republic of the Congo,
July 25,
1:38pm (Congolese and UK time)

Lance was waiting at the computer when Pod walked in, an excited look on his face.

'Lancelot! You are stronger. I knew you'd be good. You're strong.' As the boy approached, Lance nodded, smiled briefly and pointed to the screen at the front of the room and began to type in French.

I am going to speak to you. Can you read this?

Pod nodded and took a seat close to him, the enthusiasm he had on entering seemed to be fading quickly.

'Firstly. I want to thank you for coming to rescue us in the forest. Quent and I owe you our lives. So I'm grateful for your bravery. So thank you.' Lance let the child take his time to read and as he did, so a look of pride spread across his face. He smiled sincerely. 'Of course. You saved us, I save you. That is what friends do. And we're good friends, aren't we, Lancelot?' Lance nodded and began to type.

'We are good friends. I am glad we met. But it also makes me sad that I have to leave in the morning.' Pod's face went from proud to shocked. Lance gave him time to process what he had just been told. Guilt began to creep into his head, as he saw Pod's young face quiver with emotion. 'You're leaving?' His voice was strained as if he was fighting back tears. 'You have not been here long. I thought you would stay longer. You need to get better.' The pleading note in the boy's voice only added to Lance's feelings of guilt. He shook his head and typed more.

'I am feeling better thanks to you. I would have liked to stay longer but I need to get back to England. I need to help some people there. They need me to make sure this beautiful place stays protected.'

Tears began to well up in Pod's eyes as he read further. 'We need you here too.' The desperation in his voice was difficult for Lance to hear. As he was about to type more, Pod suddenly spoke again. 'I could come with you.' The words fell heavily in Lance's ears. He was worried this might happen. He had been the first person to show the boy any kindness in such a long time, it was natural he would form an attachment. Throughout his adult life, Lance had never considered the prospect of being a parent or guardian. The mere idea of it rarely occurred to him. He had enough problems coping with life. A child, he always knew would only add pressure to his fragile mentality. He had never disliked children, but firmly believed he was incapable of looking after one. Add to that, his life was spent on the move, rarely staying home for any length of time. And he also knew that if he did decide to bring Pod back to England, the legal implications of the boy's care would be equally as stressful for himself as it would be for Pod. Bringing him home with him was not an option. He was careful with the next words he typed.

'Pod. You are brave and strong. And we are lifelong friends. But right now, you need to stay here. Doctor Santu needs you to help him. I am always travelling, often to dangerous places. I do not want you to ever be in danger again. You have been through enough.' Even as he watched Pod's watery eyes read what he had written, Lance wished he could feel more empathy towards the boy. The child needed love. Deep unconditional love and Lance knew he could not provide it. His feelings towards the boy were strong, but they mainly felt dutiful. He had felt a firm obligation to help Pod and the others the moment they had met, to protect them with his life if he had to. But he felt he could not love the boy as a son. A friend, yes but not a son. He could not be what Pod so desperately needed right now. Lance had too many emotional barriers up, which would always prevent Pod from getting the affection he needed and deserved.

The boy stared at Lance once he had read. What was written probably felt quite cold and unfeeling in Pod's interpretation. In the boy's mind, Lance was basically saying, 'I'm leaving, you stay here.'

Pod tearfully nodded his head. Guilt rushed through Lance so fast he felt queasy. He was about to type more but was at a loss of what to say. As he pondered this, Pod let out a high-pitched sob and ran crying from the building. It was pointless going after him. He had no LANSPEAK and clearly, the boy did not want to talk any more.

Lance slumped back in the chair. *I am utterly useless at human interaction,* he jadedly told himself. He closed his eyes and tried to focus his thoughts. His mind was scrambled and it unnerved him. Thoughts of Pod's crestfallen face haunted his thoughts. His mind played different scenarios of how differently he could or should have handled his conversation with the boy. Whichever way it played out, the boy would always be disappointed.

The minutes began to add up and before he knew it, he had been sitting for over an hour. His body ached but his mind hurt more. He sighed and looked up to see Dan standing in the doorway, the solid frame of the man blotting out most of the sunlight. His face had a weary but serious look. Without saying anything, he tossed something to Lance. He caught the camera, which he had recently retrieved from the skeletal hand of Duncan. Dan and himself had viewed the final recording and it was horrific viewing. It showed the terrifying last moments of Duncan's life. It also proved the existence of the J'ba Fofi. This recording was firm evidence of the most important and incredible zoological discovery of modern times. It also showed a man being killed. Lance felt ghoulish watching it. Both men were sickened after seeing it. They both agreed that nobody should ever see the recording. Dan's deep voice echoed through the room.

'Someone's awake and wants to discuss what's on that camera.' Lance sighed, as he saw Quent, limping with the aid of crutches, enter the schoolroom. His red face full of excitement, as he brushed past Dan and hobbled towards Lance. The younger man faced the keyboard. *Well*, he thought. *I might as well destroy the hopes of two lives instead of one whilst I am on a roll.*

Rivertown School,
Rivertown,
The Democratic Republic of the Congo,
July 25,
2:48pm (Congolese and UK time)

As the man weakly shuffled over and sat near him, Lance knew this would be another guilty action to add to his day. But at least he knew he was morally justified. Dan had left, knowing what Lance had to do. Quent at least deserved some privacy.

'Man, I feel rough. This place doesn't agree with me.' Quent's face was red, though not as severe as it looked this morning, Lance thought, glancing briefly at the man. He was surprised at his mental state though. Quent had seen unimaginable horrors and been close to death numerous times just as he had. Lance thought the older man would mentally be more like Rufus when they had returned. Though there were two reasons why Quent's sanity had remained largely intact, Lance mused.

Firstly, neither of them had witnessed the horror Rufus had. They had managed to escape with their lives. Rufus had seen his soulmate attacked and killed by giant spiders right in front of him. Spiders, which should not even exist in reality. That was enough to destroy even the strongest mind.

Secondly, Quent's very reason for being here had been proven to be right. Years of ridicule and mockery were about to be turned around. He was going to finally be vindicated, as he saw it. Proving the existence of the J'ba Fofi would bring long overdue fame and fortune in Quent's eyes. Which made what Lance had to now do all the more difficult. He began to type.

'Could you give me your bank details please?' Quent was immediately puzzled by such a question.

'My bank details? Why?' he asked curiously.

'No time to explain. We have to sneak out of this country. My bank account could be being watched. I need to transfer funds into your account to cover our tracks.' Quent looked even more confused. But when Lance typed nothing more, he reached into his belt, which had many attached pockets and pulled out his bankcard. Lance's own bank account flashed up large on the screen. With a few pushes of buttons, he transferred two hundred thousand pounds into Quent's account.

'Whoa! That's a serious chunk of cash. Why would we need so much?' Lance sighed and typed some more.

'Actually, it's compensation. For you.' Quent shook his head.

'I don't understand.'

'I am compensating you.'

'Compensating? Me? For what?' Quent's voice began to rise with uncertainty. Lance held up Duncan's camera and pressed the play button. The small screen began to play the grisly demise of the unfortunate man. Quent gazed at the screen with morbid fascination.

'That's my proof. The proof I've been searching for my whole life.' A sly grin spread across his face. Lance felt sickened by the man's lack of empathy about what he was watching. Quent then let out a scream as the younger man pressed a button and deleted the entire gruesome scene from existence.

Rivertown School,
Rivertown,
The Democratic Republic of the Congo,
July 25,
2:50pm (Congolese and UK time)

'Nooooo!' Quent's anguished cry filled the room, as the man lurched forward in a futile attempt to stop what had already happened. His weakened state caused him to stumble forward, his flaying hand knocking the camera out of Lance's grasp. The device smashed loudly on the floor. Lance stood to steady the other man, who aggressively shrugged away any attempts of help, choosing to clumsily stumble backwards into another chair. His red face was panting and his entire body shuddering, with what Lance guessed was a combination of anger and exhaustion.

For what felt like hours, both men sat in silence. Which for Lance was easy. It was Quent who broke the peace. 'Why? Why?' was all he could ask weakly. Lance began to type as Quent looked up.

'I think you know why. Those animals need protection.'

'Protection? From whom? From what? From where I was standing, they looked like they were planning an invasion.' His voice began to rise with emotion.

'Quent. You know as well as I that if news of those creatures reaches the western world, this whole area will be put at risk. This whole country possibly.' Quent shook his head.

'You're wrong. It'll be like discovering a dinosaur. People from all over the world will want to come and study them. Find out more about them. Who're we to deny them that? The world deserves to know about them.' This time, it was Lance who shook his head. The naivety of this man staggered him at times.

'The last thing these animals need is for the world to know about them. The less people know about them, the better. You know that if they were discovered, this whole place would be overrun with people. Rivertown would be taken over. Its inhabitants probably moved around, their homes lost. Too many people would probably do more damage than the planned mining operation here. The gorillas would probably become extinct, with so many people destroying their habitat by

marching through it to get to the spiders. And do not get me started on what some people would like to do when they found them.'

Quent shook his head again. This time appearing confused as to what Lance meant.

'How long do you think it would be before rich trophy hunters descended on that place? Fat rich dentists and similar from America and other places would pay top dollar to hunt and kill these things.' Quent shrugged.

'Not necessarily. They'd have a lot of publicity. People would just want to see them. Study them.'

'And people would pay blood money. Men with powerful guns would come here to prove how tough they are by killing the biggest specimen they could find. Then have it stuffed and mounted on their wall. You know this would happen. It would be inevitable.' Quent looked down, as if pondering on whether this would happen. He again shook his head and looked up.

'We could stop all that. These creatures are unique to the world. They're incredibly rare.'

'There lies the problem. The rarer the animal, the more valuable they become. Capturing one of them alive to take back to a zoo would make a lot of people extremely rich. You know this to be true. Quent, exposing the existence of these animals would seal their fate. No matter how well they were protected, they would soon become extinct through greed and cruelty. It is a harsh truth, but the only outcome. They must remain a secret.' The older man's face was deep in thought. His mind mulling over what he had been told. Lance hoped to have convinced him.

'Okay. So why are you so keen to expose the gorillas? You said yourself they're just as rare. Why show them off to the world? Don't they need protection too?'

Lance stared at the man aghast. He was beginning to lose patience with him.

'The evidence of the gorillas needs to be made public to ensure their survival. Proof of these animals needs to have as much public support to prevent CES from commencing mining operations here. If the world knows they're here, CES will be forced to abandon their plans, no matter how much money they've invested.'

'But what's the difference?' Quent's question sounded almost laughable to him now.

'The difference is that the world has already seen gorillas. And most importantly, don't want to see any more of them killed as they're becoming rarer and rarer with each passing year. People have already accepted the existence of these animals. Asking them to simply get used to the J'ba Fofi would be impossible. You said it yourself; it would be like discovering dinosaurs or even aliens. They would never be left alone to live in peace and thrive. Unlike the gorillas who would be given that chance.'

Quent was silent for a long minute. Without saying anything, he stood up, and wobbled for a moment before limping over to the camera on the floor and groaned as he leaned forward to pick it up. Without a word, he sat back down and studied the camera, a mirthless smirk on his face.

'Well, this is broken,' he said flatly. He looked up, a vague defeated expression on his tired face. 'So what do we do now?' His voice almost devoid of any emotion.

Lance typed some more.

'I leave tomorrow. I'm taking an alternate route out of the country. I have booked a flight for you in a few days. A commercial flight back to London.' Quent stared ahead and nodded wistfully. 'Well, okay. I guess I'll see you around.' With that curt comment, the older man stood shakily and hobbled out of the building without looking back.

Lance leaned back in the chair, concerned by Quent's sudden apparent acceptance of the situation. He found it hard to believe that a man who had spent many years trying to prove the existence of mythical animals, then to finally find them only for it to be snatched away would accept such a decision. Lance had a strong feeling that he had not seen or heard the last of Quentin Roth.

Rivertown,
The Democratic Republic of the Congo,
July 25,
9:19pm (Congolese and UK time)

The darkness brought little relief from the heat Lance thought as he settled down onto a hammock, which was tied up in one of the buildings near Dan's office. The two men had spent most of the day discussing what had happened earlier and what was planned for the days ahead. Lance was still feeling incredible guilt about Pod and Quent. Dan did his best to reassure him that he had done the right thing, which unfortunately did not alleviate these feelings of remorse.

The two men had walked around the village, as they talked and Lance was surprised at how large the place was. It did not seem so big when he first arrived here, largely due to the fact that the place seemed to be a very narrow settlement squeezed in between the river and the forest. It was narrow but also very long. As the men travelled the length of the village, Lance discovered it had shops, small workshops, a library, a post office and some small offices similar to Dan's.

He wondered how much Fim had contributed to the place, though it appeared that Rivertown's inhabitants were quite self-sufficient and enjoyed a seemingly peaceful existence. On seeing such a vibrant place thriving, Lance's resolve to keep CES away from here strengthened even further.

When they neared the banks of the river, he noticed a boat slowing down as it headed for the small wooden dock, which was further east along the river from the area he and the boys had arrived in. The boat looked similar to a canal longboat, with one man controlling the vessel as it slid alongside the dock. A few men were waiting on the bank to unload what appeared to be essential supplies.

Dan informed him that this was a weekly delivery of goods needed to keep the village going. He said men took it in turns to collect and deliver the stock. When the boat returned, it would take with it some locally produced items, along with raw materials such as wood and hay, which traders would sell at the markets in Kisangani. It was a mutually beneficial deal and ensured the survival of the village.

Dan told him that it would be Hursan's turn to take the boat back the next day. The boat would dock quite a distance up river, where the stock would be loaded onto a waiting truck, which would travel to Kisangani. Lance was informed that this was his way out of the village in the morning.

This low-key method of transport pleased him as he found it hard to believe that CES would be able to track him through such a wilderness. Lance began to mentally plan the onward journey. The hardest part would be finding The Monsoon and hoping it would be available for hire. Dan had reliably informed him that his friend in Lubumbashi would be able to transport him to South Africa as quickly and as secretly as anyone could.

Once they had returned from the river, both men had a meal together. Dan had supplied Lance with non-perishable food for the journey, though he insisted it was only for emergencies. They agreed to meet at the dock at sunrise. Lance tried to clear his head so he could get the rest he needed prior to the next step on this journey.

Rivertown,
The Democratic Republic of the Congo,
July 26,
6:11am (Congolese and UK time)

Lance had been awake for over an hour before he got up, ate a light breakfast and headed towards the docks. Even though it was still quite dark, he could remember his route to the boat as clearly as when he was actually there. The first light was beginning to break through the trees on the horizon, as he walked towards the river. The day was already warm, though it has not really cooled down overnight and the red sky in the distance was an indication of another hot day to come.

To his pleasant surprise, Dan was already waiting for him, a warm welcoming smile on his face. As he approached, he waved his hand at a young man sitting at the helm of the boat. 'This is Hursan, your guide for the next day or so.' The man, who looked no older than eighteen, waved and smiled broadly. Lance held up a hand in greeting as he descended the slight incline leading to the river. As he got closer, he noticed a smaller figure standing next to the boat, whose presence had remained hidden due to their outline being disguised by the silhouette of the boat from a distance away. Lance was pleased to see that it was Pod.

The boy was smiling shyly, which made Lance feel a huge sense of relief. As he approached Dan, the boy ran up and threw himself at Lance, almost knocking him off his feet. Glancing down at the embracing boy, he could see tears in his young eyes. Though his face did not have the distraught look it had yesterday. It was a face filled with emotion but not bitterness.

'I could not let you leave without saying goodbye to you, Lancelot. My good friend Lancelot.' His voice was breaking with emotion, as he tightened his grip around the man's waist. Lance felt slightly helpless, knowing that he could not reply to the boy.

'My friend, my good friend.' He repeated through gentle sobs. Lance hugged the boy back, hoping that was enough of a response to Pod's poignant gesture.

It was almost a relief when Dan walked over. ‘It’s okay, Pod. You know Lance loves you very much, but now he has to go with Hursan to start his journey home.’ Lance felt the boy nod fiercely through muffled sobs. Dan put a comforting hand on his young shoulder and he eventually broke apart from Lance, though looked up at him with red eyes. ‘I know I cannot come with you, Lancelot. But I am glad we will always be friends.’ Lance was struck by the sheer bravery of this boy. It was clearly incredibly difficult for Pod to accept that Lance had to leave without him, but it was obviously incredibly painful to even admit.

Dan put a reassuring arm around the boy. ‘It’s all going to be okay, Pod. In fact are you going to tell Lance what you would like to do when you’re older, provided you study hard?’ Pod looked up at Lance with a look of hope in his eyes.

‘I am going to be a doctor, Lancelot. When I am big, I want to help people.’ It was now Lance’s turn to feel overwhelmed with emotion, a feeling he never liked, as he had no control over it. He hugged Pod tightly, as he felt tears well in his own eyes.

When they parted, Dan raised a hand, which Lance gratefully shook. ‘You’d better get on board; you’ve a long journey ahead.’ Lance nodded and made his way towards the boat. As he was climbing onboard, Dan’s voice spoke from behind.

‘Oh just a couple of things. Firstly, you never asked the name of this river you’re about to travel on. Lance thought for a moment. Dan was right. He had no idea which river this was, though he knew it was not The Congo. He shook his head and raised both hands in acknowledgment.

‘Well, I’m still not going to tell you. The fewer people who know this exact location, the better.’ Lance smiled and nodded in agreement.

‘And secondly, when you see Fim again, tell her I’m still waiting for her answer,’ Dan said, adopting a sly grin and winking at the younger man. A cheeky almost childlike look spread across his face before he laughed knowingly. Lance had no idea what he was talking about, but smiled and nodded. Giving Pod and Dan a little wave, Lance took a seat in the chair next to Hursan, who extended a hand in greeting, which Lance accepted.

The boat then gradually pulled away from the tiny dock. He felt waves of emotions as the waving figures of Dan and Pod slowly drifted further from view. *Two incredible people*, he thought, as they disappeared when the boat turned in a bend in the river. He was in awe of such people. His entire life he had struggled with his mental health, emotions and coping with life in general. It was upon meeting such people as these, who had endured more pain and suffering in their lives than anyone should be put through, but still remained positive, optimistic and still saw the good in this world. He felt truly humbled by his newest friends, as the boat chugged its way through the river towards his next destination.

**A river,
The Democratic Republic of the Congo,
July 26,
1:29pm (Congolese and UK time)**

They had been travelling constantly for over seven hours. The heat of the midday sun was intense. Lance felt awkward that he could not readily communicate with Hursan, though he guessed that Dan had informed him about Lance's lack of communication. The young man had made no attempt to engage in conversation at any time, though he kindly offered him food and drinks and even a wide brimmed hat when he could see Lance struggling under the intense glare of the sun.

He pointed at Hursan's watch, hoping he would realise that Lance was wondering how much longer they were going to be travelling for. The young man held up a hand with three fingers, which Lance took to mean three hours. He nodded gratefully. The total time they would spend on the river indicted just how isolated Rivertown really was. Which actually gave it an advantage in many ways. He hoped companies like CES would leave this place alone once they discovered the remoteness of the place.

Despite the stifling heat, Lance found himself feeling more relaxed than he had been in a while. He was grateful he had made peace with Pod. As he rested on the river and gathered his thoughts, Hursan's voice startled him.

'So you saw the spiders too?' He spoke French with no accent behind it. And the lightness of his voice reminded Lance how very young this man still was. He glanced over at the man, who was still staring at the river. Lance nodded, unsure if Hursan had seen the gesture. Though he quickly nodded a reply.

'You met the warlord too?' Lance again nodded.

'Bad man, very bad. But I tell you this. I would rather face the spiders again than the warlord.' Lance nodded heartily in agreement. It was at that moment when he realised that Hurasn was possibly the only person in the world (apart from himself) who had come face to face with both the warlord J'abs Fofi and the J'ba Fofi spiders. The young man also reminded him of Pod, which was an encouraging thought.

Hursan had spent a lot longer in the company of the warlord than Pod and the other boys had. And had likely seen more horrors than they. So it was a testament to this man's strength, courage and positivity that he had been able to turn his life around to such an extent. He hoped Pod's life would also continue to flourish, which he was certain it would.

The rest of the journey was made in silence, which Lance appreciated, but did feel mildly awkward that he could not communicate properly with Hursan. The younger man did not seem to mind; in fact, he looked extremely contented, as he steered the boat through an endless unspoiled wilderness, clearly finding real peace in such a beautiful place. He was more similar to himself than he realised, Lance mused.

The remaining few hours passed quickly and quietly. It was late afternoon when the boat slowed and pulled into another wooden dock, though this one was much bigger than the one back in Rivertown. Surrounding the dock were numerous mud brick buildings, some with smoke rising from them. It looked like a much smaller settlement than Rivertown and also much less developed, which gave the place an added charm.

Several men were waiting on the bank to unload the stock onto a small lorry, which was parked nearby. No sooner was the boat moored up than the men scrambled on board and began unloading the small cargo. A majority of the men took the bulk of the stock and began loading it onto the lorry. A small number of them took what appeared to be food and wood and disappeared into the settlement. Lance guessed this was possibly their payment for their services. *If only life was this simple everywhere,* he thought wistfully.

It took a surprisingly short time to load up the vehicle. Lance had tried to help, but by the time he had managed to climb off the boat, the task was virtually completed. Some of the men glanced at him with curious, even puzzled looks, though he did not feel uncomfortable or threatened at any point. He trusted Dan to have arranged a safe route to the city.

Hursan chatted briefly to a couple of the men, causing one of them to laugh out loud whilst glancing over to Lance. The younger man then waved him over and they both climbed into the lorry. One of the men gave Lance the thumbs up sign as he passed them.

The vehicle roared to life, the loud engine sounding like it required urgent repair. Hursan was smiling, as they drove out of the village along a single dirt road.

'Don't worry, my friend. He wasn't laughing at you.' Hursan had to almost shout over the noise of the engine. 'I told them that you stole one of the warlord's boats. They now say you are welcome to have a drink with them anytime,' he said whilst breaking into a laugh.

Lance could not help but smile as their transport gathered speed along the tiny road.

Kisangani,
The Democratic Republic of the Congo,
July 26,
9:27pm (Congolese time)

The journey through the forest road had been much more arduous than the previous journey along the river. The noisy lorry shuddered with very rock and bump it drove over. It was difficult to feel a moment of comfort throughout the entire trip. The progress had started slow but when the wider roads were found they made faster progress. Lance was surprised at how long it had taken to get to the city.

Roughly, five hours by road had ensured every bruise and injury on his body was hurting considerably more now. It was dark, as they entered the vast sprawling city. A large body of water could be seen to his left as the main road took them through the endless buildings. It was strangely comforting to see civilisation once more, considering Lance actively avoided large cities if he could help it. Large crowds unnerved him, even though he lived in London. But his home city was familiar to him and the space his large house had, offered some sanctuary from the hectic world outside.

He was relieved that the city was quite quiet at this time of night. Unfamiliar cities, which were densely populated, made him feel quite panicked if he had to spend long periods in them.

'I will take you directly to the airport. I know the way. It's where I met Doctor Kazadi when she once used this aeroplane.' Hursan's voice startled him from his thoughts. Lance was beginning to understand why Fim based herself in London and left the running of things from this side to Dan. Even though he was a seasoned traveller, he did not fancy making this journey on a regular basis.

The lorry powered through the city, the traffic was sparse as they headed east. It did not take long before they were heading out of the city. The surrounding area seemed more rural, though it was too dark to see much. Various lights were dotted around near the road. Lance increasingly found it difficult to believe that they were headed towards an airport. The area seemed far too quiet and undeveloped.

His doubts ceased when after a few miles the lights of a large structure could be seen in the darkness. As the men approached the building, they turned left onto a side road and followed it round, taking them around the back of the airport. There were many lights on but the place seemed eerily quiet.

The lorry passed the entire length of the building and came to shuddering stop near a cluster of dimly lit buildings at the far end. A tall wire fence separated the road from the interior of the airport. Lance noticed a small gate where a man was sat in a chair reading a book. From this distance, he looked like a security guard.

'Here you are, my friend.' Lance nodded and gathered his bag and opened the door to the vehicle. He extended a grateful hand to the young man who shook it firmly. 'Good luck, my friend. It was nice meeting you,' Hursan said kindly. Lance nodded appreciatively and jumped out onto the road. His whole body ached as he landed. The night was still hot and as he watched Hursan drive away, Lance was overcome by a deep sense of loneliness, which was rare for him to feel such an emotion, as he always preferred working and travelling alone. But right now, he felt like a vulnerable stranger in a large and unforgiving world.

Kisangani Bangoka International Airport,
Kisangani,
The Democratic Republic of the Congo,
July 26,
9:59pm (Congolese time)

Lance pushed any negative thoughts to the back of his head. He had it on good authority from Dan that The Monsoon would be here on this day, so wasted no time in walking towards the gate. The man looked up from his book, a look of puzzlement spread across his face. He was middle aged but still looked fit. As Lance approached, he shone a torch at him and held up a hand.

'Are you lost?' The deep, French speaking gravelly voice cut through the night. Lance was prepared and handed him the letter he had retrieved from his bag. It was a letter Dan had given him. A single sheet, with a message typed in French. The paper was headed as an official government document. Dan and Fim said that often such simple methods could open many doors in this country.

The fake letter simply read that the person holding it should be given access to the next flight available, as it was important top-secret government business. He hoped that it would work, as he had no other documents to prove he was who he claimed to be. The man slowly read the brief letter, then shone the torch in Lance's face. Time seemed to pass slowly and Lance began to think that this man was not convinced by such a basic letter request. *Why would he be,* Lance thought realistically.

As it seemed like the man was becoming increasingly dubious, Lance put a hand into his pocket and pulled out one of the banknotes Dan had given him. The look on the man's face was one of almost disgust. He sneered and waved a hand away. Lance was about to offer more when the man opened the gate and motioned for him to walk through. Lance nodded in gratitude, the man curtly nodded back, though the same look of distaste was still on his face.

Walking towards the small buildings, Lance noticed a bright light coming from one of them. As he approached, he could hear a raised voice. The voice was deep and speaking English in a strong French accent. The view into the building was obscured by wooden roller blinds. He got close enough so he was able to listen to what was being said.

'Forget it! You've caused me enough trouble. I wasn't counting on almost crashing like that. Come back to me when you've sorted your own problems out. I try and operate a discreet service here and you've almost messed the whole thing up. You're rapidly running out of friends in this country because of your screw ups.'

Lance was intrigued to know more about this conversation, but just then, the door opened and the tallest, thickset man who walked through was briefly startled to find himself almost bumping into Lance.

'Whoa. Where'd you come from?' The deep voice was now suddenly recognisable, as Lance had heard it once before. His name was Frederic and he was the pilot of The Monsoon. Frederic looked to be probably in his late thirties, with a baldhead and a neatly trimmed goatee beard. He was wearing a smart pilot's uniform. The man stared at him for an uncomfortable few seconds before he spoke.

'What do you want?' He continued speaking in English, clearly not knowing which language Lance spoke. Not wanting to waste time, he handed the letter to Frederic. He barely glanced at it before nodding.

'So you need to get to Lubumbashi? When for?' His direct questions came as a relief to Lance. He took out his note pad and pencil and wrote, deciding for some reason to write in French.

'I am sorry, I am unable to speak. I need to get to Lubumbashi tonight. It is most urgent.' Frederic shook his head.

'Night flights cost more, my friend. How much you paying?' Lance knew he had to haggle, so wrote down a price.

'$20,000 US dollars in cash.' Frederic whistled and shook his head.

'You understand that landing an unscheduled flight incurs extra costs.' He grinned but it was not menacing in any way.

'$25,000.' Frederic sighed and looked up.

'Forty-thousand is the best I can do. All to be paid up front.' His manner was business-like. Lance did not want to spend this much money, but if this was the price of getting south quickly and undetected, it was the only way. He nodded and held out a hand, which Frederic shook.

Lance proceeded to take out what he did not need and gave the brown envelope full of cash to the man. 'Cash always works for me. We're friends now!' he said winking before chuckling to himself. He shouted over to one of the other buildings, this time in French.

'Obed! Obed!' At the call of his name, a much older man emerged from the building. His long white hair and beard and the large pipe dangling from his mouth gave him a wizard-like appearance that would be if wizards wore boiler suits. He slowly wandered over to Frederic, who handed him the envelope.

'Are we fully fuelled?' asked Frederic. Obed nodded casually. 'Good. Give that to Rosy to count.' Obed nodded once more and headed back to the building.

'If it's all there, we leave. But I don't give receipts I'm afraid.' He winked and smiled once more. Lance took the time waiting to glance around. He spotted the tail of The Monsoon about thirty feet away. He had not noticed it on his arrival because it was largely in the dark. His body ached all over and he began to notice how tired he was. He was looking forward to sitting in one of the comfortable chairs he knew were inside The Monsoon's cabin.

After a few minutes, a shout came out the building Obed had entered just before. Lance did not understand the cry, but it clearly meant something to Frederic, who turned to him, a broad grin on his face. 'You can count, my friend,' he said laughing heartily. 'You can climb on boar—' Frederic's instruction was cut short by a loud familiar voice, which came from the building Frederic had only moments before.

'You've got to be kidding me!' Lance's heart sank as he turned and looked at Brenton Stanmer.

Kisangani Bangoka International Airport,
Kisangani,
The Democratic Republic of the Congo,
July 26,
10:06pm (Congolese time)

For what seemed like hours to Lance, nobody spoke. Time seemed to stand still and he felt lightheaded. The man who he had come to despise was marching towards Frederic and himself, a look of confused anger spread across his face. His suit and hair were untidy. This unkempt look was a far cry from the sharp crisp image he normally had.

'I didn't believe it when it was suggested. You're alive? How?' The older man's voice was angry and disbelieving. Lance did not need the loss of his LANSPEAK to be speechless right now. A thousand questions swam through his head. Thankfully, it was Frederic who stepped in. The pilot raised a hand and squared up to the approaching man. Lance had a sudden feeling of satisfaction when Stanmer suddenly stopped, though continued to glare furiously. Lance guessed that Stanmer used his physical height and build to intimidate people, even bully them. It was gratifying to see him meet his physical match, as Frederic was younger, taller and even more powerfully built than the CES man. And the pilot was clearly not impressed with his bravado. Lance realised it was with Stanmer who Frederic had been arguing with just as he arrived.

'Stop right there, Brent. Our business is concluded. My business is with him now,' the pilot said, nodding towards Lance. A look of frustrated fury shadowed Stanmer's face.

'Do you not know who this is, Frederic?' Stanmer asked incredulously. Frederic half smiled and shook his head, clearly neither knowing nor caring, who Lance was. Stanmer looked at Frederic aghast.

'He's the man we'd been tracking. He's the one who almost crashed your plane!' It was Frederic's turn to look shocked now. He looked over to Lance then back to Stanmer. A look of amused disbelief on his face.

'This is man here is the one who jumped outta my plane nine days ago?'

'Yes! It's the same man!'

'You're telling me this is the guy who fell from thirty-thousand feet outta my plane without a parachute?'

'Er, well, yeah,' Stanmer replied, suddenly realising how foolish his words now sounded. Fredric leaned forward, a serious look on his face.

'So tell me one thing, Brent.' His deep voice sounded menacing.

Stamner nodded nervously.

'If he fell outta my plane with no parachute, how on earth is he not a red splat stain on the forest floor?' With that, Frederic burst into loud uncontrolled laughter. Stanmer looked to the floor, shaking his head. Frederic's laughter echoed through the night and Lance found himself smiling. He was also grateful that Frederic was already in the cockpit the first time he boarded The Monsoon.

Once the laughter had died down, the pilot stared at Stanmer with a look, almost of pity. 'Ah Brent, you really have lost your grip, it's no wonder they sacked you.'

Lance glanced at Stanmer when those iconic words were spoken. But before he could contemplate them, Stanmer glared back, his reddening face shaking with anger.

'How did you do it?' Lance knew even if he had the LANSPEAK, he would not have answered. This man had no right to ask or be told anything. It was then Stanmer noticed the absence of the LANSPEAK. 'Oh so where's your little walkie-talkie gone?' Some of the bravado was returning to his voice. 'Where is it, your little speak and spell? Not so bold without your voice, are you? So much easier to act dumb now, eh?' The offensive comments had no effect. Stanmer had lost his power now, not that he ever had much over him in the first place. Frederic looked at the older man with bewilderment as he continued his attempts to belittle Lance.

'This isn't over, Knightly. You'll get what's coming to you. Mark my words.'

Frederic motioned for Lance to board the aeroplane.

'Where are you taking him?' Stanmer asked, a hint of desperation in his voice.

'That's none of your business!' the pilot shouted back without turning around. Lance did turn around, as he climbed the short steps up to the aircraft. Stanmer looked deflated. A broken man. He stared at Lance, a glazed tearful look in his eyes. Lance almost felt pity for him. Almost, but not quite.

Aboard the Monsoon,
The Democratic Republic of the Congo,
July 26,
10:10pm (Congolese time)

An uneasy feeling of déjà vu overcame him as soon as he entered the cabin. It was similar to as when he had left, quite dramatically, over a week ago. Two orange parachutes hung near the door. Once Frederic had shut the cabin door, Lance checked both bags out of curiosity. They were both empty, but padded out to make them look like they were real parachutes.

Frederic's voice boomed over the tannoy. 'Ladies and gentlemen, please take your seats and fasten your seatbelts, as we are preparing to take off.' Lance then heard a laugh, which he could not decide was concerning or reassuring as the engines roared into life.

He did as he was instructed and strapped himself into his chair. The aircraft wasted no time in gathering speed and as it took off, he was finally able to sigh with some relief. They were safely in the air and he was now one-step closer to getting back to London and concluding this incredible journey he had been on.

As he relaxed, he felt sleepy, though his mind was still awake. His thoughts focused on Stanmer. He had been sacked by CES. That was hardly surprising as he had lost their prototype drone and failed to prevent him gaining vital evidence of the area, which could (hopefully) halt their mining plans. Lance also wondered how Stanmer had found out he was still alive. Though as the man himself had stated, he was clearly not convinced Lance *was* alive up until tonight.

A few ideas popped into his head regarding Stanmer's inside information. The obvious one could be that for the remainder of the flight, which he had jumped from, Stanmner and Quent continued to track him. Another could be that the man had seen a copy of the video he had made, which Dan had sent to Fim.

Knowing CES's skills at intercepting e-mails, Stanmer could easily have seen this new evidence. Though knowing that Stanmer was not employed by CES at this point, it was anybody's guess at how the man found out.

Though right now, Lance did not care how he knew. He felt sleep quickly overcome him. His body, which still ached terribly, was grateful to be resting once more.

Lance slept peacefully and, thankfully, nightmare free. His dreams involved him being back in London, speaking to Tristan, Blake, Ezzy and Fim. The dream was quickly shattered by Frederic's deep voice booming over the tannoy.

'Lubumbashi Airport! Sorry about the delay. We had to wait on the runway for a few hours before we had clearance.'

A few minutes later, the door opened. The warmth of a rapidly heating up day rushed into the cabin. He stood, though felt groggy and his body still ached, despite the long sleep. He picked up his bag and stepped out onto the tarmac. It was early dawn and the hot sun was about to reach over the horizon. He had slept longer than he thought. Frederic was smiling up at him. 'Feel better?' he said grinning whilst pointing towards a set of doors leading to a terminal building. 'That's your way out, no questions asked.' Lance nodded gratefully, managed a half smile and walked towards the building. 'And thanks for staying onboard for the whole flight this time.' Frederic's comment stunned him for a moment and he turned around to see the grinning man wink and give Lance the "okay" sign before he climbed back into his aircraft. *People never cease to surprise me,* he thought, as he headed blindly into the nearby building.

Lubumbashi International Airport,
Lubumbashi,
The Democratic Republic of the Congo,
July 27,
6:09am (Congolese time)

Lance walked through the doors into the terminal building, which was, thankfully, air-conditioned. There were a small number of people in different areas of the building and all appeared to be staff. A few glanced at him briefly, barely acknowledging him, which he was grateful for. They were clearly used to seeing people using this entrance at unusual times of the day or night. Despite having had a full night's sleep, he still felt weak. His body had not physically recovered from his arduous journey and there was still a long way to go before it was over.

Lance wearily headed for the exit of the building, hoping it would not take long for him to find Dan's friend Leopold. As he emerged into the morning heat once more, he noticed a man at the far end of the outer building. On approaching the lone figure, Lance noticed that the man was holding what appeared to be a small sign. When he was close enough, he could read the words, written in English on the board.

FRIEND OF
DR S.

Relief swept over him. Leopold Faida was a similar age to Dan, though his greying hair was much shorter. Wearing thick, black boots, khaki coloured shorts and matching shirt, the man had the appearance of a park ranger. The man was smiling as Lance neared him. Before Lance could reach for his notebook and pencil, the man held up an index finger to his mouth, instructing him to stay silent at the moment, which Lance always found easy.

The older man motioned for Lance to follow him, as the two men walked towards a side road near one of the outer gates to the airport. He followed Leopold towards a huge lorry that was parked at the side of the road. Much larger than the one he had travelled in with Hursan the day before. And hopefully, more comfortable, Lance thought.

The huge lorry was a heavy goods vehicle. Leopold climbed into the driver's seat and Lance joined him in the passenger side. Once the door was securely closed, Leopold finally spoke.

'I'm Leo. And you must be Lance,' he said in a deep French voice whilst extending a hand, which Lance gratefully shook and nodded. 'I could see The Monsoon from here. I thought you were never going to disembark. Red tape is surprisingly thick in this part of the world too I'm afraid. Though fortunately for you, the rest of the journey is my territory. We should have no hold ups,' he said with a confident smile. Lance nodded, thankful for someone else to take charge of his journey for a while.

'I know you don't speak, so I'm going to tell you our plan. We stay in this cab as much as possible. We get out only for food and to use the toilet. We sleep in the compartment above our heads. At each border, I'll of course do all the talking, if anyone asks, you're working for me. I know the route to South Africa like I know the inside of my truck. But there's one more thing. Dan told me you'd have some spare border passes.' Lance was momentarily confused, until he figured out what Leo was implying. He handed the brown envelope to the man. 'How much is left?' he asked, feeling the weight of the remaining cash. Lance opened and closed his hand twice.

'Ten thousand?' Leo whistled, looking disappointed but not wholly surprised.

'Those flights are getting more expensive each month I swear.' He picked up a few loose notes and sighed. 'It should be enough. Though if we have to use it all, I'll tell Dan he'll still owe me my usual fifteen percent,' he said whilst smiling. Lance could only nod once more. Leo secured the money in a compartment above his head and started the engine. The powerful vehicle roared to life, steered the lorry out of the airport and headed towards the border with Zambia.

The Road,
The Democratic Republic of the Congo –
South Africa,
July 27–July 30

The journey over the next few days was, for Lance, the smoothest and least disruptive on his entire trip. Leo was clearly an experienced traveller and knew all the routes intimately. They passed through the borders of Zambia and Zimbabwe with virtually no disruption to their travelling.

Leo knew the first names of many of the (largely unofficial) border staff, having even friendly relationships with them. He never argued over the costs, so it was clear to Lance that it was a mutually beneficial arrangement. Everyone involved profited from allowing the lorry through with minimal questions. Only on one occasion did a man ask to see inside the container being towed behind the lorry, though Leo informed Lance that sometimes they have to pretend that they were working within official parameters.

The majority of the time was spent on the various roads, which covered vast distances of the huge continent. Leo was clearly used to working alone, so having a silent companion suited him fine. He played jazz music constantly, which Lance enjoyed. Relaxing in the cab of the lorry, watching entire spectacular countries pass by whilst listening to the likes of Duke Ellington, Miles Davis, Louis Armstrong, Billie Holiday and many others ensured Lance's mind was calm, focused and positive.

When they arrived in the South African town of Louis Trichardt, Lance had initially intended of continuing to Cape Town by some other means and as Leo stated, he did not normally travel that far into the country. But the man insisted on driving them all the way to Cape Town. He informed Lance that Dan had suggested that it would be safer and quicker to get Lance to Cape Town himself.

The natural beauty of South Africa never ceased to please Lance, as he had been here twice before. The vast city appeared before them and the lorry joined the heavy traffic, slowly heading to their destination. Lance was so relaxed he almost considered spending some time in the city, enjoying some of the beautiful sights and experiences the place had to offer. He pushed such pleasant carefree thoughts aside. He was still on a mission to return to London as soon as possible and conclude this incredible story he had become entangled in.

Finally, the huge lorry pulled up at a car park.

'Well. The end of the line, my friend,' Leo said smiling. Lance shook the man's hand gratefully, before reaching up for the envelope of money, which had less than two thousand dollars left in it. Taking out a single one-hundred-dollar bill, Lance then handed the rest to Leo. The older man looked almost embarrassed. 'No, my friend. I've made enough money on this trip, that's far too much of a tip.' Lance shook his head and swiftly climbed out of the lorry. He looked back up towards Leo. 'Well, thank you,' he said humbly. 'You take care, young man. It's a dangerous profession you've chosen.' With that, the man closed the door and eased the juggernaut slowly back onto the road. *Another unassuming person who had been invaluable to him on this journey,* Lance thought, himself now feeling humbled. He took a deep breath of morning air and headed towards his next destination.

Van Schalkwyk Safe Deposits,
Heerengracht Street,
Cape Town,
South Africa,
July 30,
10:22am (South African time)

Lance wasted no time in getting to the Safe Deposit building. Known as the VSSD, he stored in places such as this items that he hoped he would never have to use. And up until today, never had to. He entered the opulent foyer of the building, immediately noticing two armed security guards standing either side of the heavy door and went straight up to a plush counter, which looked to be made of solid marble. An immaculately dressed woman looked up from a computer screen, her professional smiled wavered momentarily, as she looked up at him. His dishevelled appearance looked very out of place in such a grand room. The polished smile returned quickly as she spoke. 'May I help you, sir?' The language was English but with an accent, Lance was unable to place. He held out a small identity card, which the woman took and scanned it through a machine next to her computer keyboard.

She nodded and then handed Lance a thin screen, which was attached to a wire. Roughly the size of an iPad, the woman smiled, her perfect white teeth beamed from her flawlessly complexioned face. 'Just now confirm your identity please, sir.' Lance placed his right hand against the screen, which scanned his palm. The woman waited for a moment. Her smile never dimmed as he stood up and said. 'This way, sir.' Lance followed the woman as she took him through a set of double doors. Two more security guards were in the next room. It was a circular room with no windows. The metallic floor, walls and ceiling reflected the harsh artificial light, giving the room a cold clinical feel. There also appeared to be no other door apart from the one they had entered through.

The woman pressed a few buttons, which were almost completely camouflaged in a section of the metal wall next to the one of the guards. A large portion of wall opened up between the two guards. It was secret door, which led to a long artificially lit corridor. The woman handed Lance a thin black plastic strip, roughly the size of a mobile phone. 'Number seven hundred and seventeen, sir. Take as long as you need.' With that, the woman nodded courteously and returned to the foyer.

Neither security guard looked at him, which he was grateful for. He walked through the newly revealed doorway. The corridor was full of safety deposit boxes of similar sizes. He found his own one and pressed the card against a small scanner. A metal box, about the same size as a small suitcase, was pushed out into the corridor. He picked it up and took it to a room at the far end of the corridor. Once inside he closed the door and opened the box.

He took out what he needed. These items consisted of a pack of contact lenses, a pair of spectacles, a passport, a bankcard and some local currency. He quickly checked all these items. They were all as they should be. Finally, Lance reached into the box and pulled out the last and in his opinion, the most important item right now. It was another LANSPEAK.

What he had now was a secret identity. Lance wasted no time in putting the contact lenses into his eyes. They were a pale green colour, which made a considerable difference to his appearance, as his own eyes were almost unnaturally dark. He put on the spectacles to help disguise his face slightly. The passport was in the name of Ethan Krige. Mister Krige had his own moderately healthy bank account, private e-mail, a bogus home address and even a fake business in his name.

Lance looked around the imposing room. He never liked having to use such places as this. He knew how depositories all over the world, were used by various nefarious people and companies. Secrecy and anonymity was why he was using it. But it was also a perfect hiding place for criminals too. Though right now, it served an important purpose.

Lance had nine such safe deposits spread across the globe. Each one contained a different identity. They also contained a LANSPEAK. The speaking device of his own design, which had been damaged beyond repair by the J'ba Fofi was the original prototype. But there were nine more. He now strapped this model to his right arm (Lance was virtually ambidextrous) so which arm it was attached to did not matter. Like the eight other devices, this LANSPEAK could be disguised as a medical cast, which Lance proceeded to do.

He placed everything in his bag and before he left the room, checked the power of the speaking device. It was fully charged. The LANSPEAKs were designed not to lose power as long as they were turned off. Everything was going well so far. Lance returned his box and left the vault corridor. He handed the key back to the receptionist. She smiled her practiced smile and if she noticed the sudden difference in his appearance, she did not acknowledge it. He nodded appreciatively. And the green-eyed man, who was now known to the public as Ethan Krige left the building, the LANSPEAK7 now firmly in place. It was good to have a voice again, he thought, as he headed out into the warm morning sun.

Hotel Verde,
Cape Town International Airport,
Matroosfontein,
Cape Town,
South Africa,
July 30,
5:16pm (South African time)

Lance spent a few hours buying a few essentials from various shops. He bought a complete change of clothes and some toiletries as well as a cheap laptop. He paid cash in the shops, whilst testing the LANSPEAK7, which worked as well as the prototype. The real test of his false identity was when he booked into a hotel right next to the airport. There was no problem checking he was relieved to discover.

Once in his hotel room, Lance had his first hot shower in a long time. Before dressing, he looked at his body in the mirror. He was initially shocked but not surprised to see the amount of scratches and bruises on his body. The worst bruising was on his right shoulder. The arm, which had been dislocated twice on this trip, was almost one large bruise. The discoloured skin spread across most of the right side of his chest and also down his arm almost to his elbow. Black and blue he thought to himself.

Despite his shocking physical appearance, he knew it could have been a whole lot worse. His thoughts drifted to Rufus and Duncan. They were not as lucky as him. He sat in his chair and suddenly felt an overwhelming feeling rush over him. It felt like his entire body was shrivelling up, like a crisp packet thrown onto a fire. His heart pounded and his head swam. He stood up, feeling like he was about to die. He walked back into the bathroom and stared into the mirror. A haunted distant face stared back. He closed his eyes. He knew it was an anxiety attack, as he had experienced them before.

Focus. He concentrated on his breathing. *It has come from nowhere, it will go back to nowhere*, he told himself. One of his counsellors had told him this and it had worked well in the past. After a few minutes, the feeling of impending doom began to subside. He lay on the bed and focused his mind. He was safe he told himself over and over. After a few more minutes, he drank some water. He needed to keep his mind occupied so he went over to the laptop and logged onto the e-mail account of Ethan Krige.

He sent a simple message to a well-known contact. He had booked a flight for early the next day back to London. Lance typed a cryptic message.

ULBOXALLCLINTCY-EGLL-16:00(E)

He waited for a reply, which was not long in coming. And the response was exactly how he imagined it to be.

You're alive? Thank God.
You idiot!
Of course, I'll be there.
M

Lance felt overwhelmed with emotion at seeing the simple reply. He knew the contact could not risk saying more. But what they had said was enough. He suddenly felt safe for the first time in weeks. He ate an evening meal in the hotel restaurant and went to bed early. First thing in the morning, he would board a flight, which would take him back to London. Despite his earlier anxiety attack, Lance slept well. His mind had taken comfort knowing that he was never alone. He had love and support whenever he needed it. How lucky he felt as the night hours obliviously rolled by.

Cape Town International Airport,
Matroosfontein,
Cape Town,
South Africa,
July 31,
7:00am (South African time)

Lance felt refreshed after a good sleep the previous night. He checked out of the hotel early. His desire to get back to London suddenly felt even more urgent. He checked in at the earliest time. Mister Ethan Krige had no trouble getting through the security checks. His eyes stung from putting the contact lenses back in but they had to remain in, as they matched his false passport photograph.

The anxiety attack from last night weighed heavily on his mind. He hated flying, but took flights regardless, as his journalism required swift travel to destinations. Though when his flight number was called, his heart began to pound and he felt the anxiety rise in his head once more. *Focus*, he told himself. It is a safe way to travel. He had survived much riskier activities this past week. Focusing on the previous dangers and near-death experiences he had recently survived gradually helped in calming his fevered mind.

I am no longer in immediate danger and I am returning to London, where I will feel more in control. I am safe he kept repeating to himself. Mister Krige entered the cabin of the aeroplane and then found himself fighting feelings of claustrophobia. Quickly finding his seat, he closed his eyes and concentrated on his breathing. His mind began to calm after a few minutes.

The engines roared to life and his heart pounded once more. As the huge aeroplane taxied along the runway, he struggled to control his panic. Anxiety shot through his body making it feel cold. As the huge craft lifted up off the runway, he felt faint. After what seemed like hours, he looked out of the tiny window at the vast country of South Africa quickly becoming smaller as the aeroplane continued its rapid ascent.

After the initial panic, the smooth flight began to help with his anxiety. The sheer size of the aeroplane helped keep any turbulence to a minimum, which also helped him relax as much as he was physically able. Once they reached the cruising altitude, he felt more or less in control and despite having a good sleep the previous night, once Mister Krige closed his eyes again, he drifted into an exhausted sleep.

Heathrow Airport,
London,
July 31,
10:28pm

The relief he felt as the aircraft landed safely on the dark runway was immense. He began to wonder why the fact that he had fallen out of an aircraft with no parachute and lived, had not lessened his aerophobia, but clearly it had not made any difference. Mister Krige exited the aeroplane with renewed vigour. He swiftly made his way through customs and various other checks and headed straight for the car park.

Even though it was almost August, the night was significantly cooler than the weather he had been recently used to. It actually felt refreshing as he breathed deeply whilst walking towards a re arranged location. The previous day, he had emailed someone who knew his plans for the next day due to a few lines of code. The code revealed which airport he was travelling from and what time he would land. It was known as plan number seven. And the person who had received the email knew the location to meet and Mister Krige was hugely relieved to see the person waiting for him in a specific parking space.

Tristan Knightly subtly raised a hand in greeting as his younger brother jogged towards him. The men embraced each other tightly then both said nothing until they were both inside Tristan's car, the doors and windows securely closed.

'You look like hell. I had no idea if you were alive or dead for over two weeks.' His deep voice broke with emotion, as he spoke. Lance felt overwhelmed with emotions, one of them being guilt. His older brother had been his constant support, his rock, throughout his life. It felt almost insulting to return his love and support with such anguish. Tears filled Lance's eyes and he wasted no time in removing the uncomfortable contact lenses, though it was not the lenses that were making his eyes water.

'I am sorry,' was all he could say, which felt wholly inadequate. For a long minute, the two men sat in silence until Tristan spoke. 'I'm not going to say I told you so. And I'm not going to ask about what happened on your trip right now. Those questions can come later. In fact, I'll only ask one thing right now. That is, did you find what you went looking for?' His voice was weary, strained. Despite the upset he had clearly caused his brother, Lance was relieved that he did not now have to lie to Tristan. The less people on earth who know about the existence of the J'ba Fofi, the safer those spiders will be.

'Yes, I did. And the evidence has been posted to the relevant person. Duncan did not survive the forest. But hopefully his death will not have been in vain.' Tristan nodded grimly and continued, his voice now more light-hearted. 'Well, I'm really glad you didn't end your days in a giant spider's web. I mean I had started to worry. Lance Knightly, the human fly,' he said whilst breaking into a smile and laughing dryly. Lance smiled and sighed with relief.

'So what's your immediate plan?' Tristan enquired.

'First thing tomorrow, I contact a doctor Fimi Kazadi at London zoo to discuss how quickly we are going to make our findings public. The sooner, the better.'

'Okay. But tonight you don't stay at your own place. The secrecy level of your email has only confirmed to me that you have to remain low key right now. So you're staying with me at the barracks tonight. And that's not up to negotiation.' Lance gratefully nodded. For the first time in weeks, he felt safe. And more importantly to him, he felt in control. Tristan started the car; they drove out of the airport and into the busy London night.

The Office of Doctor Fimi Kazadi,
London Zoo,
August 1,
9:56am

Lance's first night back in London for over two weeks was strange and unnerving. It felt like he had been away for a year. So much had changed in his head. Having seen and experienced in the past fifteen days what most people could not even imagine in their entire life began to overwhelm him. It was only the long talks he had with Tristan and some of the other soldiers at the barracks that had prevented Lance from having another anxiety attack.

They talked about the warlord, Rivertown, Pod, the other boys, Dan, Fim, Quent, the gorillas, Duncan, Rufus, jungle survival, heat exhaustion and feeling lucky to be alive whilst living in a safe country, free of war, famine and pandemic diseases. It was easy to omit the truth about the giant spiders, as almost nobody on the planet would seriously believe the existence of such animals. He was relieved that when asked what actually happened to Rufus and Duncan, it was one of the soldiers, not Tristan who questioned him. Tristan did not ask out of respect for Duncan in particular but some of the other men could not help their morbid curiosity. It was easier to lie to them than Tristan, telling the soldiers that it was the warlord who had attacked Rufus and Duncan, with fatal consequences. He did feel more than a little awkward when talk of Quent led to them discussing his belief in the giant spiders, which in turn led to a lot of laughter about how deluded the man clearly was. And for some reason, it hurt slightly to see Tristan join in the hearty laughs. Though it did help to offload the experiences of the trip onto people who were happy to listen. And when Lance finally went to bed, he slept surprisingly well.

In the morning, he wasted no time in taking a taxi to London Zoo. Tristan had offered to drive him, but did agree when Lance said the more inconspicuous the transport the better. He had not messaged Fim when he arrived back in the country, nor had he this morning. Lance just hoped that his friend was at work this morning. He sighed with relief when a familiar voice said 'come in' when he knocked on Fim's office door.

Doctor Fimi Kazadi, one of the most respected primatologists on the planet smiled her warm smile as she opened the door to him. Before she even invited Lance in she held out her arms 'This time I get a hug.' She said, her smile widening even further. He leaned in and hugged her tightly, finding himself pleasantly surprised at how easily it was to receive affection from someone. They broke apart and the doctor invited him to sit down. 'I was about to have some tea, so you're just in time.' They both sat and he savoured the flavour of the fruit tea as it refreshed his pallet. Fim was still smiling as she looked at Lance, though careful not to look him directly in the eye.

'Before we discuss our plan of action, I just want to say a few things. You, honey, are one of the bravest people I've ever met. And the lengths you've gone to for our cause will put me forever in your debt.' Lance held up a hand, as he hated receiving praise and right now Fim was placing him on a very high pedestal. He appreciated the gratitude but felt uncomfortable at the same time. The doctor seemed to wisely pick up on this and subtly changed the subject. 'So thanks to your recording of those beautiful magnificent animals, you've given us enough evidence to challenge CES and others like them. The footage is clear and irrefutable. It's exciting but also frightening. Gorillas in the Salonga National park are extremely rare, so this footage is pure gold. But it's not only CES we have to protect them from. These animals will now be at high risk from poachers,' Fim said with a look of disgust and anger he had never seen on her normally cheerful face. Lance sat back in the chair. He had never considered poachers being a risk, though he was unsure why. Possibly due to the fact that he was so set on preventing CES getting a foothold in the place he had not considered other equally evil people.

'So the speed in which you returned is greatly appreciated. For now, with you as a witness to the discovery, you're able to back up the evidence on the recording.' Lance was slightly unsure of what Fim was talking about until she elaborated.

'Oh yes, once Dan had sent me the vital proof, I wasted no time in speaking to a contact at UNSESCO. The Salonga is already a world heritage site, though sadly not one of the most protected. But with evidence of previously undiscovered primates in the area for the first time, they'll be forced to take action. Which should include barring CES from going near the place and employing rangers to give the animals twenty-four-hour protection. Though in the meantime, Dan has arranged for some volunteers to guard the area as much as they can, which I'm grateful for.' The mention of Dan's name brought a different smile to Fim's face. Though Lance knew that Fim and Dan shared a long history. 'So I've managed to set up a press conference here tomorrow. It's in the Huxley lecture theatre at midday, where a member of UNESCO will be present, along with anyone else who wants to come along. Once this story is made public, it will hopefully go viral on the Internet and social media. CES will have nowhere to hide. And you'll be there to give an accurate, honest account of actually being there.' These words suddenly fell into the pit of Lance's stomach. He paused for a moment before he managed to type with a shaking hand.

'How many people will be at the conference?' Fim shook her head.

'Well, I've no idea. But I'm hoping for over fifty people.' He felt nauseous at the thought of merely *standing* in front of fifty people. The thought of speaking in front of them made him want to vomit. Lance never liked crowds, but he tolerated them in his working life. But the very thought of public speaking had always filled him with a palpable dread. When he was younger, he was actually diagnosed with severe glossophobia. He did not want to let Fim, Dan or anyone else down, but he knew he simply could not stand in a room with more than six people and speak to them publicly. Fim astutely picked up on his sudden panic. 'Oh honey, you've just gone three shades whiter. You hate speaking in front of people, don't you?' Lance could only nod quickly, feeling weak and foolish. 'Honey, it's absolutely nothing to be ashamed of. It's an extremely common and recognised phobia. And I wouldn't want to put you through that.' Fim's kindness and understanding touched him. 'So, let's think of a way around this.' Though as Fim spoke, Lance had already considered an alternative.

'I would happily do a video call from a nearby location. Similar to what some witnesses do in court.' Fim broke into a broad smile and nodded. 'Now that's a good idea. In fact, it might even seem more authentic. We could pretend you're out of the country. Let's say Paris, in my offices there. We could live video link to the conference and the people would be merely distant shapes on a computer screen. Would you be able to do that, honey?' Lance genuinely appreciated Fim's uncondescending way she spoke to him. Although he would still struggle, he believed he could do it. Lance nodded positively.

‘Excellent. Any idea where you could call from?’ Lance nodded again. He knew just the place. Fim nodded, her excitement hard to contain. ‘This is it, honey. Tomorrow is the day we push CES out of the DRC for good.’ Lance smiled at the prospect. Fim then leant towards him, a more serious look on her face. ‘You have to know that you won’t be the only witness there tomorrow.’ Lance guessed at whom she was referring.

‘Your friend Qunetin Roth will be there, which I am actually pleased about as he can actually be seen in the recording. Acting like a fish out of water, I might add. But he’s agreed to speak about the discovery tomorrow also.’

‘So he has been in contact then?’ Lance asked, mildly shocked at Quent’s sudden reappearance, though he knew roughly the day the man was returning to London, which was the day before him.

‘Oh yes. He’d been on the phone to Doctor Drachman as soon as he touched down. He bored the ears off Drach, trying to tell him about this gigantic spider he’s claiming to have seen when he was in the forest. Which is pointless in telling Drach, as that man has been all over the world searching for spiders. He’s seen it all. The biggest, the smallest and all of the ones in between. I’m only surprised they’ve not named most of them after him,’ Fim said chuckling slightly. Lance listened intently, wondering if his name would crop up. ‘But in the end, Quentin has actually agreed to attend the conference tomorrow.’ His name was not mentioned, but Lance was highly dubious about Quent’s real reason for attending the press conference. In fact, he had a good idea why he appeared willing to help. A feeling of guilt came over him once more. Quent was going to face more ridicule here if he continued to talk about the J’ba Fofi in any academic circles. But if he were to look at Lance to back the story up, he would forever be disappointed.

‘So Dan said you met a warlord. The one that attacked Rufus and Duncan.’ Fim’s question was asked with a renewed seriousness. Dan had continued the story that it was the warlord who was responsible for what the spiders had done. Lance was grateful that Fim believed the necessary lie, though he was sure Dan disliked lying to someone he respected as much as Fim. He nodded in confirmation, whilst wondering if Dan had ever revealed to her that the warlord was his own twin brother. Fim shook her head sadly.

‘People like him are like an infected wound in my beautiful home country. And their infection spreads all too easily.’ She looked up, her eyes bright with tears. ‘Thank you for helping get at least a few of those young boys out.’ She smiled thinly, knowing, as he did, that there were many others just like Pod who remained at the mercy of wicked people and were forced to do evil things. He shuddered inwardly. Without another word, Fim stood and leaned towards Lance. His body stiffened slightly. Fim then gently put a hand on his shoulder and kissed him lightly on the cheek. He automatically stood and hugged this amazing woman. She suddenly reminded him of Ezzy, another amazing strong woman. 'Thank you, Lancelot. You're one of the good guys.' Fim said with tears now rolling down her face. He nodded at the great compliment and headed towards the door.

'I will arrange my link to tomorrow's conference later today and give you details.'

Fim smiled and nodded.

'Blake Cudjoe, the editor of the magazine I often work for will be keen to attend tomorrow's conference. I will message him.'

'That'll be great, the more the merrier,' Fim replied gratefully.

'And finally, Dan asked me to tell you, that he is still waiting for an answer.' Fim laughed loudly. 'Ha Ha. Oh that dear man, he is persistent. Sending messengers now. He can wait just a little longer,' Fim said, that knowing smile having returned to her face. Lance nodded and headed to the door. '*I will message later, Fim.'* He left the office, confident that the end of this difficult journey was now in sight.

A Public Telephone Booth,
Camden Town Tube Station,
London,
August 1,
10:47am

Lance placed the telephone as close to the LANSPEAK7 as he could and dialled a well-known number.

'Hello, My Earth magazine, editor's office.' The familiar voice of Blake Cudjoe was hugely reassuring to hear.

'My friend. I am back in London. I have much to tell you. But right now I need to you to listen.'

'Lance! Where've you been? When did you get back?' The excited surprise in the man's voice was evident.

'I am good. I have much to say. But right now, you must listen.'

'Um. Okay,' Blake replied, sounding slightly confused.

'Doctor Fimi Kazadi is holding a press conference tomorrow at the Huxley lecture theatre in London Zoo at midday. You need to be there. And publish an article in the magazine as soon as you are able regarding the content of the meeting.'

'What's this all about, mate?' his friend asked, sounding even more perplexed.

'All will be revealed, my friend. Please do this for me.'

'Well, of course. But will you be there?'

'I will via a video link.'

'Sounds good. And of course I'll attend. Anything to find out about your adventure.'

Lance knew he could rely on Blake to be reliable and trustworthy.

'Okay, my friend. I'll be there for twelve. I'm keen to find out all about your trip when you're free though.'

'Of course.' Though Lance guiltily knew he would have to lie about large parts of his trip to a man he had the highest respect for. But it was for the best, he kept telling himself.

'I will be in touch.'

'You'd better,' the man said light-heartedly. 'Oh and Lance. I'm very pleased you managed to avoid getting eaten by any giant monster spiders.' His friend was laughing as he hung up, leaving Lance shaking his head grimly.

He spent a few hours losing himself in some of the quieter parks in the capital city. Though even the most tranquil places could not compare to the sheer unspoiled forest of The Salonga National Park. Despite all of the horrors he had encountered there, nothing could take away the feelings of being surrounded by such raw nature that he had during those rare undisturbed moments. He guessed it was his appreciation of the stark beauty of the forest, which had probably balanced out the horror he had experienced.

Quent's distraction from the ghastly sights had been his aggressive quest for fame and fortune. *Whatever gives you protection from such extreme circumstances,* he thought. As the afternoon became evening, Lance felt a renewed peace as he headed to another place where feeling safe was always guaranteed.

Ezquerra Residence,
Floor 57,
The Shard,
London,
August 1,
8:12pm

Wagner Ezquerra gasped when she opened the door of her apartment to see Lance standing there. She knew he was on his way to her, as she had to allow him access to this part of the building. It was not a gasp of surprise but mild shock at his appearance. He had lost some weight and the stresses of the journey had taken their toll on his face. Small scratches and bruises dotted his pale face.

Everyone else he had seen since his return had made no mention of his shocking appearance. Out of respect or politeness, he guessed. But Ezzy was the closest person he had to a mother and her greeting was one only a mother could get away with.

'Oh my goodness. You look terrible!' Ezzy almost shouted, as she stared up and down at the young man, who seemed to have aged considerably in a matter of weeks. He winced when she placed a hand on his injured shoulder. She shook her head despairingly as she took his hand and led him into her apartment. It felt like an age since he had set foot in this luxury home, when in fact it had only been twenty-two days.

Lance sat down in a chair Ezzy offered and she sat immediately opposite. She knew not to look him in the eyes, but her intense concerned glare was almost uncomfortable to him, though he let her run appraising eyes over him, as she was clearly worried.

'You look like you've been through hell,' she stated, her voice much calmer and filled with concern. *Hell*, Lance thought. Yes, he literally had been through such a place. He shrugged and tried to smile.

'Yes. It was a rough trip I have to admit, Ezzy. But like you always instil into me, it was a story worth seeking.'

The older woman nodded stiffly. Ezzy had always encouraged Lance to get to the truth of a story he was following. But right now, she could not contain strong feelings of guilt. She had actively encouraged him to follow the story regarding Rufus and Duncan, which now appeared to have been a considerably dangerous one. Ezzy knew Lance was more than capable of coping in some extreme and hostile environments, just as she had been when a similar age to him. But there comes a point when brave becomes reckless and determination becomes dangerous obsession. Up until now, she was always confident that her young friend knew where to draw the line. She guessed that the involvement of Rufus had made it personal, which had forced him to cross lines she thought he never would.

'No story is worth your life, Lancelot.' Her voice began to break with emotion as tears welled in her eyes. Now it was Lance's turn to feel guilt. She rarely called him Lancelot and her doing it, she was looking at him like a mother who had nearly lost a child. He swallowed a hard lump in his throat and nodded humbly.

They sat in silence for a long minute, which was broken by Ezzy standing and walking over to the man, who also stood and embraced the woman who understood him as well as anyone could. She sobbed quietly into his shoulder for a few minutes. Ignoring the pain the powerful hug caused at times, as he needed the hug as much as she did. She turned and sat back down, her eyes were red but her face was now more composed. She grinned. 'You're lucky I was free to see you, I could've been entertaining a male guest,' she said slyly and winked. He smiled and shook his head.

'I am sorry. I should have phoned ahead.'

Ezzy laughed, which was a beautiful sound to him right now.

'All right. I appreciate the social call, but I know you too well to know you're not finished with your journey just yet.' He nodded and was reminded once again of how Ezzy knew him better than most people ever could.

'I need to stay here tonight and need access to your computer. I am going to video link to a press conference at London Zoo tomorrow. I did not trust the one at my home right now.'

'Of course. What's mine is yours. And this will always be a home whenever you need it.' Lance nodded gratefully. It was practical to stay here tonight so he could ensure the link was set up in plenty of time for the conference tomorrow. But there was another reason, which took him by surprise. Tonight was one of the extremely rare moments in his life that he would rather not be alone. It was a curious feeling, though he did not dwell on it.

'You'll have plenty of time to set up the link in the morning. Right now, you need to relax and have a cup of tea. And if you're happy to, tell me all about this journey you're on. Even if it's going to be painful for me to listen to at times.'

Ezzy's face was now one of almost professional interest. She was eager to find out what had happened to this young man who she loved as much as any son of her own.

Once Ezzy had gotten drinks for them both, Lance made himself comfortable in the chair and began to tell his incredible story once more. Like Tristan and the soldiers, he left out the part where he fell out of an aeroplane without a parachute. That would be too much for Ezzy to hear. And of course, he omitted the discovery of the gigantic J'ba Fofi spiders by simply replacing them with tales of the warlord. She winced when he told her about Duncan, smiled when she heard about the gorillas and shed tears when she learned of Pod and his other young friends.

Ezzy looked physically tired when Lance had finished his edited version of the story. He only felt slight guilt by not giving Ezzy the full story about what happened. But like he had agreed with Dan, the fewer people who knew the real truth, the better.

'Well. I'm not surprised you look in such a state. You encountered the very best and very worst of humanity on your trip. Which, to be fair, is quite normal in your line of work. In fact, sadly it's more often the worst. But you've triumphed in the end. You've fought the good fight and won. And I've never been prouder of you as I am at this moment.' More tears flowed down her elegant cheeks. Lance made himself take the compliment and nodded quickly.

'So, tomorrow you'll be a key witness at that press conference. And you'll get your chance to tell the whole world what an evil corrupt company CES really is.' When she said the word CES, Ezzy looked as if she had just tasted something foul. 'CES. Sounds like it should be short for cesspit.' Lance then almost spat his tea out as the refined, eighty-year old Spanish lady swore as loudly and brazenly as any of the soldiers in Tristan's unit. He smiled broadly, as colour suddenly flushed through his pale cheeks.

UNESCO/Doctor Kazadi Press Confrence,
Huxley Lecture Theatre, London Zoo/
Ezquerra Residence,
Floor 57,
The Shard,
London,
August 2,
Midday

Lance had benefited from sleeping well the previous night and wasted no time in preparing the computer for the link to the conference. The technical side took minutes. His mental preparation required much more time and patience. He knew what he had to do and focused his mind on what was required of him. He tried not to overthink the situation and constantly reminded himself of the importance of the meeting and how much depended on his contribution.

He had a good link with Fim who was the first person to arrive at the lecture theatre. The computer, which Lance was addressing the conference from, was on the front desk facing the chairs, which quickly began to fill up with an impressive amount of people. The view of the audience was clear and, thankfully, not as intimidating as he had feared, though he was still glad not to be there in person.

A majority of the people were unknown to him. In fact, there were only three faces he recognised. Blake Cudjoe, Doctor Jonathan Drachmann and finally, sitting at the back, as if trying to be inconspicuous, a very tired and awkward looking Quentin Roth. None of the men acknowledged his image on the computer screen, which he found he was glad about for some reason.

Once the theatre was full, the doors were closed and Lance heard Fim's strong clear voice echo around the room.

'Ladies and gentlemen, thank you all for coming here today at such incredibly short notice. I know how busy many of you are. And before we start, may I introduce Karla Ntumba, who's generously taken time out of *her* busy schedule to be here today. For those of you who don't know, Miss Ntumba is a member of the delegation of the DRC to UNESCO. And in a moment, you will realise the importance of her presence today.'

Many members of the audience nodded greetings towards the front desk.

Lance was relieved that Fim had not yet highlighted his involvement yet. The less public speaking he was required to do, the better.

'So without wasting any more time on small talk, let's have a look at the reason we're all here.' With that, Fim pressed play on a screen, which was hidden from Lance's view. Though as soon as the short recording began running, he recognised it immediately. It was the recording from his GoPro of their first encounter with the gorillas. Each sound was familiar, though it brought memories of that place flooding back and he had to control a feeling of mild panic.

The looks on the faces of the audience quickly distracted him. They were not looking at a hostile dangerous place. They were staring at real evidence of some of the rarest, most beautiful animals on the planet. Faces stared in awe. Mouths opened in astonishment. Tears of joy welled in numerous eyes. The whole of the audience were transfixed by what was shown on the GoPro recording. Lance himself began to feel emotional at seeing so many reactions. It *had* been worth it, he told himself.

When the roar of the alpha male gorilla cut through the theatre, a few people jumped, though most looked on in excitement. Fim then stopped the recording.

'So there you have it, people. Firm evidence of a troop of gorillas, previously unheard of in that part of The Salonga National Park.' Fim's voice was met with an enthusiastic round of applause. The audience cheered and whistled, which was something Lance had not been expecting. Once the excitement died down, Fim's powerful voice once again commanded the room.

'I'll reassure you all that both men in this recording returned from their journey alive and are here today. And I will address them now, as they are the only ones who can confirm the exact location of this wonderful discovery. Ladies and gentleman, may I introduce mister Lancelot Knightly, a freelance journalist who was behind the camera during this historic moment.' This introduction was met with another round of applause, which Lance was not prepared for. He closed his eyes and waited for the sound to stop. Once it had, he began to do something he never had before in his life. He looked up and, as much as he was able to, mouthed the words coming from the LANSPEAK7 as he typed, to give the impression he was actually speaking.

'Ladies and Gentlemen. Thank you for such a warm welcome.' So *far so good,* he thought. '*I am sorry I am unable to be there in person. I am busy in Paris. But as Doctor Kazadi had mentioned, it was I who recorded these magnificent apes. It was a privilege to be the first person to document such a rare and precious sight.'* If anyone found his slow controlled speech strange,

they did not show it. Some of the people assumed that the odd word, which appeared out of sync with his mouth's movement was due to the slight time delay from the remote meeting. He continued, eager to be out of the spotlight.

'We were hoping to find the gorillas, as there had been unofficial sightings of them. But Fim needed concrete evidence to ensure their protection and survival, as there are too many factors putting the lives of these animals in danger. One danger being poaching. Myself and my companion encountered a warlord operating in a nearby part of the forest. If this man discovered such rare animals, their lives would be in grave danger for obvious reasons. Another even more destructive risk to their habitat is evidence we found of a business called Company Expansion Services. They are known as CES. And they have been making plans to mine the area close to the gorillas' habitat for cassiterite. I do not have to tell you the devastating effect that mining would do to this part of the forest.'

The last comment was met with many people shaking their heads in disgust and anger. This is exactly the reaction Fim and everyone involved wanted. Lance hoped nobody would begin asking questions as it had taken every ounce of self-control to get him through that dialogue. Thankfully, Fim came to his rescue.

'Thank you very much, Mister Knightly.' More applause, which caused Lance to wince inwardly. 'Your bravery has given us hope. And what you have learned has given us all food for thought. This company, CES, have had their dirty hands in this beautiful part of my homeland for far too long. They have bribed corrupt government officials in the DRC to bypass any protection UNESCO have given to this area and made plans to begin mining without consent. In fact, they were actually planning on dropping explosives into the area from a drone, to make a start to the mining.' Fim's words were spoken with an anger Lance had never known in the woman. And her rousing speech was met with open shouts of anger and shared revulsion of CES's despicable plans. 'I have it on good authority that this drone has been destroyed. But companies like CES have limitless resources. I even asked a spokesperson from CES to attend this conference to try and explain what their plans are. Alas, she didn't reply to my numerous emails.' This was met with grunts and snorts of mutual loathing for CES and similar organisations.

'As most of you clearly noticed, the colouring of these gorillas is unique. Their fur is like nothing I have ever seen in any primate of this size. Which tells us that this discovery is a first in zoological terms. They are possibly the rarest of their kind on earth, so as mister Knightly rightfully pointed out, these apes will require the highest level of protection. Now that their existence is public knowledge, they have, unfortunately, become a valuable target for poachers or collectors of exotic animals. That is why, in conjunction with UNSESCO, the preservation of these animal's habitat is now an urgent priority. And everyone here has a part to play. By making this discovery known throughout the world, we'll quickly gain an immeasurable amount of support. But going public is not without risk. Due to the increased risk, it has been agreed that the exact location of these gorillas is to remain a secret, known to only a small number of people who need to know.' The audience nodded enthusiastically, agreeing with Fim's assessment of the discovery.

Lance's mind thought back to when he first saw the apes. To him, they were beautiful magnificent animals, but looked much the same as any gorilla he had seen. Obviously, to professionals such as Fim and her colleagues, these animals were an exciting new discovery. He felt a renewed surge of pride at being a part of such a momentous occasion. But the significance of such a discovery made him think about that whole area in which the gorillas live. He began to wonder if the place were some sort of microenvironment. The existence of two entire species of animals, which were not meant to exist there, or even exist at all, could mean that this section of forest was literally like nowhere else on earth. *The main reason that the area should be protected now more than ever,* Lance thought.

'Ah yes. Now let's hear from the other brave gentleman who we now owe so much to.' Fim's voice broke his train of thought. And he began to feel anxious, as he saw Quent stand weakly and wave a hand in greeting. Another round of applause greeted the man, but unlike Lance, Quent embraced the attention, in fact, he revelled in it. The louder the applause got, the more contented and almost smug, the man's face became. *The fame he was hungry to receive,* Lance thought cynically.

The clapping died down and Quent stood proudly, as he addressed the audience.

'Thank you for that kind introduction, Doctor Kazadi. And yes, I accompanied Mister Knightly on that rather gruelling expedition. But in reference to those magnificent creatures, I can add nothing more to what that young man has already said. Apart from the fact that after we first saw those wonderful animals, we were immediately chased away by a very angry alpha male.' He laughed slightly and a number of people laughed briefly as a courtesy. 'But where they chased us to was an even more incredible place. Populated by even more amazing creatures.' Quent's voice began to rise with excitement. A few confused murmurs rippled through the seated people. This was Lance had been expecting and dreading in equal measure. 'You see, after we barely escaped the gorillas with our lives, we came across an even deadlier foe.' Lance still held out a trace of hope that he was not going to reveal the hidden truth of their journey. Quent dashed that hope with one sentence. 'You see, my learned friends. Mister Knightly and I found ourselves face to face with the J'ba Fofi! The mythical giant Congolese spider!' Quent's voice was raised to a shrill almost manic sound when he spoke. Utter silence descended on the room. Lance suddenly felt anxious and nauseous and he saw Drach put his hand to his forehead, a look of pity, mixed with despair etched across his face. Before anyone else could even comment, Quent's voice had changed into a desperate, almost pleading wail. 'Lance! Tell them! Tell everyone what we found! What you and I saw! The J'ba Fofi are real!' Lance could only shake his head. Overwhelmed with guilt and pity for Quent, he could only look down, shaking his head. 'Lance please! Those giant spiders are real and we both saw them!' Quent's emotional voice cut through Lance, but he had to protect the area at all costs. He continued to shake his head, unable to even look at Quent. 'Please, mate!' His voice was cracking with emotion. Lance could barely listen to the man's pitiful outburst. Once again, Fim stepped up.

'Mister Roth. Everyone appreciates what you have done for us regarding this new discovery. But I think your recent journey has taken a huge toll on you, as it would for even the strongest person. I know you and Mister Knightly suffered from the effects of heat exhaustion on this trip, which can cause even the strongest minds to suffer. Dehydration can cause delirium and even hallucinations. Believe me, honey, I've seen it in the most experienced travellers.' Her gentle voice was calm, and sympathetic and in no way mocking. Lance had huge respect for Fim's response to Quent's "revelation". She could have reacted in anger and asked him to leave the conference but she chose kindness instead.

'No! I'm not mad! We saw them! Spiders as large as dogs. Bigger even! Huge hairy beasts with leg spans over five or six feet in diameter!' Quent spread his arms wide when describing the size of the spiders, like a fisherman boasting about the size of his prize catch. The crowd began to shake their heads. There were many expressions in the crowd. Pity, shock, disbelief, anger and curiosity. And worst of all, ill-disguised derisory laughter. 'Mate, please! Tell them what we saw!' Tears were forming in the man's eyes, which merely added to Lance's feelings of guilt. Fim spoke once more.

'Honey, please, you've clearly been through Hell and back. What you need now is rest. We all want you to take time out and—'

'No! I'm not sick and I'm not crazy!' Lance was shocked at how Quent aggressively cut Fim off. And he was not the only one who felt it. Angry raised voices now filled the room.

'Sit down, you idiot.'

'Stop wasting everyone's time!'

'Who is this guy?'

'He's been reading too many fantasy books.'

A majority of the words merged into one barely subdued disgusted voice. Drach could be seen waving at Quent to sit down and be quiet, but the frustrated man was too riled up now. 'It's all true! We even saw a giant queen spider!' This comment was met with large pockets of laughter, much to Quent's annoyance. He glared at Lance. 'Tell them! Tell everyone here what happened to Rufus and Duncan who made the same journey as us a few months before. They know what happened. Duncan certainly did!'

'You're out of order!' An angry voice replied to the last comment. Lance knew he had to end this now. He typed and mouthed the words.

'J'ba Fofi is the nickname of the warlord I mentioned earlier. He uses the name of a local myth to instil fear into his enemies. It was he who attacked Rufus and Duncan. Duncan was tragically killed and Rufus barely escaped with his life. This is what happened. Both Mister Roth and I suffered from heat exhaustion on our trip. It has clearly affected Mister Roth worse than myself.'

Lance felt wretched writing those words but he knew it had to be done. The existence of the J'ba Fofi spiders must never be exposed to the rest of the world. He forced himself to look at Quent who had a defeated, blank expression on is exhausted face. An awkward silence was broken by a female voice, which cut through the heavy atmosphere.

'Do you have any proof of these giant spiders? I've just googled giant Congolese spider.' This question was met with a few nervous laughs, as it was unclear whether this was a genuine inquiry or a mocking one. Quent's face began to redden and without a word, he placed his left leg on the back of the chair in front of him, much to the surprise of the person sitting in it.

'You want proof lady? Well, here you go!' He lifted his trouser leg to reveal the angry wound, which, according to Quent, had been caused by the fang of a creature that should not exist.

A few people winced and took a sharp intake of breath at the sight of the nasty wound, which was now looking infected. 'Here's your proof! This is where one of those monsters bit me! How's that for evidence?' His voice had a renewed confidence, as he clearly believed that a cut on his leg was conclusive proof of the existence of the J'ba Fofi. The people disagreed.

'Proof? I got a worse injury than that from my lawnmower last week.' The room resonated with laughter. Quent looked crestfallen. His fight had left him. He put his injured leg back on the ground and shook his head sadly. Lance's guilt lay heavy in his heart. Despite everything, Quent did not deserve this.

'Honey, that leg looks infected. It needs seeing to as soon as possible.' Fim's loud but measured voice quickly subdued the laughs. Though still concerned, her tone had adopted a slightly firmer edge. Her patience with the man who had basically hijacked her meeting was growing thinner. 'Get some help, honey.' Quent nodded at Fim and looked around the room like a humiliated child who was facing a group of bullies. He said no more and as he limped miserably from the room, under the gaze of various academics and learned people, leaving Lance with a heavy sense of self-loathing. The man did not deserve this. He always thought of himself as someone who fights for the underdog. He was the person who would always stick up for anyone who could not fight for themselves. Lance utterly loathed bullies and right now, as he saw the tragic figure of Quent hobble out of the lecture theatre, it felt as if he had been complicit in the mocking of a man who was merely standing up for what he believed in.

He sighed as he listened to Fim wrap up the conference, knowing she too felt bad for Quent, though she had no idea that everything the man said, no matter how outlandish it sounded, was true. Sighing again, he flinched as he felt Ezzy's hand squeeze his shoulder reassuringly. She had been watching the conference from a distance as to not break his concentration. Saying nothing, Lance took her hand in his, grateful for the support, but nothing could ease his guilt right now.

He felt that he had made a true enemy today. How could Quent not feel anything but hatred towards him now? And that hate was well justified, he grimly told himself.

The Benedict Hospital,
West Didsbury,
Greater Manchester,
August 3,
2:51 pm

The previous day's events had been more emotional shattering than he could have imagined. The conference wrapped up almost as soon as Quent had "caused a scene" and Fim spoke to him briefly afterwards about the next steps they were going to take. It was a relief to have some of the burden taken from him. The illegal activities of CES, along with the discovery of the gorillas, were now very much public knowledge. In fact, by early evening yesterday the footage he had filmed of the rare apes was already on YouTube and other social media sites. It felt like his part in this story was finally concluded. Though there was one person he still had to see.

Lance spent the previous night at Ezzy's apartment and took the earliest train from Euston station to Manchester. He no longer had concerns about using public transport or even hiding anymore. The official story was now exposed and what happened next was out of his hands. He doubted CES would actively pursue him now. The exposure of their illegal activities in the Salonga National Park was irreversible. They had nothing to gain by gagging him now.

CES was not his present concern, as he exited the train and boarded the tram to his destination. The imposing Victorian manor house, which was a short walk from the tram stop, brought back vivid memories for Lance. Pushing them temporarily to one side, he walked through the grand public entrance of The Benedict Hospital, which was one of the most prestigious psychiatric hospitals in the country. And this was not the first time Lance had set foot in the place.

He approached the reception desk and typed into the LANSPEAK7.

'Good afternoon. I am Lancelot Knightly and I am here to visit Rufus Walcott if possible.'

The female receptionist did her best to be professional and hide her surprise at the speaking device.

'Of course. Are you a family member, sir?'

'No. I am a good friend.'

'It's only immediately family visits for all our patients at the moment I'm afraid, sir.'

Lance had been expecting this, as he knew how the place was run.

'Mister Walcott has a brother visiting. Could you please get a message to him and let him know Lance Knightly is here?'

'I'm sorry; we have a strict policy that states—'

'Please. I have come a very long way.'

The woman paused for a moment, nodded then stood.

'One moment please, Mister Knightly.' She then disappeared into the room behind her. After a few minutes of standing there, Lance began to imagine a couple of burly security guards turning up, ready to escort him off the premises. Eventually, the woman returned and sat back down.

'He's on his way down, Mister Knightly,' she said smiling professionally.

'Thank you very much.'

'Lance! Oh, mate, great to see you!' Myles Walcott strode across the square foyer towards him. His arms were raised, his eyes wide with excitement. 'I saw you were back. Your video is doing the rounds on the Internet. I'm so glad you're safe.' The man looked in better shape than the last time he saw him, but the strain on his face was still there, though not as severe. Lance held up a hand to prevent the man from coming too close.

'Hello, Myles. I have come to visit Rufus.' Myles stopped a few feet in front of him. His face changed from excited to sad, though not as despairing as Lance had seen on his face the last time they met.

'Well. He's making some progress, mate, but it's a slow and painful process.'

It felt like a lifetime since he had rescued Rufus from Stanmer's grasp, though in fact it had only been twenty days. Tristan had arranged for Rufus to be covertly brought here, as he knew the hospital would keep his admission strictly confidential. Often soldiers and even people under witness protection programs would be treated safely and privately here. Lance knew it was the best place to bring Rufus, as he knew Stanmer and CES were eager to have control over him, for reasons, which were now very clear.

'Of course. May I visit him? Is he well enough to receive visitors?'

'If it's you, definitely. Follow me.' With that, Myles turned and headed towards a wide staircase behind the foyer. Lance followed him to a room on the first floor. Myles did not knock on the door and just walked in. 'Rufus! You have a special visitor!' he shouted, as he led Lance through a surprisingly spacious self-contained apartment and into a small lounge. A man was sitting on a sofa, his legs pulled up to his chest and he was rocking slightly.

Lance was shocked at the appearance of his friend. Rufus Walcott seemed to have physically shrunk. It looked as if he had lost half of his body weight in a matter of weeks. His pale face was pinched and drawn. Wearing a loose-fitting tracksuit, Rufus looked like man three times his age. A different person to the one who had set off on that fateful trip so many months ago.

'The weight loss was from his catatonic state. He refused to eat so we tried tube feeding him but it was too traumatic. I thought we were going to lose him, but a week ago, he finally let me feed him. I think his previous fitness managed to sustain him long enough. But his mind, I just don't know.' Myles's progress report on his brother was painful to hear, but sadly, it was what Lance was expecting.

Rufus did not look up when the men entered the room.

'Rufus. Someone you know is here,' Myles said, sitting in a chair opposite his brother. Lance cautiously sat beside his friend. He had no idea what to expect. He touched the thin man on the shoulder, something he rarely did. The man flinched but did not look around.

'Rufus. It is Lance. Do you remember me? Your friend.' The man twitched and turned his head. His haunted eyes bored into him, but Lance determinedly held his gaze, desperate to get through to the tortured man. A flicker of recognition possibly flashed in his stare, though it was impossible to tell. The man's mouth fell open and he seemed to look through Lance at something distant. Then suddenly, Rufus spoke.

'Lance. Yes. I know Lance. My friend Lance. He has dark eyes. My friend Lance. Yes. Yes.' His voice was unrecognisable to the one Lance knew. It was strained. High pitched and croaky, as if he spoke very little.

'That's right, Rufus. Lance. He's here. You're friends with him.' Myles's saw this as real progress, but Lance was shocked at the damaged state of his friend's mind. Myles stood and was going to approach his brother but Lance held up a hand.

'Rufus. I am your friend Lance. You have experienced a terrible ordeal. But it is over now. You are safe. You are with your family and friends.' As he typed, Lance realised how hollow the words sounded. Rufus had made progress but his mind was incredibly damaged. Having had a first-hand insight into what had happened to him and Duncan, he at last understood. The horror the man had seen was beyond comprehension. Rufus was facing a mental battle. A battle he was unsure he could even hope to win.

He squeezed his friend's shoulder and stood slowly. He felt like he should stay longer, but seeing the man in this devastating state was too much for him to witness right now.

'I will visit soon, my friend. And next time, I want to see you put on some weight.' Myles followed him to the door.

'Thanks for coming. It looks grim but he *is* making progress. We have to be thankful for that.' Lance could only nod. He had seen an improvement since he had last seen his friend. He was unsure at what condition he would be in, but somehow was not prepared to see such a strong person reduced to such a pitiful state. Myles grabbed his arm and led him to the doorway, his face suddenly serious. 'So it's true like you said. Rufus and Duncan were attacked by some warlord. That's what he's talking about when he keeps saying J'ba Fofi?'

Lance nodded. Rufus had been added to the list of people who had to be told the edited version of what actually happened. 'But you met this J'ba Fofi man. How come you didn't come back a basket case?' Lance was shocked to hear Myles use such a derogatory phrase but said nothing. The past few weeks had clearly taken their toll on him too.

'It was what happened to Duncan. We can only imagine what happened to him. But I think we can be sure that it was horrific and that Rufus witnessed the whole thing.'

Myles nodded. 'Yeah, that makes sense. Look, it may not mean much to you now. But thank you, Lance, for everything you've done for me and Rufus.' The man held out a hand, which Lance gladly shook.

'That is what friends are for.' Myles nodded gratefully, as Lance left the room and headed back to the reception. There was one more person he felt he had to meet. The same woman on the reception looked up to greet him.

'Could you please inform Doctor Dankworth that Lancelot Knightly is here please?'

'Do you have an appointment with the doctor, Mister Knightly?'

'No.'

The receptionist was mildly surprised at the abrupt reply, but picked up the telephone and pressed a number.

'Doctor Dankworth. I'm sorry to disturb you, but a gentleman by the name of Lancelot Knightly is here. He says he wishes to see you. He doesn't have an appoint… Oh okay. I'll send him straight through.' The receptionist pointed to a corridor where a number of closed doors could be seen. 'Last on the left, her name's on the door.' The receptionist said, barely looking up as if seemingly eager to now match Lance's abrupt manner. He nodded and headed along the dimly lit corridor.

The Office of Doctor Felicity Dankworth, MRCPsych MBBS,
Consultant Psychiatrist,
The Benedict Hospital,
Greater Manchester,
August 3,
3:01 pm

'Come in!' The cheerful voice called behind the closed door after Lance had knocked. He stepped into a typical, if quite lavish, doctor's office. A woman stood from behind a large, wooden desk and smiled. 'Long time no see,' the woman said smiling. Doctor Felicity Dankworth had been a psychiatrist for over twenty years, which was often surprising to hear, due to how very young she looked. Lance had never tried to figure out her actual age, though he did also think that the woman looked younger than she actually was. Slim and attractive to him, her thick red hair was neatly tied up in a bun. She wore a colourful dress and it was similar to type she wore when he was under her care. Which was now ten years ago. His mother, Anaisha, was killed in a publicity stunt for the Knightly Empire thirteen years ago. The fourteen-year old Lance watched his mother die in front of him. And he had not spoken another word since that day. It was when he was seventeen that they brought him here to Doctor Dankworth to try and get him talking again.

'Come and sit down. I hoped you would come and see me if you visited your friend. Is this acceptable?' she enquired, holding out a hand, which he shook happily whilst nodding. 'But still no eye contact, I see,' the psychiatrist commented, as they both took a seat.

'Are you going to charge me for these assessments?'

'Ah. That incredible speaking device. I must say I'm disappointed you still need it. And I'm not assessing you, merely making a few observations. You're not my patient anymore,' she said, still smiling. 'And as you're no longer under my care, please call me Liss. I take it you go by Lance still?' He nodded.

'So. You have just visited Rufus?'

'Yes. What can you tell me about him?'

'Well. Absolutely nothing, due to patient confidentiality,' she replied professionally. He nodded.

'Of course. Well, let me add something then. I have returned from the exact same part of the Congolese jungle that Rufus was in.'

Liss nodded. 'Okay. So you're prepared to shed some light on some possible explanations for his condition?'

'Yes. He and Duncan were attacked by a warlord. He goes by the name J'ba Fofi. You may have heard Rufus mention those words once or twice.'

The psychiatrist nodded once more but said nothing.

'I believe that this warlord tortured and killed Duncan in front of Rufus. And that he barely escaped with his life. That is why Rufus is so mentally damaged. Many people may not have been aware that Duncan and Rufus were more than good friends. They were soulmates if there is such a thing. They were totally devoted to each other. Duncan was his life.'

If Liss knew any of this information, she did not let on. Before she could comment, Lance spoke again.

'That is why I think he is suffering a severe form of PTSD. But you probably have many other words for what he is suffering.'

Doctor Dankworth had also joined the growing number of people who had been fed the unofficial version of what had happened to Rufus. To Lance, it was easy to not tell Liss about the existence of the spiders, as he guessed she would probably not allow him to leave this hospital ever again. The warlord story was plausible and made sense to anyone who heard it.

'Why do you think he's suffering from PTSD?' The question did not surprise him. In fact, he was expecting it.

'Well, I know what PTSD is like. Having suffered from it myself.'

'Suffered or are still suffering?'

'Well, you are the doctor. You tell me.'

'Of course you were traumatised by what happened to your mother. But thirteen years later, I feel you still haven't grieved properly. Instead, you have built up walls around yourself. Not talking being the obvious one.'

'I had problems speaking before her death.'

'Hardly. You had a mild speech impediment. A slight stammer, which according to your notes, you were being successfully treated for. I doubt it impacted on your life as much you think it did. I mean you managed to learn numerous foreign languages.' She paused before continuing. 'You know, here at The Benedict, we have some of the best speech and language therapists—'

'No. I appreciate that, but no.' Liss nodded, knowing a final word when it was said.

'I know it goes deep, your fear of speaking. But whatever has caused this, it can be undone.'

'I thought you were not going to analyse me.'

The consultant sighed. 'I know. Forgive me. But the way I see it, you ended your therapy with me when we were making progress. And Lance. I still feel I could help you. I think you hide behind your autism, treating it as simply another barrier to not let people in.'

'You always said you would never label me. In fact you always said you found it difficult to diagnose any of my behaviours.'

'At the time, I couldn't. You were, are unique. So by understanding and classifying your…differences, could benefit many others who are struggling like you.

'You make me feel like your personal project. So what have you diagnosed? I am now intrigued to learn what I am officially.'

The doctor leant back in her chair, shaking her head.

'Please don't feel this way. I always told you if I could understand your various conditions, I could help you.'

'Okay. What are my various conditions? List them.'

'If it'll get you thinking, then yes, I can give you some of my thoughts. You *are* autistic, Lance. Though it would take considerable time to find your place on the autistic spectrum. Leading on from that, I must conclude you are also a savant. An autistic savant if you want the full title. That much was obvious years ago with your incredible grasp of languages, mathematics and science. Plus your memory is almost photographic. The construction of that thing wrapped around your wrist merely confirms what I would professionally consider a genius level of intellect.'

Lance listened intently. He had researched all of these facts and theories and agreed with some of them. Though he never considered how they could be scrutinised so deeply. But this was her job, he conceded.

'I also believe you have selective fake mutism. Which sounds like a harsh analysis but it would could be connected to your autism.' Lance shook his head. He came here to try and discuss Rufus, though he knew Liss would want to discuss his past but he was not expecting such a cross-examination. It brought back memories of the therapy of ten years ago. The doctor was clearly frustrated at how little she was able to help back then. It was clear he had never been far from her professional curiosity this past decade.

'And then there's your eyes. One of the reasons you hate making eye contact. Is it because you hate their appearance? The fact that people stare at them makes you feel uncomfortable or embarrassed?' Lance did not even look up.

'This is what I'm talking about. I showed a colleague of mine a picture of you when you were much younger. He was fascinated by your unnaturally dark eyes. Like I said earlier. You're unique in so many ways, Lance.' He flinched when she said "unnaturally dark eyes". It began to feel like the doctor has been passing his details around her professional peers like some sort of scientific conundrum.

'You are beginning to make me feel like a mutant.'

The psychiatrist shook her head. 'As I was saying, one of my colleagues actually came up with a diagnosis of your eye condition. He classed them as bilateral ocular hyperpigmentation. Which isn't even a recognised condition. Don't you see? You're potentially a new scientific discovery.' The doctor was now beginning to sound excited, which he knew was an unprofessional emotion to feel in front of someone she still viewed as a patient or client.

'Forget mutant. You see me as a laboratory rat. Your laboratory rat.' Liss could not hide her disappointment.

'You've got me wrong, Lance. I've only ever wanted to help you. And through you, help others.' Despite her over enthusiasm, he did believe she wanted to help, but he could never return to the therapy she clearly was offering indirectly. He had no desire to stay any longer. A doctor such as Liss could literally spend many years examining his mind and still not find the answers they were so confidently seeking. Lance stood up but it was the doctor who spoke first. 'I am sorry if I've offended or upset you. It wasn't my intent. But from a person in my position, you have to see yourself from my point of view. It's just that you're so—'

'Unique. Yes, you have repeatedly told me,' Lance interrupted.

The doctor did not offer her hand as he turned to leave, though he guessed it was out of embarrassment rather than rudeness.

'Actually. I do have a question.' Liss looked up intrigued.

'Why is it that I am closer to my adopted brothers, particularly Tristan, than I am to either of my biological sisters?'

The psychiatrist thought for a moment about the random question.

'Well, there could be many factors. The loss of your mother when you were a child could have caused you to create some coping strategies which you—'

'No. It is because they are my brothers. And I love them.' Liss stared, looking quite bemused.

'You see, doctor Dankworth, not everything in life has to have a deep complex, professional, psychological reason behind it. I hope that clarifies a few things.'

As he got to the door, he turned.

'I know you will do the best for Rufus and I thank you for that.'

Then Liss nodded courteously, her professional interest in the man who had just left was now even higher, something she never thought possible. She smiled. *No, we do not know everything,* she humbly mused.

Lance felt a huge relief once he left the hospital. It was as if he had found some closure of a part of his life and it felt good. He wasted no time in boarding the train bound for London. The carriage was quiet enough for him to make a call. He took out something he had never used before on the prototype LANSPEAK device, as it was just that. A prototype. The LANSPEAK7 and the remaining eight had had the ability to be used with headphones. Why he never designed the original without this capability, he had no idea.

Plugging the headphones in he used the device to make a call.

'Lance. How're you doing?' Blake answered almost immediately.

'I am fine. I have seen Rufus and Myles. Rufus has improved slightly but he has a long way to go.'

'He's strong. He will get through this, mate.'

'I am certain. But right now, I need to discuss where I go from here.'

'How do you mean?'

'Well firstly, I will continue to report back to you and your magazine just as I always have. And I appreciate you will still publish my reports under my pseudonym of BLACK-EYED BOY.'

'Of course. I hoped you would. But I'm sensing a "but" coming.'

'BUT. I will also be writing separate reports from my new blog.'

'Er. Go on.'

'I realised at the conference how much so-called cryptozoologists such as Quentin Roth are not taken seriously. And I saw an opportunity.'

'An opportunity for what?'

'To be able to hide in plain sight. I am going to make it public knowledge on my blog that I am also a cryptozoologist. It will go a long way in explaining why I am seen in some exotic places around the world. I am hoping that my new reputation as a cryptid explorer will act as a cover for my real intentions.'

'Right. Let me get this clear in my head. You announce to the world that you're this cryptozoology person, when in fact you aren't. Which means whilst you're searching for all these mythical imaginary creatures in certain parts of the world, you're *actually* a serious reporter, working in said place on a genuine story. So as you say, you're hiding in plain sight as someone looking for monsters or whatever and anyone observing you see you as nothing more than a bit of a joke. But secretly, you're digging the dirt on what's really going on. Is that the gist of it?'

'In a nutshell, yes.'

Blake's laugh forced Lance to remove the headphones for a moment.

'Ah, my friend. I always knew you were a genius. This is an inspired plan. But what is your blog called? And what's your cryptozoologist's pseudonym?'

'I am going by the name SILENT KNIGHTLY. So my real name is public.'

'Inspired! And the blog's name?'

'I have not decided. I thought perhaps you could come up with a name.'

'Hmm. Now that's pressure.' Blake paused for a moment.

'Got it. Your blog will be called "Undiscovered Nature". What do you think?'

'It is really lame. Which means it is perfect thank you.'

'Lame? It took ages to come up with that cool name.'

'I know. I am grateful. We will still meet in our usual place to discuss my next journey. I think it would be wise not to talk about plans of action over the phone or email. This is a new LANSPEAK so it is pretty secure for now. But for how long, I do not know. Secrecy is one of our strengths now. There is much wrong in this world of ours, Blake.'

His friend sighed. 'I know, mate. But thanks to people like you, we *can* make a difference.'

'No. People like you us.'

'Right. Okay. So this has been a strange conversation. And a first for me. I don't think I've ever met a fake cryptozoologist before. Or maybe I have and they just didn't tell me.'

'It is a first for me too. I will be in touch. Stay safe.'

'You too, Silent Knightly.'

Blake hung up and he sat staring at the blank screen of the LANSPEAK7 for a number of long minutes. How safe is anything in this modern cyber world? Keeping things private was becoming almost impossible for many people. Companies like CES have so much power it was frightening. And people like TEX seem to be able to access anything, anywhere at any time.

Lance felt like he had opened Pandora's Box the moment he became known to CES. He admitted to himself that he was afraid. Sitting there, asking himself why he had gotten so involved, his mind quickly offered reasons. There was a small minority of people in this world who lived by their own agenda. And for some reason, they literally cannot have enough wealth or power. Nothing will ever be enough. CES, Stanmer, his bosses, the warlord. And countless others like them in every part of every country. A famous quote came to him. "Bad men need nothing more to compass their ends, than that good men should look on and do nothing."

A shiver ran through his body. His fear and doubt abated. Lance knew many good people. Tristan, Blake, Ezzy. And some he had met recently. Fim, Dan, Pod, Leo, Hursan. Good people were everywhere. He suddenly felt less alone than he had in a while. *As long as good people keep fighting the fight, then I shall to,* Lance told himself.

He began to type into the LANSPEAK7. In capitals, he wrote what felt like a mission statement to himself.

TODAY I WAS DESCRIBED AS AUTISTIC. I WAS CALLED A SAVANT. I WAS ASSESSED AS SOMEONE WHO HAS SELECTIVE FAKE MUTISM. I WAS INFORMED I HAVE BILATERAL OCCULAR HYPERPIGMENTATION. I WAS DESCRIBED AS MEDICALLY UNIQUE. SOME OR ALL OF THESE OBSERVATIONS MAY BE TRUE. BUT THEY ARE NOT ME. I SHALL TELL YOU WHO I AM. I AM LANCELOT KNIGHTLY. I AM LUCKY ENOUGH TO BE YOUNG, FIT AND HEALTHY. I HAVE LOVING FAMILY MEMBERS AND GOOD FRIENDS. I HAVE THE PRIVILEDGE OF BEING INDEPENDENTLY WEALTHY. AND I SAY TO THIS TO THOSE OF YOU WHO SEEK TO DESTROY ALL THAT IS GOOD IN THIS WORLD. NO MORE! FOR TOO LONG, I HAVE SEEN THE DEVASTATION AND SUFFERING YOU LEAVE IN YOUR WAKE. YOU KNOW WHO YOU ARE. I AM COMING FOR YOU. FOR TOO LONG, YOU HAVE REMAINED ANONYMOUS. HIDING BEHIND LAWYERS, POLITICIANS AND CORRUPTION. NO MORE! I AM COMING FOR YOU. I WILL EXPOSE YOU. I WILL RUIN YOU. IT IS NOW YOUR TURN TO BE AFRAID. IT IS NOW YOUR TURN TO KNOW FEAR. IT IS NOW YOUR TURN TO STAND UP AND BE COUNTED FOR THE EVILS YOU HAVE FOR SO LONG BEEN IMMUNE FROM. I WILL TEAR DOWN YOUR PROTECTION. I WILL DIG YOU OUT OF YOUR HOLES AND HOLD YOU UP FOR THE WORLD TO SEE. I AM COMING FOR YOU. I HAVE A GENUIS LEVEL OF INTELLECT. I AM FLUENT IN MANY LANGUAGES. MY TECHNOLOGICAL SKILLS ARE VAST, AS ARE MY SURVIVAL SKILLS. I HAVE ONE OF THE MOST DANGEROUS COMPUTER HACKERS ON MY SIDE. I HAVE SECRET IDENTITIES IN CITIES ALL OVER THE WORLD. I AM AN EXPERT AT REMAINING

ANONYMOUS. AND I AM COMING FOR YOU. I KNOW MOST MARTIAL ARTS. I CAN SCUBA DIVE, BASE JUMP, FREE SOLO CLIMB, PARACHUTE, HANG-GLIDE, SKI AND HAVE TRAINED ALONGSIDE SAS SOLDIERS. I CAN HOLD MY BREATH UNDER WATER FOR OVER FOUR MINUTES AND EVERY YEAR, I RUN TWO SOLO MARATHONS BACK TO BACK. AND I AM COMING FOR YOU. YOU ARE ILL-PREPARED FOR A MAN LIKE ME. I AM UNEXPECTED. I AM RELENTLESS. I AM YOUR NEMESIS. I AM YOUR DOWNFALL.

I AM LANCELOT KIGHTLY.

AND I AM COMING FOR YOU ALL.

Epilogue

The Office of Jonathan Drachmann,
London Zoo,
London,
August 6,
3:23 pm

'Come in!' Drach shouted at the person knocking on the door. He sighed inwardly, as he saw Quentin Roth enter the room. 'Quent. What can I do for you now?' he asked wearily.

'Actually, it's what I can do for you,' the younger man replied, a barely restrained look of excitement on his face.

'Right. Look. I feel bad at the way you were treated at the press conference the other day.'

'You mean being laughed at? Oh, I'm used to that. Had it my whole life,' he said, though smiling.

'You have to understand, that room was filled with actual academics. People who have studied, researched and worked hard to get to the top of their chosen field. Fields, that are recognised scientifically and professionally. For you to stand up and spout what you did was frankly insulting to them, Quent.'

The man merely smiled. 'Oh, I know I don't have the credentials all of you lot have but I was merely speaking the truth.'

Drach shook his head. 'We've gone over this. These spiders you claimed to have seen do not exist. Not *might not* exist. They *do not* exist. Fact. They couldn't support their weight and they wouldn't be able to breathe. It's basic biology.'

'Well, they *do* exist. Lance was lying. He saw them too.'

'And just why would he do that?' Drach's patience was now wearing very thin.

'No idea. To protect them he said. But he saw them. He even saw the queen.'

Drach shook his head. 'Oh boy. Your fantasy really is complete. Spiders don't have queens. They're not eusocial creatures. Oh, why am I even discussing this nonsense? Could you please leave? I have real work to be getting on with.'

'You don't believe I saw them?' Quent's smile was almost mocking.

'You didn't see them. You had heat exhaustion and your fevered mind did the rest. End of story. Goodbye.'

'So you won't want to see my proof?'

'A cut leg isn't proof of anything as you well know.'

'No. But this is.' With that, younger man took the rucksack off his shoulder and fished out a cardboard shoebox. He opened it and approached the doctor.

'Behold,' Quent said confidently, as Drach found himself staring down at a small, perfectly intact J'ba Fofi egg.